Black Camelot's Dawn

& The Return of Madame Hot Temper

By

Darius Myers

FERO SCITUS BOOKS

WEST NEW YORK, NEW JERSEY

Books By Darius Myers

Published by

Fero Scitus Books

The Publisher's Dilemma: A Big City Tale of Privilege, Power & Murder

Black Camelot's Dawn & The Return Of Madame Hot Temper

Black Camelot's Days of War

Black Camelot's Dazed By Death

Black Camelot's Skeletons & Secrets

Fero Scitus Publishing

6115 Boulevard East

West New York, NJ 07093

Visit our website at www.dariusmyers.com

First Edition: November, 2020

Second Edition: July 2022

Revised 9781637320860
9781087906645
978-1-63848-396-0

The characters and events in this book are fictitious. Any similarity to real persons, living or dead, is coincidental and not intended by the author.

Printed in the United States of America.

In Memory Of:

Carlyle Gainey

Quincey Simpson

James Horace Simmons, Jr.

Dr. James Mahoney

Karen Coward Mills

Doug Picker

Cover Credits:

Raina Andrews. Thank you, dearest cousin.

&

Damien Dufour

Part One

Chapter One

Walt Bigelow rapped on Chief of Detectives Teddy Walker's door twice and hard. It was a loud knock that Walker had come to know from their years together, and it always meant bad news.

"I hate it when you pound on my door like that, Walt. What's going on?"

"Teddy, we've got a problem. Some of our friends are under attack."

The Chief wondered whom Bigelow called their friends. He'd been the top detective in New York for nearly a decade. Bigelow was his top aide during that stretch, and they'd made many friends over those years.

"Friends? Who are you talking about, Walt?"

"It's the former Harris Simmons guys, Teddy. Donald Alexander, Kwame Mills, and their buddy, Tom Wilson, the music executive. Their attacker wants to bring an end to Black Camelot."

"Attacker? What do you mean, Walt? Is everyone okay?"

Walker took a deep breath and braced for bad news. Bigelow was right. The Black Camelot crew were friends. They were also important leaders in the city.

"Yes, everyone is safe, but it was a real scare," Bigelow said. "All three had bombs delivered to their apartment buildings today. The packages looked suspicious and got picked off by their building's security. The guys weren't home, and the bombs were fakes."

"Thank God for that," Walker said. He let out a long exhale with the news that the bombs were fake and crossed his heart with the sign of the cross. "We don't need anything bad to happen to these people."

"Yeah, Teddy. We could lose the city if they got taken out by a bomb. I can't imagine the chaos that would follow," Bigelow said and sat down in a leather chair opposite Walker's desk.

The attack, even with fake bombs, made Bigelow nervous and jittery. The detective tried to sit still in the chair, but his nerves were a mess. Sitting was the last thing he could do. He got up and walked in circles in front of Walker's desk. The Chief had seen this quirky, frantic version of Bigelow numerous times over the years. Moving around helped him to think when he was under stress.

Finally, Bigelow stopped and said, "The Harris Simmons guys don't know yet about the attack, Teddy. I asked the building security guys to give us an hour to get back to them with a plan. I think you should take the lead. This is what you do best."

The Chief looked at his loyal, top assistant and nodded appreciatively as a thank you to the compliment. Bigelow nodded back and resumed walking in circles.

Like Bigelow, Walker was upset by the news, but he wasn't surprised. As a black man, he loved Black Camelot and their inspiring success stories. But he hated the nickname the press created for Alexander and Mills and their impressive collection of friends.

"That name Walt is rocket fuel for white supremacist groups. It makes them targets."

"Rocket fuel is right, Teddy. Haters live to hate, and that means we have a problem that may never go away."

Bigelow then read to Walker from a notepad. Teddy, each bomb had a letter and the same warning. It said, 'There is no such thing as Black Camelot or Black Royalty. End this now, or next time the bombs will be real. You'll be warned only once.' The letters were signed, 'A Proud American For How Things Should Be.'"

Walker turned to Bigelow, who was still nervous and jittery but stopped his manic circle walk. He moved to a large windowsill and sat down.

"Walt, You said the guys don't know yet, right?"

"No, boss, they don't. I wanted you to know first," Bigelow said, and leaned forward from his windowsill seat, and waited for instructions.

"Okay, thanks. Here's how we are going to handle this. Call the building security guys back and tell them that we will send teams to their places to conduct a complete investigation. Tell them that we'll contact the Black Camelot guys too," he said and looked up to the ceiling as he framed his thoughts. Bigelow knew he hadn't finished but interrupted him.

"When will you be free to talk to the guys?"

"Give me a second, Walt," Walker said and held up his hand for Bigelow to pause and let him work. He opened his laptop and clicked on his calendar. A typical day awaited him filled with meetings for the city's top and most respected cop. He began to reschedule and cancel appointments until an image of a huge explosion flashed in his head. Then the image flashed again and again, with each flash revealing more chaos and destruction.

The Chief of Detectives closed his laptop and looked at Bigelow. His eyes had turned into piercing slits, and his jaw tightened into a menacing scowl. Bigelow knew that look, Teddy Walker was hot.

"Nothing else matters today, Walt," he barked. "A racial bomb threat in my town and against our best people. I'm not having it. Let's get the Black Camelot people on a call, right now."

Chapter Two

Three years ago, shortly after the Harris Simmons Murders and trial, the Celebrity Hack Patrol met at Café Cielo. Their work on the story had turned them into celebrity journalists.

Each had a private table at Café Cielo and held court there daily. The tables cost $10,000 a year. Celebrities, business leaders, politicians, and society people flocked to Café Cielo, hoping to receive a mention in the columns and be seen at one of their tables.

The breathtakingly beautiful Jennifer Kung, a star gossip columnist from *The Ledger*, called the meeting. Her peers nicknamed her "TV" because of her movie-star good looks. But being a television reporter wasn't for her. She liked being in the streets. They sat at her table.

She said to her colleagues, Luke McFlemming from *The News* and Mike Desanctis from *The Post*, "Guys, we've done well with the Harris Simmons stories. Luke, you won the Harlowe writing prize for your coverage. Mike, you increased your audience by 25%, and I grew mine 30%. And not for nothing, I still believe I should have won the Harlowe."

"Me too," Desanctis said with a frown. "My editor Pete Colon called up the Harlowe committee and told them I got robbed."

Luke looked at them with a smug smile, "You two are just poor losers. The committee knows who the star is in this town."

"They know who has the biggest ego," Kung snapped. "You are a horrible winner, Luke. You could show a little grace, you shmuck."

Luke looked at her, considered her reprimand, and decided to partially agree, "I guess I should be more humble, TV. It's just hard with all this talent."

Kung snickered at him. Desanctis gritted his teeth and shook his head dismissively. Luke never hesitated to rub in his victory for the industry's most important journalism award.

The three writers were important allies of Teddy Walker's. They had helped him find Gill Harris' killer in the Harris Simmons Media Company murder mystery.

Desanctis said, "I know we may never again have a story with murder, romance, illegitimate children, a corporate power play, and then for good measure another murder. The story was like an old school soap opera with one cliffhanger after another."

"You are right, Mike, but that was then, and this is now. So what's on your mind, TV?" Luke asked and glanced at his watch. "I'm meeting some VIPs in a few minutes."

"Guys, the city fell in love with Donald Alexander, Kwame Mills, Tom Wilson, their friends, and their lives. They are handsome, hip, smart, and straight out of central casting. If we package them right, we can keep their stories going for a long time."

"Package them? What do you have in mind?" Desanctis asked.

She responded with a question. The idea had been on her mind for a while, and she wanted to walk them through the opportunity.

"Would you agree, Mike, that they are the princes and princesses of the city?"

Luke cut off Desanctis before he could answer. It was typical of him. He was a grown man who had never learned how to wait his turn or play well with others. Desanctis wasn't bothered. He let Luke speak.

"I agree 100 percent," Luke said. "Donald is Gotham's top dog and owns the city's limelight. Do you want to do a series on Donald Alexander as the King of New York and his Court? Is that the story angle?"

Kung flashed an approving smile. "Now you are with me, Luke. Except it's bigger. New York needs a magical essence, a crew of people the city believes are worthy of exceptional adulation. Donald, Kwame, and Tom have the unique celebrity cool, charm, and style to pull it off. I say we dub them Black Camelot. Every story will brand them as the Kings, Queens, Princes, and Princesses of New York City. We follow their lives closely as the city's royal family. We write about how they brought the spirit of Camelot to New York."

Desanctis nodded his approval of the idea, "I think you are on to something here. Readers would love this, Jennifer,"

Luke added, "It is a killer idea, Jennifer. But why are you sharing it? I wouldn't share."

Jennifer picked up her glass of water, rolled her eyes, and took a long drink. "Thanks for being honest, Luke. You wouldn't share because you can't see the big picture. There are seven people in the Black Camelot crew. They are all living fascinating lives. If you write a story, then when I have a Black Camelot story, my readers would want to read it. Same for you, Mike."

"Who are the seven again, TV?" Luke asked. His curiosity was piqued and he liked the idea even more than he let on. It might even be a way to steal readers from his friends and grow his audience.

"Donald, Kwame, Tom, are the guys. The women are even more fabulous: Donald's girlfriend is the former investment banker Carrie Alexander; Kwame's lady, Michelle Nubani, is a world-renowned economist; and the supermodel Danielle Jackson dates playboy Tom. The one with the most interesting back story is Samantha Rivers, the illegitimate daughter of Cornwall Harris."

"Yes, TV, they are a great crew, and you're right, the women are just as interesting as the men," Desanctis said. Black Camelot would provide readers with the kind of stories and gossip they covet. "Will we share story leads?"

She glared at Luke before turning to Desanctis, "We'll see how it goes, Mike, but don't expect Luke to share."

Luke shrugged sheepishly and didn't bother to protest. He knew she was right.

Kung continued, "If we do this right, our editors will be happy, and our peers in the newsroom will stop calling us the Celebrity Hack Patrol and put some respect on our names."

"I'd love that, Jennifer. I can't tell you how much I hate being called a Celebrity Hack," Desanctis said.

"No one in my newsroom would dare say 'Celebrity Hack Patrol' to me," Luke barked with a defiant tone. It was a lie. Most of his colleagues despised him and called him worse. But, like Desanctis, he liked the idea and was on board. "This is brilliant. Let's do it."

Kung nodded to note their acceptance of her idea and then glared at Luke. McFlemming was a glory hound and wouldn't hesitate to exaggerate or steal credit for others' ideas. She put him on notice. "Thanks, Luke. If you tell anyone this was your idea, you will regret it. Please don't do it. You don't want me holding a grudge."

"C'mon, TV. You know I won't take credit for it," he said, but it was a lie. He knew it when he said it. Being a team player wasn't in Luke McFlemming's nature.

Chapter Three

Donald Alexander sold Harris Simmons Media for $75 billion. The sale made him and Kwame rich. As CEO, Donald earned two billion dollars, and Kwame, as President of International, took home a half-billion dollars. Samantha Rivers, the illegitimate daughter of deceased and corrupt family leader Cornwall Harris, also became richer. She received $200 million from the deal.

Teddy Walker told them three years ago that their wealth would not protect them from hate. If anything, it would make them even bigger targets.

"Lady and gentlemen, hate groups are one of our biggest problems in this country. They remain huge threats to racial harmony and are one of the leading causes of violence domestically. You are rich and powerful people of color. They will come after you. It's not a matter of if. It's a matter of when."

He reminded Donald, Kwame, and Tom of that conversation today. "Well, gentlemen, we talked about this day coming. The good news is that the bombs sent to your places were duds."

Also on the call was Charlie Humphrey, the head of security at Harris Simmons. Oliver Harris had mandated lifetime security protection for Donald, Kwame and Samantha as a benefit following the company's sale. They only used it on occasions like public events. Humphrey shared how he would put his team to work and be a primary contact point.

"Donald and Kwame, we are going to post teams at your place and assign you armed drivers until we get through this. The same will be done for you, Tom. We'll take the lead on this and provide you guys with all the protection you need."

"What about Sammy?" Kwame asked.

"She did not receive a bomb or a threat, but yes, we are going to assign a detail to her as well," Humphrey said.

Chief of Detectives Walker added, "We've got our best teams on this fellas. Finding who's behind this could take a while. We need you guys to be careful and allow Humphrey and his force to do their jobs. We'll be there to back them up when needed."

"Do you have any leads?" Donald asked.

"The packages were delivered by a courier. We are trying to identify the vehicle that delivered them."

After the phone call, Walker closed his eyes and rubbed his temples. He bowed his head and began to pray, "Lord Jesus, you are a God of love, not hate, and I know these threats are not by those who believe in you as the highest power. Keep our officers, Donald, Kwame, Tom, and Samantha, under your protection. I pray in your name. Amen."

He then picked up his phone and dialed a private number. It was a call he'd rarely had to make during his tenure with the NYPD. The recipient answered during the first ring. "Hi Teddy, how are you, my friend?"

"Well, not so great, Voice. I have a problem and need your help. My guys can't handle this."

"Then talk to me, buddy. The Voice is always here to help you."

"Donald, Kwame, and Samantha need the Society, Voice. The bad guys have taken their first shot. We can't let anything happen to them."

Chapter Four

Two days after the bomb threats, 23-year-old steroid addict Richie Pointer, a heavily muscled white male, walked out of a convenience store in Rome, New York. He had just worked the midnight to 8 AM shift at a plastics factory in town and stopped to pick up breakfast on the way home.

A black man leaned on Richie's pickup truck in the parking lot as he talked on his cellphone. Richie screamed, "Get off my truck, nigger! What is wrong with you?"

"Oops, I'm sorry," the black man said and calmly backed away. "I didn't mean anything."

"God damn you," Richie yelled.

"I'm sorry, I don't want any trouble. Please accept my apology," the man said and continued to walk away.

Richie shook his head in disgust and hopped into his truck. He was halfway home when he saw the homemade bomb. As he made a turn, it rolled out from under the passenger seat. The crudely built explosive was made with two sticks of dynamite, a small clock, wires, and a half-inch metal detonator box wrapped in duct tape.

"What the hell?" Richie yelled and panicked. His body recoiled from the surprise and he lost control of the cup of coffee he was sipping. The piping hot liquid flew everywhere. Most of it landed on his face and chest and his body jerked from the searing sensation as the coffee scalded him. He slammed on the brakes and barely missed smashing into a tree as he regained control of his truck.

Richie straightened up the car to the curb, shut off the engine and frantically rubbed the still hot liquid off his arms, chest and face. As the heat lessened, he nervously grabbed and pulled on the car door handle as he feared the bomb would explode. The door was locked and as he reached to unlock it, his phone beeped with a text. Richie knew it wasn't a coincidence and grabbed his phone. He read the beginning of the text, "Don't get out of the car, or the bomb will go off."

He jerked his hand off the door latch and continued reading, "Now pay attention to my instructions. Open the envelope. It's on the floor, next to the bomb."

His heart sank as he read the enclosed instructions. "It wasn't a smart move to go after Black Camelot. If you want to live, follow these instructions. Drive home. The police are there waiting for you. The bomb squad has already been in your home and removed your bomb-making equipment. They also have all of your Black Camelot files and evidence of your white supremacist activities. It's over for you. Don't think about trying to escape. If you don't go home, I will detonate the bomb. And if you don't believe me, look out your driver's side window."

He looked outside as the man he'd called a nigger in the parking lot pulled up next to his truck in a sedan. The man held up a remote and mouthed the words, "Go Home Now or Boom."

Richie's shoulders slumped. He knew he was beaten. He started the truck and drove home to a waiting posse from the Rome PD.

. . .

At the factory, Richie worked the forklift and did a lot of grunt work. The muscle mass and endurance from the steroids came in handy, but those performance-enhancing drugs also caused him to rage and bully co-workers. He'd been at the factory for a little more than a year and twice was suspended. Once, for stealing a co-worker's lunch from the refrigerator in the break room and a second-time for sucker-punching a white co-worker, Jimmy Franks.

He punched Jimmy after he excitedly announced to the workers his engagement to his longtime black girlfriend, Tanika. Richie took offense and screamed at him in the factory break room, "What is wrong with you? Tanika's a nigger. You should join me to eliminate them, not make more of them."

Franks didn't like Richie because of the way he bullied the other workers and because he was a racist. Franks was bigger than and just as strong as Richie and made it clear that he would not stand for his bigoted rants. "Don't ever use that word around me, Richie. And you better respect my woman, or we're gonna have a problem."

Afterward, a scuffle broke out, and Jimmy, a one-time boxing prodigy, took Richie apart. He bloodied Richie's nose and fattened his lip in front of all their co-workers. It was a humiliating defeat. The taller Franks hit Richie with four punishing jabs. Each blow landed with a cracking sound as it smashed against Richie's face. Franks finished him off with an uppercut to the gut that caused Richie to fall to his knees and double over, gasping for air. He kneeled on the floor and raised his hand in defeat. "You win, Jimmy. I quit."

Everyone thought the matter was over after the thrashing, but ten minutes later, Richie snuck up from behind the six-foot-three, 240 pound Jimmy as he ate his lunch. Richie punched him in the face, breaking an eye socket, and yelled, "I'll blow you and the nigger bitch up, Jimmy. I'm a nigger killer, you nigger lover."

The bosses called the police, but Jimmy did not press charges. He told the police, "I'll handle this on my own. I just hope you will look the other way when I do."

The incident, four months back, was a local news story reported by the *Rome Journal.* The headline, "I'm An N-Word Killer, You N-Word Lover," was how The Voice learned about Richie Pointer. The Voice kept a file on racist acts. The act that landed Richie in that file placed him on a short-list of suspects in the Black Camelot bomb threats.

The day after Richie's arrest, Walker, Bigelow, and Humphrey had a conference call with Donald, Kwame, and Tom. "Gentlemen, I have great news," Walker reported. "We pulled out the stops and contacted all of our sources, and were able to find the guy who sent you the bombs. He is from upstate New York, a lone wolf, and will be charged with hate crimes and terrorism.

He continued, "We were able to find him with some basic old-fashioned police work. He stuffed newspapers in the boxes with all the bombs. The newspapers were from the *Rome Journal*, and that turned out to be our key lead. We were able to draw a circle around Rome and found a list of people in that area associated with hate crimes or white supremacist groups. The suspect, Richie Pointer, came up in a database. We were then able to track him down with a bridge video as he paid a toll leaving the city an hour after delivering the bombs to your places. The bombs were duds, but I'm glad we got him. When the Rome PD bomb squad picked him up, they said he had enough explosives in his house to blow up a skyscraper."

"Teddy is right," Humphrey added. "This lone-wolf, a steroid-raged guy, is capable of anything. We are lucky to have him off the street."

"That is awesome news and a relief," Donald said. "Ted, we're hoping you won't make any press announcements naming us as the targets of this attack. It's not the kind of publicity we want."

"I agree, Donald," Walker said. "We don't want to inspire copycats."

"Copycats are why we don't want our names in any story," Kwame added.

"We got this guy, Kwame," Walker said. "You can relax."

"Thanks, Teddy, this is great news and good work on your part. We're thankful." Tom said.

"My pleasure, guys. I'm glad to bring you the good news," and ended the call.

Walker called back Humphrey, after the call, "Charlie, we were lucky he didn't send a real bomb. The Voice told me the Harris Simmons security guys are from the Society of Protectors. Is that right?"

"Yeah, Teddy. Most of our guys are Society members. Everybody assigned to Donald, Kwame, and Sammy going forward will be members."

"That's good news, Charlie."

Chapter Five

All of the city's news media was on hand in the ballroom at the Millennium Club. They were excited to see Donald Alexander as the lead trustee of the Harris Simmons Diversity Education Foundation. Donald, Kwame, and Samantha Rivers were the three primary trustees of the foundation set up by Oliver Harris, Jr. Three years ago, upon his death, Oliver bequeathed the foundation $3 billion.

The fund had doubled in size since Oliver's death. Donald said to the press, "I remember Oliver telling me he was going to put the pinch on his wealthy friends to leave their money with his foundation. Never in a million years did I think we'd receive pledges to our cause from so many of these wealthy white scions of power and industry. We are now at $6 billion and have another $8 billion in pledges. Imagine what could happen once we pull in all these pledges."

Jennifer Kung whispered to her Celebrity Hack Patrol colleagues, "This guy is golden. Is there anything he can't do? First, he gets Harris Simmons sold for $75 billion. He turned Oliver Harris, Jr., into an important financier of historically black colleges and universities. Now he's out here selling the education dream for black Americans while getting the richest white people in the world to fund this vision. This guy is magical."

"He's the real deal, Jennifer. Alexander may be on his way to becoming the most important philanthropist of his generation. And as a trio, they look the part: two elegant, accomplished black men and a beautiful heiress. Hollywood couldn't cast this setting better."

Luke looked at them and agreed, "It's no wonder Donald is a recurring entrant on the most beautiful people list with his six-foot-two, lean, and muscular physique, dark brown skin, close-cropped hair, clean-shaven face, flawless white teeth, and chiseled facial features. The same goes for Kwame. He is just as tall and strikingly handsome, with mocha skin and thick curly hair, and that youthful dimpled, white smile."

"Yes, they are beautiful people Luke," Jennifer said, "and Samantha's stunning features and background stand out even more. Look at her, she's at least two inches taller than me and I'm five-foot-seven. She is regal with those big brown eyes, high cheekbones, and long, lean body with curves that cause guys to embarrass themselves. She's a sexy mama."

"Yeah, she's smoking hot," Desanctis agreed.

"Oh yeah, that woman is a heartbreaker, no doubt," Luke said. "I'd date her in a second."

"Sure you would, Luke," Kung said and rolled her eyes. "In your dreams."

They all stared at Samantha. Kung was right. She was the Black Camelot's captivating princess.

After concluding his opening statements, Donald opened the press conference for questions. Luke raised his hand and waved aggressively. Donald noticed him but didn't want to call him first. He looked to Kwame and Samantha seated behind him on the dais.

You should ignore Luke," Kwame said. "If you let him ask a question, you do so at your own risk."

"Yeah, he's a hot dog. Be careful," Samantha added.

"Well, this is our life now. We are doing what Oliver asked of us, and that is to do some good. I'll have to make sure he understands."

He turned to McFlemming with a smile and said, "Luke, how are you today? What is your question?"

Luke smiled back and said, "Donald, I am doing great, and thank you for calling on me. Congratulations on all your success with the foundation. It is becoming the largest and most important private educational foundation in the world. My question is, should it be so race-focused? Should some of this huge treasure chest go to non-black colleges and universities?"

Donald looked back at Kwame and Samantha. He cleared his throat as he momentarily regretted the decision to call on the hot-dog journalist. Kwame whispered, "I warned you. The guy's a glory hound, be careful."

As he waited for an answer, Luke stared at Donald with his arms crossed and a smug smile on his face. He enjoyed being a pain in the ass.

Kung whispered to Desanctis as she watched Luke try to show up Donald, “Only a few seconds ago, he praised Alexander. Now he’s trying to embarrass him and doesn’t care. He needs help. I swear this guy might be bipolar."

"You may be right. It would explain a lot, TV."

Donald, however, was a seasoned top executive and accustomed to being put on the spot, especially by antagonists like Luke. He answered the question with grace, charm, and a smart-aleck comeback that showed up the smug reporter.

"Have you come to battle or celebrate Luke? I feel a little hot sauce, my friend. Are you trying to raise the temperature in the room?"

A reporter in the back shouted, "You don't mean hot sauce. You mean a hot dog. That's all he is."

Luke turned and looked behind him to see if he could identify the reporter. He had a legion of haters but couldn't spot the culprit and quickly turned his attention back to Donald.

"No, Donald, I want to know if this program is discriminatory conceptually?"

Jennifer snapped at him, "Stop, Luke. You are acting like an asshole."

Donald, Kwame, and Samantha heard her, as did other members of the press. The room became silent. Luke was a jerk, but everyone wanted to hear the answer. Alexander wasn't put off. Instead, he saw it as an opportunity to educate the press on the foundation's mission.

He acknowledged Kung first, "Jennifer, I'm okay with Luke's question. He, like you, has ten million readers to serve daily. He's trying to be of service."

"My audience is actually bigger than hers," Luke gloated. The entire press corps groaned, giggled, or rolled their eyes sarcastically.

"Barely, Luke. There used to be a bigger gap until people started to realize what kind of jerk you are, and now your readers are my readers," she shouted. It was a quick-witted response that led to more laughs from the other reporters.

"That's right. Get him TV," a reporter shouted from the back of the room.

"Overrated. Way overrated," another voice barked.

Luke's right eye began to twitch as he tried again to identify his haters. It was his nervous reaction. He began to blink his eyes to stop the twitch and took a deep breath to relax.

"Okay, people. Okay," Donald yelled, quenching the barbs and laughter. "Luke asked a fair question. You guys who question his style and methods can beat him up later."

He continued, "The Foundation's name is the Oliver Harris, Jr. Diversity Education Foundation for Black Colleges. The charter and mission for this fund are targeted and specific. The money will be used for major capital expenses, specifically the construction of classroom buildings and student dormitories. It will also cover salaries and research grants for tenured professors and academic scholarships for high performers. It also includes, and this was most important to Oliver, need-based scholarships for students who come from working-class and underclass families and are otherwise disadvantaged. The

Foundation supports the rich heritage of historically black colleges and universities. Many of these institutions have outstanding alumni but small endowments. Oliver wanted to provide them with the financial backing they needed to compete as world-class institutions of higher education. The charter and mission were defined by Oliver, not by me, Kwame, or Samantha."

"Well, it is my understanding that you instructed him to support black colleges?" Luke asked.

"Are you suggesting that I forced his hand, Luke?"

"Well, yes, I am," Luke answered. He was sure he had a gotcha moment. The local television crews thought so as well, and they jostled closer to the dais with their cameras.

Donald waited for the press as they moved in for the kill. He stood calmly and let his transcendent smile light up the room.

After the press had positioned themselves, Donald said, "Thank you, Luke. Your questions will help us get the news out on our mission. Oliver was a trustee at Harlowe, one of the most historic and financially solvent universities in the world. Their endowment is $30 billion. They have more than 200,000 living alumni. He spent his final years learning about Harlowe's best practices and visited our country's great black colleges to compare them to Harlowe. He defined the use of these funds after this period of due diligence and started the living pledges program, which is why the foundation doubled its endowment. Oliver did this of his own accord. He designed it and set it all up."

"What people don't understand is Gill's murder and untimely death wrecked Oliver. He needed something to do, or as his doctors later told me, he would have died of a broken heart. Remember he lost his only son and his younger brother several months apart in a scandalous series of events."

Samantha Rivers sniffled and wiped tears from her eyes as Donald talked. Kwame shifted his seat closer and put his arm around her.

"You see Samantha here. You all read the story of this beautiful, brilliant black woman, the illegitimate daughter of Oliver's brother, Cornwall. He denied her until months before his death. Oliver fell in love with her, as did my boss and her Uncle, Gill Harris. I had talks with Gill about culture, and that's why Kwame Mills was hired three years ago. That's also why I became President of Harris Simmons and took over the company as the first non-Harris family member to serve as CEO. They were exceptional and open-hearted people, Luke."

Donald then pointed to Deirdre Francis, Sheri McCready and Steve Ryan in the audience's front row. "See these three talented media executives. They are the new leaders of Harris Simmons, two women, and a black man as CEO, COO, and President of Sales. The Oliver Harris of his later life would love this talented, diverse team running the company." The three executives all smiled uncomfortably as the camera flashes blinded them.

Desanctis said, "Damn, this guy is magical. It's clear why this city has adopted Black Camelot as its heart and champion for the people."

Donald didn't hear what Desanctis said, but what he said next made it seem as if he had. "Oliver lived a life full of riches, glory, and public adulation. He had given away tons of money to lots of causes but found his purpose at the end of his life. He asked Kwame, Samantha, and me to protect his purpose, and I couldn't be more thrilled. Doing his part to fix and present opportunities for black and brown folks who attend these schools was his way to help the least of these. I couldn't be more honored and proud to do my part in continuing this mission."

Luke then raised his hand again, "One more question, Donald?"

Donald shook his head in amazement, "I'll give it to you, Luke, you've got spunk. But you're done after this. It's starting to feel like we are doing an exclusive interview."

"Exactly, stop being a pig," Jennifer said. The reporters throughout the room groaned again. Like Kung and Desanctis, they had had enough of his grandstanding.

Luke posed the question Jennifer told him she wanted to ask, "Is it true he told you he had a dream that you, Kwame, Samantha, the record mogul Tom Wilson, and Carrie Sinclair should be the royal family of New York?"

Jennifer snapped and yelled, "Damn you, Luke. You asshole."

She was so angry that she kicked him in the back of the leg hard enough for him to shriek in pain and yell, "Ouch. Dammit."

Donald heard the commotion and asked, "What's going on over there? Is everything okay?".

"I'm fine. I got a cramp in my leg," Luke said as he rubbed his calf.

Donald sensed there was more to it than a cramp. The reason for the shriek wasn't his business, and he didn't want the hotshot reporter to get any more attention. He answered the question and crossed his fingers, hoping it would end his back and forth with Luke, "Oliver told us we are privileged, and he wants us to go and do some good. He set us up well, and we now dedicate ourselves to the causes we believe in. He said you are young, beautiful, handsome, and intelligent enough to become our city's Camelot family. But he meant from our deeds and works, not from a vanity standpoint."

"So, you don't believe in the Black Camelot thing?"

"I believe in what we're doing. The Black Camelot label is your creation, Luke. You guys created it after the Harris Simmons murders, not us. It's true, we are rich, but we are now black people living a life of service. Some people say we are powerful, but we don't subscribe to that. If being rich and focused on service means we get called Black Camelot, and if it helps us with our mission, we'll take that moniker any day."

He turned to Kwame and Samantha and asked for confirmation, "I don't mean to speak out of turn. Do you guys agree?"

Kwame and Samantha nodded their agreement, and Donald turned to the other side of the room to take a question. As he did, Jennifer continued to glare at Luke. "I hate you sometimes. There was no reason for you to do that!"

Desanctis backed her up, "Luke, you are wrong. She told you she wanted to ask that question. I was there when she did. You need to stop doing that."

Luke looked down sheepishly and offered a weak excuse, "I was on a roll, and I lost my head. I'm sorry. Jennifer, please accept my apology."

After the press conference, Jennifer approached Samantha Rivers. She wrote a spectacular first-person account of part in the Harris Simmons murders, and they'd become close friends since. Jennifer still seethed when she told her buddy and told her "Luke stole my question."

"You mean the one about Black Camelot. You kicked him, didn't you?"

"Damn right, I did. He's such an asshole and always tries to steal the glory."

Samantha stood a few feet away, Samantha pulled him into the conversation, "Kwame, come over here, please."

"She did kick him," Sammy said excitedly as he arrived.

"He's a show-off, and I'm sure he deserved it," Kwame whispered to Sammy and Jennifer.

"Luke was an ass today and he did deserved it," Jennifer said. She stayed around to say hello to Sammy, but she also had a huge request for the Black Camelot crew. "Kwame, I want to run an opportunity past Sammy, Donald and you."

"Sure, what's on your mind?"

"I'm all in with Black Camelot. Even though we started it because everybody thinks you guys are high society types, I know that's not who you are. You have a bigger purpose, and I am glad Donald spoke to it today. I also know the press is always chasing all of you, and how much of a pain we can be at times. I would love to have exclusive rights to your important future stories. You guys know me; I'm not a hot dog, and I will write stories the right way, not with Luke's drama."

Kwame thought for a second about her request. He looked at Donald, who stood a couple of feet away in an interview, at Samantha, and said, "What a wonderful idea, Jennifer. I agree we should have one primary contact for our stories. Are you okay with her, Sammy?"

Sammy's face lit up, "Heck yeah, Kwame. Jennifer is my girl. Let's give her first rights. Jennifer's a pro, and I trust her. She did a killer job on the exclusive I gave her following the trial."

Kwame nodded his agreement and said, "I agree. You've always been a pro with us. It will piss Luke off, but that's what happens when people think you're cool."

Chapter Six

Six months after the press conference, Kwame asked Michelle Nubani to marry him. He surprised her at an album release concert in New York by Rote Tunz, his college roommate.

The concert turned out to be the perfect cover. Kwame had to get Michelle to come to New York as she had returned to Chicago to continue her work as an economist at Sheraton University. They'd discussed marriage. He knew she was as in love with him as he was with her, but she had no idea the proposal was coming.

"Michelle, Rote has a new album coming out next weekend. He's having a concert for the new album release. Would you like to come?"

"Of course I'll come, Kwame. Any time I spend with you makes me happy."

"Fantastic, Baby, I'll send you a plane ticket now. Rote has just completed this jazz and R&B album. The performance will be at the Grand Ballroom."

"Wait. Isn't Rote a hip-hop guy? Can he sing? What kind of jazz?"

"It's a combination of jazz standards and rhythm and blues love songs. The name of the album is *Rote's Throwback to Love.* He's put together an amazing soundtrack with memorable love songs of the past."

"Ooh, that sounds so romantic, Kwame. I'm excited to see him perform and, of course, to be with my Man."

"Thank you, my love. I can't wait. Tom will be there with Danielle. Carrie and Donald, too. We'll have dinner at the Top Floor, the restaurant at the Grand Ballroom, and go to the concert together."

The Top Floor Restaurant at Grand Ballroom was a five-star restaurant. It was known for its rotating celebrity chefs residency program that featured some of the world's most respected culinary artists. Chef Carol Barnett was in the middle of her three-month residency. She was renowned for her Southern Soul Love menu, the highlight being her award-winning peach cobbler dessert.

Michelle found out from Carrie and Danielle that Chef Carol was the guest chef. She got so excited that she spun in a circle, rubbed her stomach, and shimmied her shoulders as she told Kwame.

"Chef Carol is doing a Chef Residency at The Top Floor. This is what I'm like after I have her peach cobbler. Her food is so yummy. It takes me to a happy place, and I do my happy dance. I can't wait for dinner."

That night, Michelle, Danielle, and Carrie rushed to their table. A bowl of cornbread awaited them, fresh out of the oven. Carrie grabbed the bowl, lifted the napkin, and deeply inhaled its warm aroma. Her eyes rolled back in her head, and she licked her lips.

Danielle grabbed the bowl and, like Carrie, took a deep inhale. As the fresh-baked smell ran through her nostrils, she said, "Oh yeah, Mama is in heaven."

"Y'all need to stop," Michelle said with a giggle. She broke protocol and, instead of taking a whiff, broke off a piece of cornbread and tasted it.

Carrie yelled, "Stop it, woman. No."

"What?" Michelle asked.

"That's like chugging a $500 bottle of wine," Carrie said. "This is a five senses experience, girlfriend. Let me give you specific instructions here, child. It goes like this, you see the cornbread, smell the cornbread, touch the cornbread, taste the cornbread. After you taste, you emit whatever sound to note your satisfaction."

"Exactly, Michelle. What is wrong with you, girl?" Danielle said with a scowl.

Michelle stopped after two chomps and Carrie's and Danielle's scolding. She knew she had broken protocol, but thought that her friends were taking the five senses experience a bit too seriously. But then, as the cornbread rested on her tongue, she realized what they meant. The flavors exploded in her mouth and she lost control of her senses as her eyes rolled back in her head, and she let out a gentle purr. She said to Carrie and Danielle, "Oh my God, that right there was the best thing ever."

"Yes, sister," Danielle exclaimed. "My mouth has been watering all day. I haven't been able to think about anything other than Chef Carol's food. I can't wait for the peach cobbler baby. I'm gonna dance it off, and if I need to, I'll run five miles tomorrow. But tonight, this model will enjoy every course. I might even have two servings of dessert."

Carrie added, "I starved myself for this and tonight I'm having catfish, yams, some greens, two helpings of the peach cobbler, and a blueberry bourbon cocktail."

"Ooh, the blueberry bourbon cocktail makes you dance," Danielle said. "We need to split one. It's mighty strong."

"We'll order two and share them," Carrie said to Danielle and Michelle.

"I will follow your lead, ladies. I love the cocktail too. Maybe we should order two and a half, to be sure," Michelle said and winked mischievously. She then smacked her lips, coughed, opened her mouth, and pointed to her throat as if she were stranded in a desert. "Cocktail, blueberry cocktail, sister thirsty, please, sister is thirsty. I need a blueberry bourbon cocktail."

Everyone laughed. The good humor and watching his lady with their friends made Kwame happy, but unbeknown to everyone he was a mess. His hands trembled, and his legs bounced uncontrollably under the table. He put his hand on his leg to stop the nervous tic, but it didn't work.

After everyone ordered cocktails, Donald pulled Kwame aside. He wanted to take a few minutes to discuss some minor developments with the Oliver

Harris Diversity Fund. Kwame's nerves were shot, and he welcomed the distraction.

He had kept the engagement surprise to himself for two weeks and realized now that it was a mistake. No one knew, not even Tom. He wanted to make it a moment Michelle would never forget and rehearsed the proposal a thousand times. But as the moment neared, his mind turned into mush. It was as if he'd never rehearsed. He couldn't remember a thing.

As they walked outside to the restaurant's terrace, he muttered to himself. It didn't take Donald long to see that something was wrong.

"You okay, Kwame? You seem like you are in another world."

He burst like a dam. "I'm a nervous mess, man, and I have to talk about it. I am proposing to Michelle tonight. It will be a surprise."

Donald broke into a wide-mouthed smile. He put his hand over his mouth and, for a few seconds, stood frozen by the surprise. He then said, "Yes, Kwame. This is such huge news. I'm glad we are here to share it. Carrie loves Michelle, and you know how she feels about you. She will be so happy for you guys. The only person who will be happier is me. You did say it was a secret?"

The uncharacteristic show of emotion was the distraction Kwame needed. It boosted his confidence, "Yeah, Donald, nobody else knows."

Donald hugged him heartily, took a deep breath, and began a metamorphosis. Kwame had never seen him this way. They'd been through a lot together, but he'd never seen him as pensive. When Alexander looked upwards to the sky, closed his eyes, and whispered inaudibly, Kwame realized that they'd just switched roles.

"Are you okay, Donald? You appear as burdened as me."

Donald closed his eyes again, took another deep breath, and said, "Yes, Kwame. I am burdened, too. It's about Carrie. I am crazy about her and think I may be ready too. I take that back. I know I'm ready."

Kwame smiled. The news didn't surprise him. He'd long hoped for it but didn't pry, especially as Carrie was his ex-wife. But he could tell Donald needed a nudge and excitedly encouraged him.

"Well, what are you waiting for? Carrie is amazing. You know what I think about her. There is no better human being in the world. She's incredible."

"You are right, but I'm a little gun shy. You guys didn't make it together, and frankly, that concerns me. Our personalities are very similar, Kwame. I'm a bit older than you, but when I look at you, I see my younger self."

"Hold up, man," Kwame said with a stern voice. He knew they were right for each other and Donald was overthinking.

"No, no Donald, time out. Don't be unfair to Carrie. Thank you for the compliment, but let me remind you why she and I didn't make it. For starters, we were very young. We fell in love too fast, and both had hard-driving careers. And let me say this honestly, with all due respect to my success, she was more talented than I am at business and most other things. That woman is a special human being."

"I agree with you, Kwame. But don't sell yourself short. You are a world-class talent. Nobody has given you anything. You've gone out and taken it."

"Yeah, but you know when you're outgunned, and that's all I'm saying. There was no way I would have asked her to put her dreams on hold. And thank God, I didn't."

They turned to look inside the restaurant at the table where Carrie was telling their friends Michelle, Tom, Danielle, and Rote Tunz a funny story that had everyone smiling and laughing.

"Look at her. There's a lot of joy in that woman. We weren't in that place, man. And because we struggled so much, we ruined any chance to get to the happiness at that table."

"You're right. Kwame, she is always that way. Carrie doesn't have bad days."

"It's why you have to make a move, my friend. Make it official like I am. That will keep her happy."

Donald was just nervous. The work and career ambitions that ruined Kwame's and Carrie's marriage were non-factors in his relationship with her. He knew and told Kwame, "We are perfect for each other, and I'd be devastated if I lost her. I wouldn't know what to do."

"That's how I feel about Michelle and why I am pulling the trigger tonight. My life is fantastic, but Michelle will make it perfect."

Michelle busted through the door to the terrace and ended their conversation.

"Hey, you two big-time executives, your work time is over. I did not come to town for you guys to talk business all night. We need to order. The concert is going to start soon. Come in here and rejoin the party."

Donald smiled and winked at Kwame and told a white lie. "You're right, Michelle. I told Kwame we needed to get back to our beautiful ladies. He wanted to share some big news."

"He tells me things are going great with Oliver's charity. Everything is perfect except he misses me," Michelle said. She then grabbed Kwame by the hand, pulled him close, and hugged him. He didn't want to let her go as her scent captivated him. She turned around and led him through the doors, back into the restaurant, to their table.

Donald walked behind them, tapped Kwame on the shoulder, and said, "Kwame speaks the truth, Michelle. Thank you for breaking up our meeting. He told me to move forward on a deal I'm considering."

She stopped, turned and said, "Well, Donald, Kwame tells me you have the best instincts for deal-making. I'm sure this one will be a winner."

"Yes, indeed Michelle, I am really excited about this deal. It's the biggest one yet."

Chapter Seven

Two beefy men exited the elevator and stood in the Top Floor restaurant's empty waiting area. The restaurant host could tell they were not there for dinner.

"Excuse me, do you have a reservation?" the host asked the first man off the elevator. He was a burly, unshaven, scruffy-faced white man wearing a dirty baseball cap.

"Oh, this is one of those fancy places, huh?" the man sneered. "I'm not surprised this is where these kinds of negroes eat. Negroes are what they call themselves nowadays, right?"

The host was shocked by the man's words and manners, he said to him, "Pardon me? What did you say?"

"Well, partner, let me take my hat off," the burly man said. "I don't want to offend you or any of the negroes. Not yet, anyhow."

"Thank you, sir," the host said. "Yes, this is a fine dining establishment. Can I ask again if you have a reservation?"

"Where are the negroes? I'm sorry, I forgot, you all call them blacks or Afro-Americans up here," the man said with a strong Southern drawl as he ignored the host.

There were two tables with black guests. One was near the restaurant's front, where two men sat quietly eating. They paused and nodded at each other but didn't say a word. At the other, larger table in the far corner, the occupants were engaged in lively conversation. The man pointed to that table when he recognized Donald and Kwame.

"Oh, I see them at the table in the back. Goodness, gracious, how times have changed. Look at them eating at this fancy place. I guess the North truly is free."

The host grew confused and nervous as he listened to the burly man. He kindly asked them once more, "Sir, may I ask again. Do you have a reservation?"

"Reservations," the man said dismissively. "Ah, heck no. That's how you all do it up here in the big city, with reservations and all."

He took his gray, dirty baseball hat off and slapped it on the leg of his blue jeans. A poof of dust emerged from the cap. He then rubbed the front of the hat and the Confederate flag logo affixed to it.

"We don't have a reservation, but if they can sit, I'm sure you can find a table for two country boys," the man said and pointed across the restaurant to Donald and Kwame's table again.

"That looks like them for sure. Let's get them now," the second white man said. He was younger, at six foot two, a couple of inches taller than the burly man and wore a gray baseball cap with the same Confederate logo.

"Hey, what are you doing?" the host screamed as the two men pulled up their pants legs to reveal ankle holsters with small revolvers.

The two black men dining near the entrance stood up. They flicked their wrists and released darts that flew 15 feet from their table across the lobby. The darts pierced and stuck in the necks of the men and immediately immobilized them.

"Ouch, oh damn. What happened? I can't move my arms or my neck," the burly man rasped hoarsely as he gritted his teeth and struggled to move, but he couldn't budge his torso, arms, or neck.

"Me too," the second guy whispered. "I'm paralyzed."

The horrified host turned toward the men who'd thrown the darts. His face paled, and he shook in fear as he tried to comprehend what happened.

The two black men approached the host and the paralyzed men. The taller man said, "Don't worry. You are safe. These guys are bad dudes. You must stay cool as we don't want anyone to know what is going on."

"Wait, hold up. Who are you guys? And what did you do? Are you like ninjas or something?"

"We are the Duncan Brothers. Yes, we are kind of ninjas. We are here to protect the table in the back. I'm Doug. Meet my brother Darryl."

Darryl said, "Hi, we need a private room to interrogate these guys and find out who sent them. Can you help us? We need to move fast before any of the other guests realize what happened."

The host nodded at them but couldn't speak. A waiter standing in the middle of the restaurant saw the altercation and ran to the lobby area. "Man, I have never seen anything like that. Martine, the host, is in shock. My name is Rodriguez. Do you want a room to take these guys? Follow me," he said and opened a door next to the elevator in the lobby. It was a private dining room that was empty.

Doug Duncan said to the intruders, "Follow him. You can't scream. You're partially and temporarily paralyzed. You can use your legs to walk. But nothing else. Follow the orders, and you may live through the night."

As Darryl Duncan and Rodriguez led the two guys into the private room, Doug turned to Martine.

"We are secret, private security for those guys in the back. For them, we don't exist and why we are ninjas. I need you to calm down. Darryl is going to stay inside with those two guys. I will stay here with you in the event any further kill crews come."

"Kill crews? Did you say kill crews? What is going on here? I'm a starving actor working for rent money. This is crazy," Martine said.

"How much is your rent Martine?"

"What? Why? Uh, well, duh, It's $2200 per month. Why?"

"What is your phone number?"

"Why?"

"I am sending you $12,000. That's rent plus bills for four months. You can quit this job or take fewer hours for a while to work on your acting."

"Uh, it is 453-20, I mean 453-2212."

Doug Duncan sent Martine the money and hoped it would relax him. He'd seen people in shock and knew he had to shake him out of the trance. He hoped the cash would work.

"How's that? Does it make you feel better?" Doug asked.

"Huh, what?" Martine said.

"Check your account, please. Trust me, we are the good guys and here for protection."

Martine nodded at Doug and smiled weakly. He was still in shock, but the money in his account did appear to relax him a bit. After a few minutes, he said to Doug, "I could tell they were bad guys. I freaked out when they reached for their ankle holsters. We could have had a massacre here."

"I hate to say it, Martine, but you are right. Everyone here could have been a victim tonight."

"Who are you? And why is this such a secret?"

"Martine, have you ever heard the expression, 'If I tell you, I may have to kill you?' Now is one of those times. Let's just say there are secret organizations to protect people who don't know they are protected. The people at that table will never be harmed by another human being. They will only die from natural causes or a freak accident, but not from assassins."

"At that table back there? Who are they? Are they famous? Are they important?"

"They are important and powerful enough that my organization has dispatched my brother and me to protect them. Remember, they don't know we are here, and that's how it needs to remain."

"Yeah, I'd be nervous if I knew people were out to kill me. I certainly wouldn't be dining out," Martine said. He was still nervous and trying to make small talk.

"We've got 20 people on the floor already, making sure the place is safe. Don't worry, none of the good guys will be hurt tonight."

As Doug talked, Martine regained his wits, and the color returned to his face. The elevator also began to ascend from the ground floor to the Top Floor restaurant. Doug surveyed the lobby area as they waited. A waist-high partition separated the restaurant's lobby from the seating area.

"Martine, stand behind the partition in case bad guys are on this elevator. I'll handle them, but if anything happens, duck."

"With those darts, again?"

"Yeah, Martine, these darts are called detaining darts. Victims can't move any of their body parts except for their legs. It also limits their vocal cords. They can't scream or talk loudly."

Martine's face began to turn pale again.

Doug looked at him and said, "Don't worry. I'll handle this. Stand behind the partition and keep your head down in case anything breaks off. You'll be fine."

The elevator arrived, and two young preppy white guys wearing jeans, tee-shirts, and sneakers jumped out.

"Everything okay?" the first man off the elevator asked excitedly. He was the shorter of the two with dark hair. The other guy was blond, and they looked like brothers. Martine guessed they were ready for action. When he realized they were on Doug's side, he relaxed again.

"Yeah, we stunned them. It was two Confederate flag-wearing Southerners; we need to find out who sent them."

Doug pointed to Donald and Kwame's table. "Darryl and I will continue our assignment. We brought the bad guys down silently. Our charges have no idea we are here."

He pointed to the room where they were detaining the assassins. "A waiter is in there with my brother Darryl and the hillbilly dudes. Can you go in there and send him out? Can you please send out Darryl as well?"

A few seconds later, Darryl and the dark-haired “preppy” came back out with the waiter Rodriquez.

"Rodriguez, I need your phone number. I am going to send you $12,000. That's the same amount I sent Martine."

The waiter's face lit up, "Are you serious? Wow, thank you. My number is 453-6545."

"There is a soundproof room downstairs that we can access," the dark-haired preppy said. "The crowd is filling out on the main floor. But there is no way we will be able to move these guys until after the show. We'd have grand ballroom security, cops, and witnesses all over us."

"So then we'll keep them up here until after the show. Do you have something to sedate and handcuff them with?" Doug asked.

"Yep, we got some stuff. We'll knock them out cold," the dark-haired preppy answered.

"Let's do it then. I need you guys downstairs. We've got about a thousand people here tonight, so I need every man on the floor."

"Roger that," the dark-haired guy said. "We'll take care of them and head back downstairs."

A few minutes later, Donald and Kwame left the Top Floor restaurant to attend the concert on the main floor. When they boarded the elevator, so did the two preppy guys. No one in the Black Camelot crew had an inkling of what had transpired minutes earlier. Doug and Darryl hid in the private room until they departed, and took the next elevator down.

Martine finally recovered from the drama. He and Rodriguez smiled broadly as the Black Camelot crew left the restaurant. The host and waiter each had $12,000 worth of reasons to smile.

Chapter Eight

The Grand Ballroom was loud. The opening act was the award-winning vocalist Fee Fee Collins and her group, That Girl Band. The crowd loved her chart-topping R&B song, "It's Too Late For You Sucka." Collins was a legendary talent and had as big a following as Rote Tunz.

As Collins' sultry, sexy voice rang through the Grand Ballroom, everyone, including Danielle, Carrie, and Michelle, sang and danced along. The song's main lyric, "It's too late for you sucka. I waited and waited, you sat on your hands, and now I'm gone," had become an anthem for women after they dumped bad boyfriends.

Donald stood between Tom and Kwame. They watched their women dance in front of them. He nudged Kwame as Michelle danced happily. The nudge encouraged him. Donald looked at him and whispered, "Ask for the order, my friend. You make your move tonight. I am buying a ring tomorrow."

Kwame appreciated the advice. He was nervous and excited, but ready for the moment, and muttered to himself, "You are supposed to be nervous, Kwame. Don't think about it."

Collins finished her performance, and there was a short intermission before Rote Tunz's set. The crowd milled around, and there was lots of noise as expected in a room of 1000 people. Michelle stood in front of him, facing the stage. He leaned forward, and her scent intoxicated him. It was another reminder of how deeply he was in love. He took a step back, then a deep breath, and said, "Hey Michelle."

When she turned around, he fell into a trance. He didn't see anyone else in the room or hear the crowd noise. She smiled as if she could tell the moment was coming and said, "I love you, Kwame. I'm so happy we are together."

"I love you too, Baby. I am crazy about you. I'm captivated and committed, my love. I have something in this little box for you that I hope you will like," he said as he pulled the ring box out of his pocket.

Kwame couldn't stop his hand from shaking all day. Now they didn't shake at all but inside, his nerves ran a thousand miles an hour. He showed Michelle the ring, and she froze in surprise. She began to shake nervously and said, "Oh my God, Kwame. What is this?"

"Marry me and make me happy forever," he said and dropped down to one knee.

A crowd of onlookers quickly gathered around them. Carrie moved next to Donald, and when she realized what was going on, she grabbed him around the waist and squeezed tight. He put his arm around her, and she whispered to him, "This makes me happy."

Danielle stood next to Tom. She was just as excited for Michelle as Carrie and whispered to Tom, "Your boy made her happy. She wanted this to happen."

As tears rolled down her face, Michelle said, "Of course, my love. I'm so in love with you."

Kwame put the ring on her finger, and the crowd of onlookers roared and clapped in approval. Rote Tunz stood on the stage and screamed, "That's my boy right there, Kwame Mills. Did I see this, right? Did he just get engaged to the beautiful Michelle Nubani?"

"Yes," the audience yelled.

"Yes," Michelle said and thrust her hand with the massive diamond into the air. The thrust drew a roar from the crowd.

Rote saw the ring and shouted from the stage, "Now that's a rock, Kwame. Way to do it right, my friend. You guys need to come up here and let me dedicate this first song to you."

The Celebrity Hack Patrol was in the crowd and shocked and delighted, Desanctis told Jennifer and Luke, "I can't believe this. I got some amazing pictures. I hope you guys got your own. It will be the story of the weekend." His colleagues stood right next to him, but Desanctis had to scream as the crowd cheers became deafening.

He walked away and yelled to Kung, "This is much bigger than a review of the new album. One of the crowned princes of New York is now engaged. My readers will love this."

"Yes, all of our readers will love this," she yelled back and asked, "Where are you going?"

"To the stage Jennifer. I am not going to miss any of this."

"Good idea, I am right behind you," she said and ran to catch up.

Luke ran ahead, beating them both. He snapped a picture of the newly engaged couple as they walked up a short flight of stairs to the stage. "Congratulations, Kwame," he said. "Very smooth moves tonight, my friend. Well done."

"Thank you Luke," Kwame said with a huge smile on his face.

As Kwame and Michelle appeared on the stage, the crowd roared again.

Rote Tunz yelled, "Ladies and gentlemen, meet the soon-to-be Mr. and Mrs. Kwame Mills."

He continued, "This occasion of my friend Kwame made this an even more special night. We are here to debut my new jazz album. It is titled *Rote's Sexy Throwback*. The album includes standards and some original songs. I want to start with an original song titled, 'Love Started For Me With You.' For many of you here in this room, when this song goes platinum, you'll remember where you heard it first. Also, tonight I am changing the name of this song. It will now be 'Michelle. Love Started For Me With You.'"

The crowd swooned as Rote began to play the song. The beginning melody was romantic and fit the moment. Kwame grabbed Michelle and danced slowly. The song immediately captured the the moment, and literally, every couple began dancing.

Desanctis said, "This is so cool, Luke and Michelle. It's the best part of my job. Check this out. We are here as one of the top-selling musical performers drops a new album. One of the top businessmen and philanthropists in the city gets engaged, the crowd is going wild, and our job is to report the story. How crazy is that? I love my job."

He then uncharacteristically threw his hand in the air and began to sway and shift his hips to the music.

Jennifer looked at him, nodded, shocked by what she saw, and voiced her approval, "Well, alright now, Mike. You have been holding back on your cool side."

She looked at Luke next, who surprised her also. He, too, was moving to the music, "Wait a minute. You too, Luke? I thought I knew you guys."

Luke responded. Desanctis didn't. Like many of the people in the room, they got caught up in the moment. "I can't help it, Jennifer. This music is fantastic. Rote Tunz has a winner with Michelle's song. That will be my headline tomorrow."

Jennifer happily started to dance next, "I love to dance. I must take advantage of this opportunity to dance with my guys."

The Celebrity Hack Reporters let their guards down and became part of the crowd captured in an epic New York moment. Donald spotted them as he slowly danced with Carrie. He whispered and pointed to the Celebrity Hacks and smiled, "Honey, check them out."

Danielle and Tom saw them also and smiled. Tom thought to himself, "This is a glorious night. I want to be next to get engaged."

As they danced, Donald whispered to Carrie, "Kwame told me about an hour ago when we were on the terrace. He pulled off a stunning surprise."

"Yes, he did. I would love to be surprised too, but it would be almost impossible to top this. I just want to be with you, Baby."

Donald pulled her tight, and they continued to dance. He also breathed a sigh of relief. Kwame's engagement surprise would be hard to duplicate, and his beautiful girlfriend let him off the hook. But it was time. The next day he would propose.

. . .

The engagement's excitement provided the perfect cover for the commotion in the back of the Grand Ballroom. A few witnesses thought it was security dealing with a small crew of drunks. They didn't pay attention as Doug and Darryl Duncan and two slightly built East Indian guys subdued four large men. The four detainees wore gray baseball caps with the same Confederate battle flag logo as the guys held upstairs. After the altercation, the security detail locked the men in a soundproof rehearsal room in the building's rear.

The East Indian guys were brothers named Keyur and Manish Patel. Keyur told Doug, "I just learned of these guys and that they belong to a racist terrorist group called BE."

"BE means Before Emancipation," Doug said. "They are dangerous and fearless if they come to New York City and try this nonsense."

"Well, they are bad guys," Keyur continued. "They got weapons in here. We took two handguns off them. We were able to take a broom from the janitor's closet, break it, make some fighting sticks, and beat them down. It also helped that they had no hand-to-hand fighting skills."

"It wasn't that much of a fight. It took about five blows each to subdue them. We then immobilized them with paralyzing darts," Manish added, "but he's right. They had guns, so anything could have happened."

"We used paralyzing darts, too," Doug said. "We have two more guys upstairs. It was easy because of the darts. Have you guys reported them to the Society yet?"

"Yes," Keyur answered. "Either way, these bozos messed up coming here. You're the lead on this job, right, Doug? What do we need to do? Are we going to finish these guys or teach them a lesson and let them go?"

Darryl interrupted, "We don't want to leave a trail of bodies. I vote we break all of their fingers and a couple of toes on each guy so they can't pull any triggers or run from any situation for a long time."

"Look at them and look at us. We're all much smaller than these guys," Darryl continued, " We will send a huge message sending them home humiliated, broken, and useless."

"That's a fantastic idea, Darryl," his brother Doug said. "Let's get the two guys from the private room upstairs and bring them down here."

Chapter Nine

The two preppy guys escorted the paralyzed attackers, held upstairs, into the soundproof room. The assassins' hands were tied behind their backs with plastic zip ties. They could move their upper bodies now, as the effects of the paralyzing darts had worn off.

Doug Duncan once again noticed the fraternal resemblance of the hillbillies' escorts.

"I meant to ask you guys upstairs before. Are you brothers? You look a lot alike."

"Yes, we are," the dark-haired, shorter brother said. He spoke fast and with a New York accent that didn't match his preppy appearance. "My name is Garry Miller, and I've been with the Society for three years. I'm an Army Ranger, and I have two black belts. It's great to meet other people in the Society, especially locals. I've done some work for the Society in the UK and South America, but this is my first time working in the States. I'm from here, born in the Bronx, but I live..."

"Garry," his brother said. He was the taller of the two. Garry immediately stopped when his brother yelled his name.

"I'm Garry's older brother, Larry, said the blonde. Garry is a talker, as you can tell. If you listen, he'll never stop," he said. Larry was a couple of inches taller and, like Garry, had a full thick head of hair.

"Well, that's what everyone says. I just have a lot on my mind, and I want to..."

Larry snapped at his brother again, "Garry."

Garry shot his older brother a glare. Doug Duncan saw the look and smiled, "We're brothers too. My name is Doug, and this is my brother Darryl. Our father is the martial artist Billy 'Death Hands' Duncan."

The Miller Brothers' faces lit up, "Oh, wow, we're huge fans of your Dad's. He's a b-a-a-a-d man," Garry said. "We should work out sometime. Did I tell you I have two black belts?"

Doug and Darryl smiled at Garry. Keyur then introduced himself and his brother. "My name is Keyur, and this is my brother Manish. We are weapons experts and fans of the legendary 'Death Hands' Duncan's, too."

"Well, right on. We have all brothers here today," Garry said.

"Yes, three sets of brothers," Larry interrupted his younger brother before he started to talk again. He also knew why they were there and wanted to turn the attention back to the assignment.

"Doug, we will follow you as the leader for this assignment. It's also a personal thrill for Garry and me to work with the sons of Billy 'Death Hands' Duncan."

Doug and Darryl smiled. They appreciated the kind words about their dad.

"Thanks, guys, for the compliment," Doug said. "So, next we are going to execute 'Project Maim.' They won't try any assassinations here or anywhere else anytime soon."

"Ouch, that would hurt, Doug," Garry said.

"This is the business we are in, Garry. You are an Army Ranger. Death is part of our work. We contemplated killing them but decided if we send them all back hobbling with broken body parts, they'll think twice before sending kill squads back here."

"Next time, there will be bodies," Darryl said and turned to the hillbillies. "At least y'all country boys will be able to go home."

Doug gave Larry an appreciative nod. He knew what it was like to manage a younger rambunctious brother. He said to Larry, "He's not as talkative as Garry, but he likes the action."

Darryl stretched as he prepared to punish the hillbillies. He also agreed with his older brother's comment, "I do like the action, and this room is soundproof. So, let's get to work. Is everybody going to participate?"

As Darryl warmed up, he began to sweat profusely. He didn't need help, nor did he want it. The other Society of Protector members politely deferred to him. Keyur spoke first, "Manish, and I will observe. We are here if you need any help. Maybe we can learn a few things."

"We'll just watch too," Garry said.

Darryl acknowledged their decline with a polite nod.

'Death Hands' son walked slowly towards the six guys. He clenched his fist and threw air punches that made sounds that only world-class martial artists could duplicate. The men sat on the floor with their hands tied behind their backs as he explained the rules.

"I'm going to untie your hands, and you can fight back. One ground rule is: don't scream for help. We're all assassins, and screaming and crying for help is conduct unbefitting an assassin. Besides, the room is soundproof, and there is a concert outside. No one will hear you. So, who is going to be first?"

Chapter Ten

Carrie carried two cups of coffee into Donald's bedroom.

Donald turned over in the bed and stared at her. He was still sleepy, and his legs were sore from the night of dancing. She sat the coffee cups on a table near the windows and opened the blinds. Sunlight from the floor-to-ceiling windows lit up the room. The glow of the morning sun was behind her, and even in her pajamas, she looked radiant. Donald was crazy about her, and his heart started to beat fast as he thought about his plans for today.

He said to her, "You take my breath away, Carrie."

She looked at him, and her face glowed, but she didn't smile. It was her look of love, "Donald, stop it, Baby. Don't make me blush. That is unfair. I have no defense against you. Nothing," she said. "See, my face is hot, and I'm losing control."

Donald knew their love was as intense as she just said. He felt the same way, and he decided not to make her blush anymore this morning.

"Alright, then Beautiful, I'll stop for now," he said with a smile.

"Thank you, my love."

"What time is it?"

"It's 9 AM; time to wake up. By the way, you slept with that same smile on your face. I haven't seen you have so much fun in..."

They were together for nearly four years, and Carrie couldn't remember a time when Donald had so thoroughly let loose. She scratched her head as she tried to recall and said, "I've never seen you have so much fun, honey."

"I had a blast. It was a wonderful evening. How could I not have had fun with my lady on such an epic night?"

His compliment made her blush again. He could still do that with the right words, touch, or look.

She continued to smile as she thought about the press being there and being kind for a change. "It's the first time I've seen you around the press and not care."

"How about that, Carrie? The Celebrity Hack Patrol saw me bustin' some moves. Heck, even they were dancing. People will remember this night for years to come, so I'm fine with them taking pictures. Are you okay with it, Honey?"

She moved both cups of coffee to the nightstand next to Donald, cuddled close, and whispered. "I really couldn't care less about what the press might say. I am with the most amazing man ever. I've known it since I met you at Ron and Marcia Cherry's dinner party four years ago, and you had me tongue-tied. When you touched me the first time, my whole body tingled. You had me at that very moment. I'm so lucky no one has been able to come between us."

Her words were timely and the encouragement he needed.

"Another woman? Are you serious, Carrie? I'm so lucky another man didn't steal you from me. I've been hypnotized by your beauty, charm, mind, and heart since I met you."

"Oh, Donald," she said.

"It's true, Carrie. The last few years have been crazy with Harris Simmons and now the foundation. And you stood by me. I am madly in love with you."

She kissed him on the lips softly, "Baby, I wasn't going anywhere, and I'm still not. I told you that you had me when I first laid eyes on you."

"I'm supposed to say that line, Carrie."

Their conversation stopped when they heard the front door to the apartment open. Donald's cook and housekeeper, Tiffany, yelled, "Good morning, Donald and Carrie. Where is everyone? Are you guys up? Oh, I smell coffee. You guys must be up."

"Yes, Tiffany, we are in my bedroom. I slept a little late," Donald yelled back.

"I have your morning newspapers. You and your friends are all over them. *The News, The Post,* and *The Ledger* all have photos of you guys on the front covers."

"Are they good pictures?" Donald yelled.

"Oh, let me go see what the newspapers are saying," Carrie said. She handed Donald his coffee cup before walking to the kitchen. "Drink your coffee before it gets cold."

Tiffany sat at the kitchen island with the newspapers. Carrie rushed in and took the seat next to hers.

"Good morning, Carrie. Everybody looked like they had such a great time. The article said that Kwame Mills and Michelle Nubani got engaged. Is that true?"

Carrie's face lit up as she told the story, "Oh, my God. It was such a fun night. Kwame surprised Michelle with a huge ring. Rote Tunz named a song for her, and you had to see Michelle. She was so happy. She is reserved most of the time, but she was in her moment last night. You could tell how much she is in love with Kwame."

Tiffany nodded toward the bedroom and whispered, "Like you love him, right?"

"Yes, like I love him," Carrie answered. She then repeated it louder for Donald to hear, "Like I love him."

Donald yelled from the bedroom, "Tiffany, I've been telling her how much I love her."

Tiffany winked at Carrie and yelled back, "You are lucky, Donald. She is an amazing woman. There is no one better for you. I hope you get engaged, too."

"That's a wonderful idea, Tiffany," Donald said. He walked out of the bedroom wearing a tee-shirt and pajama bottoms.

He turned Carrie's seat to face him, knelt to one knee, and said, "Carrie, I can't wait any longer. How about we buy you an engagement ring today? I don't want another day or another moment to pass without you knowing how much I love you. My heart has burst for you. I told Kwame last night when he told me his news that I was ready, too, and I would ask you today. Marry me. Please say yes."

They hadn't talked about marriage or rings, which made this moment a total surprise. She placed her hands over her heart as her lips quivered, and her eyes began to water. She wanted to say yes, but couldn't.

Tiffany could tell how overwhelmed she was and said, "Open your mouth, sweet girl. Let the words come out. Just open your mouth. Say yes, sweet girl."

"Please, sweet girl, say yes," Donald said.

Carrie melted emotionally. It took her a few seconds to compose herself. She wiped tears from her face, shook her hands frantically, and nervously brushed her long mane back from her face. Donald smiled at her with the smooth, assured handsome gaze that always hypnotized her.

"Of course, Donald. You make me happy. You fill my heart. My love for you is beyond comprehension. I will marry you." She pulled him upright and kissed him.

"That may be the sweetest proposal I've seen in my life," Tiffany said. "You guys deserve each other, and I'm happy for you both. Let's thank God for this moment."

Tiffany Joseph has been Donald's housekeeper and chef since he skyrocketed to success and moved to Sanchez Palace in Soho twelve years ago. Their relationship had evolved over the years, and both were devout Christians. Whenever he was going through an issue, she would give him a Bible verse and remind him of prayer's power. He respected and trusted her tremendously, and often introduced her as his second Mom. So, he obediently obliged when she said, "Let's thank God for this moment."

"Do you want to lead the prayer, or should I?" he asked her.

"No, Donald. You are the man of the house, and we are here with your future bride. You lead the prayer."

"You are right, thank you. Let us hold hands in prayer," he said.

"Heavenly Father, thank you for this moment. You've brought Carrie and me together as only a God as gracious as you could. The journey has been long and eventful, but you've been molding us for each other. Thank you for teaching and leading us. May we continue to put You first, then each other, and keep us humbled and grounded by Your words. May they guide us continuously. We pray in Your name, Amen."

"In Your name, Jesus. Amen," Carrie said.

"Amen. What a wonderful prayer, Donald."

"Thank you, Tiffany. Okay, Carrie, my fiancée. I like the sound of that word," he smiled. "Let's shower, dress, and go ring shopping."

He stopped first to look at the front cover of all three newspapers on the counter. Under the pictures of the engagement story of Kwame Mills and

Michelle Nubani, a small photograph also appeared on the cover. The photo was tagged, "Two Bodies Found in Back Alley of Grand Ballroom."

. . .

Hours after the concert ended at the Grand Ballroom, Doug Duncan and his team at the Society of Protectors dumped two bodies in the back alley. Doug explained to The Voice, "We located six guys at The Grand Ballroom, and we intended to interrogate them for information. Our plan was not to kill anyone. We only wanted to break the fingers and a few toes of all six. However, the first two guys had weapons hidden in the heels of their boots."

"What kind of weapons?" The Voice asked.

"Short knives. They twisted off the heels on their boots and pulled out two-inch knives. In the hands of someone who knows what to do with them, they can be deadly. They double-teamed Darryl, but he disarmed them and sliced them up pretty badly with their own weapons. Then he snapped their necks. He chose to relieve them of their pain. It was a merciful decision."

"Well, those are the consequences in our line of work. I understand those game-time decisions. Did we learn anything about who sent them?"

"The pair with the knives in their boots were the leaders. I'm afraid we didn't secure any information from them. But they had fairly sophisticated weaponry."

"Doug, let me tell you that was not all that was sophisticated about them. We recently confronted another team of three guys with beacons implanted in their arms beneath their tattoos. The beacons sent off an alert, and a response team of five rescuers came to their aid. Our team was prepared and handled them. You guys were lucky they did not send reinforcements."

The Voice was right. BE had a head of operations who dispatched kill teams and served in a role similar to the Voice. His name is the Confederate.

The Confederate knew the team was in trouble and sent a rescue crew to the Grand Ballroom. However, the metal and cement soundproofed walls in the rehearsal room blocked the beacons' transmissions. They couldn't figure out how to locate their team when the beacons went dead. The Confederate called them off when he realized they might be walking into a trap.

He told the rescue team, "We must live to see another day. We have no idea what is going on in that building. We have six fighters in there, and we can't locate them. For your safety, get out of there."

The difference between the BE and The Society of Protectors was immense. The Society operated as an army of professional protectors with assassin skills. The BE was a loose outfit of angry racists looking for a fight.

Bobby Joe Blain learned that lesson painfully and shared it with the Confederate.

"I'm just not built for this. I'm only 21 years old. I believe in the Before Emancipation cause, but they ruined the team and me. They killed two of us and broke four of my fingers on my left hand, three of my fingers on my right hand, and both of my big toes. They told me because I looked like the youngest that they would have a little mercy on me. I'm doing what they asked me to do. I'm telling you that we are in over our heads."

"Where are you now, Bobby Joe?" the Confederate asked.

"I am at the safe house in the Bronx. We got a taxi here, but everyone here is busted up. As I said, we weren't ready for these guys. First, they paralyzed half of us with these tiny darts. To make matters worse, the guys were average-looking physically, all less than six feet tall and under 200 pounds, but man, they were total badasses. They only used one guy, and he was unarmed. He let our guys take their knives out. He stood about five feet ten or so and 30-40 pounds lighter than our guys. That little guy fought them both at the same time. It was so tough to watch, and it felt even worse. I nearly shat myself. They couldn't touch him, and the fight wasn't even close. He disarmed them and beat the crap out of them; gave them their knives back, disarmed them again, and beat the crap out of them some more. And then he gave them their knives and took them away one last time. He sliced them up and snapped their necks. It was a massacre. We were way out of our league."

This report stunned the Confederate, but he didn't let on. He couldn't afford to have the young associate lose confidence in him as a leader.

"Why didn't you send someone to save us? We thought you were supposed to send someone to save us. Wasn't the beacon supposed to help you track us?"

"They didn't work, Bobbie Joe. I am sorry."

"Hell, man, I quit. I'll go to rallies, but no more of this stuff. I need to get my fingers and toes fixed and go back to Tennessee and enlist in a junior college or something. I've had enough."

"We'll send a team to you."

"Please come quickly. We all need to get home and go to the hospital."

Chapter Eleven

Nine months before Oliver Jr.'s death, Kwame learned about The Guiding Force. Oliver called him in London while he still served as president of Harris Simmons International.

"Kwame Mills here," he answered.

"Hey Kwame, this is Oliver Harris, Jr." His voice, as always, was bubbly.

"Wow, wait a second. Is that you, Oliver?"

"Yes, this is me, Kwame. I'm sitting in my office. My secretary gave me your number, and I called you myself. I think I last made a direct call internationally ten, 20 years ago. No, I'm wrong, let me think correct that. I've never made one. I'm 85 years old, and this is a first. Ha, I guess you can teach an old dog new tricks after all."

Kwame chuckled as he listened. "Oliver, it's always nice to hear from you, but is everything okay?"

"Oh yeah, everything is grand. I'm still rich, thanks to the killer job you guys are doing."

He continued, "Kwame, I've been working on something here. You are due in town next week on Monday for our quarterly lunch. I need you and Sammy to stay in town for a few extra days. It's a pretty important reason and highly secretive, and why I am contacting you directly."

"Okay, Oliver, I will make plans to stay through the week."

" I'm calling Sammy, next. She'll be shocked. We text and email each other, and she calls me at least once a week, but I've never called her. My secretary, or my wife Grace, always calls and patches me into her. I'm a bit of a dinosaur with all this technology stuff."

"Well, she's in the office now. If you call, you can catch her. I just had a meeting with her 20 minutes ago. She's still around."

"Okay, I'm going to give her a ring. Hopefully, she won't pass out from shock."

Kwame smiled at Oliver's comments. After recovering from his son and brother's death, Oliver enjoyed his final years working on his educational fund and his time with Samantha. He adored his grandniece. She was fiery, funny, smart-alecky, and affectionate towards him in a way he had never experienced.

The quarterly meetings with him, Donald, and Sammy eventually morphed from business meetings into Samantha's coming out party with New York business and society leaders. He filled her trips with lunches, dinners, and society events with his wealthy and influential friends. She was equally fond of her uncle and loved hanging around him.

Oliver was 85. He stood about five-foot-eleven, weighed about 190 pounds, and had an energy level that belied his years. Not even his hair betrayed his years. He thought his thick head of all-white hair made him look old, but Samantha always teases that his mane made him look younger and handsome.

When Oliver called Donald Alexander about the special meeting, the phone call was less ominous, but still alarmed his protégé. As chairman emeritus, he was a non-executive chairman. Donald had complete operating control of the company. He often told Donald, "Look, I'm never going to meddle in what you are doing. I don't need to because I'm rich beyond my wildest imagination and in the autumn of my life. I had my run at the top and want to enjoy my final days trying to make a difference."

Except for his last few years, Oliver never had any significant relationships with people of color. These three people changed his worldview. He was grateful for them and, as a gift that would extend well beyond his lifetime, ushered them into a world only a few knew.

They met at 3 PM in the historic 39th-floor conference room at Harris Simmons. The room overlooked Central Park. On this bright sunny afternoon, they stood at the window, captivated by all the activity in the park.

A bottle of champagne and four glasses were also on the conference room's gigantic table. They all wondered what the occasion might be.

Kwame asked, "What is going on, Donald? What's with all the mystery? And why the champagne? Are we celebrating something?"

"I have no idea. It's a secret to me, too."

As they unsuccessfully tried to piece together the secret, Oliver burst through the door with the excitement and energy of a man half his age. "Hey, everybody, what a beautiful afternoon, huh?"

Kwame was standing next to Donald. They nudged each other and smiled in appreciation of Oliver's joy. Samantha glanced at them and then asked, "What are you up to, Uncle Oliver? Champagne in the afternoon? Does Aunt Grace know you are drinking?"

He smiled at her and winked. "I won't tell if you won't tell. You wouldn't sell out old Uncle Ollie, would you?"

Donald then probed, his curiosity as high as everybody else's. "So what gives Oliver? Did you sell the company? You've got us all guessing."

"No, Donald, I told you the company was in your control. What I want to tell you about today is much bigger than money. This is life-changing."

Kwame, like Donald and Samantha, could tell Oliver enjoyed the suspense. He thought about how spectacular a salesman he must have been in his heyday. They were captivated and anxiously waited for his revelation.

"What's the secret, Oliver?" Kwame inquired. He wondered, what could be bigger than Harris Simmons? They were all at the top of the game. What more could there be?

"I need you all to fill up your glasses and take a seat. Trust me. You need to be seated."

Donald quickly grabbed the bottle and popped the cork. As the sound echoed through the room, an amused Oliver commented, "That's a sweet sound that I've enjoyed over the years, but today the sound is the sweetest yet."

They filled their glasses, took a seat, and stared anxiously at him. He took a sip, and after it marinated on his tongue, nodded approvingly.

"Good bubbly here," he said, and then asked casually, "Have you heard of The Guiding Force?"

They eyed each other and waited for someone to nod yes or no. Oliver suspected they hadn't, given the secrecy of the organization.

He then confided, "I am a member of The Guiding Force. It was the brainstorm of Horace Simmons, who, besides being my father's business partner, was Dad's best friend since college at Harlowe. Horace and my dad were two of the founding members of The Guiding Force 80 years ago. It is the most secretive society of American business, civic and political leaders ever. I am the third Harris Simmons member. Gill was up for a vote before his death. Cornwall was not a member. He did not fit because of his notorious public profile. The Guiding Force is too secretive and powerful to have reckless personalities as members. Corrupt personalities and characters could endanger the anonymity and sully the super secretive and discreet group of power brokers and our important work."

They did not know what to make of the news. Oliver was excited, but they were still in the dark as to why it should matter to them. He continued to explain, and they just listened.

"The Guiding Force has always benefitted Harris Simmons. It used to be how we got access to newsmakers and influencers for our editorial stories, and part of the secret sauce Horace Simmons and my dad were particularly astute in developing."

He continued, "The Guiding Force helped us close deals with advertisers, win favor with politicians, and secure lines of credit when the company was in its early stages. Its members were also very lily-white, Mayflower descendant types. There were no black or brown people or women as members, until now."

Donald asked, "What do you mean, 'until now'? Was The Guiding Force about to be exposed, and do you want us to run some stories on this? Do you want a fluff piece on this organization? I'll gladly call an editor to do some stories."

"No, that is why we have champagne here, and I asked you all to sit down. It's like this: The Guiding Force members were previously selected and pre-qualified as the best of the best. At least that is what we'd say to each other. At a recent meeting, I asked my fellow members to look at how we categorize the best of the best, and to my surprise, they did."

"What are you talking about, Uncle Oliver?"

"Sammy, I am stepping down as a member, and, as a result of your birthright, will be grandfathered in as a member."

Chapter Twelve

The induction took place on a Saturday afternoon. It started with a meeting in the lobby of Harris Simmons with Oliver Harris providing an overview of The Guiding Force's history.

"When Horace Simmons started The Guiding Force 80 years ago, its mission was simplistic. He wanted to build a great organization to do business deals. His vision was to bring the best businesses, civic, and political minds together to support each other. The initial group members were Mauldin Daniels, the legendary CEO of Team Kaos Automotive, the largest American auto manufacturer; Jackson Lee Mulliken, the domestic and international shipping magnate; John Curtin, the Texas oil baron; Hardwick "Hardy" Ewing Bivens, the Governor of California; K. Wimer Brockelman, the Wall Street financier; Wesley O'Connor, the founder of the American Symphony; Oliver Harris Sr.; and Horace Simmons."

Oliver continued, "The original members worked closely together and supported the objective of economic growth and business development. Only much later did national and global governance principles become part of its mission."

"The current members you will meet today are descendants of the founders. They are Mauldin "Danny" Daniels IV, the current CEO of Team Kaos Automotive and great-grandson of Mauldin Daniels; Jack Zell Mulliken, the grandson of Jackson Lee Mulliken and CEO of We Ship, the global shipping company; John S.P. Curtin, the grandson of John "Big Tex" Curtin, whose family's oil ownership had grown beyond Texas to 25% of all America's oil and now natural gas mining; K.Wimer "Lax" Brockelman IV, the current head of the Financial Exchange; California Senator Janet Bivens, granddaughter of Hardwick Ewing Bivens, the first female member of The Guiding Force; and Jacci O'Connor, longtime conductor for the American Symphony and granddaughter of its founder, Wesley O'Connor."

"These are some of the top guns in business and society," Donald said.

"Yes, they are, Donald. And today, as we go through the ceremony, the power and reach of The Guiding Force will be revealed. Your induction, aside from getting married or having a child, will be one of the highlights of your life."

Oliver turned to his niece, "The last member admitted was Jacci O'Connor three years ago. She was our second female member. Senator Bivens, who had been a member for 15 years, put her foot down and demanded we admit more women. Janet and Jacci are excited to have you, Sammy. They will be the older sisters you never had. And because you are a Harris descendant, that means a lot to me. They will be here to protect and advise you, long after I am gone."

Oliver escorted them to the private exit area used only by the executives. There was a table there with three boxes as well as four glasses of champagne.

"Grab a glass and the box with your name on it." They picked up the filled champagne flutes, as Oliver instructed. He then led them in a toast, "Cheers to this life-changing day. Now, have a drink and open the boxes."

The trio sipped the champagne and opened up their boxes. Its contents included a silver band watch, a matching silver ring with a black rectangle stone, a tiny screwdriver, and a book titled, *The Guiding Force Book of Order.*

"Gentlemen and Lady, read the inscription on the back of your watch and tell me what it says?"

He continued, “Donald, I will walk you through the full exercise. Everyone watch him complete these steps. Kwame, you will go second, and Sammy last. Samantha, don't refer to me as Uncle here. I am # 25 or Oliver 25 at all GF activities. You'll get accustomed to it. There is a formality to this organization."

"Okay, Oliver 25," she said.

Donald picked up his watch. It was heavier than it looked. He read its inscription: "Donald Alexander, The Guiding Force Member #40, For Life & With God's Protection."

"Awesome," Oliver said. "Now, use the small screwdriver from the box to remove the tiny screw and back cover from the watch. Place the cover on the table. This is an important step, so please follow my instructions precisely."

Donald removed the cover and placed it on the table.

"Now, press your right thumb into the black foamy mat on the back of your watch. It will leave an imprint."

Donald complied.

"This is your thumb signature. Now, use the screwdriver to screw the tiny screw back on the cover. That is it."

Oliver turned to Kwame and Sammy, "Now, you two complete the task."

As Kwame and Sammy unscrewed the backs of their watches and imprinted their thumbs, Oliver could tell they were excited but not nearly as much as he. This ceremony was his first opportunity to admit members.

"Okay, now that you've completed this task, let me show you something. Watch what I do and duplicate each step. Take the watch, turn the crown – which you may refer to as a ‘wind button’ - one revolution clockwise, and then joggle it and down twice."

As the crew wound their timepieces, Oliver said, "I know this feels like an arts and crafts class, but this watch is your identifier in The GF. You must learn how to use it properly. Watch what I do."

Oliver joggled his watch crown up and down twice, and the back cover opened.

"Look at the inside of the cover now, please." To their surprise, the inside cover now displayed their name and member number.

"This timepiece has been custom-designed. You can't use the screwdriver to open the back cover anymore. The wind button is now also sensitized to respond only to your fingertips. No one else can open your watch."

"What's the importance of this watch, Oliver?"

"Excellent question, Donald. If you are ever to meet any of the retired members, the watch is proof of membership. A member must show their watch to identify himself or herself in a one-on-one meeting."

"And what about the imprint?"

"Another good question, Donald. There are safety deposit boxes at banks in the top 100 cities globally, where you can get cash and emergency resources. There are four and five-star hotels in the top 200 cities in the world that will always admit you. There are doctors in the top 200 cities and security teams in literally every market in the world. *The Book of Order* will instruct you to each. You will have to display your fingerprint. It is like an international currency."

"Wow, this is overwhelming," Donald said.

"I told you this is the most powerful organization in the world."

"What about the ring? What does the ring do?"

"Donald, I'm so glad you are full of questions. All of this stuff can almost seem like a master spy class. The ring is an identifier for our security forces when you are traveling, particularly abroad. If you are ever in trouble, a beacon gets activated, and our forces will find you. Never travel without it."

"It's super-spy stuff and cool," Kwame said.

"You are right, Kwame. A beacon locator that will help the good guys save you from the bad guys is spy stuff," Oliver said.

"Wow, so the security forces are the real deal, huh?" Samantha joked. "I can put them on some bad guys from my past? Right?"

"No #42, please don't ever do that. Seriously, these guys are killers." He looked at her with the patented Oliver Harris glare. It was a look that made many powerful people shrivel. He'd never looked at her that way, but she had heard about it and knew he meant business.

"Just kidding, #25. I guess this is not a time for jokes."

"No. The time for jokes is later." He glanced at his watch and said, "Okay, we have a ceremony to attend. Grab your boxes of goodies. There's an SUV outside. It will take us to meet the other active members. They have come to town for your initiation."

The ride took two minutes. The ceremony was at the Millennial Club, the city's most exclusive business club, located only a few blocks from the Harris Simmons headquarters. Donald was a member, and Kwame retained a visiting membership when he lived in London.

"This is where the initiation will be? Do we have a private room?" Donald asked, surprised.

"No, Donald. I know you and Kwame have been members here and probably thought this club was paid for by the members. However, The Guiding Force are the real owners of the building, the real estate underneath, and the entire city block."

"Wait a minute, did you say the entire block? Two billion dollars of real estate is on this block: The City Museum, The Dignitary Hotel, The Celebrity Hotel, The Pacific luxury condominium."

"You forgot Kip Meenan's Midtown, the Irish dive bar on the far corner. And it's not two billion. Try between seven and twelve billion dollars," Oliver said.

He continued, "Real estate holdings throughout the world are how we pay for everything. We burn through $100 million a year. You'll see the financial details in the book, including the annual operating costs. The GF will never ask members for money. Our organization is wealthier than some small countries' entire GNPs, and if our members need money, we have it."

"This is beyond comprehension. What does The Guiding Force do with all this money?"

"Really important work, Donald. We support projects like clean water and crop development in third-world countries. We provide legal support and defense for victims against corrupt police departments and bogus arrests. One of the biggest uses of funds is to buy juries and judges in banana republics, where rigged and corrupt judicial practices are the norm. We also use our financial clout and our private army to threaten autocratic rulers and suggest they leave office. But no one outside of The Guiding Force would ever know."

"Isn't that corrupt?" Kwame asked.

"Kwame, a lot of evil people are in power throughout the world. Our strength is in letting them know that we can reach them and balance the scales of humanity and justice for good. And trust me, the bad guys receive the message. They don't want us sending our forces to visit them. Over the last eight presidential elections, we've persuaded five guys not to run for President."

"How do we do all this without getting noticed, Uncle, I mean #25?"

"That's the beauty of who we are. We've ended wars, droughts, and famines and, to do that, we must remain secret. Now let's go inside and meet your new best friends."

As they departed the SUV, the usual doorman was not there. Donald attributed this initially to the induction being on a Saturday, a typically slow day at the club. His replacement was massive and muscular. Donald guessed he was at least six feet eight and 350 pounds.

"Good evening, Member 25. I am Carlos. Welcome to The Guiding Force Members 40, 41, and 42."

"Who is this guy?" Donald asked Oliver. "He's as big as Satch Jones, if not bigger."

Donald was thinking about the extra-large security lieutenant and retired pro football tackle at Harris Simmons.

Oliver said, "He is as huge as Satch. You're right. We have a primary security team of 100 people who are on the annual payroll. They are the best of the best. They must speak three languages and have elite military training. Most of them are American Green Berets, Army Rangers, and Navy Seals. We also have members from India's Marco Force, Israeli Special Forces, Japan's Delta Force, and several other countries. Some are unassociated with any military. Those guys are the scariest. They are the fighters who walk into the darkest alleys without fear."

"Wow," Kwame said.

"Yes, wow," Oliver responded. "Our guys can get into any country and resolve pretty much any situation. We also have a secondary militia of several thousand we can access at a moment's notice. Through our primary and secondary security, we do have the capability to mobilize a small army."

After they entered the Millennial Club's massive entry hallway, Kwame said, "This place looks empty. Are we the only ones here?"

They heard the outside door close, and Carlos turning the three large locks on the massive double doors. The sound echoed throughout the empty main floor.

"The club is closed. Everyone is downstairs in the Members Quarters," he said in his thick Spanish accent.

"Downstairs, Members Quarters? What are you talking about?" Donald asked. "There is only a pool down there."

Oliver winked at Donald and flashed a kind smile, "I told you we own the entire block, and this is a secret organization. Just keep cool #40."

He turned to Kwame and Samantha and asked, "You guys okay?"

Kwame said, "I'm cool. I thought there was only a pool downstairs, too."

Samantha excitedly walked up to her Uncle and said, "This is so much fun. I can't wait to see what's next."

Oliver chuckled, and so did Carlos, who waited next to the elevator to escort them downstairs.

"You are definitely my family, #42, and remind me of myself on my initiation night. I said the same thing to my Father 40 years ago, but I remember it just like yesterday."

"Well, let's get after it then," the impatient Samantha said. "Lead the way #25, please."

"Okay, follow me and pay attention." Once they boarded the elevator, he said, "Kwame hit the pool button and hold it for a ten count until the button turns from white to green."

Kwame pressed the button, and Oliver counted off, "One, two, three, four, five, six, seven, eight, nine, and ten."

The button turned green, and Oliver smiled and his voice rose with excitement. "You guys have to understand this is my first initiation since my own. I had Gill up for membership as a gift for his 55th birthday. He was admitted, and then we had the shooting at Harris Simmons. I looked forward to it as a special Father and Son moment."

Oliver lowered his head, and his eyes began to water as he thought about the untimely murder of his son. Samantha put her arm around her uncle and pulled him closer. She kissed him on the forehead and wiped at his tears, "Uncle Gill was an amazing Man. I miss him so much. He did so much for me."

After her words, the four members of The Guiding Force stopped talking. The only sounds were sniffles as they drifted off into their private thoughts. Oliver snapped them out of it.

"Okay, guys and gal, enough of the sadness. We have a great evening planned, and in seconds you three will become part of something dear to me. Let's get ready for some fun."

The elevator door opened to a room that was half as long as a football field. Its centerpiece was an Olympic-sized pool. On the far end of the room was a seating area.

"Hurry, we have the green light," Oliver yelled as the elevator door opened. "We only have 20 seconds after this elevator door closes to make it to the other side of the room."

"Why, what's going on?" Samantha asked.

"Just help an old man along, #41. #40, go ahead, and when you reach the other end, I need you to press your member # into the phone on the wall. Do it in this order: pound sign, four, zero."

Donald ran across the room and pressed his information into the phone as Oliver instructed. The center of the wall slid open in two parts, and as it did, Donald's, Kwame's, and Samantha's jaws dropped in amazement.

Behind the wall was a room as large as the pool room. The decor was stodgy and what one might expect to find in an old-school secret society clubroom. Portraits of past and present members hung on the dark oak walls. In the center of the room sat a massive circular table surrounded by ten seats, one each for the seven active members and the three new members.

Waiting for them in front of the table, champagne flutes raised, were the six current members. They all smiled and yelled in unison, "Welcome Members 40, 41, and 42 to The Guiding Force."

Donald, Kwame, Samantha, and Oliver entered the room, and the doors slid closed behind them.

Oliver performed the honors. "Ladies and gentlemen, let me introduce you to our new members. Member # 40 is Donald Alexander, CEO of Harris Simmons. Member #41 is Kwame Alexander, President of Harris Simmons International, and Member #42 is Samantha Rivers, Senior Vice President of Sales and Operations for Harris Simmons International."

Of the current members, Mauldin "Danny" Daniels IV spoke first. "Welcome #40, #41, and #42. I am member #34, and my name is Mauldin Daniels. My friends call me Danny, and I am the oldest tenured member. It is a pleasure to welcome you as members and to call each of you a friend."

Next up was K. Wimer "Lax" Brockelman. He said, "Welcome #40, #41, and #42. I am member #35. My pals call me Brock. It is a pleasure to have you as members and to call each of you a friend."

Brock was followed by Jack Zell Mulliken, who said, "I am member #36, and welcome to this extraordinary group of people and this life-changing moment. My friends call me Zell. I'm excited to call each of you a friend."

He stepped back as John S.P. Curtin introduced himself. The energy tycoon said with a Texas accent, "I am member #37, and we change the world here at The Guiding Force. I am excited to have you guys on board and to call each of you a friend."

Janet Bivens, the senior Senator from California, was next. "I am member #38 and so glad to have you guys aboard. I have long been a fan of your media properties and have been impressed by your work. I am excited to call each of you a friend."

The last introduction came from Jacci O'Connor, the American Symphony conductor. Donald, Kwame, and Samantha all knew of her. She was an international celebrity recognized as much for her leadership of the world's best symphony orchestra as she was for her charitable work. "I am a member #39 and so excited for this moment. You guys are just what we need in this organization, and we are so proud of Oliver for presenting all three of you. I'm excited to call each of you a friend."

Donald, Kwame, and Samantha were overwhelmed by this reception by The Guiding Force members. Three short years later, they would begin to understand the power of their membership and what it meant when a Guiding Force member said, "I'm excited to call each of you a friend."

Part Two

Chapter Thirteen

Today was Luke's first time meeting her. He'd seen her in public but never this close. The drop-dead gorgeous rumors were true, so much so that he had to take a deep breath to compose himself.

She escorted him to the large living room and offered him a seat and something to drink.

"Are you thirsty? Would you like a bottled water, Luke?" she asked. Her voice had a low pitch, without any noticeable accent. It matched her urbane looks perfectly.

"No, thank you, I'm okay, Ms. Stuart. May I call you Dawn?"

"Sure, you can. But if you don't need a beverage. Let's get started."

Her first question unnerved him even more. "Luke, I have to put your journalistic skills to the test. Look at me and tell me what you see."

"Dawn, I am unclear what you are asking. Can you be a little more specific, please?"

He wondered why she asked the question, and he hadn't settled down yet from the shock of her incomparable beauty. Dawn Davis Stuart had successfully intimidated him, the rock star journalist. Nobody did that.

"Just tell me what you see," she repeated. "That's what I need you to do."

He took a deep breath and thought, "Is she asking me to objectify her and tell her she is one of the most beautiful women I've ever laid eyes on? Should I tell her I will be daydreaming about her for days, maybe months, wondering if I stood a chance to be with her? Nah, she couldn't mean that. Don't be stupid. This is a wonderful opportunity, an interview the other members didn't get, and an important city story. Be professional and take it slow, answer the question."

He chose to describe what he saw and hoped it was safe. "I am looking at a stunningly beautiful woman."

"Thank you, Luke. Now, continue," she said. Dawn didn't blush or smile at the compliment.

"I'd say you are 30 years old."

She exhaled and stared at him with a sigh and rolled her eyes. It wasn't a good answer and Luke knew right away the compliment was a fail.

"I'm 40 years old, Luke; that's sucking up. You should know my age, especially as a gossip news reporter. Hell, anyone reading the stories about me shooting my former husband knows my age."

"I do, Dawn, but I was being coy. I'm also abiding by the rule that you should never ask or tell a woman her age." He decided to throw out good manners as an excuse. It helped a little, as she didn't denounce his response.

"Well, heck, then make me 27. I always liked that age."

Dawn Davis Stuart had him off his game. Today was her first interview since she had moved back to the city. She left in disgrace after the murder of her ex-husband, served a prison sentence and remarried. The second marriage didn't work out, and after the divorce decided to return to New York. She also had an agenda and needed help from the press. It was why she had invited him there, not to exchange pleasantries.

The interview took place at the spectacular Upper West Side apartment of her father-in-law, Yancey Stuart, Sr. Luke learned about the apartment from society page articles about the city's rich and famous. He sat in the massive living room, on one of the two luxurious sofas, surrounded by furnishings that made it a showpiece home of the city's super-rich.

Gigantic floor-to-ceiling windows admitted natural light and a captivating view of the Hudson River. The vista extended, unobstructed, for miles up the

West Side all the way to the City Bridge. The river glistened on this clear, sunny day.

Yancey Stuart, Sr., was a noted art patron, and Luke was impressed by his collection. It included original works by the artists Brandao, Neal Webster, Lauren Washington Evanston, and Shaboo Jones. He knew from his research that the collection was worth $250 to $300 million, and that Yancey often loaned works to major art museums. As he admired the pieces by those famous artists, he reminded himself to remain calm and not touch anything. He wanted Dawn to believe he wasn't overwhelmed by it all, but even more importantly, he didn't want to break anything.

Dawn sat on the couch across from him and crossed her long, lean legs. He guessed her height at five-foot-seven or eight. She wore purple yoga pants and a tight-fitting short-sleeve synthetic fiber top that revealed her curvy, gym refined body.

He couldn’t tell how much she weighed but knew for sure that she wasn’t model skinny. The muscles beneath her clothes made that obvious. She wore no makeup, which made her natural beauty even more fascinating. Her auburn hair was pulled back and tied in a thick pony-tail. Her skin was tanned, and he assumed she used a bronzer or a tanning bed.

"Look at me the way I am looking at you, Luke. Tell me what you see," she asked again, staring hard at him. "You need to figure this out or, I will end this interview and go to the next member of the Celebrity Hack Patrol. I need this story done right."

He nervously looked away. Dawn had him on sensory overload, and he had to close his eyes to clear his head. After a pause, he opened his eyes and said the first words that came to mind, “I see a woman with reddish-brown hair."

"I dye it. Dark brown is my natural color, but okay, continue."

She was an enigma, one he decided to solve like a puzzle, piece by piece. He took a shot with another answer. "Your nose is full, not large, and natural, unlike those of the many society women who've had nose jobs."

"Very observant. Yancey asked me if I wanted a nose job, but that wasn't happening. I was dead set against changing it to look like everyone else."

Her response gave him some momentary confidence. Solving the puzzle was often how reporters filled in the blanks on stories. He would continue on this path but first complimented her for not getting a nose job.

"Well, I'm glad you didn't. Your nose looks perfect as it is."

She shrugged off the compliment. It wasn't that she was inconsiderate, but she wasn't needy in that way. Praise about her beauty meant nothing to her.

Luke needed more time to think and got the break he needed when the older white man walked into the room and announced himself in a loud baritone voice. The man said, "I'm Yancey Stuart, Sr."

Luke knew who he was but had never met him, either. The retired real estate baron was tall, broad-shouldered, and ruggedly handsome. Luke guessed he was six feet four and weighed a well-proportioned 230 pounds. He had thinning white hair, and Luke pegged his age to be early to mid-70s. Yancey walked over to Luke and extended his hand.

"So this is the star reporter from *The News*, the fabled Luke McFlemming, the lead guy from the Celebrity Hack Patrol?"

Yancey didn't smile, and Luke stood up to shake his hand. The coarseness and sarcasm of the greeting from the once-powerful business leader unnerved him as much as his introduction to Dawn had.

Luke was momentarily lost for words. These people had him so far off his game that he just sat down with his mind racing as he tried to process it all.

Yancey observed to Dawn, "He doesn't look like some super sleuth. $100 says he won't figure it out. I'll give you three guesses."

The old man knew the answer to Dawn's question. He didn't seem to care that he was rude. Dawn did, however, and barked at him, "You need to stop, Yancey. You are acting mean."

He responded with a shrug of his shoulders. It was an "I don't give a damn" shrug. Luke didn't like it, but he wanted the story and was afraid to react in his typically arrogant way. He knew these were the kind of people who would throw him out, so he had to continue to suck up and take the jabs.

Yancey, still unimpressed, walked to a bar in the corner of the living room to mix himself a cocktail. When he arrived, he turned around and shook his head dismissively. Luke noted it wasn't a real bar. It was a tall glass top table about four feet high, with a dozen or more expensive bottles of brown liquor, half a dozen glasses, and a large ice bucket.

Yancey plunked an ice cube into a glass and glanced at Luke again. Luke stared back but couldn't tell if Yancey was smiling or smirking. He guessed, smirking when Yancey said, "Yeah, I'm pretty sure. He's too white-bred. I'll up the ante and give you five guesses."

Luke had had enough and finally stood up for himself. "Am I in this room? Sir, let me tell you that many people don't like me because I am a prominent reporter. Typically, however, they are kind to me for the same reason."

The old man smirked again. Luke knew what it meant. The face said clearly, "So what, you think I care?"

Yancy patronized Luke further. "Okay, important reporter, whoopee," he scoffed. "Now, what are you drinking? I am having a single malt Scotch. Do you want a cocktail? Or a tissue for some tears?"

Luke glanced at his watch and gritted his teeth. It was mid-afternoon and too early to drink. Yancey saw him look at his watch and continued with the verbal jabs. "Don't look at your watch. It's happy hour somewhere. Besides, I thought all real reporters liked brown liquor."

Yancey then turned to Dawn, "Honey, I'm raising the stakes. I'll give you two to one odds this guy doesn't even drink. I told you we should've called the girl. She probably drinks Scotch, and she ain't white-bred."

Luke defiantly snapped back, "Well, that would make sense. She's Asian, Yancey. So yeah, that would mean she ain't white-bred, and neither am I, for the record."

Yancey flashed a contented smile and nodded his head. He approved Luke's response, "Oh, a little spirit. Look, Dawn, Luke is getting angry, showing some backbone."

The old man walked from the bar to the couch with the cocktails. He handed Luke his drink and sat down, with a smile that revealed he wasn't bothered by Luke's discomfort, "Touchy, are you big-time reporter?"

Dawn finally jumped in and interrupted the hazing, "Luke, ignore him. Yancey doesn't get out much nowadays, and he has a bit of a gambling problem. He's having fun at your expense. Fair warning, he likes single malt and a bet."

Yancey took a long swig from his drink. He leaned back on the sofa next to his daughter-in-law, crossed his legs, rubbed his chin, and said, "Betting and booze. She's right, Luke. A man has got to have his vices, and I'm rich, Luke. So I can bet all I want."

Dawn couldn't control her father-in-law. He had a cocktail and she hoped it would occupy him long enough for her to proceed. She rolled her eyes and turned her attention back to the initial question, "Okay, now back to where we started. What do you think when you look at me?"

"A society gal?" He answered quickly and hoped it was the end of the game.

"I used to be, but it's not the right guess."

"That's one guess," Yancey said. "This guy is thinking about it all wrong. You have to give him better hints. Otherwise, we'll be here all day."

She stared at Luke again and agreed, "I suppose you're right, Dad."

"Okay, Luke. Can you guess my ethnicity?"

Luke was tired of the game but had to play. He stared at Dawn, took a swig of his drink, and said, "Red hair would make you Irish."

"Is that a guess?" she responded.

"Yes, it is," he said anxiously. Each wrong answer ratcheted up his nerves. This game didn't make him look too bright. He hated it.

"It's wrong, but not a bad guess. At least you're thinking better."

"Yeah, Luke, I thought she was Irish when I first met her, too," Yancey added.

"Okay, you must be Italian?"

After a few more guesses, she said to Yancey, "You're right. He'll never figure it out."

Dawn stood up and walked over to him. He stared at her fit, athletic, curvy body. He looked beyond the tan and discovered her natural complexion wasn't pale. His face lit up.

Yancey saw him catch on and said excitedly, "This genius may have finally gotten it. I wish you had taken the bet. Watching him guess was some decent action, Dawn."

Luke turned to Yancey and said, "You must be really rich. The kind of rich where you don't have to have good manners."

"Oh, uh, oh," Yancey said with his half-smirk and smile face. He didn't care what Luke thought and continued teasing him, "I done made the star reporter a little angry. Poor Luke."

Luke snickered at Yancey, then turned to Dawn. "Enough of this. I've got it. You are either African-American or Latina."

Yancey put his drink down and clapped his hands as he said, "Bravo, Bravo."

Dawn shook her head, frustrated by how her father-in-law carried on, and said, "How about both, Luke? My late father was a light-skinned black man. Both of his parents were mixed-race, and my mother was a light-skinned Puertorriqueña."

"Her father passed as a white man," Yancey Sr. whispered and winked at Luke. He said it as if he were revealing a scandal. It was another part of his act to unnerve and test Luke.

"Be respectful of my father," Dawn snapped and glared at Yancey. "Yes, he was mixed-race. He didn't pass as a white man, but because of his features was able to get work as an accountant in white-owned accounting firms. He never denied to his employers that he was black, and he later opened up a small accounting practice in Harlem, where I grew up. I'll never condemn him."

"I don't either," Yancey said. "A man has got to take care of his. Anyhow, this was fun to watch."

Dawn smirked at her father-in-law, "You didn't figure it out either, Dad. You need to sit back and enjoy your afternoon nip."

Yancey looked at Luke with a sheepish grin, "She's right. I didn't figure it out, either. For the record, it didn't matter to me. She is beautiful, smart, hardworking, and wasn't a gold-digger. Dawn was a double major at Harlowe University and graduated top of her class. My son didn't have a problem with her, and that's all that really mattered."

"He's right, Luke. Yancey loved me. But, he had two problems."

"Boy, did he," Yancey said, rolling his eyes. He sighed loudly and repeated it for extra impact, "Yes, he did."

"Enough with the sound effects, Dad," Dawn said, followed by another glare.

"What, Dawn?' he said with a defensive tone and raised his arms up in a gesture that matched. "I'm here to do the confirmation, so Luke will know this is all on the level."

"Confirm what? That she's mixed race?" Luke asked.

"We got you didn't we, big-time reporter?" Yancey asked with a smile.

Luke racked his brain as he recalled the murder trial and the public spectacle. None of the reports revealed her ethnicity.

"Yeah. I didn't see it. But I must ask why is it such a big deal? We are in New York. Most people here would not object to it, and beyond that, I looked at her hard and could not guess."

"As I said before, it was a non-issue between Yancey and me. Going forward, I don't want the public to be confused or misled. I am a proud mixed-race Black Latina."

Yancey added, "As for me, I have to tell you my son surprised me. I always thought he was a little too white-bred."

Luke turned to the scandalous murder and why he thought he was there. "You've forgiven her? She did kill your son."

"I forgave her. Yancey wrecked his marriage. He also got confused about his responsibilities as a husband. He was pretty wild out there, and a few of his professional enemies learned about his cavorting and sent pictures in the mail to Dawn."

Dawn interrupted and said, "After that, I cut him off sexually, and we attended couples counseling to try to save the marriage."

"For a year, I worked with my son, too. He was in therapy for sexual addiction. Do you remember my son?"

"Yes, Yancey," Luke said. "He was a strapping, tall, muscular guy. And a big personality like you, sir."

"And very handsome," Dawn added. She smiled and drifted off momentarily in what Luke guessed was a fond remembrance. "Let me tell you, Luke, this was just a bad series of events. First, a year into our intense couples counseling, a woman showed up out of the blue and slapped him with a paternity suit. We had just started sleeping together again, and I got pregnant immediately."

"Did he know that you were pregnant?"

Luke began taking notes as fast as he could. This had now become the fascinating interview that he had hoped for.

"Of course, he did," Yancey said. "We were all excited about the news. Everyone but my son; he was nervous. He told me he wasn't certain if he could be reliable enough to be a decent father and husband."

"So how did he end up at the strip club with his pants down?"

"I kicked him out after the paternity suit came up," Dawn said and looked up at the ceiling, pensively.

Yancey said, "And she had every right. He moved to one of our properties. Everybody was pissed at him. My late wife, Tabby, died three years ago of a sudden heart attack. I believe it was a broken heart. She was livid, too. We all rejected him, and he fell back into his vice."

"Wow, so sad," Luke said and looked up from his notepad. He thought about the dramatic shooting and trial nearly nine years ago. "I covered the celebrity beat during the trial, and your wife was not very public. We never heard much from her or you, Yancey. This is part of the background story we need to make sure people know."

"Yes, Luke, that is why you are here. I'm getting another drink. Do you want another single malt?"

Luke thought for a second and agreed, "I would like one, thank you. May I have some ice this time? I need to be clear-headed and take notes, and I still have a deadline."

"Oh, a lightweight," Yancey said and smiled as he took his glass. He nodded condescendingly at his daughter-in-law. "I'm still not sure about him, Dawn."

"The old man, does he ever stop with the wisecracks?" Luke asked. He didn't care as much now about defending himself. The story was juicy, and he was more comfortable with Dawn and Yancey. He no longer feared they would kick him out.

"Not really. Yancey doesn't listen or take direction too well, and you'd better never, ever get on his bad side."

Yancey could hear them talking about him and added, "That's right, Luke, getting on my bad side is not a good move. That's why we picked you for the story and not the other members of the Celebrity Hack Patrol. We want someone who can fight back. You can fight, right? Otherwise, we'll go to the girl. I still like her."

"I can handle this story, and I need to correct you, Yancey. It is the Celebrity Press Patrol, Sir. I am a Harlowe Writing Award winner and the best in the business."

Yancey had an easy foil in Luke and enjoyed razzing him into agitation. He loved to talk trash, and Luke's big ego made him an easy mark.

"Wait, hold-up now, did you just throw out some prize stuff? Oh Lord, how about that one? Luke's a star. Did you hear that, honey?"

Dawn didn't acknowledge her father-in-law. She whispered to Luke, "Don't respond. He'll eventually settle down."

Luke ignored the jab, as Dawn suggested, and when Yancey handed Luke his drink, the old man's focus turned to why the reporter was there. "Well, Luke, Dawn and I have a score to settle, and we want to set the record straight. It's the kind of scandalous stuff Celebrity Hack, I mean, Celebrity Press Patrol readers covet."

Luke smiled. He'd finally had a breakthrough with Yancey. "Thank you for calling us by our proper name. Now sir, what is the score you want to settle?"

Luke took a long swallow from the single malt. His brow lifted as he was surprised by its taste. He was too nervous as he drank the first cocktail to notice, "By the way, this is quite good."

"Thank you, Luke. It's an 18-year-old that comes from a private maker in Scotland. I have a small stake in the company -- only 20 barrels are released each year. It's one of the benefits of my wealth."

"Focus, please, Yancey," Dawn snapped, and turned the focus back to the meeting, "Luke, have you heard of Bronson Pagent of Pagent and Roth?"

"Yes, they are big-time real estate guys with assets in New York, London, Chicago, and Brazil. They have a blue-chip name and reputation."

Yancey yelled, "Blue-chip my ass. He's a punk. I hate him. My son competed against them and killed them on deals. We won a huge waterfront development project in Rio. The woman in the paternity suit was part of a setup orchestrated by Pagent. She came from an influential family in Rio but was young, just 20 years old. The affair was legal, and had she not gotten pregnant, it may have gone away."

"Not if I had known about it," Dawn said and grimaced at her father-in-law.

"I'm sorry, Dawn," he said sympathetically. "I meant to say the chain of events would not have gone as they did."

Luke could tell from the exchange how much her husband's affairs still pained her.

Yancey continued, "They set him up. The Brazilians hate American business people who go down there and take advantage of their women. We lost the deal and got barred from projects in Brazil for ten years by Brazil's government. Bronson Pagent, the head partner at Pagent and Roth, used the story in backroom conversations whenever he thought it would be advantageous for his firm in deals."

"Was he successful?" Luke asked.

"Yes, we lost deals in Toronto, Honduras, Nicaragua, and London as a result. It crippled our international business."

As they revealed more, Luke busily took notes and realized that there was far more to the story.

He interrupted Yancey and Dawn. He had to take a break from his furious note-taking and process all that he just learned.

"Sir, this is a lot more than I expected today. It sounds as much about illegal business practices as it does about a horny, bad boy business tycoon. What do you want me to do with all this information?"

"I want you to tell the whole story. We are an open book. We want Bronson Pagent, his partner Sy Roth, and their part in designing this conspiracy to be exposed."

"I need to show you something," Dawn said as she walked to a table on the other side of the living room. On top of it was a pile of folders.

"Bronson Pagent is a despicable human being. He went to great lengths to destroy my husband's life."

She pointed to the folders, "These files will incriminate him. There are 25 women he's had affairs with over the last decade. I put the same amount of energy into finding out every piece of dirt on that creep that he put into destroying our lives. I have files for bank fraud, extortion, and the women he sexually harassed and assaulted."

"A scorned woman is a bad enemy to have, and if there's anything we know about my daughter-in-law, it's that she has a hot temper," Yancey said.

Dawn looked down at the floor as her shoulders slumped. Yancey's comment pained her. "I am Madame Hot Temper no more. Jail makes you think about how you need to channel things."

"But you do want revenge, don't you? That's why we have Luke here, correct?"

"I guess you're right," she answered. "I want to destroy him and, if possible, start police investigations that would put him in jail."

"What do you mean? For sex crimes? Sexual assault? I don't understand."

Dawn leafed through the pile of incriminating files, pulled one out, and showed it to him. The cover read, "Bank fraud. Downtown, New York Project."

She pulled another file that read, "Bank fraud, Chicago Loop development project."

"Pagent and Roth are not what they purport to be," Yancey said. "We got into a couple of projects with them as co-managers and found out quickly they were not paying back loans and past debts, and had fabricated financial statements that suggested they were solvent enough to complete their part of the projects. On several occasions, we fronted them cash to complete their portion."

"In other words, you became their bank?"

"Yes, but after the first incident, we charged them interest and took a huge portion of their profit margin."

"Was that illegal?"

"Not on our part. We never signed any documents that noted us as a lender to them. We ended up in the role on a deal-by-deal basis. I didn't like it and told my son I wanted him to stop. We didn't need the money from the interest. He said it allowed us to keep an eye on them and their evil practices."

"We think this is why Pagent tried to set Yancey up with all the sex stuff. He wanted the interest money back and came up with a blackmail plan," Dawn added.

"Why not go to the authorities when all of this broke out?"

"There was a huge potential for us to lose face with a lot of clients and city governments. If it got to finger-pointing, we could have lost our licenses. I was letting my son run the company and frankly should have kept a better eye on things."

"And he, Bronson, is a sexual deviant. That creep groped me at our home while Yancey was making cocktails. He grabbed me and fondled my breast. I screamed, and my husband came running into the living room."

"Oh, he shouldn't have done that," Yancey said. "Huge mistake. Madame Hot Temper is not to be touched."

She shot her father-in-law a piercing look and said, "You need to stop calling me that name."

"Why? Remember, I hate him as much as you do. Do you want to tell Luke what happened next, or should I?"

Before Dawn could speak, Yancey continued, "Luke, she's a badass, a legitimate Kung Fu mama. She punched his lights out."

Luke was now fully engaged in their unique back and forth. The crazy stories were so captivating that he asked, "Can I get another drink, please? Whoever said rich people are boring needs to come hang out here."

"Sure, another round is a great idea. Coming up," Yancey said. He sprang up and walked to the bar.

Luke excitedly wrote notes while Yancey made the drinks. He said loud enough for Yancey to hear him in the far corner of the living room, "There is a lot of drama here, and the reveal is like peeling an onion. Every time I ask a question, you give an answer that leads to two more questions."

They both glared at Luke, and neither smiled. He could tell by the cold glares they were still angry. The iciness continued while Yancey made the cocktails.

"You only get half a cocktail Yancey," Dawn yelled. "You've had enough for the afternoon."

The former real-estate baron smirked at his daughter-in-law. He had no intention to have only half a cocktail and ignored her order as he continued the discussion, "Are you going to tell him how you kicked his ass? Or should I give the play by play?"

She looked at Yancey and sighed. Luke could tell that she didn't like the story and was reluctant to talk about it, "My husband was a retired pro football player."

Yancey returned with two full drinks. He handed Luke his cocktail and took over the storytelling, "My son was a brute. He would've snapped him in half."

"Yeah, I would've guessed that," Luke said. "He played for the New York Bombers and was a tight end for ten years."

"As Dad said, he stayed in shape and physically could easily beat the crap out of Bronson."

"That runt attacked her on purpose," Yancey snapped and took a long gulp from his drink. He stared into the glass. The stare revealed his enduring pain and anger.

"Yancey came running into the room, and I told him what happened. He went nuclear, smacked Bronson around, and then he suddenly stopped and said, 'This creep. He wants this to happen. The ex-pro football player beats up the runt. I can't do this, Dawn. You have to beat his ass.' He then walked over and locked the door so Bronson couldn't get out, and I beat the crap out of him. And I admit, it was fun."

"Bronson is the devil," Yancey added. His face and gestures became animated as he got up from the sofa. Luke could see from his facial expressions how much Yancey still hated Bronson as he recalled the fight. "He'll do anything to get an edge on his competitors. My son threw him out of the apartment on his ass after Dawn tore him a new one. A piece of paper fell out of his jacket pocket during the beat down. It was a document intended to extort Yancey for assaulting him. My son was right. He attacked her on purpose."

He continued, "And the guy comes by it honestly. He's a second-generation scoundrel. Here's what you need to know about the father, Rowan Pagent. He was a notorious slumlord who owned dozens of low-income housing apartments throughout New York City, Westchester, and Long Island. He was indicted for illegally hiking rent rates at his government-funded apartments in Brooklyn. His partner in the scam was a friend who worked at the federal housing authority. They were arrested, tried in court, and convicted. Rowan refused to cooperate with the Feds and was believed to have pocketed upwards of $50 million. He served seven years in jail and barred from future government contract work. After jail, Rowan left the city and lived the rest of his life off the money from the housing scam. He died five years ago. I hope he is in Hell."

"Wow, I never heard that story. He does sound scummy," Luke said as he wracked his mind about Rowan Pagent. He recalled the story and trial but it was before his time as a Celebrity Hack and more of a straight news story and not a gossip feature.

"My husband wasn't an idiot," Dawn added. "He knew their family history and that they were evil, and so Yancey decided to tape the beatdown. Afterward, Yancey Jr. told Bronson that if he pressed charges, he would have to explain why I kicked his ass. He also told him he was going to be just as nasty. The video, as well as documentation of his firm's insolvency and doctored financial records, was evidence that could refute any charges by Bronson."

"Oh damn, that's the dramatic gossip my readers would love. But I must ask, why do you want to air all of this in public now? It's been almost nine years since the murder. The press did a job on your character, Dawn. We now spend a lot of time following the lives of Donald Alexander, Kwame Mills, and the Black Camelot crew. You could just let sleeping dogs lie. Do you want that public glare again?"

She gritted her teeth and glared at Luke, "I want Bronson Pagent to pay. He ruined my life."

"He was behind all of the nonsense and my son's death," Yancey Sr. added. "And my wife, Tabby, as I said, died of a broken heart too as a result of all this. He has to pay."

"Okay, I understand. You should know this is front-page stuff, not gossip. If we can get the story out, it will put the glare on Pagent and Roth and their bad practices. You'll steal some of the headlines from Black Camelot because whether you like it or not, you remain infamous here in the city."

"I know, and it pains me to no end, Luke. I shot my husband, and I should have controlled myself. I'll never be able to live that down, but I can't let this creep get away with his part. I'll never forgive him."

Yancey cleared his throat, and his voice turned cold and sinister, "I'm worth half a billion. I am finished with my real estate business. My son is gone, and my wife is gone."

He pointed to Dawn and said, "I'm going to leave her a lot of money and the rest to charity. Let me be clear, I may have been a bit light-hearted and teased you today. But don't be mistaken. I have vengeance in my heart. Bronson Pagent must pay. I want the world to know how corrupt he is. I will use all my power to expose him. That is why you are here. I hope you can help us."

"This could be your next Harlowe Writing Award," Dawn added.

"Yeah, that would be nice. I'd like that." Luke said and shook his head in agreement.

As he put his notes together and prepared to leave, he said, "I do have a small favor. For now, I need you guys to trust me to do this story as an exclusive. Please don't go to Jennifer Kung at *The Ledger* or Mike Desanctis at *The Post*."

Yancey said, "Do a good job, and you won't have to worry."

"That's fair. Remember, I am a Harlowe Award winner. I'll be sure to do a good job."

Chapter Fourteen

After the death of Yancey Stuart, Jr., Bronson Pagent and his partner Symon Roth became the leading real estate developers in both New York City and nationwide.

Pagent heard rumors about Stuart's return to the Big Apple. When he read the article that confirmed she was back, he dismissed it. He didn't see her return as a threat to his business or standing as a prominent member of New York society.

His partner Sy Roth was far more concerned. When he arrived at work, he made a beeline to Pagent's office.

"Did you see the story by Luke McFlemming of the Celebrity Hack Patrol? He has more than ten million followers. What do you think this is about, Bronson?"

Pagent snickered, dismissing his partner's worries with a shrug. "Come on, Sy. Why are you worried? Luke's a gossip hack, and the article is just a PR story. The woman did kill her husband. If she comes back and wants to be accepted, she has to clean up her reputation."

Roth did worry about everything. Pagent knew he exaggerated his worries at times, too.

"Yeah, I suppose you're right," Roth said as he held his copy of *The News* and stared at the headline, "Madame Hot Temper Comes Back To The Big Apple."

"Sy, I don't need to see that article. I remember what happened. She was a rich socialite who shot and killed her husband in a strip club."

"Yeah, I remember. But what if they come after us?"

Roth was Pagent's equal partner in their firm, but Bronson was the business' face. Roth needed his partner to lay out a plan if Dawn Davis Stuart came after them. They had a lot to lose.

"You need to stop worrying, Sy. My father told me punks lose in business and life," he said, referring to his disgraced father.

"He also told me if there's anything I want, I have to take it. And that's what we've done with our business. Now to protect what we have, we must keep our presence. Our vendors and partners have to believe we are still tough and unscrupulous. They come to us because we do the dirty work they can't and won't do."

"Well, that's not all true, Bronson. They come to us because we are loaded. We have money to lead deals they don't. Yancey was our bank back in the day. We are the bank for so many of these guys now. If those guys can find financing without us, we will lose our stature. What if they choose to leave us?"

"Sy, we won't allow that. I've been pretty good at intimidating them with the consequences of trying to find other partners. We'll do what we do. Stop worrying. Nobody will leave us because of this article."

Roth still didn't buy his partner's confidence. He asked nervously, in his nerdy, nasally voice, "But what if Yancey Sr. and Dawn want to be the bank now? If they want back in the game, they can take all of our partners easily."

Pagent snapped at his partner in the fake, tough-guy, New York accent he had perfected over a lifetime. "Sy, Yancey Sr. has been out of business for eight or nine years. Dawn has never worked in the business. I'd be surprised if they wanted a comeback. Why would you say that?"

"Because the article makes a huge deal about how the two of them resolved their old issues. Yancey holds no ill feelings and is in support of her return to

New York. It also said she is single again. She divorced her second husband. It appears she's back in town to be a player."

Roth opened the newspaper to a stunning full-page photo of Dawn in a designer pantsuit, seated on a sofa with her legs crossed, hands folder in her lap and her hair pulled back. She stared straight ahead with the no-nonsense, intense look that unnerved Luke during the interview. Yancey Sr. stood behind the sofa with his hands on her shoulders, clad in a blue blazer, slacks, and white shirt. He too had a no-nonsense stare for the camera. It made the point that scared Roth. They would be a power to be reckoned with in New York City.

Roth plunked down the photo in front of Pagent and attempted to objectify Dawn. "She is hot, Bronson. Madam Hot Temper is still very hot and tempting. And they are a powerful family," he said, in a failed attempt to make a joke. Pagent didn't laugh.

Sy then brought up the subject that sent his partner into a nuclear rage. "Yancey said he taped the fight when she beat you up and would use it as evidence to destroy our reputation. That can't get out."

Pagent's face turned red. His breathing became short and loud and sounded like a snort. The subject made him lose his cool. There was one sure way to make Bronson Pagent angry and lose control. Bringing up his beat down by Dawn Davis Stuart was that subject.

He yelled at his partner, "That never happened, Sy. I fought Yancey Jr., not her. He was a former pro football player, and yeah, he roughed me up. I'm no punk. I would've kicked that woman's ass."

Pagent had lived this lie for nearly a decade. If the tape were released, his reputation as a gangster real estate tycoon would be destroyed. His partner knew it, "Look, Bronson, I'm not you. I'm skinny, and Lord knows, I'm not intimidating. I've never had a fight in my life. I also know if people didn't fear you, we'd be where we were when Yancey took us in."

"Yancey was a sucker, Sy," Bronson yelled through a snort. "Everybody thought he was so smart. You see what that got him."

Sy shook his head in agreement and said, "I understand why you hate him, Bronson, but all I'm saying is if there is a videotape, we have a problem."

Pagent snorted and screamed again, and this time Roth saw the fire in his eyes, "I'm telling you there's no damn videotape. I would have knocked her out. Do you hear me, Sy? It did not happen."

Sy knew Madame Hot Temper beat his partner up. He knew this because Yancey Jr. told him the day he beat up their bodyguard Chopper Brown and Bronson in front of New York's real estate leaders.

Roth had to motivate Bronson to get the videotape. Goading Pagent made him angry enough to turn red and snort in anger. Roth hoped he'd agitated him sufficiently to act, or he might need to do it himself. And he had to do it before McFlemming finished this series of articles.

Chapter Fifteen

"Our boy Luke McFlemming is back at it, Teddy, and this one is a doozy," Walt Bigelow said as he walked into Walker's office with a copy of the Dawn Davis Stuart article.

Walker grabbed the article, read it quickly, and said, "Madame Hot Temper is back. I have to admit, I'm not into this gossip fare, but I like her. Like everyone else, I believe her husband was an idiot and got what he deserved."

"Me too, Teddy. The story was straight juicy tabloid sensational. She had the best nickname ever, too."

"Yes," Walker said and laughed, "Madame Hot Temper. Her nickname goes into the convict moniker hall of fame."

"Well, she knows what she's doing. Luke is writing her stories. It's a month-long series to appear every Wednesday. She's back and ready to take our town by storm."

Walker shook his head and smirked. They both knew how obnoxious McFlemming was and how incorrigible he could be.

"I've got to say, Walt, with his ego, I'm surprised Kung or Desanctis hasn't taken Luke out, Madame Hot Temper style."

"Teddy, now that would be a great whodunit. Besides Kung and Desanctis, there'd be a long list of suspects. We might even make it. I'd certainly enjoy 15 minutes alone with him in a padded room. That dude takes the term pain in the ass to a whole new level."

"Yes, he does, but I have to admit, he's good at what he does. They are all excellent reporters with huge followings now. I'd like to think with the Harris Simmons story we helped make them stars, too."

"No doubt we helped them, Teddy. McFlemming, though, pushes buttons. One of these days, somebody is going to punch his lights out."

Those were Jennifer Kung's exact thoughts as she walked to her Midtown office. "That scrawny piece of crap. I am going to hear from my editor about this. If Luke calls or texts me this morning, I will kick his ass." Desanctis wasn't any happier during his morning walk to work. His newsstand guy, Smitty, could tell it would not be a fun day for him.

Smitty said as he handed him a copy of *The News*, "I wanted your take on this and didn't see a story from you. I hope that guy didn't scoop you on this one. He's a clown. And I bet a bad winner, too."

A jolt of stress ran through Desanctis's body as he read the headline. He looked at Smitty and said meekly, "Oh, he's the worst, Smitty, the worst kind of winner imaginable."

Smitty unfolded a chair and placed it in front of his small kiosk. "You okay, Mike? You might want to sit down and catch your breath."

"Thanks, Smitty, I'm okay. This is why I don't take newspaper home delivery. It's 7:30 in the morning, and my stress level is already too high. I have to talk to Luke."

Like Kung, Desanctis knew what to expect from his editor if he didn't have any leads on this story. It made him talk to himself. "Two stories still captivate New Yorkers. One was the Harris Simmons murders, and the second was Madame Hot Temper."

He knew it was going to be a long day as the headline Smitty showed him continued to flash in his head, "Exclusive by Star Reporter Luke McFlemming: Madame Hot Temper Comes Back To The Big Apple."

Luke still hadn't left his apartment in Greenwich Village. He had been following the readers' comments online and felt good about the response the story generated. He expected his colleagues to be upset, and he was right. His first phone call of the day came from Kung.

"Come on, man, we are way too old for this grandstanding, petty competition stuff. You could have given me a heads up. Now I am going to walk into a hail of gunfire."

"I know, TV, you have every right to be pissed. Dawn and Yancey called me and told me they wanted me for the series. My ego got the best of me again. I should have told you and Mike."

He continued and shared, "I'm running four more stories over the next four Wednesdays. It will provide new facts about what drove her to shoot her husband. It's serious stuff. I can't share much now, but I promise to make an introduction for you and Mike once I write a couple more stories."

Dawn expected more showboating from Luke. The offer to make an introduction caught her off guard and calmed her down. It gave her something she could tell her bosses.

"Okay, I'm still pissed at you. If you can do an introduction, it'll soften the blow with my editor. But it is unusual for you to share this much. Why are you now being a classy winner? Did you find Jesus this morning or something?"

"Ha, no TV, I'm still looking. Please pray for me. I am a work in progress. I'm doing this because this story is not what I thought."

He didn't want to stay on the call too long, lest he might spill something about the scandal with Bronson Pagent. He knew it was a big story and one he needed to flush out.

"TV, I need to call Mike. I'm sure he's pissed, too, and if I'm right, panicking. He's probably slow-walking to the office, trying to figure out what to say to his editor, Pete Colon. That guy hates me."

"How do you know Colon hates you? Wait, I take that back. It makes sense. Everybody hates you."

"Even you, TV?" Luke said.

"All right, you are allowing me to save a little face on this, and so I hate you less than everyone else."

"Thanks, Jennifer. Let me call Mike. Trust me, there's enough fat on this bone to feed all of us. We'll talk later."

Luke hung up and called Desanctis. As suspected, he caught him on his slow walk to work. Desanctis answered the phone with an attitude as Luke expected.

"I'm usually a gentleman, but if you're calling to brag this morning, I swear, Luke..."

"Easy, Mike," he interrupted. "I'm calling to apologize. This one dropped in from nowhere. She called me and asked me to come in for a visit. I've got a series of stories to run over the next four Wednesdays."

Desanctis cut him off and accused him, "You sound like you're boasting."

"Look, Mike, you have every right to be angry with me. I'm trying to give you something so you can save face. Just calm down for a second and listen, please."

Desanctis put the phone down and took a couple of deep breaths. He'd had enough of Luke and his grandstanding over the years.

The deep breaths helped, and he returned to the call, but his voice was low and cold. It revealed his anger to Luke, "Okay, what is it you want to share?"

"Dawn Davis Stuart came back here to settle some scores. I can't give it all away, but I will tell her that it is in her best interest to bring you guys in. I've got the main story, and it is wild. I would be happy to do an intro for you with no strings attached, but I need a couple more weeks. You can tell that to Pete Colon when you get to the office."

"You know he's going to have my butt on this. He hates you, Luke. But if you are on the level, I owe you thanks."

"Pete Colon's hating me is the worst secret in New York, Mike." It was true. Colon did hate Luke. He wanted the low-key Desanctis to be flamboyant and reckless like Luke.

Colon was super-competitive and hated Luke because he had a larger audience than Mike. Luke had ten million daily readers; Desanctis 9.8 million. It was a bragging rights fight for Colon. He was best friends with Luke's editor, Zach Goldberg, since graduate school at Harlowe University. Goldberg always needled him, and it kept him in a perpetual bad mood.

The offer calmed Mike down. He now had something to tell Colon. "Okay, Luke, thanks. You tell me how you want to move forward. Maybe, I'll see you at Café Cielo tonight, and we can talk about it?"

"That sounds like a plan, Mike. Best of luck with Pete this morning."

Luke ended the call and began to think of how important the series could be, "If I do this right, New York will fall in love with Madame Hot Temper, and this Bronson Pagent spin will captivate the city. I've got a shot at another Harlowe if these stories come together."

It was a fantastic morning. The initial feedback was strong, and the city was excited about the return of Madame Hot Temper. When he got to the office, he told his editor, Zach Goldberg, "I knew people were fascinated by her when she was in the headlines, but after all these years, this is surprising."

"Remember this is New York City, Luke," Goldberg said. He sat back in his office chair with a contented look. Luke had won the news cycle for the morning and that made him happy. Goldberg was also a great storyteller, not a pain in the ass like Luke, but never missed a chance to offer advice. He reminded Luke that New Yorkers had long memories, especially for stories about the rich and famous, and that applied to their fascination with Dawn Davis Stuart. She would always remain an important story in the city.

"Luke, we like second acts from notorious characters. And with the fabulous nickname Madame Hot Temper, Dawn Davis Stuart is one of the all-time greats. You better believe your readers are curious as to what she will do next. Heck, I'm even curious, and I've seen everything."

Luke's phone beeped all morning with texts from friends and colleagues. He was too busy to retrieve them. But when he did, the five messages in sequence stopped him in his tracks. "Walk away from Madame Hot Temper. Leave this story alone. You are warned. Destroy any files and move on. You only get one warning."

Chapter Sixteen

Chopper Brown never had to say much. At six foot eight and 300 pounds, his massive size did all the talking. He also was the muscle man Bronson Pagent used to extort and intimidate real estate foes and partners. But he wasn't invincible, and the fistfight he lost to a much smaller man was a moment Bronson Pagent, Sy Roth, and the New York real estate community never forgot.

The day after Dawn Davis Stuart beat up Bronson Pagent, Yancey Stuart, Jr. called him and said, "I am giving you six months to disentangle your affairs with my firm. My lawyers will be in touch to make sure you don't try to steal anything. You crossed the line when you put your hands on my wife. If I ever see you in public, you should cross the street. Dawn beat your ass, but that wasn't enough for me. I want a piece of you, too."

Pagent used Chopper for occasional work as an enforcer, but after Yancey Jr.'s threat, Pagent hired him as a full-time driver and bodyguard.

Chopper had redeemed himself since, but nine years ago he didn't stand a chance against Yancey Stuart, Jr., a former pro football player who stood six foot five and weighed 250 pounds.

Yancey saw red when he spotted Pagent leaving the Crescendo, a hotel that hosted the Annual West Side Realtors Conference. He ran for the exit, surprising Pagent and Roth. Chopper couldn't help him. He was behind the wheel of their SUV, which left them without protection.

"Pagent!" Yancey yelled at his sworn enemy. "I told you when I see you in public. I am going to kick your ass. Today is that day."

"Wait, wait, don't hit me. Okay, I'm sorry. I shouldn't have," Pagent yelled, as he turned pale in fear and ran to the SUV.

Yancey ignored Pagent's plea. He grabbed him by his collar and pulled him backward as he tried to open the locked car door. Witnesses later said Yancey dragged him from the car like a lion, dragging his prey into the bush. As Yancey dragged him, Pagent screamed frantically with his feet and arms flailing haplessly, "Chopper, please help me. Help me, Chopper!"

Chopper was large and imposing, but not very fast nor agile. When he heard the screams, it took him a while to move his enormous body from the driver's seat to the sidewalk. Yancey Jr., by that time, was working Pagent over.

"Let him go!" Chopper yelled as a crowd of onlookers formed, and a petrified Sy Roth watched.

"I'll let him go in one second," Yancey said calmly. In football practices and games, he had many fights with massive men and often emerged victorious. He wasn't intimidated by the enormous man at all.

Yancey picked up Bronson with one hand. He held him up in the air at his six-foot-five eye level and with his free hand grabbed his nose with his thumb and index finger and twisted it. The twist broke his nose instantly. Yancey then dropped him, and Pagent fell to the ground like a rock. Pagent was in so much pain from his broken nose that he forgot to use his hands to break his fall and fell hard on his ass. The crowd of onlookers, many of them business enemies, roared with laughter.

Bronson screamed, "You broke my nose. Oh, man, this hurts! Why would you do that, Yancey? You broke my nose."

Yancey, however, was just getting started. He looked at Pagent and said, "Don't you move. I'm going to take care of the goon and come back to you."

The former football star turned his attention to Chopper. He asked him calmly, "Are you sure you want to do this? I promise you it won't end well for you, either."

"I told you to leave him be!", Chopper roared.

Yancey was now a comical sight for most of the witnesses. With one hand, he held his bleeding nose, and with the other, he rubbed his bruised ass. His real estate foes couldn't get enough. They whipped out their phones, took pictures, and continued to laugh, many hysterically.

"Chopper, kick his butt! This is the guy I told you I needed you to take care of," Pagent yelled, as he held his blood stained nose.

That command made Yancey angrier, and he said, "Well, that was a mistake, Pagent. You hired a goon to fight your battles because my wife kicked your ass. And yes, everybody," Yancey Jr. yelled to the crowd, "my beautiful wife beat this fake tough guy's ass, and I have it on videotape."

The crowd roared again in laughter as they pictured tough guy Bronson getting thrashed by Yancey's wife.

Yancey then stepped on Pagent's calf, applying his full weight. "Yancey, stop. Please get off my leg, Yancey."

Bronson tried to push Yancey off of him but was not strong enough. He was at least 50 pounds lighter than Yancey and didn't have the muscles to move him. Fighting a brute like Yancey was why Chopper was there. Bronson yelled angrily at his bodyguard, "What are you waiting for, Chopper? Get him!"

Chopper charged at Yancey but didn't stand a chance. Yancey nimbly, like a football player evading a tackler, sidestepped the bodyguard as he ran at him and tried to corral him in a bear hug tackle. He stuck out his foot, tripped the big man, and threw a hard punch that landed flush on the side of his head. Chopper stumbled and crashed headfirst into the building's cement front. The crash, as loud as an auto collision, drew gasps from the crowd.

Stunned, Chopper shook his head and staggered blindly. Yancey didn't let him rebound; he grabbed him from behind and put him in a chokehold.

The bodyguard resisted valiantly but couldn't break Yancey's vice-grip lock on his neck. Finally, Chopper gasped, "Okay, you win. I'm done. Stop, please."

"I need a couple more seconds," Yancey said calmly. He even winked at a few of his real estate colleagues in the crowd who were rooting for him.

"I'm going to put you to sleep in case you have any more ideas."

As Chopper slowly crumbled and fell to the ground, Yancey said to the delight of the crowd, "Go to sleep, big boy. Nighty, night."

The real estate pros cheered in glee. They were ecstatic to witness Bronson and his enforcer publicly and savagely humbled.

After finishing off Chopper, Yancey looked at Sy Roth, who stood frozen in his tracks. "I'm not going to hurt you, Sy. The beatdown here wasn't about business. It was personal."

"Thank you, Yancey," Roth said in a trembled voice.

"You should kick his ass, too," someone yelled from the crowd. "They're partners and equals as far as I'm concerned. They do a lot of bad things."

"That's why I'm cutting them off. I'm going to do everything I can to put them out of business."

Yancey returned his attention to Bronson and said, "I wish your goon or you had put up a better fight."

He then reached down and, with his left hand, lifted Bronson off the ground once more.

"I'm sorry, please stop. Please stop," Pagent begged.

Yancey smacked him twice with an open hand on the head. The second blow knocked him out cold. The crowd cheer became deafening as Yancey held him up with one hand like a rag doll. Many took out their cameras to record the moment.

Yancey then carefully laid the bloodied, unconscious tyrant on top of his bodyguard and stood over them both like a conquering hero, admiring his work. The cheering continued until they heard the sirens of an approaching police car. An onlooker said, "Come with me. I'll get you out of here."

A voice from the crowd yelled, "Don't worry, Yancey, we'll tell them you were defending yourself."

"Thanks," he said as he escaped to a loud ovation.

Chapter Seventeen

Walt Bigelow dialed Teddy Walker's number and looked at his watch, "I hope he's up. I don't want to drag him out of bed."

Walker answered on the first ring, "It's midnight. How bad is it, Walt?"

"Well, it's crazy, Teddy, and tomorrow the gossip columnist wars will resume with a twist."

"Huh, what do you mean?"

"We've had three incidents tonight, and they may be related."

"What are you talking about?"

"Remember the Madame Hot Temper story? Well, about an hour ago, somebody attempted to break into her apartment, and it didn't go so well."

"Walt, she just got back to town."

"Oh, it gets better, Teddy. Luke McFlemming got mugged at his apartment. An EMT unit is taking him to the ER. They beat him up badly."

"Wow, Luke McFlemming. Say it ain't so. It wasn't you?" Walker chuckled. "Remember what we talked about earlier today?"

"I have an alibi, Teddy. I'm in the clear," Bigelow laughed.

"Good, I need you on the job Walt, not behind bars."

Neither wanted Luke hurt, but both smiled as he recalled their conversation hours before. Walker then turned to the reason for the call. "So, why do you think Luke was attacked?"

"I don't know, but they took his laptop and his cellphone. That means they were looking specifically for files."

"And wait, Teddy, we had a third event. There was a strong-arm burglary at *The News.* A couple of guys with masks ran in through the entrance and overwhelmed the night security guard. They went to the editorial floor, grabbed the night editor, and made him show them Luke's desk."

"Okay, now I understand why you think Luke was involved. What happened next?"

"They snatched all his electronics. His computer, a smartphone, a tablet. They smashed his monitor and walked out of the building to a getaway car."

Walker then considered how Bigelow had started the conversation, "Walt, I'm sorry, let's go back. Did you say the break-in at Dawn Davis Stuart's didn't go so well? What do you mean?"

"My bad, Teddy. I was so excited about this crime spree because it all seems related. I'm guessing it's related to her story today."

"What are you talking about?"

"Madame Hot Temper is fully back. She shot the intruder. He's dead."

Walker needed a moment. He walked to his sofa and sat down.

"Teddy, are you there?" Bigelow barked into his phone.

"Yeah, man, I had to process all of this. You're right. She is fully back. Where are you now? Was she hurt?"

"I'm on my way to her place on the Upper West Side now. I don't think she was injured. Mac McClellan is at the scene and said she was fine."

"Are you leaving from the headquarters Downtown?"

"Yeah, I should be there in ten minutes."

"Stop by here on the way, please, Walt."

Walker lived in Midtown, halfway between headquarters and Dawn Davis Stuart's apartment. "I want to make sure everything is proper with her. She's a convicted felon. How did she get a gun?"

"The gun belongs to her father-in-law. McClellan said the intruder broke in and assaulted her. The old man came out with his gun and got into a scuffle with the suspect, and she shot the intruder in self-defense."

"I don't know what to say. I hope they are buttoned up. If not, we may have to bring her in. The press is going to have a field day with this, so we can't give her any benefit of the doubt. Ring me when you get here. I'll be ready

. . .

As Bigelow shared all the details of the night's burglary, mugging and shooting with Walker, Luke McFlemming was being rushed to City Hospital in an EMT unit. He was subdued and did not display the bravado he typically shared with his Celebrity Hack Patrol friends.

The EMT team remembered him from his years hanging around in the City Hospital parking lot waiting for an ambulance to bring in a high-profile celebrity. Tonight, he was that celebrity, "Hey Luke, I am EMT Johnson. We worked on the Harris Simmons murders a few years back. Meet my partner Roy."

"Hi guys," Luke murmured. The beating was so severe that talking was painful.

"Oh boy, you sound like you are in pain," Paramedic Roy said. "Don't worry. We'll get you to the hospital in a hurry."

Roy continued, "Nice article on Madame Hot Temper today. I understand this series will continue for the next four weeks. I'm looking forward to it."

"Thank you," Luke muttered.

Roy continued, “Her pics are awesome, by the way. She's still hot stuff, and doesn’t seem to have aged a bit. She's my celebrity crush."

"She might be hot, Roy, but bad luck follows that woman for sure," Johnson said.

"Thanks, fellas. You may be right. She's still hot and bad luck is right," he whispered as the ambulance rushed through the streets to City Hospital.

Chapter Eighteen

At 10 PM, Mike DeSanctis and Jennifer Kung were still at Café Cielo. Luke hadn't shown up yet. Today, of all days, they expected he'd be there to brag. As they were seated, their phones beeped. It was from the text group they shared with Luke.

"Oh my, this is not good," Kung said.

"Somebody finally kicked his ass. I'm sorry, TV, I know that is insensitive, but if anybody had it coming…"

"You don't have to explain, Mike. It was bound to happen. What goes around comes around. But I do want him to be okay. He's an ass, but you know, he's our ass," Kung said.

She shook her head as she read the text, "Hey Guys, your leader is on the way to the hospital now. I was mugged and roughed up badly. It was a home invasion. I got caught unawares and am on my way to the ER."

Desanctis shrugged, "That guy can't help himself, TV. Even on his way to the hospital, he's still Luke."

Their phones beeped with another text from him. "I guessed you both are still at Café Cielo. Can you bring me an order of the pasta Bolognese and a tiramisu? I'm hungry."

"Like I said. He's our ass, Mike," Jennifer said.

"You are so right. I guess we should go and check on him. You realize he doesn't have any other friends. Are you up for it?"

"Yeah, Mike. I'll pay for the food. You pay for the car."

. . .

Luke was nervous about what landed him in the ambulance. Native New Yorkers had a sixth sense for danger. He grew up in Hell's Kitchen, and while he couldn't remember when he was last in a street fight, he was upset this time he'd been trounced.

"Was this someone I wronged in the past? I didn't realize I made the kinds of enemies who'd stoop to this. Maybe this is a random assault?"

His mind raced as he tried to think of potential suspects. His thoughts were interrupted as they arrived at City Hospital.

"We're here, Luke. It must be different for you now as a passenger," Paramedic Johnson observed as he looked outside and saw the crowd of press and photographers gathered around the ambulance.

"Yeah, and it's a view I don't like at all."

A paparazzo recognized him when the EMTs unloaded him from the ambulance. "Oh wow, is that you, Luke? What happened?"

Another yelled, "Damn, Luke, you got jacked up! I hope you got a punch or two in."

"I got robbed, and my ass kicked too," he said. Luke instantly regretted the comment. It angered Johnson and Roy as the cameras flashed.

"Bad move Luke. Never engage with the press," Johnson snapped. "Now we have to fight through this crowd."

He was right. Within seconds, the 30 or so press hanging around the parking lot swarmed around the stretcher, forcing the paramedics to respond aggressively.

"Get out of the way!" Paramedic Roy yelled. "Move people. He's one of you guys. Let us get him inside. He's not critical. He'll be back out here with you tomorrow. Let us do our job and get him inside."

Johnson moved to the front of the stretcher, lowered his shoulder, and muscled through the crowd. The press and paparazzi walked alongside them until they reached the emergency room entrance. Luke could see and hear the non-stop camera clicks and flashes.

"A little bit of karma, huh?" Johnson said after they made it inside. "You'll be on the 11 o'clock news. I can imagine the headline now. "Star Reporter Got His Ass Kicked."

"I should have kept my mouth shut. This is not a good look for me. For a day that started so well, it is ending terribly."

Seconds later, a curvy, attractive, redheaded Irish-American nurse ran toward them. She said with a high-pitch voice and a New York accent.,"Who we got here, Johnson? How bad is he?"

"This is the star reporter, Luke McFlemming. He was mugged and has bruised, if not cracked, ribs. It was a home invasion as he entered his place," Johnson said as they gently moved him from their EMT stretcher to a hospital gurney.

Luke knew her from his days raiding the emergency room and trying to sneak his way into a hot story. He smiled weakly, "Hi, Nurse Dulany, I'm on this side today."

She shook her head with a concerned look as she assessed his fat lip, swollen jaw, and puffed-up eye, "Yeah, man, they went to work on you. I hope you didn't let those paparazzi take your pics."

Johnson said, "Oh, he'll be on the news tonight and over the Internet tomorrow for sure. He's yours now, Dulany. We've got to go back to our unit. Hopefully, we won't be back again tonight."

"Yes, pray for a quiet night. Thanks, guys." Dulany said.

"Bye, Luke, and good luck. Listen to Dulany. She's the best," Johnson said. He patted Luke's hand as he and Roy walked towards the ER exit.

"Thanks, fellas," Luke said.

He heard the door open, and one of the paramedics yell, "Move out of the way, or I will ram you with this stretcher. He'll be fine. Now move the hell out of the way."

"I now see how annoying we are," Luke told Dulany.

"Hey, you are only doing your job, just like those guys are. We'll take some X-rays to ensure nothing is broken and then give you some antibiotics and a sedative to help with the pain. We'll hold you overnight."

Dulany yelled out to her team, "Guys, we have a celebrity here."

Luke smiled when Dulany called him a celebrity. Within seconds, a male and female nurse ran towards them and stood at attention.

"He was assaulted. I need you to X-ray his chest area."

She checked his eyes and asked, "Did you lose consciousness at any time during the assault?"

"Uh, no, I don't think so."

Dulany didn't like the answer and barked to her team, "He is not sure. Let's run a cat scan, too, and check all his vitals."

As she finished her commands and the nurses began to wheel him off, Luke said, "Thanks, Nurse Dulany. My colleagues Jennifer Kung and Mike Desanctis are on their way. They're bringing me dinner and are worried about me. Tell them I will be okay."

"I hope they have enough for two," she yelled back and smiled. Luke mustered a grin in return.

On their way to the hospital, Mike Desanctis called Walt Bigelow to ask if he had any news to share about Luke.

"Hey, Mike. Are you calling me about the crime spree?" Bigelow asked.

"What crime spree? I called you to find out if you had any scoop on what happened to Luke?"

"Yeah, don't worry. Your boy got mashed up but should be okay. This was an interesting night as there was a series of burglaries. Luke's story this morning may have set things off."

Desanctis could tell from Bigelow's voice that he wasn't worried about Luke. Indeed, the detective knew Luke would be okay. The Chief of Detectives had bigger concerns.

"What do you mean, Walt? Jennifer and I are on our way to the hospital to visit him. What is going on?"

"Okay, let's do a quick conference call. I'll give you two some scoop, but everything is off-the-record as we don't have any definitive news yet on any of the crimes."

"Hold on, Walt," Desanctis said and turned to Jennifer. "Walt wants us both on this call, but it is unofficial. I'm putting the phone on speaker."

She spoke first, "Hi Walt, Jennifer here."

"Hey, Jennifer. We don't have any official news yet. But Luke's Madame Hot Temper story this morning seems to have set off a series of crimes. Besides Luke's home invasion, there was a strong-arm burglary at *The News*. A couple of tough guys walked in, beat up the security guy, and took all the computers and electronics off of Luke's desk. And brace yourselves, we had a shooting at Madame Hot Temper's residence."

Bigelow intentionally did not tell them about the dead body.

"Are you kidding? Dawn Davis Stuart's? Is she okay? We should go to the scene of the shooting, Mike. We'll check on Luke later."

"No, Jennifer, please don't go there. I am on my way to pick up Teddy, and you guys cannot be there. Go to the hospital and check on Luke. I need a couple of hours. I promise I will share with you what I have later."

"You promise?"

“Yes, Jennifer, I got you. There are a bunch of dots here. But I need you to give us time to connect them."

She looked at Desanctis, who nodded his agreement. "Okay, Walt. We'll do as you asked."

"Thanks, guys, give me a couple of hours. I'll meet you at Café Cielo and fill you in. Tell Luke I said to feel better. Check that, don't tell him anything. I don't want him to know what is going on, not tonight."

They arrived at City Hospital as the call ended. The ER was busy and loud, and fortunately for them, Luke was sedated. Nurse Dulany recognized them from their columns and greeted them.

"Hi Jennifer and Mike, I'm Nurse Anna Dulany. Luke told me you were coming to visit. He also said you would be bringing food."

They both smiled at her. Mike asked, "How is he?"

"Sedated. He's in a fair amount of pain. Bruised ribs are the most serious issue. We gave him something for the pain. He'll be fine in a day or so."

"Probably a bruised ego, too, right?" Jennifer asked.

"I guess, but he's an excellent patient. Pain does that to even the toughest men. They all want pain relief. I'll take you to his room, and you can check him out. Follow me."

She led them past the emergency room stalls to a small section with private rooms. "Luke's asleep. He tried to wait up for the food, but we sedated him."

Jennifer grabbed Mike's arm. She had to turn away when she saw Luke's battered face, "Oh damn, they worked him over good."

Desanctis crossed his heart and said a short silent prayer, "I hope he got in a punch or two. You did say he will be okay?"

"Yeah, we've taken X-rays. He'll need to slow down for a few days."

"Thank God. Then we'll let him sleep. Would you mind giving him this food? We brought him some pasta and tiramisu," Jennifer said and handed her the take-out.

"Sure," Dulany said. "It's tastier than our food and will make him happy."

"Tell him we prayed for him and will come back tomorrow. Will you?" Desanctis asked.

"Happy to do that for you guys," the head ER Nurse said with a smile.

Dulany placed the food on the nightstand as the reporters departed. They had made the car wait and, after jumping in, directed the driver to take them back to Café Cielo.

Having the car wait turned out to be a smart move. The Celebrity Hacks avoided the crowd of reporters who saw them and ran to their car. They knew they were there to check on their buddy.

Bronson Pagent was the last person to learn about the strong-arm burglaries. He poured himself a bourbon and became enraged as he listened to Chopper explain all the evening events.

"This was an idiotic idea, Chopper. Why didn't you come to me? Have I not been loyal to you?"

"Yes, Bronson. I apologize. It was a one-time thing with my cousin Petey and a couple of other guys. It was supposed to be a wham-bam thank you, ma'am thing. It's now almost 11, and Petey is silent. I'm afraid he got arrested."

"Or he could have gotten shot and is dead!" Bronson yelled.

"Don't say that, Bronson. Petey is my first cousin. I'll be jammed up with the family if he gets hurt."

"Chopper, now you think about that. I swear if I had a gun, I'd shoot all of you."

"I'm sorry, Bronson. That's why I'm calling you. What should I do? I have to go see him."

Bronson was furious. His partner's worries about Luke's article put them in a fix that could destroy everything.

"Look, Chopper, if Petey gets arrested, these walls will come tumbling down. Sy Roth will not take the fall for you."

"I know, but it was his idea," Chopper said.

"Wake up, Chopper. Don't be a fool. Sy is rich. He'll hire a powerful lawyer and sell you out. You need to make sure he gives you enough money for you and your crew to live out of town for a few months. Make sure you get at least $20K and leave town tonight."

The more Bronson thought about Sy's move on Dawn Davis and Yancey Stuart, the angrier he became. He understood Luke McFlemming's story could be embarrassing and possibly hurt business, but theirs were white-collar crimes. These burglaries and attacks were different. Sy had taken their evil deeds to a new level.

Bronson ordered Chopper, "If he doesn't have money for you, kill him. If Petey gets arrested, you may need to kill him, too."

"I don't want to kill him, Bronson. A killer is not who I am."

"Chopper, Petey is a two-time loser, and this was a crime spree. You will go to jail if you get arrested. I don't know for how long. You have tough decisions to make."

Bronson took a long swig from his bourbon and closed his eyes as he tried to figure out if there were any easy angles or ways out. He didn't have an answer and couldn't think clearly. He only saw red as his fury at Sy grew.

"You need to call Sy and get enough money for all of you," he repeated. "Throw your phone away, too. Buy a burner, and call me before you go to Sy, and I'll let you know if he lives or dies."

Bronson ended the call and angrily thought about the mess Roth started. Chopper Brown was having the same thoughts, but he had his limits. He wasn't a killer and didn't want to go to jail.

He spotted a convenience store, dropped his phone on the ground, crushed it with his heel, and walked into the bodega to buy a burner, worried about his cousin Petey and what Bronson would tell him to do next.

Chapter Nineteen

Dawn Davis Stuart sat sullenly on the sofa in the living room. Yancey sat on the couch opposite her, and Mac McClellan stood between scribbling on a notepad. Nobody looked over at the den. It was adjacent to the 1000 square foot living room and nearly equal in size. A long marble counter about four feet high separated the two rooms.

She stared out the floor-to-ceiling window in front of her. The nightlights of the city offered a postcard view of the river and the City Bridge and rivaled the daytime view Luke marveled at the day before. Dawn was petrified, justifiably, because the perpetrator's dead body lay on the other side of the marble counter.

"I can't believe this happened," she said. "I haven't even been back here a month. All I want is to make a new start. I can't go back to jail, Yancey. Please help me."

Yancey got up and sat next to his daughter-in-law, "Don't worry. The shooting was purely in self-defense. An intruder attacked us. Stand your ground laws should apply, right detective?"

The old man looked at the detective. The intruder did break into their apartment and attack them. What ensued was clearly self-defense, but they needed the detective's assurance that Dawn didn't have to worry.

McClellan said, "Technically, Sir, the law for these kinds of cases is called the Castle Doctrine, but loosely based on the same rules for self-defense. Both allow you to protect yourself and your home against illegal entry and fear of a deadly threat."

Yancey put his arm around his daughter-in-law to console her, "I told you, sweetheart. Don't worry. My gun is legal, and this was an illegal break-in and attempted robbery."

She shook her head, sighed, and fell back onto the sofa. Her face was tear-stained from crying. She laid down, curled up, and began to cry uncontrollably again.

"She's been like that since we called you guys," Yancey said.

"She may need medical attention. It appears to be a panic attack. I've seen this from people who were in shock after traumatic events."

"Jesus, help me. Lord, have mercy on the soul that I took. Lord Jesus, I need you right now. Mercy, mercy, mercy," she whispered as she cried.

"I'll call my friend Dr. Clarence Ewell. He's the head of surgery at City Hospital and lives around the corner. If he's home, he'll come over and take a look at her."

"Okay, I'll keep an eye on her," McClellan whispered and walked away with Yancey Sr., a few steps away from her. "She needs a doctor. There's a new diagnosis called Grief Suicides. It happens when people involved in accidental shootings turn guns on themselves, cut themselves, jump out of windows, crash their cars, and jump in front of trains. I'm not a doctor, but from what I learned the first 24-48 hours after traumatic events, all bets are off."

Yancey then walked to the corner of the den to make the phone call. He needed a quiet place as Dawn Davis Stuart's cries echoed throughout the apartment.

As he spoke, there was a knock on the door. It was smashed in during the break-in and couldn't be fully closed. At the entrance were Bigelow and

Walker. Bigelow announced himself, "Hello, Walt Bigelow, Assistant Chief of Detectives, here."

McClellan heard them and yelled back, "Hey, Walt, it's me, Mac McClellan over here! Come on through."

Bigelow entered, followed by Teddy Walker. McClellan met them in the entry foyer that overlooked the apartment's living room and den.

"Hey, guys. Thanks for coming. Let me give you a quick overview," he said and pointed to the far corner of the den. "Yancey Stuart, Sr. is there on the phone. He's calling a doctor friend who lives in the neighborhood."

McClellan turned to the muffled sounds they could all hear coming from the living room.

"Ms. Stuart is on the sofa. She's crying and needs medical attention, and on the floor over here in the den is the guy who broke into the house," Mac said and pointed to the body.

"Dawn shot him twice, once in the head and once in the heart. We have an EMT coming, but since the intruder was already dead, we wanted to do a comprehensive crime scene investigation before moving the corpse."

Walker and Bigelow had seen dead bodies hundreds of times. It didn't bother them. The rules for homicides said that they were not supposed to touch the body. They eyeballed the corpse and confirmed that he was dead. The Medical Examiner would do that officially, but for them, he passed the eyeball test.

"What else can you tell us?" Bigelow asked as they looked away from the body and admired the spectacular apartment. It was quiet except for Dawn's sobs and Yancey's phone conversation.

"This was a strong-arm robbery attempt. The intruder overcame the doorman. He pistol-whipped him but did not knock him out. And as you can see, he busted through this door. He was a dumb criminal, though. He asked for Yancey Stuart's apartment number and beat up the doorman until he gave it to him. The doorman rallied and called the Stuart's as the guy broke in the door. Ms. Stuart ran to the door with a bat. He knocked her down and said, 'I want all the financial papers.' He then hit her hard and said, 'That's a payback blow,'" McClellan said as he read from the notes and statements he got from Dawn and Yancey.

"I came running out with my gun right after he busted in the door," Yancey added as he entered the conversation.

He had finished phoning the doctor and introduced himself, "I'm Yancey Stuart, Sr. I never used the gun, and I didn't want to shoot him. I had him under control and made him put his gun on the floor. I lowered my gun just a little. He charged me, knocked me down, and took my gun. Dawn was still on the ground. She picked up his gun and yelled at him to stop. He turned and pointed my gun at her, and she shot him twice. He stumbled into the den, collapsed, and died right there."

The Chief introduced himself and Bigelow, "I'm Teddy Walker, Chief of Detectives, and this is Walt Bigelow, my assistant chief."

"Thank you for coming," Yancey said. "Twenty years ago, I would have kicked his ass. I'm not the man I was. He smacked her hard, and that pissed me off. A man is not supposed to put his hands on a woman like that, and he roughed me up, too. He had bad intentions. I'm glad that she was able to rebound. She saved both our lives."

"Well, based on what I'm looking at - the fact that there were multiple witnesses to this being a strong-arm robbery, and she shot him with his gun - she won't face any charges. When a guy enters your habitat with a loaded gun, you do what you have to do," Walker said. "Beating up the doorman, breaking an apartment door in, and brandishing a loaded weapon is the definition of a strong-arm robbery."

"I agree," Bigelow added, nodding and then asked, "Yancey, you said he asked where the files are?"

"Yes. We didn't have a chance to ask what he meant before he got rough. As you can see, he's massive, and he wanted to kick some ass."

Walker and Bigelow stared at the body sprawled against the counter. Bigelow said, "I'd guess he's about six foot five and weighs well over 300 pounds. I'd say that is indeed massive."

Before they could ask another question, there was a knock on the door. "Yancey, Dr. Ewell here," their neighbor announced.

"Come on in, Dr. Ewell," Yancey said.

"Hi guys," he said. "Oh, wow, it's Teddy, Walt, and Mac. Tonight might be the first time I've seen you outside of the hospital."

"Unfortunately, it still has to do with work, Doc. We have a body here," McClellan said.

"Oh really, Yancey said it was about Dawn. What is going on here?" Dr. Ewell asked as he surveyed the apartment. "Busted door. A beat-up doorman downstairs. A dead body, and my favorite New York City detectives. This sure looks like a crime scene."

"Yeah, Doc, that sums it up pretty well. We are waiting for the Medical Examiner to come in and the paramedics to take the body out. Yancey called you because Dawn had a panic attack. She shot the guy and is not doing well."

"Where is she, Detective?"

Dawn overheard Dr. Ewell and sat up on the sofa. "I'm in here." When he and the detectives came into the room, she retold her version of the events. "It all happened so fast. I didn't know what to do. He was so violent, and when he began to beat up Yancey, I did what I had to do."

She curled up on the sofa and began crying again.

"Do you have anything you can give her?" Yancey asked.

"Sure, I can give her something to put her to sleep. But are you guys done with the questions? It will put her out till the morning."

"Yeah, we're good for now," McClellan said. "We have the initial statements. There are video cameras in the lobby and the hallway. And we have the gun, which belongs to the suspect."

"This is a Castle Doctrine case. She's not going to have any problems with the law. The press will have a field day with it, but she's in the clear with us," Walker said.

"Now I know what he meant when he asked about the files," Yancey said. "He wanted the files we shared with Luke McFlemming."

"Yancey, you should know that McFlemming got mugged earlier tonight. He should be at the hospital by now because of his injuries. We don't think they are serious, but he was beaten up pretty badly," Bigelow said.

"This is all my fault," Dawn said through her cries when she heard about Luke.

"Excuse me. Let me take a look at her," Dr. Ewell said. He walked over and sat next to her.

The doctor looked at the bruises on her face from the big guy's roughing her up, "He smacked you around, I see. Are you feeling any pain anywhere?"

"No, I'm not in pain. I am okay," she said between sniffles.

"Dawn, the attack was traumatic, and I'm sure your adrenaline is flying sky high. I will give you a shot that will calm you down and allow you to sleep. Okay?"

"Thank you, Doctor," she said and resumed her fetal position.

Dr. Ewell spent the next couple of minutes carefully checking her over. Yancey stood with the detectives and watched pensively as the Doctor examined Dawn. The doctor smiled when he was done. Yancey read it as good news and let out a sigh of relief.

"Your vitals are okay, Dawn. Your blood pressure is a little high, but to be expected. I'm going to give you a sedative now that will put you out. It'll help you sleep through the night."

After sedating Dawn, he called out to Yancey, "Come on over here, buddy. Let me take your vitals. I need to make sure you are okay."

Yancey walked over and said, "I'm fine Doc. More embarrassed than anything else. He roughed me up some, and I haven't had a street fight since my 20s. I wish we could have stopped him without deadly force."

As he spoke, Dr. Ewell took his heartbeat and blood pressure. He finished and flashed another smile.

"You're going to be okay, buddy. When we leave, I need you to take these two pills. They will help you sleep."

Walker said, "You did great, Yancey. You both are alive, but yeah, it would have helped our investigation if he were alive. Not only for this shooting but the two other burglaries tonight."

Yancey glared at Walker. "Oh, this is an easy case, Detective Walker. You can solve this one tomorrow. This is Bronson Pagent's handiwork. We were hoping to expose him through this series of articles. The back story is how Bronson used organized crime methods to grow his business. He attempted to extort my son. Pagent sexually assaulted my daughter-in-law in a hair-brained attempt to make Yancey attack him. If Yancey had put his hands on him,

Bronson could have blackmailed him, but Yancey instead had his wife beat the crap out of Pagent and videotaped it."

They looked at the sofa and Dawn. She still lay in a fetal position, but her sedative had kicked in, and she now slept peacefully.

“You mean her?" Mac McClellan asked. "Not her? She's a sweet soul."

Yancey looked at McClellan with a raised eyebrow, "Yeah, but she's also Madame Hot Temper. She's mild now, but Dawn has great martial arts skills and beat the crap out of Pagent. They didn’t work against this brute,” Yancey said, glancing at the massive corpse in the den.

He continued, “Bronson doesn't want any of this stuff to go public. It would destroy his mystique and business. It is part of the reason I wanted her to come back to New York. There's a lot more to it, but it's all in the files. The series of articles was to be part of the revenge of Madame Hot Temper. ”

Walt Bigelow heard enough and said to Walker, "Well, alrighty. Shall we pick Pagent up tonight or tomorrow morning, Teddy?"

"Get his address, put a unit outside of his house, and let's knock on his door at 7 AM. Tell him not to leave town and to come in tomorrow afternoon for questioning," Walker said.

Chapter Twenty

"Don't kill him. Get the money and high tail it out of town. Make sure he gives you $20K, and rough him up. Hell, if he has a bag of cash, take it all," Bronson told Chopper when he phoned from his new burner.

"What about you, Bronson? Are you going to be okay if the police get involved?"

"I'm in a dilemma, my friend. Either way, I'll be in a fix. If Petey gets arrested, the cops will come, and it'll be my word against Sy's word. You worry about yourself now. Take the money and go."

"This was a stupid plan. Again, I'm sorry, Bronson."

"Yes, it was Chopper. Let's hope everyone gets out of this okay."

. . .

Across town, Sy Roth paced the floor in an empty factory. Everyone had checked in with him except Petey. Sy promised to pay them $2000 apiece, and he knew that Petey wouldn't miss a payday.

His phone rang, and he was relieved when he heard Chopper's voice. The relief, however, was momentary. Chopper said, "Sy, I'm leaving town tonight with the rest of the guys."

"Wait, what do you mean, Chopper?"

"I'll be there in an hour. I need $20,000. I am taking the guys and heading to Canada for a month. It's time for us to disappear."

"I don't have $20k on me, Chopper. And why are you leaving?" Sy asked.

That was the answer Chopper expected from the nerdy Roth. He wasn't as vicious as Pagent, but just as cheap and manipulative. Chopper growled, "Get the money, Sy. If the police round us up, you're going to big boy jail, and you're not a jail dude. Do you understand?"

The prospect of jail scared Sy. He also sensed Chopper's nervousness and knew it wasn't time to argue, "Okay, I'll get the money. Don't worry, that's not a problem."

Sy hung up the phone and caught a taxi to his Midtown office. He emptied a safe where he kept cash for emergencies. Also in the safe was a small handgun. He took it, too.

Pagent knew Sy kept the cash on hand to do under-the-table deals. Banking authorities could question large withdrawals, and their business operated with too many bad actors to leave bank paper trails. Sy always kept at least $50,000 in the safe.

Sy took all the cash and the gun because he was nervous. Pagent gave him the gun as a gift and for protection, "We deal with tough guys. Neither of us will ever win a fistfight, so take it, just in case."

Sy hoped he wouldn't have to use it tonight and nervously took a taxi back to the factory. The stress of the evening, and now the wait, tortured the nerves of Bronson's nerdy partner.

Finally, Chopper arrived, and when he slammed the door to the 5000 square foot factory, the sound echoed like a cherry bomb. Sy sat on a metal chair in the middle of the factory and jumped up when Chopper entered.

He could tell immediately from Chopper's face that he had no good news. "Sy, we still have not heard from Petey? And Bronson told me you probably had more than $20,000."

"What are you talking about, Chopper? And what do you mean, Bronson? Have you been talking to him?"

The big man began walking towards him with the menacing scowl that made their real estate foes crumble in fear.

"Yeah, I have," Chopper said. His voice now dark and sinister. Sy began to shiver in fear as he suspected Chopper was no longer on his side.

"How much cash do you have? I told you we have to skip town. I'm not interested in going to jail. How much money do you have?"

Sy opened the bag as his heart raced. Chopper stood only a few feet away and could squash him with one blow, but at that moment, he feared his partner more than the menacing giant standing in front of him.

"Why did you call Bronson? You weren't supposed to tell him. Are you double-crossing me?"

"I called him because you have no idea what you are doing," the giant bodyguard barked. "Petey probably got arrested. He's my cousin, and I'm not going to let you pin all of this on me. Now, how much money is in the bag?"

"Stop and step back, Chopper," Sy said. He got up from the chair with the gun in his hand and tried to point it at Chopper but fumbled the weapon.

Chopper rushed forward and smacked him hard across the face with a backhand blow. The blow lifted the five-foot-five 150-pound Sy from the floor. He flew five feet backward and fell clumsily on his ass. The gun fell to the floor, and Sy grabbed his face, cringed through his pain and spat out a bloody wad.

The longtime bodyguard looked at Sy, shocked, "You pulled a gun on me. Come on, Sy, what is that about? You are not a killer. Were you really going to shoot me?"

"No, Chopper, but you scared me. And you knocked my tooth out!" Sy yelled as he clutched his jaw. The pain was excruciating, "Jesus, this hurts."

Chopper picked up the gun off the floor and grabbed the bag of cash.

"This is not your world, Sy. It's not mine anymore, either. If I make it out of this, I'm cutting ties with both of you guys. You and Bronson are not decent people. I'm taking the money and getting out of town. If I get arrested, I'll throw both of you under the bus. I was a fool to be a part of your world all these years. You both can go to hell as far as I am concerned."

"Wait, wait, Chopper. Please!" Sy pled as he walked out.

The bodyguard got into the van. He peeled off from the factory, his adrenaline sky high. After two blocks, he pulled over to calm down and think about what just happened. Sy Roth, the epitome of a weakling, pulled a gun on him. He closed his eyes as he imagined how badly that moment could have gone and admonished himself for his longtime association with Roth and Pagent.

"I need to change my life and get a new job," he said and opened the bag. In it were eight stacks of bills, all hundreds, wrapped in seals marked $10,000.

His anger from the showdown a few moments ago was lessened by the haul. "Wow, this is a lot more than even Bronson suggested he might have on hand. I guess I won't have to worry about a new job for a while. "

He excitedly called Buck, another of his cousins and part of the strong-arm crew at *The News*.

Buck picked up on the first ring. "Who is this?" he barked.

"It's me, Chopper. I got a new burner phone. I had to smash the other phone. What have you heard about Petey?"

"Damn, Chopper. You had me sweating bullets. I've been calling you for an hour. I stopped by the location to pick Petey up. He got shot. There are police over there now. I hate to tell you, but Petey is dead."

All the blood rushed from Chopper as his body fell limp. His heart began to beat so hard that he could feel it as he placed his hand on his chest. His mouth was dry and pasty and his tongue stuck to the roof of his mouth.

He brought his cousin into this caper, and that made Petey's death his fault. They had known each other all their lives and were more like brothers than cousins. His mind raced, and he panicked as his grief rose. He didn't know what to do, but the news broke his heart. He leaned on the steering wheel and cried like a child.

As he wept, Buck realized there wasn't anything he could do but stay on the line until Chopper got himself together. He searched for consoling words but had none. He listened until Chopper composed himself.

Finally, Chopper said, "Buck, call Marco and both of you meet me at my place in Harlem. I have a lot of money here, enough for us to hole up for six months to a year. Give me an hour. I need to make a stop first, and then we gotta get going and cross the Montreal border by the morning."

. . .

As Chopper, Buck, and Marco met, Walt Bigelow joined Jennifer Kung and Mike Desanctis at Café Cielo. "Is it true you guys have VIP tables, and celebrities show up here?"

"Yeah, and the tables are expensive," Desanctis said.

"How expensive?"

"$10,000 a year and, we still have to pay for all the liquor and food. It's expense account money, though. The cost of doing business. I'll have you and Teddy here after this is over."

"I'd love to have you as my guest, too," Jennifer added.

"That's great because at $10,000, I'm never going to be able to afford a table. That's almost a month's salary for me," Bigelow said.

Jennifer then got down to business, "What you got for us, Walt? My paper is put to bed, but we can put it online with a huge follow-up tomorrow."

"Same here," Desanctis added. "Our newsstand issue is printing, but my column, like Jennifer's and Luke's, is constantly updating. What gives Walt?"

"Hold your britches. You know from Luke's story today that Dawn Davis Stuart is back in town, right?"

"Yeah, we both wish we could've gotten a piece of that story and the series Luke is writing," Desanctis said.

Bigelow looked at them both with a stern glare.

"No, you don't. Or I should say, maybe you should rethink that. I already told you somebody got shot. I didn't tell you somebody died. Are you ready?"

"Oh, hell, no," Jennifer said, shocked. "Was she the shooter?"

"Yes, she was the shooter."

"You're kidding me," Desanctis said, stunned. "She just got back here. The legend of Madame Hot Temper grows. This is unbelievable."

"Yes, it is, unbelievable," Bigelow said. "We're all in shock, to be honest."

Desanctis raised his hand, "Hold on, Walt. I must call my editor. Have you heard of stopping the presses in our business? Well, this is one of those moments."

"Me too," Kung said as she dialed her editor. "We need to get the story in, even for a limited press run for tomorrow morning. This story will be all over television tomorrow. We need to get it on the front cover to win the scoop. It will be old news by tomorrow evening."

Bigelow understood. "Go ahead," he nodded. "Do what you need to do. I'll be right here."

He ordered a cocktail while Kung and Desanctis called their editors. Their conversations were brief. A few minutes later, they returned to Bigelow.

"I'm good. We stopped the presses, but I need to turn this story in by 2:00," Desanctis said. It was 1:15.

Jennifer chimed in. "Same here, Walt. My editor is holding the trucks. I have a 2 AM deadline too. That's just enough time for a print run the news trucks can pick up at 4 AM."

Bigelow then gave them a full account. "I told you about the break-ins at Luke's and *The News*. We know the bad guys were after files. We are looking at Bronson Pagent as the ringleader of this crime spree. That is off the record, of course. What we know for sure and what you can say on the record is Dawn Davis Stuart shot a yet-to-be-identified armed burglar to death with his own gun."

Desanctis asked, "How'd it happen?"

"Luck. He overpowered her and knocked her unconscious. Then her father-in-law, with his licensed gun, aimed at the intruder and made him drop his firearm. The intruder then rushed Yancey and took his gun. Dawn revived, picked up the bad guy's gun, and ordered him to stop. He pointed the weapon at her, and in self-defense, she shot him in the head and heart with his own gun. He's dead."

"Wow," Desanctis said. "The Stuarts were lucky. Do you know who the intruder is?"

"No, Mike, not yet, but we expect to do so shortly. We took fingerprints and hope to identify him through facial recognition."

Kung, like Desanctis, typed away as Bigelow shared details of the shooting. She looked up from her laptop and the draft of the story she'd already put together. "Yeah, Walt. Mike is right. They were lucky. They easily could have gotten shot. What is next?"

"We are going to visit the real estate tycoon Bronson Pagent in the morning. He is a person of interest. Today's article and the series of articles to follow are about how Bronson Pagent attempted to extort Yancey Stuart, Jr. He also sexually assaulted Dawn, so she beat the crap out of him."

"Right on. Women power!" Jennifer yelled. Her screams echoed as there was no one else in the restaurant except for the bartender and manager. They smiled at her.

"There's another story," Bigelow continued. "A financial one about Bronson being broke and rescued by Yancey Jr.'s largesse. Nonetheless, Bronson purposely drove a wedge through Yancey Jr. and Dawn's marriage that led to the fateful strip-club incident. Bronson is a bad guy, and the Stuarts wanted to expose his white-collar crimes through this series."

"And she came back to clear her name," Kung said. "Wow, but this is not a good way to start."

"I know, but the Father-in-Law loves her. She's a mess now, and while we were there, a doctor came in to give her a sedative. We need you guys to run with the story. She's in the clear with us, but this case adds to her infamy."

"Oh, poor Luke, he's going to miss this one," Desanctis said.

"He's going to check out of the hospital when he sees the headlines tomorrow. I guarantee you," Bigelow said.

This last comment was met with a thumbs up from Desanctis and a smile from Kung. They both sat in Café Cielo in the early a.m. and wrote their stories after the presses stopped. Luke won the news cycle today, but they would be the star reporters in a few hours.

Chapter Twenty-One

Bronson Pagent stood outside the East Side factory. He hid in the shadows, dressed in a hooded sweatsuit with a backpack draped over his shoulders, and waited impatiently for Chopper Brown to leave.

The real estate tycoon was incensed with his partner's decision to order the strong-arm burglaries, and because of it, even after 20 plus years of partnership and the prospect of jail, decided he couldn't trust Sy anymore.

After Chopper drove off, Bronson, an electrical engineer by education, rigged the factory's doorknob with 40-milliamp electrical currents from a battery in his backpack. It was a lethal current. Once he rigged the doorknob, Bronson receded into the late-night shadows and stood behind a tree a short dash from the building.

Five minutes later, Sy Roth grabbed the doorknob to leave the factory, and a short, loud buzzing sound rang out.

"Oh, God. Uh," Sy yelled as his hand stuck on the doorknob. He stumbled outside and fell on his face. The current killed him instantly. Bronson emerged from his hiding spot and disconnected the battery and wires. He looked at the body and immediately recognized his mistake. There were burn marks on Sy's hand. The currents were too strong, and a diligent cop might detect that he was electrocuted. Bronson pulled out his handkerchief and nervously wiped the fingerprints off the door, then off the battery and wires before putting them in his backpack. He walked away from the building, dropping the battery and cables into trash cans over several blocks, and thought, "If I'm lucky, all of these parts will be in a landfill by tomorrow morning."

He jogged home after he ruled out taking a subway or taxi. "This will take a while, but if I take a subway or a taxi, someone may see me."

Bronson was right. Dressed in a warm-up suit, he looked like a late-night workout fiend. No one noticed him, and as he made his way up Eighth Avenue, he saw the lights on at Café Cielo. He'd been there before and knew its reputation as a place to be seen in the city.

"That's Jennifer Kung and Mike Desanctis," he noted as they sat at a table. They were talking to another man he didn't recognize.

The sight of the Celebrity Hacks made his heart beat faster, and he picked up his pace until he made it to his Upper West Side block. His heart raced again when he spotted a police cruiser parked across the street from his brownstone mansion.

"Why are they outside?" he wondered. "Have they already knocked on the door? Are they here to keep an eye on me entering and leaving?"

It also meant he needed to enter without being seen. He jogged around the corner and, through an alley entrance, entered through his basement door.

"Leave the lights off as you go upstairs," he cautioned himself.

The wood-burning fireplace had embers from a fire he started earlier in the evening. He stripped off his sweatsuit, threw it into the embers, and poured himself a glass of bourbon as he watched a piece of evidence go up in flames. The fire blew strongly in his face, and the smoke from his clothing wafted across the living room until he opened the vents and redirected the smoke up the chimney and outside. The fire and the stench from his clothes left an unpleasant smell in the living room, and he moved the facing designer sofas and a coffee table from the fireplace to the window. He was manic about such things and feared the smoke would destroy the expensive furniture.

After the fire died down, he walked up to the second floor, showered, and then nestled in the bed next to his wife.

As he drifted off to sleep, Sy Roth's body lay on the ground undetected. At 2:30 AM, a gaggle of late-night club-goers discovered it and called the police.

Mac McClellan got a call from the desk sergeant at the city precinct. "Hey, Mac, where are you?"

"I'm on the West Side. I just finished up at Yancey Stuart's house. I'm waiting for a uniformed team to post some security here before I turn in and try and catch a few hours of sleep. I have a big morning ahead with this crime spree and the dead body."

"Mac, I know it's late, and I'm sure you want to head home, but some partygoers stumbled across another body on East 12th Street. We have some uniformed officers on the scene. Can you head over there and start the investigation? Just put together enough notes to do a handoff for the morning crew."

McClellan was exhausted. His shift was supposed to end at 10 PM. But then all hell broke loose, and he was the only detective on duty at this hour. He had his hands full with the Madame Hot Temper shooting and the two other related burglaries. However, Tarlton, the desk sergeant, was a friend and always did favors for him.

When she asked, "Can you go to the crime scene?" he knew it was a call he had to take.

"Okay, Tarlton, I can do that. Can you save me some time and have the uniformed guys search the body for any identification?"

"They have already, Mac. The picture identification on the body is that of Symon Roth. He had a couple of business cards on him as well that say he is the Managing Partner at Pagent & Roth, Real Estate."

McClellan's heart nearly jumped out of his chest. "Did you say Symon Roth of Pagent & Roth? It's his body?"

"Yes, the uniformed guys say that the ID matches the body."

"Tarlton, come on now? You have to be kidding me. Sy Roth, really? And they were able to make an ID match?"

"Yes, based on the driver's license."

"Is there an obvious cause of death?"

"They did not report gunshots or bodily wounds, and that's why I need you to head down there. These guys are rookie cops and wouldn't know any better."

"Tarlton, this may be crime number four tonight and part of the same spree. Have them rope off the block and identify any security cameras that are in the area. I'll be down there in ten to fifteen minutes."

"Thanks for giving us some senior leadership on this Mac. I appreciate you stepping into the gap."

"No, thank you, Tarlton. It's a bit eerie, and I'm beat, but I need to be at this crime scene."

Chapter Twenty-Two

The city came alive as all five local news stations reported the notorious Madame Hot Temper shooting. Mike Desanctis was ecstatic because all of the news reports were attributed to him and Jennifer Kung. Three of the stations had called for phone interviews on the breaking story. Jennifer did interviews with the other two stations. Desanctis was the top dog today, and his editor was going to be excited because he won the news cycle.

He got to bed at 4 AM and grabbed a nap before his phone awakened him two hours later. He should have been exhausted, but once the television stations began calling, he got a kick of adrenaline. "Luke will be pissed at me and TV today," he boasted. He scooped us on a huge story yesterday, for sure, but today he's probably doing everything he can to bust out of the hospital."

Desanctis loved his headline, "Drama Returns to the City With Madame Hot Temper." It was a bit misleading as this was a self-defense shooting, but it sold newspapers, and readers wanted the sordid dramatics of a scandalous murder. His wife saw his headline on TV and scolded him facetiously.

"Mike, my dear, you morphed a little into Luke with that headline. That's something he would do. That woman deserves a break."

She was right about the headline, and he didn't try to defend himself. "I did become a little Luke-like, Suzie. Something came over me. I guess because we are all in this together. Jennifer, Luke, and I understand the voracious appetite our readers have for scandal. Madame Hot Temper's a perfect foil for us: beautiful, dramatic, rich, and sophisticated."

"And misrepresented and manipulated by you, my husband, the mild-mannered, Westchester County-bred, son of an accountant. What have you become?"

Mike smiled at his wife. She was a modern dance professor at Harlowe. They met there 20 years ago when she was a dance student, and he was a reporter for the school newspaper. He was a handsome nerd. She was hot and artsy. She liked geeky nerds, and when she performed in a campus dance recital, he covered it for the *Harlowe Student News*. She liked the article and began following his weekly stories.

Suzie Terry found out where he lived on campus and would stop by at all hours to flirt. Everyone on campus knew about her crush.

Finally, one day she confronted him and said, "For a reporter in training, you have the worst detection skills ever."

“Suzie, that’s not true. I understand everything going on."

"Really? Then tell me what I am talking about."

He took a deep breath, blushed, scratched his head and his chin, and looked down on the ground. Finally, he stuttered, “Uh, well, you like me."

"Well, golly gee Mike. You do understand. I've been throwing myself at you for months. Don't you like me?"

"I'm shy. Besides, you're hot, and you're popular, and all the guys on campus like you. I didn't think I would have a chance. So, I chose not to try."

"Mike, you should try. I'm into you," she said as she pressed her body against the shy reporter in training and kissed him. They have been together since.

Suzie had been his backbone and, along with his editor, Pete Colon pushed him to be more outgoing. She facetiously scolded him this morning but was excited for her hubby. "I think I finally created a monster in you, Mike Desanctis."

"Grrrr. I am a monster," Desanctis said, smiling at his beautiful wife.

"Grrr back, Baby. I have classes this morning, so I must get ready. I'll see you later, and we can celebrate."

He did a couple more television interviews and, by 8 AM, was ready to leave the apartment to walk to work. When he got to the lobby of his building, the doorman Marvin smiled and said, "Madam Hot Temper. Golly Mike. That woman is something else. Is she that cold-blooded? That lady is like a Wild West fast gun. Pow! Pow! Pow!", Marvin said and blew on his index fingers as he imitated a Western shootout.

He continued, "Dudes need to steer clear of Madame Hot Temper. She has no issues with putting a cap or two into a fella."

Mike looked at Marvin with an incredulous smile. He realized most of New York thought of her as Marvin did. To them, Dawn Davis Stuart was a gun-toting, no-nonsense, hot-headed shooter. "Marvin, this is a tough break for her. She was defending herself."

He ignored Desanctis' defense and asked, "Is she going to jail? I hope not. She's too glamorous for jail."

Marvin's comment made him stop in his tracks, "Come on, Marvin? Too glamorous for jail. Where'd that come from?"

"The picture of her in your story," he said. The photo editor at *The Post* put on the cover of the print edition. Marvin's face lit up as he showed it, "Look, man, she's like a Hollywood starlet. Check her out. That woman makes men drool."

Mike marveled at the photo too and said to his doorman, "Well, Marvin, don't worry, she won't be going to jail. There is a law called the Castle Doctrine. It's legal to use deadly force to protect yourself against armed home invaders. She shot the intruder with his own weapon."

"Well, I'm for that. If you break into someone's home, all bets are off. Mike, I bet what really happened was that she batted those beautiful eyes and pursed her lips, and he dropped his gun. She then picked up the gun and shot him in the ass. Bang, bang!"

Mike laughed and corrected him, "That would be the Hollywood version, Marvin. He roughed her up and knocked her unconscious."

The doorman snarled. "Nah, he hit her. I'm from Uptown, Mike. We have rules. If you put your hands on a woman, you've got to pay."

"I hear you, Marvin. But you should read the article. Stop looking at the pictures."

"Nah man, I like the pictures. Madame Hot Temper is a hot tamale. A spicy mamacita!" he yelled as Mike walked out the door.

When he reached his corner newsstand, Smitty greeted him with a huge smile. "Mike, this is a huge story. I only have two copies left. I had to stash them behind the counter."

"Smitty, you didn't have to do that. I can get all the copies I want at the office."

"They ain't for you, Mike. They're for me. Madame Hot Temper is back. I need you to autograph these for me," he said as he held up copies with the headline 'Drama Returns to the City With Madame Hot Temper.' It surrounded the glamor shot that excited Marvin and Smitty and was sure to captivate the city.

Smitty said, "Man, she's so beautiful and will shoot your ass in a second."

"I just told my doorman this was self-defense," Desanctis said as he placed the newspapers on the small counter and signed the front pages. "You have to read the article. She was protecting her home against an armed intruder."

Smitty looked at him with a sarcastic smirk. He was convinced Dawn Davis Stuart was a badass. Desanctis was not going to convince him otherwise. Especially today.

"She shot him dead, right, Mike?"

"Yes, but it was self-defense."

"Mike, she's gangster," Smitty barked. "The woman has been back here for a hot minute and is already mowing down bad guys." Smitty imitated a machine gun waving in the air, "Rat tat tat tat tat. She's a fly as heck, bad babe with a gun."

"Fly as heck, bad babe with a gun," Mike said and shook his head in appreciation of Smitty's description.

He was struck by Smitty's and Marvin's fascination with Madame Hot Temper. She was much bigger than he could ever understand, and it was just time to accept the city's obsession with her. He played along. "Yeah, she's different, Smitty. Madame Hot Temper is back, and she's a bad mama."

"Yes, Yes, Yes!" Smitty yelled. "That's what I'm talking about, Mike. You have a good day, big-time news reporter."

Desanctis smiled. It was a happy morning for him. He strutted to work with his head high and shoulders back as one reader after another paid him compliments.

Pattie Cunningham, the editor of *The Ledger* and Jennifer Kung's boss, was as excited as Smitty and Marvin. She called her ace gossip reporter. Kung recognized her number and picked it up.

"Boss, you never call me, especially this early in the morning. Did I do something wrong? You could have waited until I got in the office."

"Haha, I just called to say I love you, TV. You make this work look so easy. What the heck happened last night? It is a big scoop for us and you."

Cunningham was the editor-in-chief of *The Ledger* and the only female editor of the city's three large dailies. She was previously *The Ledger's* chief celebrity reporter. Kung apprenticed under her and took over after Cunningham's promotion to the editor.

"Thanks so much, Pattie. It was a long night."

"The CEO and his minions are calling and texting. They want to be able to brag like insiders. It's like that with these society stories. Everyone wants to act like they are more connected than they are."

"Yeah, Pattie. Being in on gossip is the new cool. Well, it's like this. Mike Desanctis and I got a call from Walt Bigelow, and he asked us to meet him after midnight at Café Cielo. He came through after 1 AM, and when he started talking, we both knew this was one of those rare stop the press moments."

"And it was. I'm glad you followed your instincts. If you hadn't, and Mike was the only person to get glory from this story, we'd both have been getting yelled at right about now. Instead, they love you."

"They should love you too, Pattie. You're the best editor in the business, and you always tell me to follow my instincts. I'm only doing what you taught me."

"Thanks, TV. What is this about Luke getting robbed? Now that's real gossip," Cunningham whispered. She wasn't a fan of Luke's either and was itching to hear about what happened to him. To her, it was as big a story as Madame Hot Temper.

"Yes, boss, Luke's in the hospital. He got roughed up pretty badly. City Hospital held him overnight as a precaution. You know he hates Mike and me right now. They're probably giving him another sedative to calm his jealous rage fit."

"I can imagine that. I'm happy for you to get this big story and beat him. I know he can't stand that," she said with a giggle. "Anything else you can share?"

"Tell the bosses that the real estate tycoon Bronson Pagent is involved. I don't know enough, but there's an extortion story with his company and the Yancey Stuart family."

Kung heard her phone click. She looked at the caller ID and interrupted her boss, "Hold on a second. It's Walt Bigelow. Let me see what he wants."

"Ooh, go ahead. I'm curious. I'll wait."

Bigelow said as she clicked on the incoming call, "Hey Jennifer, what a fabulous story this morning. I've got more stuff, and I'm going to need help from you, Mike, and even Luke. Are you ready for another doozy?"

"Sure, what you got, Walt?"

"Sy Roth, Bronson Pagent's partner, is dead."

"You're joking right, Walt. Are you serious? When did it happen?"

"Sometime, this morning. Partygoers found the body outside a factory the company owns on the East Side. We are doing an autopsy now. He wasn't shot or physically assaulted, as far as we can tell. All we know now is he had burn marks on his hands and a missing tooth. He might have lost the tooth falling on his face."

"What do you need from us?"

"Everybody is exhausted, but I need you guys to make it down here by 3 PM, and we'll update you on everything."

"Okay, Walt, I'll be there. I have my boss on the other line. I have to tell her."

"Go ahead and do your job, and congratulations on the article today."

Jennifer clicked the call back to Cunningham, "Pattie, Sy Roth died last night, or I should say early this morning? He is the partner of Bronson Pagent's. He died outside one of their factories, and they are now doing a post-mortem examination to determine a cause of death."

"Oh my God, Jennifer! Are you going to be okay? Do I need to hire a security detail for you?"

"No, Pattie. Luke got beat up because he had information on the extortion. At least that is what Bigelow told us."

"Well, you be careful. I don't need you to get hurt like Luke." She then whispered, "I kind of hate saying this out loud, but it brought a smile to my face after I learned that he was okay."

"What do you mean?"

"That he got his ass kicked. It was about time."

"Ooh girl, you are so right. Luke will never be able to live this down. Mike's a better person than I; I'm going to rub it in Luke's face. I'm not gonna let him forget this. Luke got whupped. A karma ass-whupping."

"Oh, that's funny as Hell. We should stop," Pattie said and let out a loud laugh.

“Why? Whupped, whupped, Luke got his ass whupped," Jennifer sang the words with glee.

"Goodbye, Jennifer. Congratulations again," Pattie said. She hung up the phone laughing hysterically at Jennifer’s song.

Chapter Twenty-Three

A weary Mac McClellan knocked on Bronson Pagent's door at 8 AM. Like Desanctis and Kung, he was running on adrenaline.

"Can I help you?" the housekeeper asked as she opened the door. The intoxicating aroma of freshly baked goods tantalized his nose and made him realize he was as hungry as he was exhausted.

"Hi, I'm Detective McClellan from the New York Police Department. I'm here to share some news with Mr. Pagent. Is he at home?"

"Yes, please wait here." She closed the front door and went to alert her employer.

"Mr. Bronson. Mr. Bronson!" the housekeeper called from the bottom of the stairs, in her thick Spanish accent. "A police officer is here at the door. His name is Detective McClellan. He wants to speak to you. Should I let him in?"

Bronson expected the visit after he saw the police cruiser parked outside his house in the wee hours. He yelled back, "Yes, Carmelita, let him in. Bring him into the living room and tell him I will be right down."

She returned to the door. "Come in, Detective, he will be downstairs shortly. He asked for you to take a seat in the living room. Please follow me."

The housekeeper led him through the long hallway that split the main floor. She turned at the opening to a spacious, sunlit living room. The furnishings included a pair of oddly-placed mid-century sofas. He found it odd that they were not in the center of the room but a few feet away from the enormous front window.

There was lots of artwork on the walls. He guessed the pieces might be expensive but paid no attention. His brain was fried from lack of sleep, and he had no interest in admiring some rich guy's stuff. He squinted as the sunglare from the window bothered him.

The room's layout also confused him, "This is awkward," he thought and whispered to himself, "The arrangement makes no sense. The massive fireplace is in the center of the room. That's where the sofas belong."

The sofa was way too hard for comfort. McClellan shifted a few times, trying to find a soft spot, but to no avail. He stared at the matching sofa on the other side of the expensive wooden coffee table. "This is definitely a style versus comfort living room," he mused. "If you ever become rich, Mac, don't ever buy this kind of furniture. It's junk."

A few seconds later, he heard Pagent walk down the stairs and ask, "Carmelita, did you offer the Detective a cup of coffee and a croissant?"

"I was getting ready, Mr. Bronson. I just pulled the pastries out of the oven and was about to offer him some."

"Well, I will do that. Bring me a cup of coffee and a croissant in the living room, please."

Pagent entered the living room, dressed in a dark blue suit, white shirt, and blue tie. McClellan guessed him to be about 50 years old and approximately five foot seven. His build was average, if not slightly portly. He could have weighed anywhere from 180 to 210 pounds. At first glance, he didn't strike the detective as athletic or impressive in any way. He also had an average face with enough chubbiness for McClellan to think he needed to hit the gym a lot more. The best thing about his appearance was his clothing.

Mac thought, "His suit looks expensive. Otherwise, he's like so many of these wimps who hide behind their money to get away with a lot of crap."

Pagent spoke first. "How are you, Detective? I'm Bronson Pagent. Welcome to my home. What can I do for you this morning?"

McClellan stood up so they could shake hands. "Thank you for your time this morning Mr. Pagent."

"Detective McClellan, can I offer you a freshly baked croissant and coffee?" Carmelita asked as she re-entered the room, interrupting the conversation.

"Oh, you must have one or even two," Bronson said. "Carmelita is a marvelous baker. You won't find a better croissant in New York. Trust me."

McClellan hadn't eaten all night, and when Carmelita had opened the door a few minutes earlier, the croissants' intoxicating fragrance had made his mouth water.

"I have to say, I rarely accept food while I'm on the job. However, the croissants smell delicious. I would love one, please. Thank you so much."

"Well, you must have a cup of coffee as well. Espresso or coffee? What would you prefer?" Bronson asked.

"Just a cup of coffee. Milk, no sugar. Thank you."

As they waited, Bronson walked to the wall next to the fireplace. He hit a button, and a shade dropped from the ceiling, covered the window, and blocked the irritating glare.

"Sorry for the sun and the odd configuration of the furniture. We had some issues with the fireplace blowing smoke into the room. We're trying to fix it and moved the sofas and coffee table here temporarily," Bronson lied.

"Oh, I wondered about that. You have wonderful taste. This is a very well-designed room with quality furnishings," McClellan fibbed. The lie was to make conversation until the croissants arrived.

Bronson was anxious. He wanted to get to the purpose of the visit.

"Now, Sir, it's not often I receive early morning house calls from the police. In fact, I've never had one. To what do I owe this honor?"

Carmelita re-entered the room with a serving tray of baked croissants and coffee. "I must say, Sir, I need to take a bite of this croissant first, please. My mouth is watering."

"Yes. Please enjoy," Pagent said. He mustered a nervous smile as it meant that he would have to wait and exercising patience wasn't one of his strong suits.

McClellan took a bite of a croissant then studied Bronson. There was tension on his face that the detective knew was a tell. He just couldn't make out yet what Pagent was hiding.

"My goodness," McClellan said after a second bite. "This is a delicacy. And you're right. They taste even better than they smell. I'm a sucker for freshly-baked goodies. I could eat these every day. How do you not?"

"Discipline, Detective McClellan, I am quite disciplined in my dietary habits, my business, and my private life. It's a key to my success."

"Ah, yes. That's why I am here. Unfortunately, I have terrible news. Last night and through early this morning, we had a horrible and deadly crime spree with four related incidents. We're now trying to make sense out of them. They included two deaths, and I'm sad to report that your partner Sy Roth was one of the casualties. There's reason to believe he may have been murdered."

Bronson spat a gulp of coffee into his cup, then choked and coughed in a fake surprise.

He got up from the sofa, walked behind it, turned around, and faced McClellan. His voice trembled, he was doing his best to appear shocked as he said, "What are you talking about, Sir?"

McClellan looked at him and didn't say a word. He chose to maintain silence and study Bronson's reaction.

What McClellan didn't know was that Bronson Pagent was really a dark soul. It took him a minute to compose himself. After he did, he asked, "Did you just tell me that Sy is dead?"

"Yes, I did, and we understand you guys have been partners for decades. We need your help. We want to rule out foul play. He may have died of natural causes, and we'll have to wait for the medical examiner to determine the cause of death. However, and I must be honest, this crime spree seemed to focus on you and him."

"Excuse me, what are you talking about? What would we have to do with a crime spree?"

"We thought it odd, after yesterday's article about Madame Hot Temper, that the reporter was assaulted."

"I read the story yesterday. You mean Luke McFlemming?"

"Yes, and his apartment and office space were burglarized. And then there was a strong-arm robbery attempt at Dawn Davis Stuart's house. She shot the robber dead."

"Whoa. I have to sit down. This is terrible," Bronson said as he walked back to the other side of the sofa. He loosened his tie, unbuttoned his top button, and took a deep breath as he sat down.

The news of the death at Dawn Davis Stuart's home did surprise him. He hadn't read the news or watched any television yet, and didn't know it was a headline story. The shock was such that he had to pull himself together as he continued to lie.

"I am stunned. Sy Roth was my partner and wouldn't hurt anyone. I am devastated by this news."

"Well, I have to tell you. We suspected you guys until Sy showed up dead. Even if he were murdered randomly, and it appears that is the case, his death will be beneficial for you."

"What do you mean? Am I a suspect?"

"We have to rule you out, but I'm sure that won't be an issue."

"What do you need from me, Detective?"

"Cooperation. We need you to tell us about any enemies who might want to kill Sy and bring you down. I must also be honest. Because of yesterday's article, we have to rule out if you guys had anything to do with the home invasion at Dawn Davis Stuart's."

"I guess you are telling me I should call my lawyer and come to visit you guys?"

Bronson's mind raced. He thought about Chopper and felt lucky that he told him not to kill Sy. It also meant if Chopper got caught, it could be good for him. He would testify that it was Sy's plan. He had enough going for him to keep lying. McClellan snapped him out of these thoughts when he asked, "Do you think you need a lawyer Bronson?"

He looked McClellan in the eye and responded calmly, "No, but you're talking about two people dead. One, who is my partner. I am going to call my lawyer."

"Do what you need to do. Have your lawyer call us, and please come in for an interview mid-afternoon today."

"Okay, I, I, will," Bronson stuttered. The stutter wasn't part of his act. He was genuinely overwhelmed and needed to call his lawyer.

The detective stood up and reached inside his jacket pocket, "Here's my card. Please call us and may I make a special request?"

"Sure, Detective, how can I help you?"

"The croissants were delicious. Is it too much to ask for a couple to go? You're right. They are the best in New York."

"Oh, sure, you can. Carmelita, can you pack a box of croissants for the detective to go? He loved them," Bronson yelled to the kitchen.

"Absolutely. I will, happily," she answered.

"Give him all that you baked this morning. I'm not hungry," he said and stood. "Follow me to the kitchen. Carmelita will take care of you."

As Carmelita boxed McClellan's croissants, Pagent stood in the far corner of the kitchen, McClellan at the kitchen island. Bronson pulled out his phone and sent a text. He then excused himself as his phone rang.

"Pardon me, please? I need to take this call."

"Sure. Don't forget to come through as agreed."

"I will. Carmelita will escort you out," he said and ran up the stairs towards his office and picked up the call. "Hi Phillips, I'm in a jam. Thanks for phoning me back. I'm hoping my membership in Pre-1860 can help me."

"What is going on, Bronson?" Phillips Warner, the lead lawyer for Pre-1860, asked.

"A detective is leaving here now. He stopped by to tell me there were two deaths last night. One of the people who died is my partner Sy Roth. They want me to come in for an interview."

"Is he out of the house? Don't say another word until he leaves," Warner said.

Bronson walked back to the top of the stairway and saw McClellan cross the hallway from the kitchen back to the living room.

"I just want to make sure I don't leave anything behind," McClellan told Carmelita.

Once back in the living room, McClellan pulled out his phone and quickly snapped several pictures of the fireplace."

"There is debris in there that isn't firewood. That joker thinks I couldn't tell. Did he burn up evidence?" McClellan whispered to himself. He then walked back to a smiling Carmelita.

She walked him to the door and handed him the box of croissants. "Please enjoy the croissants, Sir, and have a good day."

"You too, and thanks so much. I will enjoy these."

McClellan bounced down the stairs with a pep in his step. He was exhausted but energized. His instincts told him Bronson was dirty.

"He's gone," Bronson said as he heard the door close. "I barely held it together when he was here."

"Are you guilty? Be honest with me. Remember, I'm a fixer, and with Pre-1860, the way we interpret the law is not how the rest of the world views the law. Give it to me straight, Bronson."

"Phillips, there was a series of crimes yesterday. All orchestrated by my partner, Sy Roth."

"Roth, he's not a member, right? He's Jewish. We don't have Jewish members," Warner said.

"No, he's not a member, and yes, he's Jewish. He hired my Goon Squad to do a bunch of strong-arm burglaries. Sy is not from that world. That is what I do, not him."

"Why did he hire them, then?"

"It was in response to yesterday's Madame Hot Temper story. I guess he panicked and tried to take revenge for the story and series of articles that were supposed to follow. It was a bad move. They hospitalized one of the top gossip reporters, Luke McFlemming. One of the squad members was shot and killed."

“I saw that story. It's all over the morning news. But don't worry, based on what you’ve told me, you are good so far. You don't need a fixer’s help."

"Well, I killed Sy after I learned about it. I tried to make it look like an accident. I wired the door to the factory he was operating from and electrocuted him. I put a little too much juice in it, and he burned hands. I'm sure the coroner will figure out he was electrocuted."

"Okay, Bronson," Warner said. "Give me all the details of the night. Everything that you were involved with and how you came to know about Sy and Chopper."

Bronson and Warner spent the next 20 minutes meticulously going over the night's events.

When they finished, Phillips said, "You played this like a veteran. Telling Chopper to kill Sy and then rescinding the offer was a master move. It was brilliant."

"What do you mean?"

"It means that you were not part of the conspiracy. You did not know about the crimes, and because you rescinded the hit, it will be hard to indict you."

"But how about the fact that I killed him?"

"Unless someone saw you at the scene of the crime, you've established strong, reasonable doubt and an alibi. We have to persuade Chopper to cooperate. You know I can't help him. Pre-1860 would never lend its service to help blacks. But if you can get him immunity to testify, he might get off free."

"I'll hire a lawyer for Chopper. I need to find him," Bronson said nervously.

Phillips said, "Don’t worry. You get me a photo. We know how to find people. We have our sources in law enforcement. If he is in North America, we'll find him."

"Okay, I can do that. I will find a photo for you. What about this afternoon?"

"I will pick you up at your home and take you to the headquarters for your interview. In the meantime, don't leave the house. Just send me a photo of Chopper and relax. You are going to be fine."

Chapter Twenty-Four

Chopper was frustrated, angry, and scared. He was in the van with Buck as they neared the USA-Canada border south of Montreal when his burner phone rang. He knew only two people could be calling that number. One was Buck. The other was Bronson.

"Hey, Big Man, I need you to come back to the city. The police are on my tail. Sy died last night. The cops want me to go in for an interview this afternoon, and I need you to help me out."

Chopper pulled the van over to the side of the road and yelled, "Are you crazy, Bronson? I am not going to come back and go to jail for you."

"It's not jail, Chopper," Bronson said calmly. He tried his best to make the request sound like it was no big deal. "I'll get immunity for you. All you have to do is tell how Sy set up the whole thing, and it got out of hand. You also have to say that I didn't know anything about it until you told me."

"Bronson, I am not doing that. You must be out of your mind. This sounds totally like a set-up. I will not do it."

"It is not a set-up. I will hire the best lawyer possible and pay you handsomely for it. Chopper, please. I need you to do this," Bronson said, and raised his voice. He was feeling desperation, but also hoped the raised voice would intimidate Chopper. "We can both walk away from this without getting arrested."

Chopper yelled, his voice now with his own dark and sinister tone, "What about Buck? And Marco? What about Petey's family? He has two small kids. There are a lot of people who have to be taken care of."

"If you come back, I will put $2 million into an account for each of them and $3 million each for you and Buck. That is a lot of money, Chopper. I'm worth at least a billion, but after yesterday my business may be ruined. I may have to start selling out and fast."

"Look, Bronson, I don't trust this. I should have left you guys after the Yancey Stuart, Jr. fight years ago."

Chopper knew after last night's episode that he was on his own and couldn't return to New York. Bronson panicked and continued to try to intimidate him, "Chopper, I need you to listen to me. Have you ever heard of Pre-1860?"

"No. What is that?"

"It is the most secretive white supremacy group in the United States, if not the world. I am a member."

Chopper gritted his teeth in anger and smacked his van's steering wheel in rage, "I should have guessed. You have a black man do all of your dirty work and now you threaten me. Was Sy Roth a member too?"

"No, we don't accept Jews, Blacks, Hispanics, Asians. But you may not believe this; I am only a member because it is highly secretive and helps me in business. And, it gets me out of tough messes like I am in now."

"Well, let them find a way for you out of this jam, Bronson. Why do you need me?"

"Chopper," Bronson said coldy, "I have to find you before they find you. If they come after you, it won't be good. You may come back, but I guarantee you Buck and Marco won't."

"Bronson, Buck's my cousin, too. Marco's my friend. They are not in this life. And I keep telling you that I am not in this life either."

"You are now. I need you to keep your phone on," Bronson said. "Don't try and hide. Right now, I am your best hope. Unfortunately, this is how it's going to play out for you, Buck, Marco, and Petey's woman and his kids."

"Damn you, Bronson Pagent. I hope you go to Hell. I have to talk to Buck and Marco, and I will call you back in an hour. I don't give a hoot about some damn Pre-1860. I will send you to Hell if I ever see you again. I'm going to rip you apart with my bare hands."

Bronson ignored Chopper's threats. He said calmly, "Let's work through this, Chopper. I know you hate me. Please call me in an hour. I want to be able to call off the dogs."

Pagent hung up the phone and called Phillips Warner. "I talked to Chopper. I had to threaten him, and I think he will cooperate. I told him that I would sic the forces on him and his family. I'm going to have to pay him handsomely, however."

"We can put a hit squad on him, especially because he's black. There's a line of people who would gladly eliminate him," the lawyer said.

"No, I don't want him touched. If he helps me through this, I will owe him."

"I thought you told me that he got you in this by doing the strong-arm robberies. He's nobody Bronson, just another nigger gangster. The world won't miss him."

As Bronson listened to Warner, he began to comprehend the treachery of Pre-1860. He had a long relationship with Chopper and defended him. "Chopper was with Sy and me for a decade. We muscled a lot of guys, and he was loyal to us. I owe him a lot. I don't want Pre-1860 after him."

"Fine, it's on you then. So, this is what I want you to do. Once Chopper agrees, have him call you at 2:15 today. We'll be at our meeting at police headquarters. He can tell them exactly what happened. They will likely order him to come in and give himself up. He can clear you and decide if he wants to come in. You probably should hire a lawyer for him, too."

An hour later, Chopper called and showed cunning Bronson never suspected. "Okay, you got me good here, Bronson. Now I need you to wire money before I talk. I am going to play the game today the way you guys taught me."

"What do you mean, Chopper? I'm trying to come to a win/win solution here."

"No, you're not. Sy told me about the company's operating cash and lines of credit. I know you have fast access to more than half a billion dollars. I want retirement money out of this. You take care of me so that I can take care of my family, and I'll risk going to jail for you. But you are a long way from convincing me, with just $3 million."

"What do you have in mind, Chopper?" Bronson asked, realizing his beefy security guy had been paying attention all those years to both his hardball tactics and how Roth kept the books.

"This is how it is going to go. I want $50 million sent to three offshore accounts in an hour. I won't speak to anyone until I receive the money. If I don't, I'm a ghost. And don't send anyone around to Petey's house. If you try, you'll see ten guys posted in front of the house. There'll also be 30 more in places you'd never think to look. They won't let your guys off the block, alive."

"No, Chopper," Bronson said. "I wouldn't do that. I'm trying to come up with a plan for us both. And I have to tell you, $50 million is a lot of money."

"Yeah, but I helped you extort a lot of money and close a lot of deals. Call it a spot bonus. Plus, Pete was the real deal. He is what we call the Community Gangster. He had a lot of friends and protected a lot of people. Tell your white supremacist guys that if they come after Petey's wife and kids, Buck, Marco, or me, they will feel the wrath of God. Let them drive by, and they will find out."

Bronson's heart began to beat as fast as it did when McClellan visited him. "Chopper, you are scaring me. Why all the aggression? Is this necessary?"

"The conversation is over, Bronson. I'm texting you the account numbers for the offshore transfers. I'm not negotiating on the amount or the timetable. If you fail to comply and don't meet the one-hour transfer timetable, the amount increases to $60 million. You've got some work to do. I'll call you after I confirm receipt of the cash. Goodbye." Chopper didn't wait for a response. He ended the call.

Chopper caught Bronson off-guard. He underestimated his bodyguard and thought of him as merely a muscle man. Chopper played the perfect game of chess and called a checkmate, and Bronson marveled at how he played the hand, "Brain and brawn. Chopper is nobody's fool. If $50 million is what is going to take, I'll pay him. It'll come from Sy's side and the amount his wife is to receive. Let me send this guy his money."

Chapter Twenty-Five

By the time Phillips Warner picked up Pagent Bronson to go to police headquarters, Chopper Brown had received the wire transfer of $50 million to his offshore accounts and transferred it twice. The money was untraceable.

Chopper, however, was still nervous as he knew the depths of Bronson's treachery. Instead of accepting Bronson's lawyer recommendation, he hired the celebrity defense attorney Hollis Tassie to defend him. Tassie was on his way to the police headquarters to stand in for him.

Teddy Walker told Mac McClellan before the meeting, "This is your show, Mac. Let me and Walt know how you want us to play it. Give me a nod if you want me to play the heavy. I'll jump right in."

"Thanks, Teddy. We want a statement from him. He's slippery, though, and I want him to understand that he's not smarter than us. Having you and Walt in there will make him know that we are serious."

Bronson and his attorney, Phillips Warner, arrived ten minutes early. The desk sergeant called McClellan. "Mac, your two o'clock appointment has arrived."

"Great, I will be out shortly. Offer them a cup of coffee and escort them to the small conference room on the main floor."

McClellan wanted to interview them in a conference room as opposed to a cramped interrogation room. The conference room had windows and a large oak table surrounded by comfortable leather chairs. It was a major upgrade from the grimy industrial steel furniture interview rooms at the other end of the hall. Interviews were often psychological games, and McClellan wanted them to feel relaxed enough to make a mistake.

"Detective McClellan will be down shortly," the desk sergeant told Bronson and Warner. "I am going to escort you to the conference room. He asked that I offer you guys coffee. I'm warning you that it's not very good."

"Thanks for the warning. We'll pass on the coffee and wait in the lobby," Warner said. He didn't trust interrogation rooms at police stations.

"I'll pass on the coffee too, but thank you," Bronson said.

The doors at headquarters suddenly swung open, and a tall, lean, immaculately dressed, dark-skinned black man with salt and pepper hair entered.

"Hollis Tassie is here to represent Chopper Brown, Lawrence "Buck" Brown, and DeMarco Smith," he said in a deep baritone voice and spun in a circle, like a dancer on center stage. He smoothly tapped danced to the Seargent's desk.

The desk Seargent covered her mouth. She tried to control it but laughed loudly at Tassie's dramatic entrance.

"Excuse me. You sure know how to enter a room, don't you, Hollis. Does that work in the courtroom?"

"Not all the time. It depends on the judge," Tassie said with a huge smile. He was known for his charisma, style, and courtroom brilliance.

"Can't I have fun? The job is hard enough, Sarg Tarlton. Besides, I can strut like this when I am winning. And I know you like me. I am charming, right?"

"You are indeed charming. Yes, you are, but where you find all this energy, I'll never know."

She looked at Pagent and Warner. "They are also here for the interview. I'm going to call Detective McClellan to find out what to do with you guys."

"That's not going to be necessary, Tarlton. Tell Mac to have Teddy Walker or Walt Bigelow come down here. I'm here to work out immunity for my clients before we speak."

He turned to Bronson and Warner and said, "Don't worry, gentleman. We are not going to sell you guys out. This case warrants immunity for my clients before they help you guys."

Phillips turned to Bronson and whispered, "Chopper is one step in front of us. Hollis Tassie is excellent for a black lawyer."

Bronson was a wreck. All morning he'd been thinking about the worst-case scenario. He feared there could be a witness who saw him rig the wires to the door and couldn't hide his fear. It showed all over his face. He was impressed by Hollis Tassie, and true to his selfish nature, only concerned with the results.

"Based on first impressions, he appears to be an excellent lawyer, period. It's not about race," Bronson said. "This is about you getting me cleared. Remember that, Phillips. I'm not interested in going to jail."

They heard several sets of footsteps and looked up to see Walker, McClellan, and Bigelow at the top of the staircase. As they walked down together, Walker and Bigelow whispered instructions into McClellan's ears. The sight unnerved Warner and encouraged Tassie.

Chopper hired Tassie immediately after receiving Bronson's $50 million wire transfer. The lawyer had disdain for wealthy, connected defendants who abused their power and influence to make their minions their fall guys.

"Tell me everything you can about this guy," Tassie asked Chopper. "These are the people who deserve jail but think the law does not apply to them."

Today, however, was a moment when Tassie and Bronson were on the same side.

"Look, gentlemen," Chopper's attorney yelled to the detectives as they walked down the stairs, "this case can be solved, over and done in about 15 minutes."

"Hey Hollis, it's wonderful to see you," Walker said, dismissing Tassie's rant as a lawyer tactic. He liked the charismatic lawyer and enjoyed sparring with him and could tell today would be one of those days. "It's clear that you've got some news for us."

"Teddy, we can all be out of here in 15 minutes. I need immunity for my clients and we can wrap this up. Everybody can be home for happy hour."

"Immunity? What are you talking about, Hollis? We've got two dead bodies here, plus an assault and robberies. Somebody is going to jail."

"Nah, not today, Teddy," Tassie said in his hip soul brother accent. "This can be quick. Let's talk about this in a conference room like gentlemen. Once you hear from me, you'll agree that my guys deserve immunity. Let's patch DA Gath in on a phone call; I'm sure he will agree. Okay, Chief?"

Walker turned to Bigelow and McClellan. "Give me five minutes to figure out what he's talking about."

The detectives didn't say a word. They just nodded. The Chief of Detectives turned to Tassie and said, "Follow me, Hollis. This better not be a waste of my time."

Walker stopped and said to McClellan as they passed Bronson and Phillips, "Mac, take these guys to the second conference room with Walt and begin. I'll be with you shortly."

"Wait, Teddy, please," Tassie pleaded. "No interview should start until we understand what is going on with this immunity talk. I'm asking you to wait until we make the call."

Walker looked at Tassie hard and long. The defense attorney didn't blink and returned an equally intense glare.

After a couple of seconds of glaring back and forth, Walker relented and decided to give Tassie the private moment, "Fine, everyone, just stay where you are. Nobody go anywhere. We'll be back in a second. Have a cup of coffee? It's terrible, but have one on me."

The desk sergeant Tarlton watched all of the back and forth and said, "This is entertaining, for sure. I should have popcorn for all these theatrics."

Walker closed the door after they entered the room. He didn't wait for Tassie to sit down. "Okay, give it to me. What is this immunity talk about?"

"My guy didn't shoot anyone. That's it, Teddy, that's the straight talk. He had nothing to do with the murder. He didn't beat anyone up. I promise you that. If I am lying, you can revoke the immunity."

"What did he do, Hollis? Give me something?"

"Nice try, Teddy. Like I said, he can help you wrap this up, fast."

Walker stared hard again at Tassie. The defense attorney stared back and didn't blink. He'd known Hollis Tassie for years, and Tassie always played his hand well. Walker's gut told him Hollis wouldn't be asking for immunity if his client didn't warrant it, so the Chief of Detectives gave him the benefit of the doubt.

"Okay, let me call Gath. Sit tight," Walker said. He walked out of the room and to the end of the hall and called District Attorney Gath on his cellphone. He returned and handed the phone to Tassie, "Here's Gath."

"How are you, D.A. Gath?"

"Hey, Hollis. Walker told me that your client didn't murder anyone or rough up Luke McFlemming. If so, we'll grant your guys qualified immunity."

"Chopper Brown, Buck Brown, and DeMarco Smith. Immunity for all three, right?"

"Okay, but if you're playing me, you messed up. It means you are persona non grata forever. And we have no deal. Are we clear?"

"This is not a game. Thank you, we'll wrap this up," Tassie said and handed the phone to Walker.

"Thanks, Gath," Walker said and ended the call.

"Here it is," Tassie began. "All three of my clients warrant immunity because they worked with Sy Roth, who put this crime spree together. Petey Brown is the dead guy. He is Chopper and Buck's cousin. Sy was embarrassed by the McFlemming story and some of the files he believed McFlemming, Dawn Davis Stuart, and Yancey Stuart, Sr. had that could destroy their business. He wanted to intimidate them and get the files."

"What does Bronson Pagent have to do with this?"

"Bronson is a piece of crap. He used my clients for years as his goons, but he had nothing to do with this. Sy went to Chopper behind his partner's back, and when things got out of hand, Bronson found out."

"Did Bronson have anything to do with Roth's death?"

"No, he told Chopper to kill him but changed his mind. It was in anger after learning of Sy's plan. He told Chopper to smack the crap out of him and to take enough money to get out of town."

"Where is Chopper now?"

"He's on the run. He'll come back now that he's cleared."

Walker walked to the door, "Mac, come in here for a second?"

As Mac entered the conference room, Walker asked, "Were we able to capture anything from the video cameras in the street?"

"Nah, Chief, the surveillance cameras were garbage. There was bad lighting and nothing more than that. The tapes are useless."

"Okay, bring those guys in here. It will be quick."

McClellan walked to the doorway and yelled, "Everyone, come in, please."

They entered the room, and as they began to walk to seats, Walker said, "Stop please, Pagent and Phillips. Hollis was right. This is over. We are granting Chopper, his cousin, and his friend immunity. Based on our conversation, we will close this case. As long as Petey Brown was the muscle who assaulted Luke, and once Chopper provides sworn testimony, this is dead. Go home and pop a bottle of champagne, all of you. It is your lucky day."

He continued, "There will be no indictment, and nobody is going to jail today."

Bronson pumped his fist and exhaled a sigh of relief. McClellan gritted his teeth and shook his head in disbelief. He said nothing more.

"Thank you, Teddy," Warner said. He turned to his client and said, "Let's go, Bronson."

Bronson couldn't control his smile. He knew he had dodged a bullet. Tassie, too, but he needed a private discussion with Pagent, "Congratulations, Bronson. Allow me ten seconds with you, please, near the exit."

"Catch you later, Sarg Tarlton," Tassie said, and winked at her on his way out. She blushed and winked back. He walked to the exit as Bronson trailed him.

Tassie wanted to ensure they were out of Walker, Bigelow and McClellan's earshot. Bronson gleefully said, "Thanks for getting Chopper off and, of course me, Hollis. I appreciate it."

"I'll be sure to tell Chopper you are thankful. He asked me to tell you that he went back to the factory because he couldn't trust Sy. As he pulled up to the building, he spotted a guy in a hooded sweatsuit put some kind of gadget on the door and then disappear into the darkness. He couldn't make out clearly who that guy was, so he parked down the street and watched what was going on. He saw Sy come out of the building, and his body seize up and then collapse. The guy in the hooded sweatsuit then removed the gadget from the door. Chopper figures he knows who the guy in the hooded sweatsuit is, so as a favor, he ran an electrical short in the street pole that destroyed all the contents on the neighborhood video cameras. He wanted me to say that he took a couple of classes in trade school and is a trained electrician, too."

Bronson stared at Tassie with horror in his eyes and said, "Let's continue this conversation outside."

Warner was a couple steps away. He didn't hear the conversation but could see his client's discomfort. He waited until they got outside and asked, "What is going on here?"

"I just shared with Bronson a $100 million observation by my client."

"We already paid Chopper $50 million. How much more does he want?"

Tassie stared at Phillips, "Well, today, Phillips, on this glorious day in the year of Our Lord, you are paying a huge black tax. Let's call it an ancestral reparations payment. Your client shouldn't have threatened my client with a visit from Pre-1860. And oh, yeah, I hate you guys, so this is fun for me."

"And, Bronson, your firm probably has some corporate by-laws that include a morality clause if one of the partners steals or breaks certain rules. You stand to take your partner's entire half-billion dollar or more stake in the firm. So while this stings, I know you'll be okay."

"I am going to give his wife his full share," Bronson stuttered. He was shocked and confused as his worst fear was realized. There was a witness.

"Sure, you are," Tassie said sarcastically. "Look, this is not a negotiation. All I want is for my client to receive $100 million more. $10 million because of what he witnessed, $90 million is the tax that you will have to pay for threatening Chopper with a Pre-1860 attack."

Phillips exploded, "You slick ass, mother..."

"Uh, oh, Phillips. No foul language. This is a business deal," Tassie said calmly.

"It's not business. It's extortion."

"Ah, man, Phillips. Now you are all in your feelings. You don't want to make a scene here. I'm guessing Teddy and Walt are probably looking at you getting all red in the face. Calm down, my friend. My suggestion is that you do the transfer to my client's account in the morning. We'll send you the account numbers by eight this evening. I'd also advise you to liquidate as fast as you can because as pissed as I am for you being in Pre-1860, Dawn Davis Stuart is probably equally pissed with Sy for sending a guy to her house."

"How do you know about Pre-1860?"

Tassie rolled his eyes, "Phillips, You're an idiot, and I'm not. I'm a rich and powerful black attorney, and I have friends in high places, too. There's a lot of hate for hate organizations. I'd say it is at an all-time high."

He then turned to Bronson, "Chopper said he likes you. He doesn't believe you have hate in your heart. You just believe that being a bully in business is how you win. And guess what, he may be right. Sometimes you win that way, sometimes you lose. Today you lose. And a bit of free advice since you just paid a $90 million hate tax. You need to fire that guy and quit those dudes. This membership cost you a lot of money today."

Bronson's attorney fumed. He stepped towards Tassie with rage in his eyes. Hollis looked back at him with cold, sinister eyes. Warner cowered, and as he did, Tassie said, "Just like I thought. You forgot your man pants today. I'm wearing mine and will crush you."

Warner turned and walked to his chauffeured sedan. The driver opened the door, and once he got to the car, he yelled at Pagent, who was a couple of steps behind, "Bronson, let's go."

Walker, Bigelow, and McClellan all watched from the precinct door. "What was that? Did he really want to fight Hollis?" McClellan asked.

Walker said, "Nah, that would have been a bad move. Hollis looks refined and sophisticated, but he's a street hustler. He would have busted him up good. Plus, Warner belongs to Pre-1860, the worst, so-called secret hate group. I'm sure Tassie wanted to smack the crap out of him for being part of the organization."

McClellan then asked, "Is there more to this case? Do you think we played this one right Chief?"

"You got the testimony Mac, and my gut tells me they didn't lie to us. They probably left a little out. We don't have a video for what happened to Roth, right?"

"Yeah, it's a piece of crap."

"Let it go. Let Madame Hot Temper take care of him. Walt, I need you to call the Celebrity Hack Patrol. Find out if McFlemming is okay and push the meeting back to 4 PM. We'll tell them the case is dead. Mac, you can lead the press event and get recognition for all your good work. How's that?"

"Thanks, boss," McClellan smiled.

Part Three

Chapter Twenty-Six

A month after Kwame and Donald's engagement, Tom Wilson proposed to supermodel Danielle Jackson.

He didn't tell Kwame until two weeks later. "It happened on the spur of the moment. We got stuck in a rainstorm without an umbrella and couldn't catch a taxi, so we took the subway home. Danielle hugged me as we stood soaking wet on the train and said, 'I love you, Thomas.'"

"I responded, 'Not as much as I love you,' and she said, 'I'm sure you believe that, but it's not possible. I am crazy about you.'"

"She looked me in the eye and I knew it was the moment. It wasn't about finding the right romantic setting for Danielle. I saw that look in her eye, brushed her hair back from her face, and said, 'Then marry me, Danielle, and let me love you for the rest of my life.'

She smiled and said, 'Okay. Let's do it.'"

"We kissed and I put one on her. Somebody yelled, 'That's the supermodel Danielle Jackson and she looks dizzy from the kiss that guy put on her.'"

She loved it and said, "Yeah I am. We just got engaged and the entire subway car started to clap and congratulate us. It was a unique New York moment."

Danielle called her parents that night, but we didn't buy a ring until two weeks later. And it wasn't on my account, she wanted to ring shop. When we got home, I pulled a twist tie from a loaf of bread, got on my knees, and placed it around her finger. She cherished that twist tie and flashed it in my face every day until she found the ring she wanted."

Kwame knew Tom's engagement was inevitable and hard-earned. Tom was madly in love with Danielle, but because of his legendary past as a playboy, she made him apologize for his trail of broken hearts.

Tom had come up with the idea to author a novel under an alias and send copies to his ex-girlfriends. His pen name was My Name Is Brother Lover. It gave him the cover to apologize without having to call people directly and deal with any drama. It was a brilliant idea that worked and Danielle liked it.

He told her, "I sent the same note to all my ex-girls. It said I didn't write this book, but the guy in this book sounds a lot like the man I used to be. I'm sorry I tugged at your heartstrings and wish you a future filled with love. Afterward, when women would contact me and ask if I were the author, I always denied it."

The book was titled *Getting Over My Broken Heart*, and its main character, Victory Scores, quickly gained a cult readership. Tom modeled Victory after himself, a tall, suave, extremely handsome playboy with a revolving door of suitors and a world-class roster of conquests. Victory had a hole in his heart, which meant no one was good enough he found Jesus. The book became a best-seller and later a blockbuster movie. He created a mystery around the many characters and conquests, and because it was promoted as a true story, it sold out in droves. The book made Tom millions, and to this day, only a few people know he was the author.

Chapter Twenty-Seven

"This is my suggestion," Cathy Martin, the celebrity party planner, said to Carrie Sinclair, Michelle Nubani, and Danielle Jackson. "Donald and Carrie will be the first to marry. I hope you can agree because, respectfully, he is the most well-known. Tom and Danielle will be second because of their music and entertainment backgrounds, and with Danielle being a model, many of the guests will be different and will shake things up a bit. Michelle and Kwame's wedding will also have more of an international flavor as your family will be coming in from Ghana and many of your parent's friends from across Europe. You guys will be last."

Michelle and Danielle were okay with Cathy's plan. Carrie, however, was uncomfortable and didn't want to overstep any boundaries. "Michelle and Danielle, you are two of my best friends. I already told Donald this Black Camelot thing is flattering, but I won't allow it to come between us. We need each other. Our lives have changed and will be different forever."

"Don't worry," Michelle said. "This order is perfect."

"I agree," Danielle said.

"Fantastic!" Cathy exclaimed, relieved. "Now, let's go over some details. I understand that Black Camelot is a media creation. But as far as the weddings go, these are big deals. America does not have any royalty. We do, however, realize how crazy the world is about the English Royal Family and all things royal."

"The City accepted you as its royal family, and now America is watching. The weddings will be classy and elegant. I will design and oversee all the elements. For you guys, there won't be any worries about the details. That is my job. Just be your beautiful selves," Cathy said.

"What would be those elements?" Carrie asked.

"Yours will be summer daytime weddings. The day will start with a horse and covered coach carriage ride to and from the church."

"Oh, that sounds fabulous," Michelle said.

"At the church, a quartet of trumpeters will do a trumpet salute, followed by announcements as each carriage arrives. He will introduce each member of the wedding party as they depart their carriage."

"That sounds very regal," Carrie said and once again looked at Cathy with a tense look on her face. "I'm going to have to grow into this. It's not who I am."

Cathy expected this kind of objection from the women and had a ready answer.

"Carrie, this is your Cinderella moment." She looked around the table at Michelle and Danielle. "Didn't all of you ladies want to be Cinderella as a child? "Think of all the beautiful black, brown, and underprivileged girls in this country and across the world who will see you as their princesses."

Carrie smiled and said, "Gee whiz Cathy Martin, you are an excellent salesperson. You're right, I desperately wanted to be Cinderella, but I never believed I could."

"Now you are, Carrie, and so are you, Michelle, and you, too, Danielle. These events will be spectacular and remembered around the world for decades, if not forever. Your backgrounds as three very accomplished women of color makes them more important stories. You should lean into this moment and have fun with it."

Michelle looked at the wedding planner and her two friends. She was just as nervous about the spotlight as Carrie but Cathy Martin's words made her embrace the moment, "Cathy, you are amazing. I was concerned and frankly didn't want all this limelight. But, you're right. Carrie and Danielle, let's enjoy this."

Danielle stood and walked across the room as if it were a runway. She moved gracefully, flaunting excellent posture refined by years as a supermodel. At the door, she stopped, turned, and posed, her shoulders arched back, and head held high. She walked and waved, turning her hand at the wrist like a princess, and said, "I am Cinderella. I found my Prince in Tom, and I'm all in. I am not shy or ashamed and will have the time of my life, with my main girls in the greatest series of weddings ever."

Carrie turned to Cathy and with a bright smile said, "Well, I guess it's pretty clear she's all in. That girl ain't nervous, at all."

Everyone laughed. As a supermodel, Danielle was most accustomed to the public glare, and her comfort helped Carrie and Michelle as they were still getting used to being celebrities.

"You bet I am. This sister is all in," Danielle said, with a wink of her eye and flash of her million-dollar headshot smile.

Cathy continued, "Now, I know you and your fiancés are Christians, so are we all good having the church services at Freewill Baptist?"

"Yes, we are," Danielle said for them all.

"The wedding ceremonies will be officiated by Reverend Hall. Two songs will be performed during each service. You couples can each pick your favorite hymns and performers to be performed at your service."

She continued, "The ceremonies will be tightly scripted and short, no longer than 30 minutes. Afterward, we will take pictures in several locations in the city. First, we will depart the church in horse-drawn carriages to take photographs in Central Park's Grand Gardens. Next, the carriages will take us up to Harlem to 125th street and Amsterdam, after which we will ride back down Park Avenue to 59th street. We'll cross to Fifth Avenue to the entrance of the Major Museum on 59th Street. We will depart the horse-drawn carriages there for the receptions ".

"These carriage rides will be for the public. Tourists and fans will want to get photos and see as much of the events as they can. All three of the receptions will be at the Major Museum."

Cathy continued, "We'll use the first three floors of the museum. The first floor will host a welcome reception for all the guests. The primary reception and dinner will be on the second floor, and the third floor will become Club Black Camelot for an after-party and where the festivities will end."

"That sounds amazing. I love the Major Museum. It's perfect for large receptions and parties," Carrie said.

"And it's so fitting: the facade resembles a castle," observed Danielle.

"It was," Cathy nodded. "A Dutch king named Norsworthy constructed it during the early settlement days in New York. At one point, it was the largest structure in the city. Most of the exterior sconces and carvings are part of the original building. It is a historic landmark, so they can't be removed. The building is a hidden gem, and as a former royal dwelling, it's perfect for your weddings."

Carrie turned to Danielle and Michelle, "Girls, we have the right person in charge of this."

"Cathy Martin, you are the boss," Danielle said. "And I'm going to enjoy my Cinderella moment."

"Thank you, Cathy. I trust you'll make us all look amazing, and our guests will have an amazing time," Michelle said.

"Thank you, ladies. It's a huge honor for me, too," she said and looked up in the air wistfully. "Black Camelot, who would think in our lifetimes there'd be black royalty here in New York?"

Chapter Twenty-Eight

Luke was worried about his next big story. Jennifer and Mike had stolen the buzz from his Dawn Davis Stuart series. The strong-arm break-in and shooting at the Stuarts' home had shaken Dawn and her father-in-law so much they decided to put a hold on the articles.

A month later, no one talked about the night Luke got mugged, Petey got shot dead, and Sy Roth died. All the attention in the city had turned to the Black Camelot weddings.

And then Kung called to brag. She wanted to tell Luke about her exclusive, torture him, and make him beg. “Luke, I called to tell you that you have a problem.”

"What are you talking about, Jennifer? Why would I have a problem?"

"Well, it's like this. Samantha Rivers and I have become close friends. Through her, I'm also now friends with Carrie, Danielle, and Michelle, and with Donald and Kwame."

"Whoopee doo, TV. I still don't understand," he snapped.

"Well, buddy. I could drag this out and torture you, but I won't. Let me get right to it. I have exclusive rights to cover all three of the Black Camelot weddings. I am running all the press stories."

Luke didn't respond. She didn't say anything else either. She waited for him to explode, and when he didn't, it surprised her. After 15 seconds, she broke the silence. "Do you mean I have finally shut up the star?"

He then responded as she expected, "You sly, cheating..."

"Oh, no, don't you dare swear at me," she said, cutting him short. "Cursing is not professional. You need to learn how to lose with grace."

Luke gritted his teeth and but couldn't control his fury. He yelled, "I hate you, TV. I really do."

He took a deep breath and tried to calm down. Kung had the upper hand, and he knew it. He couldn't afford to be shut out of these weddings and began to lobby her.

"Come on now, Jennifer. This is too important of a story for you to have the exclusive. I have a public to serve. You have to let me in on this one. These weddings are public events."

"Public to serve? You are such a prima donna. Your ego is a pain in my ass."

It was not unusual for one media source to cover celebrity events, and he knew it was a common practice. It saved the celebrities from being overwhelmed by media requests. But even in defeat, as opposed to showing grace, his immediate response was to lash out with a petty attack.

"Well, I do have the biggest following in town. It's a fact. I have more readers than you."

"And that petty response is why I hate you sometimes. I'm going to love peeling off your readers with my exclusive coverage."

He responded with muffled words Jennifer couldn't comprehend. She figured he had covered the phone and cursed her out in a juvenile fit.

"I don't understand what you are saying, but how about this to make you even madder. I am a bridesmaid at Michelle Nubani and Danielle Jackson's weddings and a guest at Donald Alexander and Carrie Sinclair's wedding. I'll be writing first-person accounts for all three as part of my exclusive agreement."

Luke pulled the phone away again and muttered angrily, "Man, she has everything. I have to give it to her. She has everything wrapped up pretty good."

He then made a move she never expected. The big star begged for mercy. It was an about-face so abrupt that she nearly dropped her cup of tea.

"Okay, TV, you win. I need in on this. Tell me, when did you get the exclusive? And how can I get in?"

Kung was stunned, but she wanted more glee from the reveal. He had given up too fast . She needed to enjoy this more and began to toy with him, "What, hey, what is it that I hear? Is that the sound of you begging? I expected more of a fight from you."

Luke knew why she was giving him the business and that she had every reason to torture him. He not only begged for access, but also mercy, "Come on, Jennifer, be nice. I give, okay. Take the foot off my neck. You got me."

She smiled and wished she could see his face, humbled and begging, "Luke, I set the wheels in motion months ago right after you hot-dogged me at the press conference for the Oliver Harris Diversity Education Fund. I talked to Kwame, Donald, and Sammy. That's when they approved the idea of me having the exclusive rights to their projects."

"Well, congratulations, TV. You deserve this, but freezing me out is wrong. I need some of this. It's the biggest story of the year, maybe the decade. You can't freeze me out."

Kung asked again, "Are you begging Luke? Are you on your knees yet? I want to hear you say. Are you begging dude?"

Finally, he said, "Yes, I am Jennifer. I have to get something out of this. I know I'm an ass at times. Okay, I admit I am an ass, and I'm sorry. Give me something, anything. I'm begging."

Kung enjoyed the moment and took her time to respond. While she did, she put the phone down, spun in a circle and did a happy dance. There were a lot of past offenses she was getting revenge for with this admission.

Afterward, she picked up the phone and said, "I like this begging, humbled Luke. Now let me see what I can offer you."

Kung wasn't a sucker, though, and decided not to give him something juicy. She decided to treat him the same passive-aggressive way he would treat her. "I can't give you anything specific now, but I can give you a lead."

He jumped at the offer, "Okay, I'll take it. What you got?"

"In two weeks, I'm going to a bachelorette party on Saturday, the last weekend in May. There is a bachelorette party for each of the brides and a party for each groom. Carrie's party is here in New York. Donald's bachelor party might be here, or it might be somewhere else. You can't crash the ladies party, but...."

He interrupted her, "If I can find out where the guys' party is and show up, I get my story."

"Yes. If you are the reporter you say you are, make it work."

"Thanks, TV. This is not much, though," Luke whined.

"That's the point, Luke. I wish you could see my face and how much I am smiling right now."

"I would never do you like this TV, ever. This is not cool. You're shutting your boy out of the biggest story of the year."

"Man, you would freeze me out. Wait a second? You just did it to me with the Madame Hot Temper scoop. You didn't share it with Mike and me until after you ran the story. At least I'm giving you this. I've got to go. Do some real newspaper work for a change and dig up this story. Goodbye."

Luke's blood pressure rose after the phone went dead. Jennifer Kung was going to blow up with this exclusive coverage. He also knew she fit in with this crowd better. The Black Camelot crew tolerated him, but they liked her, and it made sense to have someone they liked to cover the events. It didn't mean, however, that he was going to lie down.

"She's right," he said aloud. "It's time for me to do some real investigative reporting. How hard could it be to find out where three of New York City's most respected business and society leaders were having bachelor parties? I can figure this out."

Chapter Twenty-Nine

Tom yelled to the driver, "Sir, can you switch the radio to a hip-hop station and turn the music up loud?"

"Sure, Sir, no problem," the driver said, and turned the radio to several stations until he found one Tom liked.

Kwame had seen this version of Tom a thousand times and reminded him that their wilding days were behind them, "Tom, remember we are going to be grown-ups this weekend. We are not in our 20s. We are in our..."

"In our late 30s," Tom interrupted. "Donald is in his mid-40s, and Ron is ancient, like in his late 50s. We'll let them act their age."

Kwame disagreed with his best friend's attempt to mock their elders, and as he shook his head, Tom said, "You know I'm right, Kwame. I love those guys, and they are cool as heck for elders."

"Are you kidding me? You do know those dudes were players in their day."

"I know Kwame, but they are retired."

"You are too, Tom. Remember, this is supposed to be a fun weekend. Nothing crazy, just good clean fun with the fellas."

Twenty minutes later, they arrived at the airport, and their jaws dropped. They saw Donald Alexander, Ron Cherry, and Luke McFlemming of *The News* walk into the terminal together.

"This dude? What is he doing here?" Tom asked as they looked at McFlemming.

"I have no idea. We'll ask Donald and Ron later. It can't be their idea. This has to be a coincidence."

They checked their bags with the private plane valet, and as they finished, Luke walked up to them, "We are going to have a blast this weekend. Yeah, that's right. I'm joining you guys."

Tom stammered an almost incoherent response, "What, huh, uh, nah man. Nah. Oh hell no, you ain't. Who invited you?"

He then turned to Kwame to verify this was not happening. Kwame was just as surprised and shrugged at him.

Luke enjoyed their meltdown. He cackled as they tried to make sense of his joining them. Finally, he said, "I am kidding, guys. I will be in Jamaica for a beauty pageant this weekend. Maybe we can catch up for a drink. I wish I had my camera handy to record your reactions. Do I scare y'all that much?"

"McFlemming, yes, you do, and jokes like that won't make us friends," Kwame snapped.

"We are not available to hang out. We're playing cards and golf most of the weekend," Tom yelled so loudly that other people in the small terminal turned around to look at him.

"Well, your loss Tom. I know you like the ladies, and the ladies like you. Nice try with the boring getaway story. I know it's Donald's bachelor party weekend. I'm not buying boring," McFlemming said as he walked away.

Kwame and Tom watched McFlemming. He did scare them, and it sucked how much he knew it. They finally regained their wits as Donald and Ron approached them. Cherry said, "Fellas if that wasn't the biggest sign to be on guard. You never know who will be watching."

"You look like you saw a ghost, Tom," Donald said.

"Playing cards and golf most of the weekend. Where'd you pull that one from, Tom?" Ron asked.

The two old guys Tom clowned on the ride to the airport looked at Tom and Kwame and laughed.

"McFlemming is a killjoy. I'm seriously considering going back home," Tom said, still stunned.

"Oh, come on now, Tom, we'll still have fun. We'll make sure of that, right, Ron?" Donald said and winked at Ron. "Forget about that guy."

"Grown man's fun. Are you youngsters ready to learn some veteran moves? Kwame, bring your boy, Scared Thomas," Ron said.

Kwame shoved his buddy and whispered, "Come on, man, get your head right, and forget Luke. You need to be ready for Donald and Ron. I told you they were players. We're about to learn something from these dudes."

Tom whispered back, "You're right. I take back everything I said about those two. They are gangsters."

On the plane were JoJo Littlejohn, Kurtis Van Weston, Steve Ryan, TJ Melendez, Miki Nomura, Rote Tunz, Phaethon Malone, Greg Smith, Rick Alexander, and Juan Mendoza. It was an all-star collection of their famous and well-to-do friends. Kwame and Tom were excited to see them all. They became more excited when they saw Juan, the convenience store owner in Tom's neighborhood.

"Oh, yeah!" Tom yelled and forgot about his meltdown a few minutes earlier. "The party is on now. Juan is in the house. Let the trash-talking begin."

"You can't have a party without Juan up in this piece. There's no way I was going to miss these shenanigans," Juan said as his face lit up seeing his friends. He walked over to Tom and Kwame with a cocktail and gave them both a hug and a hearty soul-brother handshake.

Tom asked him, "Have you met the fellas yet?"

"A few, but who is your boy over there? The dude with the movie star face made this drink. He looks familiar. He's playing bartender and is better looking than you, Tom."

"You mean JoJo Littlejohn. He's a Hollywood D-List actor. Thank God he's got that face, because the brother is only an okay actor," Tom said loud enough to catch JoJo's attention.

Littlejohn was accustomed to Tom's trash-talking. He exaggerated a yawn and patted his mouth. He loved to remind Tom that he always bested him on the lists of best-looking people.

"Oh, damn," Juan said. "I kept trying to place his face, but my mind is mush. I had to pull an all-nighter at the store for this trip. I've seen all of his movies. "

Tom turned to the group as he, Kwame, Donald, and Ron still had to say hello to everyone. "Let me introduce you to him and the rest of the guys. They know about you and your store, and how close you are to Kwame and me."

As they approached JoJo, Juan said, "There was an article in *Celebrity Profiles* naming him the most desirable man in Hollywood. And in an article in *The News* a couple of years ago, readers voted him the hottest male in New York. Tom, you finished fifth. Donald was second."

Tom shook his head and frowned, "Juan, I know about that article in *The News.* Kwame, JoJo, and even my fiancé remind me. They all tell me I'm slipping. How do you remember that? It's gossip, Bro."

"Gossip, gossip, gossip. My wife Lillian tells me that's all I do, especially when the fellas come in."

"Ha, she may be right, Bro. I mean, the coffee is good in your spot, but I go there more for the trash-talk," Tom said.

"And gossip," Juan said.

Tom nodded his head and admitted, "You're right. Trash-talk and gossip."

They arrived at the bar, where JoJo was still making drinks, "JoJo, meet my good friend Juan, here. He just complimented your amazing bartending skills. I told him it's your fallback gig, and you have to stay in practice because your acting is only so-so."

"Oh, I can see the game is on already," JoJo said and stared down Tom. It was a don't bother me kid look. JoJo was as fast with the jokes and one-liners as Tom and snapped back, "Tom is trying to bring the jokes, and we haven't lifted off yet. I'm glad being a comic ain't your main gig, Thomas. You'd starve, Bro."

"Whatever," Tom said as they continued to playfully glare at each other.

Juan laughed at JoJo's quick retort and their snap battle that he guessed would continue for the weekend. JoJo looked away finally and turned to Juan and said, "It's a pleasure to meet you, Juan. I heard a lot about you from the fellas."

"Nah, you are lying? Really?" Juan said as his face lit up with surprise. "Oh, hell. That just made my day."

"No, really! Tom tells me your store is where the action is, but I can't come by."

"Why not? You have to visit, JoJo."

"Well, Man, you know Tom can be petty. He likes being the most handsome guy in the room. Every time an article comes out, and he is voted less handsome than me, the brother has to visit his therapist. And whenever I'm in the same room with him, he starts acting out. Like he is now."

"At least I can hoop," Tom snapped back.

JoJo rolled his eyes, then winked at Juan before responding, "There you go with hoop stuff, again. Today we got Phaethon Malone on this plane. So, you finish second there, too."

"He's right," Juan said, "Phaethon is a basketball legend, a ten-time all-star."

"But don't worry, Tom, you're straight with the music business," JoJo said, then quickly corrected himself. "Well, you are a top music executive, but we have one of the best talents in the business on this plane. Juan, do you know Rote Tunz?" Littlejohn asked as he turned and pointed.

"Hey, Phaethon and Rote, raise your hands and meet Juan. You all have heard Tom and Kwame talk about their boy Juan, right?"

"What's up, Juan?" Phaethon yelled. "I have long wanted to come by your store for some coffee talk."

"Hey Phaethon, I'm a huge fan," Juan replied. "I was there the night you scored 60 against the Barons."

"Thank you, Juan. I was on fire that night. We need to get you some tickets for next season. We'll make that happen before this weekend is over."

Phaethon and Rote walked over to shake Juan's hand. Rote said, "The brothers love your place, Juan. I've been there once before. I had a blast and need to come by again for some more coffee and laughs."

"Oh, I remember. You're always welcome, Rote. You have to give me a heads up because my wife Lillian will kill me if any of the three of you come into the store and she's not there. She'd be so mad she'd bring me back to life just to kill me again. I need some advance notice."

They all cracked up with Juan's joke. Rote said, "Well, let me set you up with some tickets, too. I understand how important it is to keep the ladies right."

"You got that right, Rote. Lillian is my queen. We've been married for 15 years. She's my third wife. It took me three times at the altar, but I'm happy now."

Greg Smith, a retired hall-of-fame football player and now one of the game's top television announcers, walked over to introduce himself to Juan. He was with TJ Melendez, the other A-list Hollywood actor on the plane. They both lived in Hollywood and were close friends. Greg introduced himself first. "So this is the famous Juan. Tom and Kwame told me your place is where all the cool people in New York must visit."

Juan's eyes bulged as he looked at Greg. "Oh my God, I'm here with Greg Smith, a 12-time All-Pro running back for the New York Bombers and our team's all-time leading rusher. You retired from the Bombers after your 15th season and became a broadcaster and product pitchman, and now you are one of Madison Avenue's most coveted celebrity endorsers."

"Wow, Juan, you are indeed a fan. I should hire you to be my PR agent."

Smith attended Grande Pointe College with Kwame and Rote. When he was single, he also ran around New York with Tom and Kwame.

Juan, continued after he composed himself, " Greg, I'm a huge fan. How are you connected with these guys?"

"Well, Juan, Kwame, Rote, and I are college aces."

Juan said, "You are my favorite Bomber of all time, #25. Led us to four championships in ten years." He excitedly clapped his hands five times and stomped his feet five times.

It was an imitation of the fan's cheer every time Smith scored a touchdown or got a first down. A chant of "Go, Greg!" followed the cheer.

Watching Juan in his glory was TJ Melendez, who, like JoJo, was on every most handsome man's list. He attended Calvary College with Donald in Ohio.

Juan was about five foot six and weighed about 150 pounds. He was strikingly handsome with a big, contagious personality that instantly made him everyone's friend.

TJ listened with a smile as Greg and Juan continued their conversation, and waited for a moment to introduce himself.

"Tom told me about your spot," Greg told Juan. "But I live in LA now. My wife moved us out there when we got married after I retired from football. She wanted to separate me from Tom and Kwame. You know those guys, the famous bachelor playboys," he winked. "I play a lot of golf with TJ when he's in town and not shooting a movie."

Juan was like a kid in the candy store as he met all the celebrities. He introduced himself to TJ Melendez with a review of his latest movie. "Ooh, TJ. You are the Man. I loved the movie where you played the badass, corrupt, smooth playboy executive in *Silicon Valley Wars*. JoJo was good in that movie, too. It should have won an award."

"Thank you, Juan. I'm glad you like the film and my art. I see everybody loves you here. I am looking forward to hanging out with you and having some fun this weekend."

"Man, my wife Lillian loves you, TJ. You have to come by the store when you come to New York."

"Of course, I will. I have to visit this great spot."

While Juan was in his glee, Kwame glanced over to the bar's far end and spotted Steve Ryan chatting with Donald. He was excited to see his old buddy. Steve was now the President of Sales at Harris Simmons and the #3 executive under Deirdre Francis and Sheri McCready. Kwame walked over as Donald asked how things were going, "How are the boss ladies?"

"Deirdre and Sheri are outstanding. They are happy and deserving. Some guys are a little envious. It's what you'd expect. Just envy and hate."

"They're taking care of you. No problems, right?" Donald asked.

"Everything is fine, Donald. They give me the rope I need to succeed. I couldn't be happier working with and for them."

"I love them, they are deserving and my favorites, too," Kwame said. He hugged Ryan and whispered, "Thanks for coming. I'm glad to have you here and to hear everything is working out well."

Kwame glanced at the front of the plane as the Captain emerged from the cockpit. He excused himself from the conversation and walked to the Captain. After a brief chat, Kwame shouted, "Hey, Fellas. Give me a second for a few words."

As the plane became silent, he said, "Let me introduce you to Captain Stevens. He is taking us to our destination for this weekend and the next two weekends of parties. Captain Stevens, please say hello."

"Gentlemen, my name is Captain Geoffrey Stevens. We are excited to have you as our guests. We'll take off in about five minutes, so finish your cocktails before takeoff, and you'll be able to refresh once we're airborne. I'll announce from the cockpit when it is okay to remove your seat belts. The weather is perfect for a safe flight today. That's all I have for now. With that, I'll turn you back to Kwame."

Kwame continued, "Guys, one last point. Ron set us up in some first-class accommodations on the island. We are staying at Big Stan's Big House. I've never been, but I understand there is no place like it in the world, so get ready for some fun. Also, before we boarded the plane, we spotted Luke McFlemming, The Celebrity Gossip Reporter, in the terminal. He's headed to Jamaica this weekend. Tom and I had a moment with him already. So be careful."

Tom nodded in agreement, then interrupted Kwame, "McFlemming wants to hang out with us this weekend. I told him, 'No way, we don't like him.'"

"Yeah, guys, we nearly lost it when McFlemming told us he was on his way to Jamaica. So be on the lookout. We are still going to have fun, but don't give McFlemming any reason for you to end up on the front cover," Kwame said.

"He's an ass," JoJo said.

"I never liked him, and he's banned from our locker room and team facility," Phaethon added.

"I like the girl in the Celebrity Hack Patrol, Jennifer Kung. She's hot and cool. Talks a lot of trash," Rote said. "McFlemming is pushy. He's interviewed me before and acts as if he's a star."

“We can’t go to Cafe Cielo without a PR person, even for cocktails,” Kurtis Van Weston said. “He’s put the fear of God into our c-suite at the Minnion Bank.”

Miki Nomura, the Japanese restaurateur, added, "Jennifer Kung is the one. She's been to my place and paid for her meal. McFlemming came in one day. He ordered a couple of single malt Scotches, appetizers, ran up a huge bill, and offered to write a story to pay his bill."

"No, he didn't!" Kwame exclaimed, shocked. Everyone else on the plane shook their heads in disgust. But no one was surprised.

"Yes, Kwame. I called his editor Zach Goldberg and told him. He apologized and told me the dude has a $50,000 expense account. Goldberg promised to reprimand him and, most importantly, told me he'd prevent McFlemming from writing any negative press about my restaurants for two years."

"Wow, Miki. I think Luke tried to play you with a power move," Kwame said as he referenced Miki’s renowned conversation starter with the girls.

"No, Kwame, he tried a sucker move. Miki Nomura is no sucker," he said and winked at Kwame. Everyone laughed.

"No, you are no sucker, Miki. I'm sure he understands now," Kwame said. "Let’s hope he stays out of our way on the island, gentleman. Let's buckle up and get ready for some fun."

The guys took their seats and prepared for lift-off. As they did, Ron, who had been silent, thought to himself. "McFlemming might be an asshole, I am glad he is because he put the fear of God in these guys, and now they will behave. They are too important to become part of some tabloid scandal. Now we can all go and have some fun."

As the plane sped down the runway and took off, Cherry had no clue how desperate McFlemming was for a story.

He paid a private detective $5000 to find out that the bachelor party would be in Jamaica and another $5000 for a private flight, just to be in the same terminal after he found out they were flying from Private Airfield. He didn't, however, have any idea about the secret location.

. . .

The Confederate was just as anxious as Luke to find out about the Bachelor parties. He had a contact number for Phillips Warner, and when he called, Warner excitedly shared what he knew about the events.

"I'm glad you called Confederate. The story is that there are three bachelor parties, and they will all be out of town. The first one will be in Jamaica this coming weekend, the second in Cabo, and the last in Vegas. They are taking private planes to each."

"Where did you find this scoop?" The Confederate asked. "This can be good. We can get them all in one fell swoop."

"Oh yes, that would devastate them. I have a contact at Private Airfield, a private airport outside of the city. They have already set up logistics for the three flights. My contact is one of Private Airfield's owners and a Pre-1860 member. He called me when he saw Donald Alexander and Kwame Mills' names on the flight plans, listed under the group name TBC's with the group contact Ron

Cherry. I guess they thought it was their way to be discreet. Cherry is a big-time investment banker here in New York and regarded as the group's consigliere."

"This is awesome news, Phillips. I'm going to get my guys down to Jamaica this weekend and see what kind of hell we can raise."

"Good luck, Confederate. I guess I'll know if you had success if there are any headlines."

"Yes, you will, Phillips. Thanks for the good luck."

The Confederate hung up the phone and called his A-Team of assassins, known as the Frat Boys. When their leader answered, Confederate told him, "Get packed and your team ready. I need you guys to head down to Jamaica this weekend."

Chapter Thirty

Carrie Sinclair and Jennifer Kung sat on the sofa in the gigantic living room of Samantha Rivers' penthouse apartment.

Jennifer showed her a picture on a tablet, "Oh my, you need to check this pic out, Carrie."

Carrie blushed at the image of the muscle-bound dancer and said, "Chocolate Thunder! Jennifer, you have got to be kidding me."

"What, you don't like? I thought you'd drool at his sinewy, muscular body. Come on, girl, tell me you don't like those popping chest muscles and ripped six-pack? And tell me he's not fine with that dark-skinned, square-jawed face, those big brown eyes, and dazzling smile? This brother is dreamy."

Carrie glanced again, "Yeah, he's good-looking, but he looks too much like JoJo Littlejohn to me. I can't have a half-naked JoJo Littlejohn prancing all around me."

"Half-naked works for me. I'm ordering one JoJo Littlejohn. He's my celebrity crush, in case you didn't know," Jennifer said unapologetically.

Carrie called out to her buddy, "Oh, Debbie, you need to check this out. There's a dancer on this site. He's a JoJo doppelgänger with more muscles."

Debbie Techelle was Carrie's college roommate, sorority sister, and maid of honor. She was also JoJo Littlejohn's lawyer and manager. Her eyes bulged and a look of fright crossed her face when she saw Chocolate Thunder's picture on the Male Dancer website.

"Oh damn, we can't have this. Tell me it ain't so," she said and grabbed the tablet and stared. She handed it back to Carrie and said, "I am going to need to contact the studios to make sure there is no confusion here. All we need is for his fans and the studios to think JoJo was once a stripper."

"I'll tell you what, Debbie," Jennifer said. "If we order him, I'll run a story tomorrow that there is a stripper who is JoJo Littlejohn's double."

"Well, then one order of Chocolate Thunder it is. But, I can't be here. I'll hang out on the other side of the apartment and watch a video," Techelle said with a frown. "Give me a bottle of wine, and I'll be okay."

"No, way Debbie, you don't have to leave. He's an appetizer dancer, and there is a strict, no phone or camera policy at this party. The other ladies are aware, and just in case, I'll confiscate everyone's phones before the first guy arrives."

Debbie grinned widely, "Oh, bless you, Jennifer. I've waited for months for this party, and I don't want to miss one second of anything."

"Of course, Debbie. We want everyone to have a great time today, and we can't have the maid of honor sitting on the sidelines. Now, Carrie, I need you to check these three other dancers out. I need your approval."

Debbie hurriedly grabbed the tablet, and Carrie yelled, "Hey Roomie, I thought this was the party for the bride-to-be?"

"Relax, my sister," Debbie said as she placed the tablet close to her chest and raised her index finger to let Carrie know that she needed a minute to check things out.

"Let me put my lawyer hat on for a second. I need to make sure all these guys are proper. I could have another client lookalike in the mix," she said with a mischievous smile.

"Yeah, right, Debbie. You know I know you. Don't get carried away and order a whole page of men."

Debbie ignored her old college roommate. She busily began scanning the catalog of muscled male dancers. "Oh my, Jennifer, are these the other three guys you're thinking about ordering? They are dreamy."

She squealed as she ran off their names, "Bronze Bomber, White Lightning, and Mango Surprise."

"They are hot, right, Girl?" Jennifer said. "Sammy, you have to check these guys out."

Sammy was in the kitchen, opening bottles of wine. She returned to the living room, "I heard you guys talking about the JoJo Littlejohn lookalike. I need to take a peek."

Her face lit up as she checked out the pic, "Oh yeah, that man is fine. He does resemble him, but JoJo has a tattoo on his upper thigh."

All the ladies stopped and looked at Sammy with their mouths wide open. They expected her to continue and make a scandalous revelation. But when she didn't, Techelle, the lawyer, began a cross-examination.

"Wait. Hold up? He did ask me for your phone number a few months back," Debbie said. "Is there a story here?"

Sammy smiled mischievously. It was a look that teased them, as was her answer, "Well, he did call, and we did go out and had a fun night. He's charming. JoJo Littlejohn has got game."

Jennifer joined the questioning, "What are you hiding with that smile? He's got game? I told you he's my celebrity crush."

"Don't worry, TV. He's gorgeous and nice and rich and damn near perfect, but not for me."

Sammy was a heartbreaker. Men dropped to their knees because of her incomparable beauty. She knew it and played the dating game like it was a blood sport. She shared a bit of her philosophy when she said to the other women, "All I know is that dating is a battlefield out there, my sisters. And I make no apologies for my casualties."

She turned to walk back to the kitchen to open more bottles of wine, and sauntered with an exaggerated cool strut. Her exit and comments stunned the women into silence. It stayed that way until Debbie yelled, "You, Girl, are just gangster."

"I just call it straight, ladies." She said with an indifferent shrug of her shoulders about the fuss over her attitude. Sammy had been that way for so long as a single woman that she didn't get the ruckus. The women got a close-up and further demonstration of her in action when the doorbell rang.

"Come in," she said and turned around and walked back to the living room and apartment entrance..

The door opened, and a twenty-something, extremely handsome black man walked in. His black warm-up suit clung tightly to his fit, muscular body. He had a Mohawk haircut and carried a bowl in one hand.

"What's up, Eric?" Sammy asked. He strutted into the room like a hipster and talked like one.

"What's up, Baby Girl? I'm bringing back the bowl I borrowed last week."

Sammy smiled and introduced him. "Thanks, Eric. Everybody, this is Eric. He's a musician, poet, artist, soccer player. Anyhow, he's rich, and as you all can see, he's gorgeous. Right, girls?"

He stood there and smiled as she continued with the compliments about his looks, "I love his handsome little caramel-toned face and those go-go hazel eyes. He lives across the hall with Paul. Eric, meet my friends Carrie, Jennifer, and Debbie."

Eric continued to smile, nodded at each of the women, and said, "What's up, ladies? Y'all look lovely tonight. How's everyone?"

All the women nodded hello. They could tell instantly that he was a player and as confident a flirter as Sammy. They smiled curiously but remained speechless as they stared at him.

Eric didn't know what to make of the silence, but was unbothered as the women ogled him.

He turned to Sammy and said, "Anyhow, here's your bowl, beautiful Sammy. Paul and I've got a livestream video tournament going, so I've got to head back. Have a good night. It's a pleasure to meet all you beautiful ladies."

He bowed to Sammy, Jennifer, Debbie, and Carrie and walked backward to the door.

Sammy said, "You too, the most handsome Eric. I hope to see you soon, Sweetie Pie."

He opened the door, flashed a dazzling smile, and said, "You need to stop flirting with me, girl. You know I am a man."

She giggled and said, "Haha, get out of here before I put some whipped cream on you and start eating you up."

As the door closed, Carrie shrugged her shoulders and raised her glass in a salute. She like the other women, was awed by her cool, "Cheers to Sammy. This sister is cold-blooded."

"You ain't right, Sammy. Guys should only date you with a warning sign. This lady can be hazardous to your ego," Jennifer added. "And, I have to say, I make no apologies for my casualties. It's a tee-shirt. You can make money off of that."

"Wait, Woman," Carrie said. She didn't want the moment they just witnessed to go by without attention. "Who in the hell is Eric? Right across the hall. He is a cutie."

"Oh, Eric is like a rich kid. He hangs around all day with Paul, playing video games. I think they made a ton of money writing code and don't have to work. I only flirt with him like that because he is gay."

Carrie shook her head vehemently, "You are out of your mind. There is absolutely nothing gay about that young man. He's a Tom Wilson playboy type and will break your heart. And what is this go-go-eye business? You a trip, Sista."

"My bad, Carrie, go-go means gorgeous eyes. Eric is a hottie, though, isn't he? I just call it the way I see them."

"Sammy, those are assassin eyes. Carrie is right. That man is a lady killer. He ain't gay," Debbie said.

She then stopped and wondered for a second if she may have missed a cue, "Really, Debbie? Do you think? I could be mistaken. I've been known to miss it on the gaydar."

Jennifer added, "Yeah, well, your gaydar needs an adjustment for sure. That man is a walking heartbreaker. He's not gay. He kisses girls and makes them cry. And since you have your hands full, can I still have JoJo Littlejohn?"

"Oops, then. I guess I should stay away from Eric, but then again, maybe not. No rush, I like flirting with him. I'll make up my mind later."

She looked into the air as she contemplated Eric as a choice and smiled. "Thanks for the gaydar adjustment, ladies. As for JoJo, he's all yours, Jennifer. But I do know about his upper thigh. It's a birthmark."

Debbie confirmed, "She's right about the birthmark, Jennifer. Nobody in the business knows about it. Is there something you want to share, Sammy?"

The women rolled their eyes in exasperation and disappointment. They wanted there to be more to the story.

"Wouldn't y'all love it to be a juicy hoe confession?" She said and winked at them as if she might have one.

As she saw their faces light up, she smiled and stopped the tease, "Sike, I have no hoe confession. The truth is, he told me, as he shared one thing a true friend would know that a fan wouldn't. I could make it more scandalous, but I'd have to lie."

She changed the subject when she picked up Jennifer's phone and said, "I want to check out these other dancers. They have the best names."

"Ooh, yes, Sammy, I think I am in love with the Bronze Bomber," Debbie said. "His likes are curvy, full-figured, dark women with thick natural hair and bright smiles. It says I am a curvy-girl lover, man."

"Well, we are going to order him for you, Debbie," Sammy said. "Carrie, we have to put these orders in, or we won't have any entertainment. Are you okay with these choices?"

"I'm fine with whomever you pick. I'm just saying in advance that I don't want these guys rubbing all over me. I'm not kidding. I got prayer oil and holy water in my pocket. I'm ready to release some evil spirits."

"Don't you start with the prayer oil bit, Carrie," Debbie said.

"What do you mean, Debbie? In fact, I think I need to start with you guys. Debbie, you first. Sammy, you're second. And Jennifer, I need some extra time, a refill for you and a Bible verse or two."

They laughed at Carrie as the doorbell rang. Danielle Jackson and Michelle Nubani barged in wearing expensive, form-fitting cocktail dresses and holding empty champagne glasses. They'd already finished a bottle during the drive over.

"Turn the music up!" Danielle yelled, "Let's get this party started, ladies."

Over the next hour, the apartment filled up with the other guests. Sammy's apartment was jammed with 20 beautiful women drinking wine, champagne and fancy finger food. They were primed and ready for fun when the four muscular men walked in. The women squealed in glee.

Chocolate Thunder, the JoJo Littlejohn's lookalike, hypnotized all the women, but Debbie tugged at her best friend's arm when she saw the next dancer. "Damn, Carrie. Check out Bronze Bomber. That man is fine."

Carrie whispered, "Ooh, wee roommate, no joke, that brother is hot. Let me find my wallet and get you some singles."

The Bronze Bomber spotted Debbie. He flashed his brilliant white smile and approached her, ignoring all the other beautiful women in the room. Carrie returned and stuck a wad of cash in Debbie's hand. She whispered in her ear, "I hope this is enough singles."

Debbie whispered back without tearing her eyes from the male specimen before her, "Don't worry, I've got some 10s and 20s for that man, a pocketful of them."

An hour and a half and three drinks later, a drunken Carrie raided the refrigerator and walked into Sammy's bedroom to take a nap. It was her habit after she got drunk, which only required three drinks. Sammy and Danielle sat on the living room floor next to Michelle. Debbie sat next to the Brown Bomber, squeezing his biceps and whispering in his ear. House music blared loudly throughout the apartment. All the women and men were now in a spirited game of best dance moves. Michelle was the surprise winner after she kicked off her six-inch heels, spun in a circle and broke out in what she called her Ghana dance. It was a series of sexy shoulder dips, followed by a swivel of the hip and a roll of her arms in a circle in front of her. Everyone wanted to learn it and started to do it together like a line dance.

Across the hall, Eric, Paul, and two other Society of Protector members were on duty. Eric let Sammy think he was gay. It was easier to keep his cover. He liked it when she flirted with him, and that's why he flirted back.

They watched the bachelorette party through video monitors the Society had secretly placed in Sammy's living room, dining room, kitchen, and the hallway leading to the apartment. The Voice had them on high alert. He'd cautioned: "Be ready for anything. If you spot any activity in the hallway, take them down. I don't want anyone entering that apartment who might be a threat."

The four men sat tensely with loaded guns and paralyzing darts, and stared at the video monitors while the four dancers entertained the women. They were ready.

But the Confederate wasn't focused on the women tonight. He had his eyes on Jamaica and getting Kwame, Donald, and Tom.

Chapter Thirty-One

"They would only stay at the best hotels or resorts in town," Luke thought as he rode in a limousine to Five-Star Platinum, the top luxury hotel in Jamaica. Luke was a VIP member, not because he traveled so much, but because he shamelessly plugged Five-Star Platinum whenever he traveled. The luxury chain awarded him VIP status as a thank you. "Maybe they are staying there. That would be cool, and I could easily crash the weekend."

There were crashers, like Luke, that Ron Cherry had in mind when he planned the bachelor party. His job was to get the guys through the weekend without scandals or incidents. Cherry needed discreetness that even the best hotels couldn't guarantee and decided to take the group off the grid. He booked the compound of his friend, the former Jamaica Minister of Finance, Stanley Ralph. Ralph went by the name of Big Stan and called his home Big Stan's Big House.

After his government stint, Ralph became a Managing Partner at Minnion Bank in New York. His 30,000 square foot waterfront mansion in Ochos Rios was often empty, and he lent his place to close friends in the States when they wanted a discreet getaway.

Ralph told Cherry, "You are going to have a bachelor party weekend? Ooh wee. I'm too old for those kinds of shenanigans, but please, take the house. I would appreciate it. We need people in now and then to run water through the pipes, turn on the electricity, make sure everything still works."

"Thanks, Stan. It's exactly the solution we need. I appreciate it, and I'm sure the guys will, too. Can you suggest some people we can hire to cook and clean the place up?"

"You mean servants? You want the VIP treatment, huh, Ron?"

"Yes, there'll be about 15-16 guys. I'd like to keep them together in one location as much as possible. I recall that you've got enough bedrooms at your estate to accommodate us."

"Twelve bedrooms, six full bathrooms in the main house. Two guest houses with two bedrooms each, and a six-car garage in case you have to kick somebody out," Stan said with a laugh.

Cherry said, "I've got two movie stars, professional athletes, an award-winning musician, and top businessmen. Keeping party crashers away is a must. Your place would be perfect."

"I'll also give you guest access to my club," Ralph said. "Island Country Club is the most exclusive on the island. Your guys who golf should enjoy it."

Ralph continued, "I have to tell you the island has a busy gossip press. Two, in particular, Dickson Weeks and Roscoe Vonnie, are rivals, like Luke McFlemming and Jennifer Kung up here in New York. I'll find you some cooks, servers, and maids to come to the house for the weekend, but it is going to cost you."

"Did you forget who these guys are, Stan? Don't be surprised if you get an offer or two to buy your house."

"Oh, my bad, Ron, I forgot these are the Black Camelot guys."

"Exactly, and when you throw Melendez and Littlejohn in there, you've got Hollywood royalty, too. Money is no object."

"Ron, then you must bring the party to my place. Don't go out. Jamaica can be just like New York. Some people will do anything to be in the news."

"Yes, we want to be as discreet as we can. My job is to get these guys home without a scandal."

"They know how to behave, right? They won't be sneaking out on you, will they?"

"Listen, they are all cool guys, and most are either married or engaged, but they are excited to have a great weekend hanging out with each other."

"Ron, I don't have to remind you there are no more beautiful women in the world than those in Jamaica. I think I showed you," Stan said, and let out a loud laugh.

His deep-voiced chuckle gave Ron a flashback to his bachelor party 25 years ago in Jamaica. "Oh, my Brother, that was a lifetime ago, and I still smile when I think of that weekend."

"Me too. Thank God for friends who know how to keep a secret," Ralph said with another laugh as he thought about Cherry's bachelor party. "Anyhow, they'll be fine if they stay on the compound."

Luke was oblivious to Ron's plans to keep the weekend clear of people like him. The reporter had no strategy other than to get to the island and play it by ear. Now that he was on the ground, he took it as a positive sign when he saw kiosks for Jamaica's two newspapers in the Ian Fleming Airport terminal.

"Dickson Weeks from *The Jamaica Times* and Roscoe Vonnie from *The Jamaica Daily*. I know them both, and now I can do some old-fashioned reporting, as Jennifer advised."

Luke opened his phone directory and found numbers for Weeks and Vonnie. "If I can play this right, we can find the Black Camelot guys and force my way into the weekend."

He called Weeks first. When he picked up, Luke said excitedly, "Dickson, this is Luke McFlemming from *The News* in New York." Everybody in Jamaica called Weeks "DW" because he hated his first name.

His response was not what Luke had hoped for, "Oh, hell no. Not Luke McFlemming from the Celebrity Hack Patrol. Didn't you leave me with a $400 bar tab at Café Cielo in New York a year ago?"

"What are you talking about, Dickson? I thought you were traveling on an expense account."

"Nah, man. I thought we were sitting at the table of the star New York gossip reporter. You have a bigger expense account than we small guys here on the island."

"That's why I'm calling. I'm on the island. I may have a story brewing. You got time to catch up?" Luke asked and tried to change the subject.

"Do you have my $400? It was a sucker move, McFlemming. In fact, if you don't have my money, you'd better grab the first plane off the island. Otherwise, I will send some guys from around the way to visit you."

Luke thought quickly. He had money, plenty of it. It didn't make sense not to pay, especially with Dickson's threat. "I got $400 for you and a story brewing. Can you meet me tonight at the Five-Star Platinum?"

"If you have my money, I'll be there. Otherwise, I have a meeting, and I'm not breaking it."

"Meet me at 8 PM, and be ready to hang out. I'll have your $400. Plus, I'm buying."

"I'll be there. And Luke, don't try to con me to buy drinks with my own money later. You're in my town now. Believe me when I say, I'll make some phone calls, and bad things will happen."

"Don't worry, Dickson. I'll have your money. I have another phone call to make. See you later."

He thought after the call, "This may work out well. I have Dickson. If I can connect with Roscoe, I'll have a shot at getting into the festivities."

As he dialed Roscoe Vonnie's number, he thought, "Did I short this guy on a tab, too?"

He couldn't remember but scolded himself, "I've got to stop. I'm a grown man with an expense account. Dickson deserves to be pissed. One of these days, I'm going to get myself in trouble."

"Hello, Vonnie here," the reporter said.

"Roscoe, this is Luke McFlemming from *The News*. I'm on the island. How are you? Are you up for a drink tonight at Five-Star Platinum?"

Vonnie didn't respond. Luke knew right away he'd pissed Vonnie off, too. "Roscoe, it's me. Luke McFlemming. Are you still there?"

Finally, Vonnie said, "Luke, how dare you call me while on the island. Don't tell me where you are. I may call some people."

"What are you talking about, Roscoe? Did I do something wrong?"

"Are you serious? You left me with an $800 tab at Café Cielo. My boss wasn't having it. You told me you would have Robinson Dawson, the Jamaican ballet dancer performing with the North American Ballet, meet for an exclusive. Not only did he not show up, but my boss Sherrod Dawson told me he is Robinson's first cousin. Robinson told my boss he never met you."

"No, wait," Luke protested.

Vonnie continued, "Luke, we have a nickname for my boss. We call him Shitty Dawson because he's always in a shitty mood. He denied the expenses I filed for that trip to New York. One more, and I'm fired. I almost lost my job because you lied to me."

"Wait, I didn't...." Luke began.

"How about stopping with the crap! You owe me triple damages, plus an email of apology from you to my editor before I continue this conversation. Bring me $2400 and send me an email explaining to my editor what you were thinking when you said you were going to have Robinson Dawson meet us at Café Cielo, or else."

Luke didn't argue. Vonnie was right. He made him look bad and had to fix it. "I'll bring you what you need, Roscoe. Just meet me at the Five-Star Platinum at 8 this evening."

"You'd better Luke. I'm not playing," Vonnie said and hung up.

Vonnie called Weeks after the call from Luke. They were tight friends and had previously discussed Luke's Café Cielo cons.

"Hey, DW. That freeloader Luke McFlemming is on the island tonight. He's trying to hook up. Has he called you yet?"

"I just got off the phone with him. He said he would have my money. I could use the $400. He wants to meet at the Five-Star Platinum, and he is buying drinks."

"I could use the money, too. He owes me $800 but has to pay triple damages because of the hell it cost me. He sent me an email that is going to get me out of jail with my boss. I wonder if he's here for the bachelor party. We don't need him messing it up for us."

"Probably," Dickson said. "I'm meeting him in an hour. Don't bring your wallet. I don't want to deal with him trying to con us into paying for his drinks again."

Vonnie snickered and said, "That ain't happening, DW. He's in our hood."

"Yeah, Vonnie. I made it clear that if he tries that down here, bad things will happen. Anyhow, I'll meet you there in an hour."

As Vonnie and Weeks prepared to make their way to the Five-Star Platinum Hotel, Luke sat at the bar drinking a single malt Scotch.

A gorgeous blonde sat nearby. Luke used the otherwise empty bar as an ice breaker for conversation.

"Where is everybody tonight?"

She smiled and said, "It's still early, and the party people don't show up until after dinner and much later. At least, that's what they tell me."

"Are you not from here?"

"No, I'm from New York, like you. I know who you are."

Her answer stumped him. He told himself, "She knows me, I hope for a good reason, and hope I didn't stiff her, too."

He smiled. "Well, who am I? I like it a lot when a beautiful woman knows my name." She was hot, and he figured he could give her a line. He had nothing to lose.

"You are Luke McFlemming, the star reporter from *The News* and a member of the Celebrity Hack Patrol."

"You're partially right. I am Luke McFlemming, and I am the star of the Celebrity Press Patrol. Only haters call us Celebrity Hacks."

"Oh my bad, Luke. No offense intended. I am a model, so I am sensitive, too, to how the public perceives me."

"I was going to say that. You look very much like a model."

Models were very much Luke's type. Especially young blonde models.

"Why are you sensitive? Tell me why?"

"Perception, Luke. Men think we are easy, vain, drug heads, or gold diggers. I am far from such a person."

"Well, I can tell you are none of those things," he said in another attempt at sweet talk. "Tell me, what is your name, and can I buy you a drink?"

He moved to the seat next to hers, "Do you mind if I sit next to you?" He continued, "And vain, I would never think that."

"Thank you, Luke. But I am vain. I have a degree in advanced mathematics from Harlowe University. This face is a blessing and a curse." She reached over to shake his hand. "My name is Monica Viola."

"That is a wonderful name for a beautiful lady."

Monica smiled weakly, "I hope you don't take offense, but if I had a dollar for every time I've heard that, I'd be rich."

"I take it back. How about a beautiful name for a good-looking mathematician who models on the side and might be fat in 20 years."

"Better, Luke," Monica said. "At least you are paying attention this time around."

"What do you mean this time? Have we met?"

She nodded. "Yes. Jennifer told me there'd be no way in hell you'd remember me. Hold on for a second. I have to send a text."

As she sent the message, Luke's mind spun as he thought of where he'd met the stunning model. Monica turned to him and said, "I sent her a text telling her she was right."

"Where'd we meet? How does Jennifer know I am here?" He was still bitter about Kung's exclusive and her making him dig up his own story.

He asked with contempt in his voice, "Are you friends with Jennifer? She's a bad winner."

Monica ignored the question. Instead, she laughed and read Kung's reply. "Jennifer said, 'Good reporters track down people and stories. Because I gave you a hint, I knew you'd be in Jamaica.' She also said, 'Good luck in finding the guys. They're not staying at the Five-Star Platinum.'"

Luke bristled and downed his drink in frustration. "I told you she's a bad winner."

Monica's phone beeped with another text message. She smiled as she read the text and looked at Luke. "You're right," she said. "She's having fun now at your expense. She said to tell you I was going to be at the party, but I couldn't cancel this shoot."

And it beeped again. As Monica read the message, an embarrassed smile crossed her face. "She asked me to give you the phone and let you see the pics."

Luke gritted his teeth. There were three photos. One with Carrie Sinclair and Debbie Techelle hugging each other, the second with Michelle Nubani and Danielle Jackson in their cocktail dresses holding bottles of champagne, and a third with Jennifer and Samantha Rivers making a toast.

She wrote, "The party has started here, and we are having a ball. I hope you can find the guys. And don't make a move on Monica. She is a black belt and will kick your scrawny ass. I'm going to post an article on this party tomorrow or Monday. Which day depends on my hangover."

Monica still looked embarrassed. "That's Jennifer. She talks a lot of trash. Sorry, Luke."

"So, she knew you were going to be here and set this whole thing up?"

"Yeah, Luke. She figured you'd be staying here and asked me to look out for you, but if it means anything, I am enjoying our conversation. It is way better than the time you looked past me at her table at Cafe Cielo."

It was his turn to be embarrassed. "Ouch, I can be a bit of an ass at times. I apologize." His mind drifted for a second as he thought about how often he self-sabotaged.

"You said it. Not me brother, maybe you should tell Jennifer to clear the air. She went through a lot of work to rub it in tonight."

Chapter Thirty-Two

Roscoe Vonnie and Dickson Weeks arrived at the Five-Star Platinum together. Vonnie saw Luke seated next to Monica Viola and said, "I see you, Luke. I want cash, or I'm walking out."

The reporters weren't the only two people to arrive. Four young, thickly muscled white guys walked in behind them and sat on the opposite end of the bar. They loudly ordered several rounds of beers. As fast as the bartender served them, they chugged them down. One of the guys yelled to the bartender, "Turn up the music. Play some reggae music."

Monica was annoyed by the loud guys and whispered to Luke, "Southern frat boys. They were here last night and had the worst manners. I had to leave the bar because they wouldn't leave me alone."

The guy who looked like the leader said on cue, "Hey Monica, how are you doing, Mama? How was your day? Let us buy you a drink."

"I'm fine. I'm here with friends tonight," she yelled back to the guy with a polite smile but with enough attitude to make the guy back off.

Monica quickly turned to face Luke and the two Jamaican reporters. The guy didn't protest. He returned to drinking beers with his friends.

Luke turned to Roscoe and Dickson as they took a seat next to him, "I've got your cash, guys. I understand that you are pissed at me. How about saying hello first to Monica Viola? She's a model friend of Jennifer Kung's and is in town for work."

The Jamaicans introduced themselves. "Hi Monica, I'm Roscoe Vonnie, and I'm a reporter with *The Jamaica Daily*, and this is Dickson Weeks with *The Jamaica Times*. It's a pleasure to meet you. Any friend of Jennifer's is a friend of ours."

She smiled and said, "Hi, Gentlemen. It is a pleasure to meet you both."

Vonnie then asked Luke, "You're here for the Black Camelot bachelor party weekend, I bet?"

"Yeah. I'm hoping we can work together on this."

"You want to tell him, Roscoe? We probably should get our money first," Dickson said.

"Yeah, DW, you are right. Hand over the money, McFlemming, and we'll tell you what we know," Vonnie said.

Luke pulled out the cash and settled up. Afterward, he asked, "Okay, fellas, I've paid up. Now, why the mini-drama?"

"We are going, Luke. Jennifer invited us to the party," Dickson said. "It's just for cocktails tonight. Media from around the world will be there. We suspected you'd be on the island, but because you owed us money, didn't think that you'd call."

"And we don't like you," Vonnie added, his voice still filled with contempt.

Monica interrupted, tapping Luke's shoulder. "Here's one more text from Jennifer."

He looked at the phone and read aloud, "Mike Desanctis is on the island and invited to the men's reception. We have a shared arrangement for the bachelor and bachelorette parties. I will share my column with *The Post*, and he will share his column with *The Ledger*."

Luke's face turned ghostly white. He returned Monica's phone. "Oh, I think I may throw up. Jennifer is being downright mean now."

"Well, not too mean," Dickson said. "She's cool with us and calling the shots. Vonnie and I have rights to all the wedding-related events in New York, too. I'm not going to risk that privilege. We can't bring you to the party without her permission."

"Yeah, McFlemming," Vonnie added. "Black Camelot has already increased my readership by 20%. My career will be ruined if I take you to the party and Jennifer cancels my access."

Luke knew he was beaten and said, "She's got me, fellas. What shall I do? I need to get into that event."

"Beg," Roscoe and Dickson chimed in unison.

The Jamaica reporters were right. Luke had no choice but to beg again. He turned to Monica. "Would you mind if I texted her from your phone before calling? If I call or text from my phone, I am afraid she won't answer."

"Sure, go for it. Remember, be humble Luke, not pompous ass Luke."

"I will try," he said as he composed the text. "Jennifer, it's me, Luke. I acknowledge that I messed up. I'm sorry, and I'm begging now. I understand that you can arrange for me to go to the cocktail party tonight. May I call you?"

She responded immediately, "Sure, I'll give you five minutes. Call now."

The bachelorette party was going fabulously well, and as his luck would have it, a good time to call. Jennifer teased Luke a little to start, "So, are you begging properly now for access?"

"Yes, I am. I'm sorry. You do hold all the cards. I need to stop being an ass."

The apology was all she wanted. Jennifer didn't make him beg more. She gave him access and even offered some advice, "Look, man, I'm a bit drunk, and

I may regret this, but okay, I'll let you in on this. There may be other restricted opportunities in the future. Some of those guys, like Tom Wilson and Miki Nomura, are not friends of yours. The movie stars JoJo Littlejohn and TJ Melendez don't like you. So, show them a kinder, humbler side of yourself. You think you are popular, but these guys are known throughout the world."

He said, with a humble, thankful voice, as relief began to set in on him that he'd be able to get in the party, "Jennifer, you are right. Thank you."

She continued, "Luke, Ron Cherry, the investment banker, is in charge of the weekend. I'll call him and try to wrangle an invite for the cocktail party. Kiss his ring, but be warned: if he says anything cross happens, you'll be shut out of everything else. Oh, and don't give Mike Desanctis a hard time, either. Other than that, kiss some ass, and maybe you'll have some fun, and they'll give you a good story or two."

"I appreciate this, Jennifer. Thank you. I'll be on my best behavior."

Luke hung up. His smile revealed his relief. "I guess you worked it out," Vonnie said. "You were so pathetic looking that I almost gave you my money back."

"Thank you, Vonnie, and you too, Monica. I guess charm works. Thanks for the master class. Jennifer is getting me in."

"I'm glad. She's a better person than me," Monica said.

"You are so right, Monica, and that's why one day, we will all end up working for her," Roscoe said.

"Luke, go have some fun, but before you leave, can you walk me to my room? I don't trust those guys. They make me nervous." She said and looked to the four guys at the end of the bar.

"Absolutely, I'd be honored to walk you to your room."

As Monica and the three reporters left the bar, the guy and his friends at the end of the bar did, too. He plunked down three one-hundred-dollar bills then ran to the parking lot. His buddies followed. They didn't care about Monica Viola. They were there to follow Luke McFlemming and the Jamaican press reporters to their next destination. It was their assignment.

Chapter Thirty-Three

"I need a huge favor from you," Cathy Martin, the event planner, asked Ron Cherry.

"Hi Cathy, how can I help you? Aren't you guys at the bachelorette party now in New York?"

"Yes, everything is excellent. The ladies are having a blast. I do, however, have a huge ask on the publicity side of all this."

"Sure, Cathy, what do you need?"

"Luke McFlemming is on the island. And..."

Ron interrupted, "Oh, hell no. It is not happening. We will not have him here. He will destroy the mood."

"Wait, Ron, hear me out, please."

Cherry could hear that it meant a lot to her. So he listened. "I think this can work out. Jennifer Kung is responsible for the press coverage for all the weddings, receptions, and activities. Luke has ten million readers, and she wants him to post an article in his column. It can help us tremendously."

"Oh, boy, Cathy. McFlemming? That's a tough one. Nobody likes him."

"Yes, I understand. You have a cocktail party from 8:30-10:30 tonight that is open to the press, correct?"

"Yes, but McFlemming is a different animal. I'm going to have to run it past the guys. If they say no, I won't push it. I am not going to allow him to ruin the weekend."

"Can you ask, please? We'd greatly appreciate it."

"Okay, Cathy. Give me five minutes. I will text you, and when I do, you can call me back. Will that work?"

"Thanks so much, Ron, that's fair."

Cathy said to Jennifer, "He's going to run it past the guys."

"Tell him I said, 'Thank you.'"

"Cathy relayed the message, and said, "We'll wait for your follow-up."

Ron hung up and looked across the room. He thought mainly of Tom Wilson. He remembered the shock from the airport a few hours earlier and figured Tom would be the least likely to agree. The guys were communing over cigars and cocktails in the great room. Most were seated at Big Stan's main bar. Tom and Kwame were playing 8 Ball at the custom-designed pool table.

Cherry yelled, "Tom and Kwame. Hold the game for a minute. I need everyone to huddle over at the main bar for a quick powwow."

After they gathered, he said, "I got a request from New York. Everyone understands how this Black Camelot theme has taken over, and the press wants to cover as many of the activities as possible. The reason we have cocktails from 8:30-10:30 is to give them an inside peek into your lives and equally fabulous friends. The request is to allow Luke McFlemming to attend tonight's press conference."

Ron looked at Tom first. Tom scowled at the floor and crossed his arms. He shook his head no but didn't say a word.

JoJo Littlejohn spoke first. "For Hollywood actors the press is part of our daily routine, and I like being part of the Black Camelot universe. I'd say it's about time black folk got treated like royalty. I have no objection."

TJ Melendez said next, "Black and brown people, don't leave us out. I'm already angling to bring the Harris Simmons murder story to Hollywood, so I want to get to know him a little better. I want to play the low-down, slimy Wynne Shields. I am fascinated with his story as the other illegitimate Harris family member, and his death, makes him sympathetic. I'm with JoJo. Let him come, Ron."

"Thanks, TJ. Well, Tom, these are your guys. They are okay with it. I'm sure they'll keep McFlemming busy most of the time anyhow. What do you think?"

Tom turned to his best friend, "What do you think, Kwame? I was a bit nervous when I thought McFlemming would be spying on us for the weekend. But this seems kind of tame, and I could always use a positive spin from the press."

"Yeah, Tom, you need it with all the women's hearts you've broken over the years," Juan Mendoza joked, breaking the tension.

He looked at Juan and scowled, "See now, that's what scares me. Juan knows everybody's secret, and HE's the guy who shouldn't be allowed around a reporter."

"Tom, I ain't telling him crap. I am working on my own book. You brought all these guys into my place and made it into the store. I've got a best-seller. I'm saving all my stories for the book. However, if you really want peace of mind, I would happily accept payment to guarantee my silence," Juan said and winked at JoJo Littlejohn and Kwame. They held back their laughs as they knew Juan's payoff ask was just a tease.

"What's the book's title?" Tom asked. He didn't see the wink and gave Juan a skeptical side-eye glare. "You didn't write a book, and I'm not paying you squat. Forget you, man!"

Juan shrugged, "Can you fault a brother for trying? I'm not rich like you guys. The book is real, though, and titled, *The Country Club Bodega: My Life With Guys Who Are Big Deals.* I have stories of all the interesting people who have come in over the years and conversations I've had with them."

He continued, "Do you remember when you brought Rote in while you were trying to sign him?"

"I remember," Rote interrupted. "The negotiations were pretty intense, and I came close to signing with the Glasshouse label. We had so much fun. My side ached from laughing so hard, and you were so cool, Juan. You reminded me that I need to be with friends because while my art is my business, this is the most important work I will do, and I need to do it with people I like."

Tom remembered the night too and he exhaled and smiled at his friend in appreciation, "Juan, I guess I owe you a commission."

"And if your book becomes a film," Rote said, "you can count on me to write the soundtrack."

"That's a bet, Rote, I'm calling you for sure, and Tom, I got you. You know that buddy. I'll keep that press guy away," Juan said.

"I want film rights to your book. I'm going to play you," TJ Melendez added.

Juan grabbed his heart. His eyes began to water at the instant love and support for his book idea.

Phaethon Malone raised his hand, "McFlemming's been badgering my agent for the last six months to get a story about my political aspirations. I'll give him an interview."

Greg Smith approved him next, "He was at my Hall of Fame reception. He did ask some decent questions. I guess I can give him some time."

"I already told you what I think about him," Miki Nomura shouted angrily. "But for you, Tom, I'll give that cheap pain in the ass five minutes. One-two-three-four-five-minutes. No more."

Everyone cracked up laughing after Miki's rant.

Ron turned to Donald Alexander. He knew Alexander wouldn't object, but wanted him to be on the record. It would make the other guys okay with their yes votes." I don't have a problem with him," Donald said. "We don't have any strippers or pole dancers here, and nothing scandalous for him to report."

"He has been trying to get to me since I became President of Sales at Harris Simmons," Steve Ryan added. "I'll gladly give him some time."

Ron returned to Tom, "See, Brother. The fellas got your back, and this will be excellent PR for all of us."

Tom nodded his approval. "Thanks guys, I appreciate you all, and everyone can benefit, so I'm cool. Let him come."

Ron smiled and said, "Fantastic. I'm glad you are all in agreement. You are 15 of the most revered tastemakers in America. So let's embrace the props that come with the territory."

"A famous tastemaker? I never thought of myself that way," Juan mused.

"Especially you, Juan. Your book is going to be a best-seller, I can promise you. People are going to want to learn about where the Black Camelot crew go when they want to chill."

"He's right," Kwame said. "It's a best-seller in the making."

"Okay," Ron said. "Then I'm going to call the people in New York and let them know it's okay for Luke to show up. If he gives anyone a hard time, we'll kick him out."

Everyone returned to their conversations, and Kwame and Tom to the pool table. Ron texted Cathy, "Don't even bother to call. The guys, surprisingly, said they were okay with his covering the cocktail party. But I will boot him if he gets out of hand."

"Thank you, Ron. I appreciate your help."

Cathy showed Jennifer Ron's text. Kung smiled at the prospect of Ron kicking Luke out if he got out of hand.

"Excellent, Cathy, thank you so much. Tell Ron I agree, kick his butt out if he gets out of hand."

Chapter Thirty-Four

The driver of the private car pulled up to a gate in the middle of a six-foot-high privacy wall. Luke looked to the left and right and guessed by the bright night lights lining the wall that it was at least fifty yards wide. He pulled out his notepad and wrote, “Grand entrance to this place. Looks very exclusive.”

The driver pressed a button on gate’s intercom. An attendant responded, "Welcome to The Ralph Estate."

Dickson Weeks was seated in the rear seat behind the driver and spoke into the intercom, "Dickson Weeks with *The Jamaica Times*, Roscoe Vonnie with *The Jamaica Daily*, and Luke McFlemming from *The News* here."

"Welcome gentleman, please have your driver follow the road. You are going to the main house. Proceed along the winding road until the end. The Black Camelot gentlemen are here. Cocktails are served, and you are the last of the invited press to arrive."

"Thank you," Weeks said. He couldn't hold back his excitement as they drove a quarter mile down the winding tree-lined road, "I'm getting psyched, guys."

"Wow!" Luke shouted as they rounded the final bend. The drive opened up to a gigantic white brick Mediterranean revival mansion. The estate was set back fifty yards from the end of the road. Landscape lights placed across the massive, meticulously manicured lawn that fronted the house were so bright it looked like daytime. The two-lane road turned into one lane that circled the enormous yard.

"This entrance puts the best homes in the Hamptons to shame," he continued, mouth agape. "If the rest of the house is as incredible, you won't have to worry about me acting out. I'll be speechless."

As the driver pulled up to the entrance, a short, stout man wearing a white linen suit emerged from the door with a tray of cocktails. "Greetings, gentleman," he said as they exited the car. "My name is Chester, and welcome to The Ralph Estate, known less formally as Big Stan's, Big House."

"Hi Chester, my name is Roscoe Vonnie; I am the society reporter for *The Jamaica Daily*. Meet my colleagues Dickson Weeks from *The Jamaica Times* and Luke McFlemming from *The News* in New York."

"Gentlemen, Mike Desanctis from *The Post* has been here for a half-hour, as has the rest of the press from around the world. There's a gigantic bar inside that is open. You can drink whatever you choose, and we made a special batch of Jamaican rum cocktails we hope you will enjoy. Please sample."

Each guy took a drink from the tray and sipped.

"What is the rum? It is quite tasty," Luke said.

"Big Stan's Exclusive White 18, I'll put money on it," Weeks answered.

"Yep, it's definitely Big Stan's EW. It has a distinctive aftertaste and is the best rum in the world," Vonnie said proudly.

"You guys know your Jamaican rums," Chester said, nodding approvingly.

"We'd better," Weeks said. "Our rums are the best, and Big Stan's EW 12 and 18 are the best of the best. Only fifty barrels of each are released annually. There are bidding wars on this stuff."

"Yes, DW and I can't afford this stuff on our writers' salary, Chester. It's $400 a bottle and an absolutely wonderful rum," Vonnie said. He suddenly stopped sipping with the realization. "Wait, why mix this? It's too expensive to drink mixed."

"Don't talk yourself out of enjoying the drink. All the rum served tonight comes from Stan's private collection. He bottles five barrels annually and uses them for charity events on the island and in the United States. Don't worry. Savor your cocktails; we won't run out. I might even be able to get you a bottle to go."

Weeks smiled and asked Vonnie and Luke, "Have you ever felt you are in a place bigger than you can imagine?"

"You nailed it," Chester said. "Stan Ralph is a world-class tastemaker. The best chefs, designers, and moguls come to this very place for private events to feature their brands and products to the most discerning movers and shakers in food, wine, spirits, jewelry, and fashion globally."

"What does that mean, Chester?" Luke asked. The New York skeptic in him thought this was merely Jamaican loyalist talk.

"I heard about these events," Weeks said. "They are closed to the press and very exclusive."

"Well, now you've finally attended one, Mr. Weeks. I hope you continue to be impressed," Chester said.

As Chester spoke, a man emerged with three black gift boxes. "Welcome to Black Camelot. Mr. McFlemming? Here's one for you."

Luke raised his hand, and the man handed him the box.

"Mr. Vonnie?" Roscoe nodded, and he handed the reporter his gift.

"You then must be Mr. Weeks," he said as he handed him the final box. The journalists had to rest their drinks on a nearby table to open the boxes because they were so large.

The man introduced himself as they opened their boxes, "My name is Corry. I will be your host for the next couple of hours. Throughout the evening, you will receive several gifts. This wristwatch is a $10,000 Maxum Amson. It is a limited edition; only 250 of the watches are made each year. Only 100 of this limited edition. It is named the Black Camelot edition"

"Wait, now. How did we get these?" Luke asked. His eyes bulged as he examined the platinum diamond-encrusted timepiece. He whispered to his colleagues, "Fellas, This is like Christmas for the super-rich. My attitude almost got me shut out of all this."

Roscoe and Dickson were also stunned, "Uh, uh, what?" Roscoe stuttered. Dickson didn't attempt to speak. He gave a low whistle and, like Luke, his eyes bulged as he stared at the box.

"Don't worry," Corry said. "Mike Desanctis responded like you did, Mr. Vonnie. He is still in shock."

The usually stoic but now very animated Desanctis emerged, "You guys get your watches? Oh my goodness, tonight is out of this world. I have to calm down. Otherwise, I won't be able to do my job.

He introduced himself to Roscoe and Dickson, "Hi, I'm Mike Desanctis, I'm with *The Post* and a member of the notorious Celebrity Press Patrol with Luke and Jennifer Kung. She might be jealous of all this swag."

Roscoe introduced himself, "I am Roscoe Vonnie with *The Jamaica Daily*. Pardon me. I need a moment to gather myself."

Dickson's face was that of a boy opening toys on Christmas, "I am Dickson Weeks from *The Jamaica Times.* You can call me DW. This is crazy."

Corry shared, "I should tell you, gentlemen, the swag bag here is worth $75,000."

"That's right," Chester added. "I told them Stan Ralph is a global tastemaker and the top brands come here for exclusive brand showcases to the top moguls, influencers, retailers, and buyers in the world."

Corry advised, "Here's the deal, gentlemen. We are going to walk to the rear of the house, down the hall to the great room. Everyone is there. Mr. McFlemming, they are okay with you being here, but Ron Cherry asked me to keep an eye on you. Is that going to be a problem?"

Luke nodded vehemently. "Not at all, Corry. I want the swag bag. I'm also here for some important interviews. America needs to understand that Black Camelot is way more than we appreciate."

"Yes, Luke, Jennifer is counting on us to do this story right," Mike concurred. "We have a chance to show these fantastic people to the world while they are enjoying themselves."

"I agree, Mike. Let's get our stories. I won't embarrass her. Are there any other rules, Corry?"

"Just a couple, I'll be in the room. Everybody is open to talking to the press. If you'd like me to introduce you to someone, find me, and I'll make the introduction. Another rule is to not use your camera phone. We have a designated photographer. Just ask for permission for a photo op, and we'll stage and shoot any shots you want. Tonight will be light and fun. Other than that, just be professional, and enjoy yourself."

Corry led them down a long hallway. They passed a huge living room and library on the left-wing, and kitchen and dining room on the right-wing. Luke made a mental note to get photographs later. He noticed some fabulous art pieces throughout the house, and he knew they would add to his stories. They finally made it to the great room and the bar. The gigantic room buzzed with laughter and conversation, light Jamaican jazz played in the background. The reporters immediately got to work.

"Oh wow, there's Phaethon Malone. He's Jamaican. Grew up in the States, but both of his parents are from here. I'm calling dibs," Weeks said to Vonnie and made a bee-line towards Malone.

"I already know Phaethon," Roscoe yelled to his friend. "He's a distant cousin on my father's side. You've got five minutes, and then I'm coming over."

Weeks grinned over his shoulder at Vonnie, gloating as he thought that he'd beat him to the punch. "Sure, he's your cousin. I'm going to need ten minutes. There are lots of celebrities here. I'm sure you'll find someone else to interview in the meantime."

Desanctis laughed at the competitive battle, saying, "Sounds like one of the Celebrity Press Patrol's knife fights for interviews. Luke never shares, however."

"Oh, no, actually, DW is my buddy. We cover for each other a lot, and we're tight friends. He thinks I was kidding about Phaethon, but he really is my cousin. I'll give Roscoe that interview as I can catch Phaethon later on."

"So, whom are you going to target first?" Desanctis asked.

"Probably JoJo Littlejohn and TJ Melendez. Movie stars are important down here. I want to learn what kind of projects they have coming up."

"I was thinking the same thing too, Vonnie. I'll take whomever you don't and catch up to the other one later."

Desanctis then turned to McFlemming and asked, "Who's your first target, Luke?"

"Mike, I heard that Ron Cherry is the guy who put together this weekend and is the Black Camelot elder. They all revere and listen to him. I know he's a big-time banker. I want to learn more about him and his role in this."

"Ooh, I like that, Luke," Desanctis said. "I may want to steal that one, too."

Luke approached Ron, who was standing next to Donald Alexander. Ron spoke first, "Hi, Luke. Jennifer Kung texted me earlier and asked if we would permit you to join us for cocktails. The guys agreed to have you here. I hope you are enjoying yourself."

"I have to tell you, Ron, this entire set-up exceeds beyond words any of the blue-chip events I've been to in the city, the Hamptons, LA, Miami, the Bay Area, Sonoma, Napa, Aspen. You've hit it out of the park. I have only gotten a Maxum Amson, but I understand the rest of the swag bag is just as amazing."

"You haven't checked out the rest of the bag yet?" Donald asked. "The goodies are phenomenal."

"We all lost our composure with the Maxum Amson, Donald. I have to do some work before I start to bask in all of these rich guy toys."

Luke added, "Donald, I want to spend some time with you, but I was hoping to grab you first, Ron."

"Sounds like my cue," Donald said. He was dressed in a dark blue linen shirt and pants and wore black leather sandals, and looked relaxed and happy. Luke made a mental note of his appearance.

He continued, "Luke, when you finish your interview, you and your reporter pals have to check out this backyard and the ocean. It has everything you could imagine in paradise. I'm going to grab one of these hand-rolled Jamaican leaf cigars and step outside to watch the waves."

Donald walked to the rear of the great room where a guy was rolling stogies. The entire rear wall was floor-to-ceiling glass. It provided a dramatic view of the property's brightly lit backyard that included an Olympic-sized pool, tennis court, regulation basketball court, golf putting green, and a massive outdoor kitchen and dining area. Beyond the yard was a white sand beach.

The two giant, side-by-side glass doors to the backyard were open, and a strong breeze wafted through the room.

As Donald walked off, Ron asked, "Have you been to his house in the Hamptons?"

"No," Luke replied, "but I've seen pictures of the former Dryden Estate. It is an architectural diamond. I'd love to visit."

Ron like Donald was also dressed in matching linen shirt and slacks. The only difference is that his outfit was tan. He also wore black leather sandals. Luke could tell that even though Cherry was in his mid 50s, the linen clothes showed off his muscles. He noted that Ron was impressively fit.

"Well, I have to say this place makes Dryden look like public housing. It is a palace, and my friend Stan Ralph spared no expense in its design and construction."

"I understand from Chester that this is a tastemaker's paradise. He said the best brands and products are introduced at events here because of the location and because of how luxuriously decadent the place is," Luke lied. Chester didn't use those words, but he tried out on Ron some adjectives that described the place.

"'Luxuriously decadent.' Those are the words of a big-time Harlowe Award-winning journalist. But you're right, and I know Stan would like that description. Let me show you around. Let's start with the private bar."

"You mean there is another bar? Is it nicer than this one?" Luke asked, and looked across the massive bar where most of the guys gathered.

"Hold your britches and follow me." They walked to the great room's entrance. Ron opened a panel on the wall and pressed a button, and a portion of the wall slid open to reveal a hidden room. Luke's jaw dropped in surprise.

"Yeah, Luke, it's impressive," Ron said as they walked into the private bar. In the room were five small round tables with two chairs each and a serving bar six feet long. "You heard about Stan's rum and tasted it in the rum punch. Well, in this room, you'll find every single malt, bourbon, port, and wine from the world's top spirits and winemakers."

"Can I get a picture of this room?"

"Sure, I think you can get the photographer to shoot a photo," Ron said and pressed a button on the wall near the serving bar. Another wall slid open. Behind the wall was a glass door.

"Stan calls this the sealed room. It is a refrigerated walk-in wine room. He left no stone uncovered. The room is sealed and bombproof."

Cherry didn't tell Luke that the was so secure that it doubles as a panic room. "Go ahead, step inside and take a look."

Luke walked into the room, and a few steps in, the room became dark. He said to Cherry, "This feels like a wine cellar."

"Yes, it is Luke and designed as such. It is 2000 square feet. We could walk in here for an hour and find bottles from all over the world. If you like wine, it is Heaven."

"How did Stan Ralph come up with the idea to build something so exclusive?"

"Stan is a proud Jamaican. He wanted to build a place comparable to any historic estate compound. He hit the ball out of the park."

"I see now why you are here. It is swankier than any five-star resort."

"You're right, Luke, and we can control who comes onto the property, which is very important. As you might imagine, discretion is important to Donald, Kwame, Tom, and their friends."

"What do you mean, Ron? Do you mean like bachelor party stuff? Strippers and dancers and those kinds of things?"

"Oh no, Luke, these guys are well beyond that. Like Stan, they are tastemakers, some of the most revered and respected men in the world. Their successes are not predicated on race. I also didn't want them in public spaces where someone might try to make a reputation off them."

"You mean like an ambitious reporter in the Celebrity Press Patrol? Or do you mean something else?"

Ron looked at Luke and said, "I told you everyone agreed to have you here, and Jennifer vouched for you. Among tonight's guests, JoJo Littlejohn, Donald Alexander, Tom Wilson, and Thomas Jorge Melendez are on countless most desirable men's lists. Rote Tunz, Miki Nomura, Greg Smith, Kurtis Van Weston, Kwame Mills, Steve Ryan, and Phaethon Malone ain't slouches either."

Luke nodded his head in agreement. "You're right. People love them all. They are the glamour princes of the city."

"I like that term, 'glamour princes,' but I'd correct it slightly. They are the Glamour Princes of the Country and are just getting started. I predict they will change the world. I don't think it will be easy for them, but they will do important things. They are up to the challenge, and that is what excites me the most."

"Even Tom? He's got a bit of a battered reputation as a lecherous ladies' man."

"Especially, Tom. You have to understand he was a gifted athlete and, yes, a ladies man who had a lot of fun for many years. Donald and Kwame are now pulling him to his greatness. His fiancée Danielle Jackson is, too. Just watch. He'll surprise you."

"It'll be good to root for him. Now tell me about yourself, Ron. Donald is the King of Black Camelot. Kwame and Tom are the princes. Who would you be?"

"Oh, that is not hard. I'm the Elder, or if you want another term, it would be a Counselor or Rabbi. They count on my experience and judgment to keep them from self-sabotaging on events like this. When Donald decided to bring on Kwame, I mentored him through the process. One of the reasons they will continue to do amazing things is because they listen and seek mentoring. I am happy to serve in that role."

Luke looked at him closely. He began to understand why the guys respected Ron. He was successful and just as handsome as any of the other men. Ron Cherry was elegant, lean, about six foot four inches, with salt and pepper hair and a thick, full hairline. His skin tone was dark chocolate, and his brown eyes and white smile gave his face a glow. In his younger years, Luke guessed, in his heyday, he was as much a lady killer as Tom Wilson.

"Ron, you are a managing director at Century Bank and a leader in the financial industry. Please, tell me about your journey."

"Why do you want to know that, Luke? I understand that you are doing your job, but this entire Black Camelot thing is about Donald, Kwame, Tom, their beautiful fiancées, and Samantha Rivers. They are the story."

"I understand, Ron, everyone knows these guys are A-Listers in New York, but my readers would like to know about the man the Black Camelot guys go to for advice."

"Fair enough. I'd like for you, however, to keep the focus on these guys. Remember, Black Camelot promises to be more than a wedding and a few parties. I believe these guys are going to change the world, so don't be slick, or I'll cut you off."

"Ron, I won't. I know enough not to try to outsmart the son of Houston Blakeney Cherry, the fabled turkey farmer turned community leader from Monroe, North Carolina."

"Nice, Luke, you've done your homework," Ron said. "What else do you know, ace reporter?"

"I know your dad was the oldest of eleven kids. Your grandparents had four boys, four girls, and three boys in that order. Your dad played for a half dozen years in the Negro league baseball and attended college at Monroe A&T. He left college to serve in the Korean War and led a black infantry group. After the war, he was able to secure a small loan. He used that loan to begin raising turkeys and chickens. The business thrived with distribution throughout North and South Carolina, Virginia, and Georgia. After the poultry business, he became a community leader and elder, of sorts, in your hometown."

"Yes, that's a pretty good account, Luke. You are buttoned up and not just a loudmouth."

"I get a bad rap, sometimes Ron. I'm a pretty talented journalist."

"I see, Luke. Well, yes, you're right, my Dad did quite well. He also became the largest employer in Monroe. He had more than 500 employees."

"Sounds as if he lived a very full, productive life. So, how did you get to New York and the investment banking business?"

"My dad's early success was phenomenal. I saw him run a fully operational business from birthing and raising birds to maturity to slaughter, packaging, pricing, and selling. I loved him and respected what he did, but I wanted to do something different. He suggested I look into banking. I found out he was doing what we now call private equity or venture capital. Back then, it was what we called local banking or, more simply, lending. Half of the businesses in town he had an interest in."

"Are you telling me your father was rich, Ron?"

"No, and as he later showed me, it was his job to keep the local dollars in the community. He would work with his banker and advise and promote local business investment. He believed the local dry cleaner should buy cleaning supplies from a local soap manufacturer, that guy should buy corn from a local farmer, that farmer should hire people from the local community during crop picking season, and those crop pickers should take their Sunday-go-to-meeting clothes to the local dry cleaner on Monday. If done right, local dollars would stay in circulation and never leave town."

"That's beautiful, Ron."

"You're right, Luke. Small towns need to learn how to keep their dollars at home and focus on community spending. It helps the small town in every way."

"Was that what drew you to banking?"

"I am a problem-solver. Like I said, I learned at my father's knee operations, pricing, packaging for consumer goods. I learned his form of banking, and how businesses should think about stretching a dollar, and civic responsibility."

"You should run for office. You can fix a lot of problems with those skills."

"No, that is what Donald, Kwame, Tom, Sammy, and Carrie will do. The Black Camelot royals all have hearts for this kind of work. Some people think this is some kind of fancy way to be pretentious and elitist, but there's a light in each of that crew. They have a chance to change the world, and that's what they are going to do. Think about what Oliver Harris, Sr. said at the end of his life: 'Take this money and go do some good.'"

"Wait, wait, Ron, you almost changed the subject on me. I do believe those guys will do special things, but let's finish with how you got to New York and the senior level at the Century Bank."

Ron took a long swallow of his rum. He took a moment to admire the taste and then answered Luke's question. "I attended Harlowe for college and graduate school. My grades were strong enough to get me into the Century Bank training program, and I've been there since. It's been 30 plus years now, and I've done well."

"Now you're going to tell me you worked hard but wish you'd made more money."

"Oh no, Luke. I'm not a billionaire, but my net worth is in the mid-nine-digits. I can fly a private plane whenever I want. Check that I can buy my own plane. I'm too blessed to play coy about that."

Luke wrote "nine digits," and when he realized what Ron meant, nodded approvingly.

"God willing, I'm going to be behind these guys for the next 20-30 years or so while they do some amazing things. Do you want to keep winning Harlowe prizes?"

"Yes, I do. As many as I can," Luke said.

"Then stand behind these guys and lift them up. These people are getting ready to take the whole world on a magic ride. Now, your time is up. Let's go back and mingle with everyone else."

Chapter Thirty-Five

"Oh, some action is coming," Larry Miller told his brother Garry as they sat in a wooded area to the left of the massive front lawn entrance of Big Stan's Mansion.

The brothers got the alert five minutes earlier. Four guys had breached the outside entrance and were approaching the main house with big guns. The invaders did not know that the compound's security system included video monitors across the front wall entrance and throughout the wooded trails and two-lane road leading to the house.

Chester and Corry received the alert and texted news of the intrusion to Larry and Garry, "Video shows four gunmen breached the front wall and coming your way. It looks like they have heavy firepower. Be ready."

Garry was dressed in a green camouflage tee-shirt, matching pants, and combat boots. His brother wore a plain gray tee-shirt, shorts, and sneakers. Garry busily rubbed matching camouflage paint on his face as the four assailants made their way towards the house. After a few minutes, the intruders emerged from the darkened woods and stood exposed on the brightly lit lawn, their high-powered guns glinting. Gary was still messing with the camouflage paint.

"Hurry it up, Garry! These guys have big guns," his brother whispered.

The sight of the guns brought the younger Miller to attention. "Oh man, Larry, you're right, he said. Those are assault rifles, probably M-16s. These guys came here to massacre."

The Millers sat in their secure position several yards into the dark wooded area to the left of the mansion's massive lawn. They were not visible as the four assailants advanced on the lawn towards the house. They crouched forward, two in front, two in the rear, their rifles pointed towards the mansion. They wore vests and helmets that Garry and Larry assumed were bulletproof.

The bright lights made them easy targets. More experienced fighters would have fallen back. These guys walked straight ahead and never looked towards the wooded area where Larry and Garry sat concealed, their guns pointed at them.

Larry whispered, "Since they are wearing headgear and vests, let's take ear shots. But let them get halfway across the lawn so they can't run back into the woods if we miss once we open up."

Garry nodded and said, "Okay, Larry. I'll take the two guys out in front. You take the others."

"Ten-four," Larry said. "Use your silencer. Let's be accurate. One-shot each and all headshots. Make them count. But first, let's say a quick prayer for them."

Garry tapped his older brother's shoulder, and they closed their eyes. He said, "Lord, have mercy on their souls, for they know not what they do. Amen."

"Amen," Larry echoed. Without another word, the brothers knelt into firing positions and squeezed off two shots that were direct hits. Each bullet hit its target behind the ear and smashed through their skulls, killing them instantly.

The dead were the four men from the bar who followed Luke, Roscoe, and Dickson to Big Stan's. They were the Confederate's top assassin crew, known in BE as the Frat Boys. But like most BE fighters, they were neither trained assassins nor seasoned combat veterans. They had more passion than know-how and smarts.

In addition to high-powered assault rifles, the team carried backpacks filled with grenades and explosives. Their assignment was to kill everyone and leave an epic scene of destruction.

Because of their lack of training, they didn't know to look for the video security system on the compound's outer wall and throughout the wooded areas that tracked their movements. They had no idea that the Society of Protectors had the house covered from every entry point.

The Miller brothers covered the front of the house. Doug and Darryl Duncan covered the back of the house from their post on the roof of a beach guest house, while Keyur and Manish Patel were two of four protectors inside the house. Leading the weekend's security were Chester and Corry, the two greeters. They were Society of Protector members who lived in Jamaica full-time and, like the other members, were deadly assassins.

After the shooting, Larry texted Chester and Corry, and they came to inspect the scene.

"Oh, my," Chester said. "These guys are babies," he said as he looked at the bodies of the guys in their early to mid 20s.

"They came here with bad intentions," Larry said as they examined the corpses, the assault rifles, and the backpacks full of explosives. "I guess they thought they had enough firepower and body armor to walk through an attack. We might have had a battle if they'd looked our way. Their inexperience cost them their lives."

"You're right. Those bulletproof vests and helmets meant they came here ready for a firefight," Chester said.

"Let's drag the bodies back into the woods," Corry said. "We have a local clean-up crew. I'll call them, and they'll be here in a half-hour."

Corry rummaged through the assailants' pockets and found their IDs. He also found a cellphone. It was on the body of the ringleader and unlocked. He found a text thread and read the last message aloud to the other Society members.

"We are at the location. We're armed, ready, and will blow up the house after we kill everyone."

Corry texted a message on the phone, "Mission failed. All your guys are dead. You sent them to a massacre. They never stood a chance. Hate lost today."

No one inside Big Stan's house had any idea about the assault nor how close hate had come to winning. They drank, told jokes, and played pool as the Jamaican clean-up crew piled the bodies from the front yard into a van.

Chapter Thirty-Six

Ron Cherry impressed Luke, and the reporter appreciated his advice. Staying close to these guys would be important news for the city, country, and potentially the world. He knew from their work at the Oliver Harris Diversity Education Foundation that Black Camelot's definition had less to do with fancy parties and "IT" people. These guys were world-changers, and Cherry's lead advisor role made him a serious power broker.

After the interview, he sat on the sofa to put his notes together. Donald and JoJo approached him as he finished. "How are you doing, Luke? Did you spend some good time with the Rabbi?"

They caught him off guard. He was still trying to measure Cherry's influence, and these two powerful guys furthered his awe by calling him, Rabbi. "What, uh, yeah. Wow, that guy is quite impressive. Rabbi, huh, that's what you call him?"

"We don't make any major decisions without calling him," JoJo said. "There's no subject on which he can't provide sage advice. Whenever he visits me in LA, I am better for it."

Donald nodded his head in agreement. "He sees things, Luke, that most people never could."

"Exactly," Littlejohn said. "I'm a confident, accomplished guy in my craft but would be lost without him. No one can top him at assessing situations and people. "

"What do you mean, JoJo?"

"Remember the adventure film *Whitewater*, about Whitewater Rapids from seven years ago?"

"I got offered the lead role on and called Ron about it. He told me the film would be a dog, the director Hugh Glinnis was on his last legs in Hollywood, and although it would be a $10 million payday, I needed to pass."

"Wow, a $10 million payday that had to be hard to pass up?"

"He gets $10-$20 million offers every month now. The Dude is on fire," Donald said.

Littlejohn smiled and said, "Do you know why, Luke?"

"Tell me, JoJo?"

"Ron insisted I pass, and that was before I was a huge star. I feared the phone would stop ringing, and I'd be teaching acting in a junior college. For five years, I was earning about $500K to $1 million a film. Then a $10 million offer came that I thought was my big break."

"Yes, I understand. That's 10-20 times what you were getting. It had to be hard to pass up."

"Oh, man, you'll never know," he said and made the sign of the cross. "Everyone in the film lost their status. That $10 million might have been my only mega paycheck. I've made $200 million since. Ron saw the future. He was spot on."

"But while he waited, he was looking back. He thought Ron had given him bad advice," Donald added.

"Yep. Oh, man, I sat home totally confused for three months. And to add to my stress, my agent wanted to fire me. He kept saying, 'My job is to find you work, and I'm making enemies with you turning down significant roles.' Man, he gave me the blues. Ron kept telling me to stay ready. He was very supportive, and then my phone rang."

"And he blew up," Donald said proudly about his friend.

"Donald's right. That's when I got *Silicon Valley Wars.* You remember the film with TJ?"

"Oh yeah, I liked that film a lot. It was an espionage story about a cartel in Silicon Valley that used mob-like tactics to extort trade secrets. TJ played a well-educated, stylish businessman who was a murderous con man. Instead of innovating, he steals all the secrets from his competitor and uses them to build a technology empire."

"Yes, and I play his primary competitor. He tried to buy my company, and during the due diligence phase, I found out he was a crook. He tried to get me killed, and I had to go on the run because the authorities didn't believe me."

"I loved that movie. You both were so good in it."

"It broke the dam for me. As Donald said, I receive ten offers a year now. Each in the $15-$20 million range. My agent doesn't fight me anymore when I tell him I have to show the script and terms to Ron. I won't make any decision without him."

"He has a sixth sense about this stuff, and by the way, he does the same for TJ."

"Donald is right. We swear by him. TJ and I have tried to get him to Hollywood. He responds that he needs to be here in New York for Donald, and now with the Black Camelot crew, he's never leaving."

"I'd be lost without him," Donald said. "Ask Kwame, and now Tom, they will tell you the same."

Donald shared Ron's impact on the other men in the room. "Phaethon Malone is counting on him to direct his political aspirations. Miki Nomura won't make any decisions about his restaurants without his advice. Rote Tunz reveres him, too. Gregory Smith's wife Shenetta has dinner with him every time he comes out to LA, and they are planning to move back to New York just to have easier access to him. Steve Ryan is now the highest-ranking African-American in the media business, and he also counts on him. We are all so fortunate to have him. He's selfless and an amazing and trusted asset."

"Luke, what do you think about this place and the night so far?" Donald asked as he changed the subject.

"It's impressive. I have to admit that I didn't know what to expect. I mean, this is a bachelor party."

"What did you expect? Girls sliding from poles?" Littlejohn asked.

"I guess I did. I was hoping to see a little something-something. After all, this is a stag party."

"Well, we did that on the plane. We are pretty secretive, as you might imagine. Things got so out of hand we had the plane circle in the air for an hour," Littlejohn said, straight-faced.

"Yeah, right. I wasn't born yesterday."

"Ask Juan and TJ. Juan and TJ, come over here and meet Luke McFlemming from *The News*. He wants to know what happened on the plane," Donald yelled to his friends.

Ron, Kwame, Tom, and Rote all heard Donald. They turned and smiled as Juan and TJ walked over.

"Don't tell him anything, Juan. Otherwise, you'll be on the front page tomorrow. Remember, what goes on in the air, stays in the air," Rote said.

"I'm not a celebrity, Rote. I could use the publicity."

"Uh oh, we are in trouble," Kwame yelled. "TJ, grab Juan's phone and toss it here. I'll erase those pics. It's in his back pocket."

TJ then reached into Juan's back pocket, grabbed his phone, and tossed it to Kwame. "Rote is right, Juan. What goes on in the air stays up there."

"Wait, I want the pic of the redhead. Don't do that, guys. I need that pic," Juan said with a panicked look on his face.

"Ha, ha fellas. Ain't no way you guys were running some girl action on a private plane. I just spent 25 minutes with Rabbi Ron Cherry. There's no way he would allow it."

"What are you talking about, Luke? Ron set it up. Two girls for every guy," Kwame said.

Luke looked at Ron. He shrugged his shoulders and said, "Luke, this is a bachelor party weekend, and the fellas are here to have some fun, so maybe I did set it up, or maybe I didn't."

"And now the evidence is gone. It's like a fish story. You had to be there," Donald said. "And a lot of fish were on the plane, Luke. And you won't see them on the island because they are all on their way back to New York on the plane."

Luke looked across the room at each of the men. Each looked back with half-smiles and shrugged. He knew that's all he would get from them. There would be no confessions.

"Okay, fellas, you got me. I'll leave it alone and enjoy my amazing swag bag."

Mike Desanctis laughed as he stood next to Kwame. "Luke hates being the butt of jokes. That was fun to watch."

"Yeah, it was. And that's why we gave him the business. The fellas wanted to give him a little payback for always being an ass."

"Well done, Kwame," Desanctis said. Vonnie and Weeks also laughed. Everybody enjoyed the razzing of Luke McFlemming.

Kwame invited them to hang out longer. "Fellas, your invite was for two hours, but you can hang as long as you want. The guys like you all. Keep an eye on your boy, Luke. Don't let him get too drunk, and have fun."

"We're not going anywhere," Desanctis said. "I love hanging out with the royal men of Black Camelot. And that'll be the headline for my story tomorrow, The 'Royal Men of Black Camelot.'"

"It has a nice ring to it," Kwame said as he walked away, "The Royal Men of Black Camelot."

Part Four

Chapter Thirty-Seven

"Honey, the fellas decided we are one and done on this whole bachelor party tour," Donald told Carrie during breakfast the day after he returned from Jamaica.

"I am so glad. This Black Camelot series of pre-wedding festivities is a lot. At the bachelorette party, Michelle and Danielle got drunk, and Sammy is too much fun and has way too much energy. I'd rather focus on the weddings, too."

Carrie chose not to tell Donald about their male dancers and that she got drunk. She instead pressed him on the guys' weekend. "You guys have a great time? Anything you want to share?"

She knew Donald wouldn't tell her but took a shot anyhow.

"Baby Doll, I made a vow to the fellas not to share anything that happened in Jamaica. You wouldn't want me to get in trouble, would you?"

Carrie asked, stern-faced, "Donald, are you loyal to your boys or me ?"

He smiled wryly before answering, "Let me think for a second."

"Oh, it's like that?" Carrie snapped. "I know that anytime Tom Wilson gets around hot girls, crazy stuff happens."

Donald nodded his head as it was part of Tom history, "In this past yes, but no, this time\it wasn't Tom. He's reformed. Danielle has his nose wide open. His playboy days are behind him."

"Tom, really?" Carrie said. She had so much drama with Tom, going back to her marriage with Kwame, that she had a hard time believing in his transformation.

“I guess everybody can change. So, tell me what happened. You all had strippers, right?" Carrie asked.

Donald realized that she was committed to an investigation and finding something scandalous, and decided to play along.

"Yeah, we did. I'm not supposed to tell you, but we had 15 guys and probably 40-50 exotic dancers--three for each guy. Ron Cherry went all out. All the women were beautiful, too."

"How beautiful, Honey?" Carrie asked, and glared at her fiancé. She had heard about bachelor party shenanigans, and she tried to read him to see if there was any truth to it.

"Nines and tens on the beauty scale," Donald answered. He pretended to strain his memory as he recalled the women, "Yeah, nines and tens. All of them."

"Did you dance with any of them?" Carrie asked, and glared suspiciously at him.

Donald knew her sistah girl attitude was brewing and deftly switched the topic to her and the women’s party.

"I don't roll like that, baby. I was thinking about you, anyhow."

"Sure, you were Donald. Now, you're toying with me. You expect me to believe that?"

"Actually, I was wondering why we didn't have dancers after we learned about Chocolate Thunder, White Lightning, Mango Surprise, and The Bronze Bomber."

"Wait, uh, ho-hol-hold-up."

"I didn't stutter, honey. I did get the names, right? Cho-Choc-Choco-Chocolate. Chocolate Thunder..."

Carrie barked, "Not fair. Who told you? Girls have a code and a bond."

"So, Carrie, tell me. Which one of the guys did you pick for Debbie Techelle?"

"I have no idea what you are talking about," she snapped back, still surprised as her mind raced trying to figure out how Donald knew about their dancers..

"Oh, I forgot the girl code," he said and winked. "What about you? Since my sources tell me you had to take a nap, I'm guessing you passed your three-drink limit pretty early in the evening. Anything else you want to admit to? Refrigerator raids, drooling, snoring?"

Carries jaw dropped, "I hate you right now, Donald Alexander. That is not fair. How'd you find out?"

He walked to the counter, refilled his coffee cup, returned to his seat to finish breakfast, and ignored her question. It was a smooth deflection that made her even more intent on finding out about any juicy news. She pulled a chair next to his and began to rub his shoulders and kiss him softly on his neck and cheek.

Donald recoiled and responded with mock astonishment, "Carrie, I can't believe you. Are you going to try to seduce an answer from me?"

"What? Can't I kiss my fiancé? I haven't seen you since you guys left for Jamaica. I miss you, Baby."

" I miss you, too. I can also tell when my lady is putting the moves on me."

"Oh, forget it. I hate you, Donald."

"Carrie? Don't be mad, Honey. It's not my fault you have a double agent in your crew of beautiful women."

"Whatever, Donald Alexander," Carrie snapped and pouted as she became frustrated.

"Stop pouting. Come back and continue the seduction. I liked that part."

"Nah, Brother, I'm pissed at you," she said as she pulled yogurt, juice, and blueberries from the refrigerator. "Right now, I'm going to have breakfast."

"But I made pancakes and turkey sausage. It is on the stove, warmed up for you."

"I'm good, Donald. I'm on my Black Camelot diet until after the weddings." She continued to pout and said, "So, you're not going to tell me?"

"Not happening, Carrie because of the guy's code, but I think y'all had more fun than we did. I can tell you we had a reception with the local press, and Luke McFlemming and Mike Desanctis were there, and y'all had more fun because this thing took on a life of its own."

"In what way, Donald?" Carrie said, swallowing a spoonful of yogurt.

"We also decided with all the parties and receptions and three weddings that once was enough. Plus, I'm too old for all this partying."

"How was Tom about it?"

"The press petrifies Tom. We are some lucky guys and are ready to just get married and put this Black Camelot wedding fanfare behind us."

Carrie gazed at Donald, and her heart melted again. The fake fight of a few minutes ago a faded memory. "That is why I love you so much. You see the forest for the trees."

She stared at his handsome face and lean body, "I can't be angry with your fine self, anyhow."

He winked and sipped his coffee. His leer made her blush, and she ran from the other side of the counter and stood before him. He pushed his chair away from the island, and she jumped into his lap, "You are my Bronze Bomber, my Chocolate Thunder, my White Lightning, my everything. I love you so much."

"I love you too. I am so lucky to have you, and I just want to make you happy, Carrie."

"I will tell the girls we need to cancel the rest of the bachelorette parties. You make sense. We have three and a half weeks to go. Let's just enjoy the weddings and receptions. Besides, Debbie exchanged phone numbers with the Bronze Bomber. I think there is a mutual attraction."

Donald laughed, "Ha, that's funny. Go, Debbie, with your bad self."

Chapter Thirty-Eight

By June 1 and just three weeks before the first Black Camelot wedding, a trail of bodies had Assistant Chief Walt Bigelow and Detective Mac McClellan concerned. According to their identification, the deceased were all out-of-towners. All the men, going back to the bodies found outside the Grand Ballroom the night of Kwame Mills and Michelle Nubani's engagement, were white men with BE tattoos.

"Normally, when you have 30 bodies brutally beaten and murdered, you have a serial killer on the loose, except these guys all have BE tattoos," Bigelow said.

"What do you think is going on, Walt?"

"I talked to Teddy and Charlie Humphrey about these tattoos. They know BE as an underground group of assassins. We have to keep this as quiet as possible. The press can't find out."

"Why not, Walt?"

"This looks like a potential race war, and in full disclosure, there have been multiple threats to Donald Alexander, Kwame Mills, and Tom Wilson since Black Camelot began. The Black Camelot crew received fake bombs and narrowly missed three assassination attempts. Teddy is very concerned and wants to be on top of this."

"Race war? Come on. We are in New York City, and this is the 21st century. That's ancient era stuff."

"No, it's not Mac. I need you to study this file," Bigelow said and handed him a loose-leaf binder. As he did, Chief of Detectives Teddy Walker entered Bigelow's office.

"Hey, Walt. Hey Mac," Walker said. "Walt, how far have you two gotten?"

"Not very far. I've shared that this has the potential to be a race war and mentioned the threats to Alexander, Mills, and Wilson."

Walker took a seat and faced McClellan, "This is our town Mac, and the best city in the world. This is not some one-mile whistle stop in the middle of nowhere. We can't have bad guys come in and wreck the peace of mind that makes this place special. We have to protect the city's image at all costs. That's why we're keeping the BE murders hush-hush. These attacks are definitely racial. The good news is, so far they've all been thwarted."

Charlie Humphrey knocked lightly and walked in, "Hey, gentlemen. I'm sorry, I meant to come in with Teddy. I had to call the office, apologies."

"No worries, Hump. We were just getting into it with Mac. I shared with him that we will not let white supremacists terrorize our town. I was about to tell him we also have to find out who the vigilantes are who have been taking out these terrorists."

Humphrey interrupted Walker, "Mac and Bigelow, that has to be the official position Teddy will take as Chief of Detectives. But..."

Walker raised his hand, and the Harris Simmons security chief stopped talking. He wasn't quite ready to tell Bigelow everything about who had killed the BE members. He then told his top assistant a lie he hoped wouldn't come back to haunt him.

"We think there's a secretive kill squad roaming New York City. In fact, we are certain. We'll identify them, but for now, we need to find out about BE and who's behind the BE threats on Black Camelot."

The lie was Walker knew about the Society of Protectors. He knew they kept Black Camelot safe, and he couldn't risk exposing them. He'd deal with the lies and the fallout after the Black Camelot weddings were over and the BE threats against them had been eradicated.

He turned his attention to the scheme that included McClellan as a mole and said, "Mac. We've come up with a plan, and we need your help."

"Me? What is it?" Mac asked with a surprised look.

"We need to make you a rogue cop."

"Excuse me. A rogue cop. Me ?"

"Yes, we need a white cop in our inner circle we can trust. This has to be a highly covert operation."

The request confused McClellan. He trusted Walker and Bigelow, but this covert operations talk surprised him. "Okay, tell me more," he sighed.

Walker laid out the plan, "It's like this. We need to create some fake stories. We'll do that with help from our friends in the Celebrity Hack Patrol. They will paint you as a tortured, racist cop fired and arrested for his role in an outlaw white supremacist group. We need you and your former partner, Bill Trombetta, to play the part."

McClellan took a deep breath and closed his eyes as he processed the request. Everyone in the room anxiously waited for him to respond.

He started with a question about his erstwhile partner, who was still a street cop. It wasn't a surprise to Walker and Bigelow.

"Will this earn Trombetta a detective's badge?" he asked after the pause. "He's still itching for one Chief and is salty that he's still on the street. He's long been worthy of a promotion."

Walker nodded, "Yes, indeed, Mac. I'll make that happen. But we need you both to help us pull this off. This is a big deal assignment. You both will be disgraced, lose your jobs, and will sit in limbo after you are arrested and fired."

"And so, while I sit home, disgraced, the BE contacts me? Is that the plan?"

"Yes, and when they do, you play hardball. You position yourself as above the low-level guys already in body bags. Tell them you're aware from your sources about the many failed BE attacks, but there won't be any failures on your watch."

"So, you think this will lead us to the BE leadership as well as their assassins?"

"I hope so. We've got to figure this out fast. It's now June, only three weeks before the first wedding. God help us if there is a successful attempt on the Black Camelot crew. The world is watching, Mac. This is an unusual undercover request, but we need your help."

Humphrey took over, "Mac, Oliver Harris asked me to take care of the Black Camelot crew. He believes they will be world changers and asked me to do my best to keep them safe. If they are hurt or killed by BE, it can start a race war."

McClellan heard all he needed and agreed. He believed in Walker and had become a fan of the Black Camelot Crew.

"I'm in, guys. I know Trombetta will be, too."

"Good," Walker said. "Let's get the Celebrity Hacks down here. We need to pull together a scuttle story to set this saga up correctly."

"Scuttle story? What is that?" McClellan asked.

"A fake story designed to mislead the bad guys," Bigelow answered. "I'll reach out to Trombetta while you call the press, Teddy."

. . .

Two hours later, Doug and Darryl Duncan, Keyur and Manish Patel, and Garry and Larry Miller of the Society of Protectors had a conference call with The Voice. He congratulated them on all their work.

"If this were a government, you guys would have earned a Presidential Medal. You've safely completed 20 missions, kept your cover, and taken out 30 bad guys in New York. But what you did in Jamaica was world-class. There were 40 people in the house that night between the Black Camelot guys, their friends, the press from around the world, and the house staff. I don't usually get emotional about our work, but we dodged a serious bullet, and it was because of your great talent and ability to work together. Congratulations."

Unbeknownst to Bigelow, Walker and Humphrey were retired members of the Society of Protectors and communicated regularly with the Voice. Walker felt guilty about keeping the secret from his long-time deputy, but it was a secretive organization, and he had a vow to honor. The Voice also kept him apprised of all of BE's attempts, the dead-body counts, and other incidents. Walker knew how aggressively and persistently BE had been coming after Black Camelot, and he hoped he wouldn't be exposed or that Bigelow or the Celebrity Hack Patrol would figure it out. These facts made him more than a little nervous when he called the gossip writers to set up the scuttle story to expose BE.

Chapter Thirty-Nine

"I need your help. We need to do a scuttle story. It is critical to protect the safety of the Black Camelot Crew," Chief of Detectives Teddy Walker told the Celebrity Hack Patrol as they sat in a conference room at Police Headquarters.

Instead of responding to Walker, Luke McFlemming glared at Charlie Humphrey and asked with disdain, "What is he doing here?"

Luke and Humphrey's dislike of each other went back to the Harris Simmons murders. Luke's rant made it clear he was still bitter.

"Get over it, and yourself, you idiot," Humphrey growled in response.

It was a stupid fight for Luke to restart, and Humphrey reminded him why, "If I recall, you won a Harlowe Award. Let it go. Your colleagues have, and you should, too."

Jennifer Kung snapped at her colleague, "He's right, Luke. Besides, if there is any threat to the Black Camelot crew, we have to work with these guys, so shut up and listen for a change."

"TV is right, and Humphrey is, too. Let's remember how important Black Camelot is to all of us, Luke. Stop grandstanding, please," Mike Desanctis added.

Luke was taken aback by his colleagues' defense of Humphrey. Walker had yet to speak, but Luke knew the Chief would not put up with him, either.

"Do we have a problem here, Luke? I don't need any grandstanding. What I need is your help. But I can just as easily get this done with two out of the three of you."

Humbled, Luke took a deep breath and decided to let the fight go, but not without one last attempt to save face, "I'm good, Teddy, but you understand if the star is not on the story, you might not pull this off."

Jennifer yelled again, "Stop embarrassing yourself. You can never stop being an ass. I thought that knock on the head a few months back might have humbled you. And remember, I can still lock you out of the wedding coverage."

Luke straightened up in his seat at this threat. Jennifer's power move surprised Walker and Humphrey, as she made it clear who was really in charge.

She looked at Walker and said, "Go ahead, Chief Walker. What do you need from us?"

Luke slumped again and rolled his eyes. When he got mugged a few months ago, it ended a lot of his tough-guy bravado. Kung brought him back to Earth with this truth. It was a fact he hated.

"Thank you, Jennifer."

"No worries, Chief Walker. Please continue."

"We've got a problem with a racist organization called BE. The acronym stands for Before Emancipation. They are a secretive domestic terrorist group of white supremacists. They are not a protest group; you'll never see any public demonstrations where they bring attention to themselves. You'll recognize them from their work product."

"Which is what?" Desanctis asked.

"They assassinate people. Often brutally," Humphrey answered.

"Yes, that's what they do," Walker continued. "They send kill squads out on missions, and most of the members are so radicalized they don't mind dying for their cause. They are a fearless and callous hate group. We have on record they are in New York now to take out the Black Camelot crew."

Walker decided not to tell them about the incident in Jamaica where Luke and Mike would have been collateral damage casualties.

Kung and Desanctis gasped. Luke quickly sat up in his chair. This news rocked them all. They had all become admirers of the Black Camelot crew and understood that an assassination would paralyze the city and destroy race relations, not only in the city but nationally.

"Oh, hell no," Luke barked. "The snowball effect of something like this could start a race war. We can't let that happen, Chief. What are you going to do?"

He then turned to Humphrey, "Please let me apologize for being a hot dog a few minutes earlier, Charlie. It was unprofessional."

"Thank you, Luke," Walker said.

Humphrey flashed a kind smile, "No worries, Luke. Apology accepted. We need a series of scuttle stories to help us find these guys. Walk them through the plan, please, Teddy."

"I have two officers, Detective Mac McClellan and his former partner, Bill Trombetta. I fired them for wrongful use of force on African-American and Latinx arrest suspects. They will do a perp walk tomorrow and will be booked and freed on bail. We have enough fake information to put them in jail for 40 years."

He then handed them a small folder. "Humphrey and I have put together a list of 15 fake crimes. Just make the stories out of these. You can also talk to Walt Bigelow or me to get statements. Bigelow and I will be doing the perp walk with them tomorrow at 9 AM. You'll be the only press allowed."

Walker continued, "We think if you run a story for three days straight based upon these fake facts, we'll have enough stuff out there to do the trick."

Jennifer said to Walker, as her voice cracked, "I have gotten to know the women of Black Camelot very well and consider the whole crew my friends. They are special people, and I consider it an honor to help you expose BE."

She turned to her colleagues, "Luke and Mike, we have to do everything we can to help."

"I agree, Chief Walker," Desanctis said. "This is important work. We can't let this happen in our town and to some of our most beloved citizens. I will use my paper and be at your side through the end."

Walker appreciated their support. He also suggested there could be some rewards for their help, "Thank you, Mike. There is probably a Harlowe here for all three of you as a collaborative project, especially if we can bring this group down. And even a Citizen Commendation that I will recommend to the Mayor."

McFlemming was in to help as well. Like the other Celebrity Hacks, he understood the Black Camelot crew's importance to the city, and the opportunity to win another Harlowe further motivated him. "I am definitely in Chief Walker. We have to do everything we can to protect our town and our people. I also like winning Harlowe's, so count me in. A Mayoral Commendation would be nice, too."

Walker smiled. Everyone else rolled their eyes. "Thanks, Luke. I appreciate all three of you, value your talent, and trust in your ability to help us pull this off. Now take your files, and we'll see you tomorrow morning at the perp walk."

Humphrey stopped them as they put their information together. "We've made it clear this is an undercover operation, so we must emphasize that no one outside of this room, not even your editors, can know about this."

"Charlie, thank you so much for bringing that up," Walker said. "McClellan is an up-and-comer in my department. He's a star, smart, a lifelong New Yorker, and has a law degree from Harlowe. He may be chief of police one day. I don't want him dead."

"We understand, Chief. We'll be sure to be discreet. Everything stays in this room."

Walker acknowledged Desanctis' comment with a nod and continued, "And by the way, Trombetta is as valued to us as McClellan. He's a tough street cop personified and a family man who goes home every night."

"We will honor these guys and protect them," Luke said.

Chapter Forty

The perp walk the following morning was a small event. There was so much secrecy that the only news sources present were the Celebrity Hacks and the few independent stringers and paparazzi who regularly hung around police headquarters.

"This is how I want it," Walker said to Bigelow as McClellan and Trombetta were paraded into headquarters, processed, and released. "We've got to control the narrative. If we had television crews here sticking mics in our faces, the story could have gone sideways really quickly."

"So what's next, Teddy?" Bigelow asked.

"I don't know Walt. I've been toying with moving the weddings out of the city to the Hamptons."

"What? Whoa? These are the biggest events the city has seen in years, if not decades. The Mayor will have your head. Plus, you're going to have to convince the Black Camelot crew this is the right thing to do."

"You're right. The Mayor would kill me, but we need to have a plan B. Let's have a meeting with Humphrey and run the idea past him before taking it to anyone else. Call him and see if he can come by this afternoon?"

"Okay, Teddy, I'll reach out to him."

By afternoon, thanks to the Celebrity Hacks' large following, the story had gone viral all over the city and online. It worked as Walker, Bigelow and Humphrey had hoped.

The Confederate learned of the scuttle stories from Bobby Joe Blain. The BE had suffered significant losses since the failed attacks at the Grand Ballroom, but the worst was the Jamaica debacle, where they lost their best team. The Confederate desperately needed some positive news. Bobby Joe's phone call was what he needed.

"Bobby Joe, how are you healing up? Are you ready to come back?"

"No Confederate, I'm healing, but I will have crooked fingers for the rest of my life. I'm finished with this assassin work. There are some stories in today's New York tabloids that you should read. Two out-of-control racist cops were arrested."

"Hold on, let me pull them up. We don't get New York news stories down here," the Confederate said as he went online to pull up stories in the New York newspapers.

"I figured; that's why I am calling. These might be the guys who have the nerve and the talent to take on the Black Camelot crew."

"Oh Lord, crack me upside the head, Bobby Joe. This is exactly the kind of news we need. It's manna from Heaven. That's what this is, manna from Heaven."

"I figured you'd like it," Bobby Joe said.

"Yes, I do, because usually, wherever we find one or two rogue cops who hate the negras, we find many."

"What did you call them? Did you say negras?"

"Yes, I did. It's my slang term for the blacks. It's just something I made up. I call them coons and niggers too, but this is a term I made up."

"I like it. Anyhow, you should see if this will help in New York."

"You're right. I will place some calls to New York and find a way to contact them. We've got a few weeks before the first wedding and have to push the fight. Thanks for this information, Bobby Joe. I'll take it from here."

"Good luck, Confederate. Hopefully, these guys are the answers for what we need."

"This might be the opportunity and opening in New York," the Confederate thought as he hung up the phone. He read the articles online, and his heartbeat sped with excitement.

He searched through an old set of files in a cabinet, found an old phone number, and said aloud, "This might be the break I need. I'm in a war and have no wins, just 34 losses. This may be my last chance to turn things around."

The Confederate compared the file information with his current database. It showed the contact as a past associate. As he dialed the associate's number, he recalled how they met." I haven't talked to this guy in 15 years. I met him at a rally when he came with a bunch of cops from New York. I hope he can help us."

He got an answer on the second ring, "Travis Pfaff here. How can I help you?"

The phone number matched the file information, "Travis, this is Beau Tappan. We met 15 years ago at an association meeting."

"Association meeting" was a code term denoting BE affiliation as either a member or associate. “Beau Tappan” was an alias. The Confederate had to vet the caller before he fully identified himself.

Travis responded with a strong New York accent. The phone call surprised him. "Ah, let me think. Yes, 15 years ago, I remember going to an association meeting in Nashville."

The remembrance pleased the Confederate. Travis had passed the vetting. The caller introduced himself, "You may remember me from my organization name, 'the Confederate.'"

"Ah, yes, I remember now. You are the desk sergeant on the force. You keep things in line and dispatch people out on jobs for the association."

"Exactly, Travis. I'm still here in that same role. Our fight continues to be hard, but we are steadfast and committed to BE's oath."

"Before emancipation, sacredly, I always pledge, before emancipation and forevermore," Travis recited.

"Oh, you remember, the end of the oath. Does that mean you still believe in the cause?"

"I do Confederate," Travis said. "Let's see what I remember. 'We take this sacred oath to keep our country what it was before emancipation. White-owned and white-controlled. We vow our blood, treasure, and honor against anyone, any force, any man, and any beast that will stand in the way of this oath.'"

"Oh, it pleases me that you remember the full oath, Travis. We need your services. May I ask why you have become inactive over the years?"

"That is simple. We have a black chief of detectives, a black assistant chief of detectives. I didn't want to work for those guys anymore and decided to leave. We have a lot of black people in power nowadays in New York City. That means we have to be careful with our associations. People are going to jail. In fact, it unnerves me to learn my name is in a database."

"Don't you worry, Travis. There are codes in this database with names and contact information. I'm the only one with the passwords to unlock them."

The Confederate lied. BE had developed a secret code, but it wasn't hack-proof. If broken, there would be a slew of arrests by authorities and assassinations by left-leaning organizations to avenge BE anarchy.

"I'm glad because I'm retired now, and I want to let sleeping dogs lie. I hope you appreciate what I'm saying."

"I totally understand, Travis. Does that mean you still believe in the cause but can't be part of the fight?"

"Yeah, exactly. I am too old now. I used to have cover when I was on the force, but not anymore. Anyhow, you didn't call an old beat-up cop to suit up."

"No, I didn't. I called for some help from someone else."

"Wait, don't tell me, you are calling about the two guys arrested this morning, Trombetta and McClellan."

"Yeah, they sound like our kind."

"They certainly do. They are some bad dudes," Pfaff said.

"Can you find a way to connect me? We have some issues in New York and need their help."

"I can probably find a connection, but I have to be careful. They are probably being watched. As I said, it's a bad time to be a racist in New York. It's going to be hard for them. But I know some people. Let me make a few phone calls. Give me a few hours. Will that work?"

"That would be excellent."

"Do you have a number I can call you at Beau? I don't see a number here on my phone."

"No, I'll call you, Travis. How about four hours from now?"

"That should be enough time for me to dig something up. It's great to reconnect, Beau."

"You too, Travis. Okay, I'll talk to you then."

Travis' heart raced. He was part of a special interstate task force set up by Walker that worked with the FBI to infiltrate white supremacist groups. His value to the racist organization was as a senior ranking white officer in the

NYPD, who doubled as a racist. His job as a BE member would be to protect BE from police investigations. He could do kill squad work, too, if called on. Nothing much ever came out of the task force. It eventually disbanded.

He had become friends with Walker during his time on the force, and called his cellphone to share the news.

When Walker saw the call, he picked up on the first ring. "Travis Pfaff, how are you doing, my friend? How is retirement life? Are you getting fat?"

"Ah, don't start with the fat jokes Teddy," Travis said as he pinched his sides and smiled. He had added 25 pounds to his six-foot frame since leaving the job and was relieved Walker couldn't see his love handles, as the teasing would have been relentless.

He got right to the call's purpose. "Teddy, remember the racist task force from way back that didn't net anything? Well, the sleeping dog woke up today, and he's hungry."

Chapter Forty-One

Retirement bored Travis Pfaff and the phone call from the Confederate energized him. He was a New York beat cop for ten years and a detective for his last 15. Like many of the cops on Walker's interstate task force, he'd had a personal reason to join.

Pfaff was German-Irish. The German side of his family hated the Irish side, and the Irish side returned the hate. He understood intolerance well from their fights that resulted in a never fully healed extended family rift.

Working on Walker's task force was cathartic for Pfaff. It helped him fight against something he experienced firsthand. His parents met in New York as exchange students at City University. His father, Gunther Pfaff, was the son of a local German politician. He shamed the family's local reputation by dating Aisling Walsh. She was a teen beauty pageant queen, the winner of Ms. Dublin, who came to the states to study and act. They met in a drama class, fell in love, and conceived Travis out of wedlock. Both families were spiteful and remained stuck on their prejudices instead of their children's happiness.

Travis nicknamed Walker's task force "Team Tolerance." Like him, many of the members had their own stories that made them firm believers in breaking racial and ethnic intolerance.

It also meant that when the Confederate called Pfaff, he walked into a trap set long ago.

"Teddy, can you believe it has taken this long for these guys to come out in the open?"

"It's desperate times, Travis. They must be desperate to call an old goat like you," Walker joked.

"Old goat! Who are you calling an old goat?" Pfaff snapped back. "If I remember, I am only two years older than you, Mr. Press Conference, Politician and Chief of Detectives. When was the last time you did some actual sleuthing?"

Walker enjoyed his friendship with Pfaff. He was one of the many exceptional people he had befriended throughout his career. Thinking about Team Intolerance and the task force caused him to flashback.

"I miss having you around, Travis. We're both old goats now. I hope we can make something out of this. These guys want the Black Camelot crew dead. They have been unsuccessful, but all they need is one decent shot. I have lots to tell you about this."

"Yes, how do you want to play this, Teddy?"

"Tell them you are not connected with most of the guys from back in the day. Blame me, the black chief of detectives. Tell him I don't play racial hate games at all. Say I have been following McClellan and Trombetta for a couple of years, and they are as bad as they come. If they were Southern cops, they would be primary candidates for BE."

"I've pretty much already told them that and said you are making it rough on racists."

"Great. You're still sharp, Travis."

"Are they that bad, Teddy? It sounds like they should be in jail. How'd they make bail?"

"Travis, we go way back. I remember your family story, and because you were one of the key members of my special task force, I'm trusting you. This entire arrest is a setup designed to flush out the hate group."

"Brilliant. Just brilliant, Teddy," Pfaff beamed. "You might be an old goat, but you haven't lost anything. I guess I have to apologize for ribbing you for not doing any police work. This is awesome."

"Thank you, but it is only brilliant if it works. We need to put handcuffs on them, Travis. And remember, if we don't, you could be exposed as a mole and be in danger. We all have to be extra careful."

"I am not afraid of a little danger. This is a worthy cause. Any other advice for me?"

"Play coy. Just say you've called around. Most of your guys are retired. Stick with the story that overtly racist cops are not as plentiful in NYC as they once were. Tell your contact Teddy Walker can become commissioner if he wants the job, and it's his presence that has put the kibosh on past practices. That is why there is no large force of rogue cops ready to step in the gap. Then tell him you were able to find out a little about McClellan. Say he is the real deal racist rogue. He might need money to pay for lawyers, so BE's going to have to pay. Tell him the DA is considering additional charges against them both, so they both need money fast. Do you think you can sell that?"

"I think I can," Pfaff answered.

"And oh yeah, tell him you think the additional charges include felony murder and that he may be remanded immediately."

"In other words, if the Confederate thinks other charges are coming, he'll act fast."

"Yes, Travis. We need them to make a move so we can secure the city before the first Black Camelot wedding, and we only have a few weeks. We're keeping these BE attacks secret. We've even kept them under wraps with the Black Camelot crew, but if I can't find the Confederate a week before the first wedding, I have a responsibility to tell them. This gives me a full two weeks to work on this plan."

"Then, we have to work fast, Teddy, and pray for quick success."

"Exactly, Travis. There's easily a billion dollars in economic activity tied to travel, tourism, and local commerce attached to the Black Camelot Weddings. The police commissioner will likely lose his job if we don't solve this. And, I don't want his job."

"You'd be better at commissioner than old Chuck Safity anyhow. Chuck is a politician, Teddy. Old Safe Chuck. He never goes to the mattresses for anyone. You're fixing the department, and he's taking all the credit."

"Don't say that to anyone Travis. You know better," Walker said with a smile. "I'm calling it as I see it, old friend. I'm right, and you know it."

Walker chuckled and appreciated his friend's loyalty. "Travis, my friend, you've always been opinionated and biased. I'm glad you called, and I appreciate this tip. I'll find some consulting money for your work on this."

"That's why people call you First Class Ted. You always do the right thing," Pfaff said as he recalled one of Walker's many flattering nicknames.

"And like I said, you're biased, Travis. I'll let you go so you can prepare for your call. I'll have the tech guys contact you after I hang up. They will set up a tracking tool to trace the call. Thanks again, you old goat, buddy."

"You're the old goat, First Class Ted," Travis snapped back, smiling as he hung up.

Four hours later, as promised, the Confederate rang. Pfaff figured the call would be as brief as the earlier one. He was right.

"Travis, I don't want to be on this call too long. A lot is going on here. I hope you can understand." The Confederate lied as this contact was critically important to him and BE.

He was also cautious because he did not fully trust Pfaff. He was going forward based on one past meeting, 15 years ago. It was a desperate, reckless move, but with the first wedding three weeks away, there was little time for caution.

"No worries. I have a golf tee-time in an hour, so I need this to be quick, too."

"Excellent, what do you have for me?"

"The articles today have a breakdown of their backgrounds and rise through the department. Trombetta is a war veteran. He's known as a bully and had several discipline complaints filed by suspects. The article didn't have all the facts. He had 20 complaints, not ten, and they were all racial."

Pfaff embellished this fact. All the elements in the story about the discipline reprimands were false. Trombetta had zero disciplinary reprimands and had a model behavior record. He acted tough but was a sweetheart.

He next shared his fake story about Mac. "McClellan was a fast-track officer and a college guy with a law degree, whom the Chief and Assistant Chief of Detectives were grooming. That's why this is a surprise. He was a trusted, star protégé of the two-highest ranking black officers in the department. The word is Walker is devastated. He feels betrayed and embarrassed as this reflects on his instincts and will hurt his outreach programs with the minority communities. It may prevent him from being promoted to Commissioner or from being elected Mayor in the future. It's a real black mark, no pun intended."

"McClellan and Trombetta sound like the guys we want. What's the word on their being available to do the work we need?"

"You mean trigger man stuff?"

"Yes, exactly. That's what we need."

Pfaff sensed anxiousness in the Confederate's voice. "I am not sure if they can be shooters. But I think they need money. I heard there are some secret indictments to come. They may need some cash to take care of their families for at least a ten-year bid."

"What is that? Straight cash? How much?"

"It looks like $150K a year each for ten years, that'll be $1.5 million apiece, in total. If you come with that kind of money, I'm sure McLennan will find a shooter."

"That's expensive, especially to kill some negras."

"Excuse me? What did you say?" Pfaff heard the slur and bristled, but he wanted him to repeat it.

"I said negras. I'm sorry, it's my slang. I should have said, niggers."

"Oh, I understand," Pfaff gritted his teeth and continued. The slur made him more determined. "Hey, maybe if you meet him, he won't be as expensive."

The Confederate paused as he considered the cost for McClellan. "I guess you are right? Can you set up an introduction? How do you suggest we move forward?"

"Give me two to three days to set up a meeting with Mac. I'll probably arrange a coffee with him and me. It is not the kind of stuff we talk about over the phone. Once I connect with him, if he agrees, we'll call you immediately and agree to terms, etc."

"Will you be on the call?"

"Yes, we'll conference you from a safe place to talk."

"Okay, this sounds like a plan. I'm trusting you, Travis. We've got to pull this off. We've had several unsuccessful attempts on their lives, and I'm running out of time. We have to end this Black Camelot excitement. If we kill one or more of these guys, it will devastate black America and nigger lovers everywhere."

"Confederate, let me get to work. Call me in a couple of days, and I'll tell you where we are."

It was the first time the Confederate mentioned that Black Camelot was the target. Travis pumped his fist with this admission. He couldn't wait to do a follow-up call with Walker as soon as the Confederate ended the call.

"Thanks, Travis. I'll call you in a couple of days."

Five minutes later, Pfaff's phone rang; it was Walker. Pfaff angrily growled, "Did you hear that pig, Teddy? I want him bad. He admitted they want to assassinate Black Camelot. This guy belongs under the jail."

"Travis, the good news is he talked too long and said too much. We were able to trace his call and to his home address. We don't have to do the call with Mac McClellan. I already had my FBI contacts down in Nashville on alert. This terrorist is going to do federal time, but first, they will bring him to New York, and we will look at him for the stuff that's happened here."

"He's coming here?" Pfaff asked.

"Yes, they will pick him up today. Once they do, they will put him on a plane, and he'll be here tomorrow. Do you want to be part of the story? It's going to be a huge press conference."

"Oh, heck yeah. You know, I do. This was 15 years in the making."

Chapter Forty-Two

Dawn Davis Stuart and her father-in-law were enjoying a late afternoon cocktail and watching the news when the story appeared with images of the rogue racist cops.

"Wait, he looks familiar," Dawn said. She reached for the remote and turned up the volume. "That detective was here the night of the shooting. Is he a bad cop? I would have never thought it. He seemed like a sweet guy."

"That's Mac McClellan. I thought he was a little sweet on you," Yancey said. "He didn't want to leave you."

Their surprise turned to relief a few seconds later when a second banner flashed on the screen, "Crooked Cop, Not So Crooked. Part of Secret Undercover Task Force That Exposed Deadly White Supremacist Organization."

"Oh, that's better. He seemed like a nice fellow. I'm glad he's not a bad guy."

Yancey teased his daughter-in-law, "Yes, Dawn, he's not a crooked cop, so is he in the mix of prospects? Do you even have a list of prospects?"

She rolled her eyes at Yancey, "He's cute, but not my type. I am happy, though, that he's not a bad guy or part of some hate group."

"Yeah, I agree. Anyhow, what is your type? It's time for you to find a husband and have a kid or two."

Dawn ignored the first part of the question. She had been keeping a secret. It was justifiable given the murder, her jail term, and second marriage, but now that she was back in New York to rebuild her life, she decided to tell him.

"Funny you should bring up having a kid. Your son had sperm harvested and frozen. It was his decision when we went through our challenges and one of the ways he wanted to show how much he loved me."

This news shocked and excited Yancey. He shot upright and yelled, "Dawn, really? Don't play games with me. Is that true?"

"Yes, it is. We have about eight to twelve frozen sperm samples."

"If that is the case, you go get those sperm moving, and I mean right now."

He jumped up from the sofa, spilling most of his cocktail on his shirt but didn't care. "We need a family. I need a grandchild. I always wanted a grandchild."

Dawn's face reddened. She covered her mouth as she blushed, "I knew you were going to say that. I think I would be a terrible mother, especially with this record, and I need a husband first, at least a boyfriend. Don't you think?"

"Nope. Why? Unless you want one. In case you are asking, you have my blessings to do anything you want. I trust you. And selfishly, I am 75 years old. You'd give me another 15-20 years of life with a grandchild or two. Maybe 25 with modern medicine."

She looked at him with raised eyebrows. Yancey, ever the character, was being one now, "Okay, whatever, Yancey, let's be real, now."

He looked back at her and shrugged, "You're right. Twenty-five years might be pushing it. I have crammed a lot of living into my 75 years. But I'm bored, Honey. Give me something to do. Money is not an issue. We'll put the boy in the best schools, get him the best nanny, the best of everything."

"Boy? How about if it is a girl?"

Yancey took a deep breath as he thought about a girl and sighed, "Oh, Dawn, you got to let a guy dream, right? I love you, and you're a girl. I'd love her just the same."

She was happy and relieved that he was so excited. They'd become close since she came back, and she was conflicted about telling him about the sperm. Now she was glad she did.

Yancey continued to make plans for the sperm. "Dawn, I've read stories about people conceiving and having twins. You could have a boy and a girl. Wouldn't that be amazing?"

"Yancey, are you trying to wreck my body? I'll never find a husband."

"Yes, you will. In fact, I'm going to do something about that, too. I meant to tell you I got an invitation last week to all three Black Camelot weddings. I've already accepted."

Her face lit up, "You're lying. Don't play around. I've been dying to go to at least one of those weddings. I have a dress in mind already. Are you serious? I need to start dieting, so I can be extra hot."

"Well, you may as well find two more dresses. The first wedding is in three weeks. The others are in July and August. Attending will be the best way for you to reintroduce yourself to New York. Lots of good-looking, eligible guys will be there."

"That sounds like so much fun. Who got the invites for us? Luke McFlemming?"

Yancey thought about his connections who scored him the invitations. "No, your Pop still has a few contacts in town."

Yancey couldn't tell her that he was #31 in The Guiding Force. After his son's death, he ended his active membership but was still a life member.

As a life member, he received invites to events like the Black Camelot weddings. Donald, Kwame, and Samantha made sure he was on the guest list as they wanted to meet all the life members.

Dawn threw out another guess as a source for the tickets. It angered Yancey. "Bronson Pagent is your secret contact, right?"

Yancey's facial features changed, his brow arched downward, and his jaws tightened. He said, "I hate him. Look, sweetheart, let me make two things clear. First, it's just you and me in this world. That is why I want you to remarry and have a family. Second, I hate that guy with every fiber of my being. I'm trying to prepare for my visit to the Pearly Gates, but when I tell you I hate him, words can't measure it. If we wouldn't become immediate suspects for killing him, I'd take a contract out on him."

"I hate him too. But you realize, we can still hurt him."

"What do you mean, Dawn?"

"Let's put him out of business. He's injured now with his partner's death. We can take over his business."

"Are you talking about a return to real estate? I don't want that life again, and I don't want it for you. Enjoy this money, be a socialite, work on charity boards, give away money. You don't need that life."

"No, I don't want it, either. What I mean is I literally beat his ass before. This time we win mentally. How about we finish what we set out to do before the break-in and his partner's death? We threaten to expose him in a way that lets him know he can go to jail."

Yancey rubbed his chin and looked at the large ice cube in the rock glass of his cocktail, before taking a long swig of single malt. A happy grin replaced his angry scowl as he emitted a sinister laugh. "So you want to mess with him? Now, that would be fun. It'll give us something to do during the day".

"Exactly," Dawn said. She looked at Yancey with a smile, nod of the head, followed by a wink of the eye that matched his sinister laugh.

"That could be a lot of fun. Do you mean his business properties? He owns world-class properties. What do you have in mind?"

"We make him sell his share to his deal partners. We take 75-80% of the profits and donate the money to charity. We'll leave him with enough to live on but force him into early retirement."

"Oh, even better. We take him to the brink of bankruptcy and take away his power. My son told me you were brilliant and ruthless. He was right. So you want to become Robin Hood. Take from the rich and give to the poor."

"Yes, that's exactly what I want to do. I say, let's go visit Bronson in the morning and inflict some misery and pain on his ass."

Yancey responded gleefully and let out his sinister laugh again.

"The morning it is, then. This will be fun."

Another banner scrolled across the screen, "Crooked Cop, Not So Crooked. Part of Secret Under Cover Task That Exposed Deadly White Supremacist Organization."

Dawn turned up the television's volume as the newscast moved to police headquarters and showed Luke McFlemming, Jennifer Kung, and Mike Desanctis on a dais with Teddy Walker, Walt Bigelow, Mac McClellan, and Bill Trombetta.

"Look at Luke," Yancey said. "He could be another guy for you. How about it?"

"Thanks, but no thanks. Luke is a hot dog. I could never be myself with him. Let's just go to the weddings. I'm sure some wonderful men will be there." She stood up and walked to the gilded full-length mirror and turned from side-to-side and checked out her figure. "I need to lose five pounds."

"Shut up!" Yancey yelled. "You are in excellent shape. You are going to be the belle of the ball. Now check out Luke. He's speaking now."

At the press conference, Luke spoke first for the Celebrity Press Patrol team. "I'm Luke McFlemming, the prize-winning reporter for *The News*. Chief Walker and his team asked my colleagues and me here, Jennifer Kung of *The Ledger* and Mike Desanctis of *The Post*, to help them run a story to set up this group of bad guys. We are here because everyone must learn that the stories were not true. We put fake news out to sucker the bad guys. We knew in advance this was not the truth. It was a smart plan by Chief Walker."

Jennifer Kung moved next to the mic. "We want all of New York to know Detective McClellan and Officer Trombetta are the good guys, and we did this as a request from Chief Walker. Tomorrow you will see stories from Mike Desanctis, Luke, and me to clear these fine police officers. We want to make sure everyone understands the officers are the good guys. They are heroes."

She stepped away from the mic. Teddy Walker took over, turned to Desanctis, and said, "Do you want to comment, Mike?"

"No, Teddy. They said all that is needed."

Walker then restated his thanks for the Celebrity Press Patrol's help with the undercover operation. "Listen, we just want everyone to know that the press helped us on this one in a big way. We've been trying to break this organization for 15 years."

He chose not to mention Travis Pfaff at his request. They both realized evil forces could still be out there, and Walker didn't want them coming after his friend.

Walker continued, "The man arrested is a member of one of our country's most ruthless white supremacist groups. They have conducted all sorts of felony hate crimes, including bombings of churches, homes, and cars; cross-burnings; lynchings; and other murders. He is being extradited to New York as we speak for questioning regarding a series of incidents that have taken place here over the last several years."

A reporter asked, "What is his name?"

"His name is Suspect A. We have decided not to divulge his name to the public at this time. There is still lots of information to be unearthed. By shielding his arrests from his fellow members, we may be able to secure more arrests. That is also why we are not sharing the official name of the hate group. It will remain confidential until the investigation is complete."

Walker also didn't share that the FBI had begun to take all the calls that came into the Confederate's operating location, a factory in downtown Nashville. They were simultaneously getting warrants and arresting thousands of white supremacists across the country.

Charlie Humphrey sat next to Travis Pfaff in the audience. "Thank you so much, Travis," Charlie said. "Teddy and I are going to sleep well tonight. BE had us tied up in knots."

"It was a stroke of luck that they called, Charlie," Pfaff said.

"I guess, but it's also what can happen when you put together a plan. It took your planting of that seed 15 years ago to get us where we are now."

Chapter Forty-Three

The day following the news conference, the Celebrity Hacks had front cover stories at their respective papers. Their editors were ecstatic. The local television teams locked out from participating the previous day made up for it with coverage and interviews that ran all morning.

"The Celebrity Press Patrol are now true celebrities. Today, we call them The Celebrity Crime Fighter Patrol," Channel 2 television news anchor Shawn Cooper said on her top-rated *The New York Morning News Show.*

"Big shout-out to my peers, known to us in the business as the Celebrity Press Patrol, for their outstanding reporting. They are our New York Stars For the Day."

Stars For the Day was a civic appreciation program started by Cooper at Channel 2. It was the most-watched segment of the three-hour morning show.

"Celebrity Crime Fighter Patrol is a nice nickname. I like it a lot," Luke said as he talked to his editor, Zach Goldberg.

"Figures you would. Just stay clear of the bad guys. It's only been a few months since you got roughed up. Be safe, Luke."

Be safe was the same caution Desanctis got from his editor, Pete Colon and Kung received during a phone call with her editor, Pattie Cunningham.

"Jennifer, I was a war correspondent, and that was the pit of Hell. But this stuff, sinister racist organizations, I covered them, too. That beat is 100 times more dangerous than covering a war. These domestic terrorists are rabid, true believers, and many will die for the cause. I am going to assign you a security team."

"I'm okay, boss. Nobody wants to hurt me."

Cunningham snapped at Kung, "Are you kidding me? Don't be hard-headed. You've been hanging around McFlemming for too long. We are talking about a white supremacist group. You are an Asian-American rock star journalist. Snap out of it. Out of the three of you guys, whom do you think they'd enjoy hurting the most?"

Kung sighed and rolled her eyes. "Jesus, Pattie, don't be so dramatic. You sound like my mother."

"I bet you had a hard time listening to her, too. Don't be so damn stubborn. You will be getting a security detail, at least for the next month or so."

Kung broke out in a big smile, "Okay, boss lady. You're right. It'll have to wait until tomorrow as I am on my way to the West Side Heliport to meet Mike, Luke, Black Camelot, and their entourage. Donald Alexander's flying us to his house in the Hamptons for a Black Camelot Wedding photoshoot."

"Wow, Girl, you live the best life. Hamptons photoshoot; did you tell me about that? How about inviting your boss to some of these fun events? I'm feeling a little left out."

"I got you, boss, for something even bigger, and you can rub this in with Zach Goldberg and Pete Colon. You have invitations to all three of the weddings with a plus one. They don't. I am in charge of the press's guest list."

"Now, that made my day. They'll both be at the Editors Club luncheon at The Millennium Club today. I'll be sure to rub it in." Cunningham said as her phone beeped. "That's my other line. Jennifer again, great work. I'm proud of you, and remember what I said, be careful."

"I will. Thank you, Pattie."

Jennifer smiled as she thought about her boss's reprimand. She then switched to the day ahead.

"Pattie is right. I am living the good life."

When she arrived at the heliport, Jennifer learned from Sammy Rivers that she would ride on the first helicopter.

"We have chartered two ten-passenger helicopters. You and I will fly on the first helicopter with the three couples, and Ron and Marcia Cherry. Luke, Mike, Cathy Martin, two photographers, a makeup person, and a two-person camera crew will take the second chopper."

Donald greeted them all. "Thank you, everyone, for coming out. Today will be a great day. Let's board and have fun."

A couple of minutes later, as the helicopters rose, two SUVs sped into the heliport parking lot. Four men armed with high-powered shotguns jumped out of the vehicles.

"We have a situation here, Darryl," Doug Duncan said to his brother as they watched the gunmen exit the SUVs. The Duncans were in the heliport terminal and in charge of ground security.

"Get your gun ready with your silencer on," Doug commanded. "We don't want to attract any additional attention."

Darryl nodded and grabbed his long range rifle..

"These guys are here to take down the choppers," Doug continued. "I've got the two in the first car. You take the two in the second. Don't give them any warning. Let's slip out and take one shot each in the back of the head. We can't afford a miss. We'll kill them and drag their bodies back in here. Remember, they can't see us."

"I'm ready," Darryl said as the brothers slipped out of the terminal.

The gunmen failed to check the terminal entrance, so they never spotted the Duncans standing guard to make sure the aircraft departed safely.

Four silent kill shots dropped the assailants as they aimed their guns at the first helicopter. The brothers dragged the bodies into the empty heliport terminal. No one on the first helicopter witnessed the shooting. Inside the terminal, Doug called The Voice.

"Doug Duncan here. We just took out four assassins at the West Side Heliport. The Black Camelot crew is safe and on their way to the Hamptons. Keyur and Manish are on the choppers as the camera crew today."

The Voice said, "These terrorists won't stop. Are they dead?"

"Yes, we couldn't take a chance. We shot all four in the head. If they had gotten off even one round and shot a pilot, we would have had a disaster. We need a clean-up crew here, right away."

"They must have followed the targets from their homes and hidden out until the choppers got in the air. Well, that makes 38 dead, including the four guys in Jamaica. Yesterday we arrested one of BE's leaders. We hoped the news would have made them stop."

"Don't worry, Voice. If they don't stop, we'll continue to take them out. It's not fun taking lives, but we're at war," Doug said.

The Black Camelot crew on the first helicopter did not hear the gunshots or see the shooting and quick removal of the bodies.

Luke and Mike, however, saw everything.

"Jesus Lord, have mercy," Desanctis whispered to McFlemming. "I just saw a bunch of guys get shot, Luke."

"I saw that too, Mike. And did you see why? They were pointing guns at the first helicopter. I'm going to assume they would have shot ours down, too."

Luke removed the lid from his empty coffee cup and vomited.

"You okay?" one of the cameramen behind him asked. "I watched that, too. Don't worry, that was Doug and Darryl. They are part of the stealth security force keeping everyone safe. We work with them. We've got you guys from here, and everyone will be safe today in the Hamptons. You can't tell anyone what you just witnessed. We need to be as invisible as possible and will only expose ourselves when necessary."

"What do you mean?" McFlemming asked as he turned to face the man, his face white and eyes bulging.

"Jesus, Mary, and Joseph!" Desanctis exclaimed.

"Please keep it down. Everything is under control. You guys are safe. The people on the first helicopter are safe, too," the cameraman said.

"What the hell is going on?" McFlemming asked. His heart raced, and he began to hyperventilate.

"I can't say too much, but I will tell you this, my name is Keyur, and this is my brother Manish. We are the good guys and extremely covert. If we tell you more, you may be killed. Either by our hands or our enemies'."

Keyur's statement further petrified McFlemming and Desanctis. They sat in stunned silence. After Desanctis recovered enough to speak, he said, "Wait, you must be joking. Did you just threaten us?"

"Yes, I did. I am sorry you witnessed this. I know you guys know Chief Walker. He knows about us. I suggest you call him once we land. He will assure you this is not a joke. He'll also advise you that we are just doing our job."

"Okay, we will. Are you a cop? Do you work for Walker?"

"No, Luke, I can't tell you anymore. Just wait until we make it to the Hamptons. Call him then, but not in this chopper. You can't tell anyone what you just witnessed."

As the helicopters made the 45-minute flight to the Hamptons, Dawn and Yancey Stuart walked from their apartment to the Upper West Side mansion of Bronson Pageant.

Yancey began to rehearse this morning's meeting with Dawn as Robin Hood, as they discussed last night. He asked her, "Who am I in the Robin Hood cast? I'm Little John, right? I can be Little John. He was Robin's #2 and a large man, just like me."

Dawn stopped and glared at her father-in-law. He responded with a confused look, "What? I can't be Little John?"

"You make me so angry at times, I swear. I'm trying to get my mind right, and here you are trying to make jokes. I'm telling you, Yancey Jr. was your son 100%. This is how he would act. I need you to be serious. Let's go, man."

Yancey shrugged and skipped along the street like a teenager. He said in a hipster's voice that didn't match his 75-year-old upper crust society lineage, "I'm just getting loose. Don't worry. He's going to feel us when we get up in there."

Dawn stopped and snapped angrily, "Enough. You need to stop, or I'm sending you back home."

"Okay, okay.," Yancey said defensively. "I was just trying to lighten the mood. Madame Hot Temper is back," he said under his breath

"I heard that," she snapped. "And you are going to see her in five minutes."

When they arrived at Pagent's doorstep a few minutes later, she turned to Yancey and said, "Follow my lead. I got this, okay?"

"I will. I'm following you, Dawn. I will be quiet unless you need me."

As she rang the doorbell, Yancey saw her facial features change. She was undergoing the complete Madame Hot Temper transformation. It so unnerved him that he took a step back and thought, "I hope she didn't bring my gun."

In seconds Pagent's maid, Carmelita, opened the door. The smell of her signature baked croissants tantalized their nostrils as she greeted them in her thick Spanish accent. "Hello, can I help you?"

Dawn answered, her voice now cold and sinister. It was a voice Yancey had never heard before, but he knew she was in control. "Yes, we are here for Bronson Pagent. Tell him that Dawn Davis Stuart and Yancey Stuart are here to visit him. Tell him that we are prepared to go straight to Chief Ted Walker if he chooses not to come to speak with us."

"Excuse me. My English is not so good. Can you say that...?"

"Carmelita, let them in," Pagent's voice blared through the door's intercom. "Sit them in the living room and offer them coffee and some of your fabulous croissants. I'll be down in five minutes, Dawn and Yancey. I see you through my front door video monitor. Welcome to my home."

"Okay, we will be waiting," Dawn said sternly.

As Carmelita escorted them to the living room, Bronson called his lawyer, Phillips Warner.

"What do you want at 7:30 in the morning? I hope you are calling to let me know that Carmelita is sending over some croissants? Otherwise..."

"No, Phillips," Bronson said, his voice high-pitched with panic. "Dawn Davis Stuart and Yancey Stuart, Sr. are downstairs."

"Downstairs, where?"

"Here at my home."

"You let them in the house? Why?"

"They threatened to go to Chief Walker unless I let them in. I have no idea why they are here."

"It's those damn files, Man. The same files Petey tried to get. The chickens may have come home to roost."

"What do you mean, Phillips?"

"Bronson, you guys have done so much dirty stuff. It comes back. That's all I'm saying."

Warner's frankness frightened Bronson, "You're my lawyer. You're not supposed to talk to me like that. You are supposed to have my back."

"That's right. I am your lawyer. And so, I'm giving it to you straight. This is not good."

"Jesus, Man. You sound like I am beaten."

"Yes, that's what I am telling you. Bronson, how much money do you have in untraceable offshore accounts?"

"$150 million, give or take."

"What's the unliquidated value of your real estate holdings?"

"A billion and a half, $2 billion. If I liquidate, I'd probably touch after taxes $750 million to a billion, and then I have to split that with my partner's wife. So if I'm lucky, half a billion."

"Okay, listen to me, Bronson. Take notes if you need to."

Bronson quickly grabbed a notepad and pen off his desk. "I'm listening. I'm ready."

The lawyer let out a deep breath and said, "The solution is simple. Don't be stupid. Give them half. You knew this day was coming. They have enough to put you in a white-collar jail for the next 20 years."

"But, wait...," Bronson started to protest.

"Stop, Bronson. You're trying to play the wrong hand," Warner shouted as Bronson continued to protest. The scream startled him and made him listen. "You have $150 million they don't know about and can't trace. That was smart. If you come out with another $250-$500 million, which I predict you will, you can buy a plane. A damn private plane, hell, even a fleet of them, and maybe even an island. How much is your home worth here? And is it paid for?"

"$15 million. Yes, it is paid for."

"Bronson, stop being greedy. You've done a lot of bad things and dodged a lot of bullets. You could just as easily be dead had your late partner decided to take you out. You have enough to buy mansions anywhere you want to live in the world. Enough cash to donate to charities and still have people kiss your ring for the rest of your life. But not if you're in jail or dead."

Bronson paused and contemplated his lawyer's advice. He knew this day was coming, but this was not how he thought it should happen. "I'm just not ready to give it all up. Can't we fight?"

"No, man," Warner yelled. "These guys are here to call in your account. I can't protect you if you want to be stubborn. And I don't know if you have been watching the news, but Pre-1860 is lying low. If you think we are going to take these guys out, forget about it. BE, our street-level militia, tried and continues to fail. There are now 38 dead bodies, including four this morning in New York City alone. Four assassins were killed less than an hour ago. We can't help you fight."

"I saw the press conference last night. Damn, Luke McFlemming and the Celebrity Hacks are everywhere."

"McFlemming and the press have nothing to do with this. It's the Society of Protectors. We don't know who they are or how to get to them, but they know how to get to BE. They are playing three-dimensional chess, and we are playing checkers. You need to stand down."

"Phillips, this is too sudden."

"I know, but would you rather it be McClellan revisiting you or Teddy Walker with handcuffs? Listen, tell them I am on my way. I can negotiate all of this for you. But let me make it clear, you just need to walk away. You are blessed to have made it through all of this alive. I'll be there in ten minutes. Don't do anything stupid."

"Phillips, Phillips, Please, I can't?"

"Bronson, take a deep breath, please, and take that pen and paper and write two words down. Focus on them and nothing else."

"What words?"

"Salvage sale. It's salvage sale time, my friend." Warner then hung up the phone.

Chapter Forty-Four

"Luke, there are beasts in the belly of this city. I'm a grown man, 20 plus years into this business, top of my game, and this week, I've seen things for the first time."

"Me too, Mike. I have to say, I've seen a lot too. Growing up in Hell's Kitchen, you grow up fast, but this is different. Assassins killing assassins, and they wanted to kill us, too."

"And all because they are powerful black people. Now we know, just a little, what the civil rights movement was about," Desanctis said as he shook his head, still in shock over what they had just witnessed.

"It's embarrassing," Luke said. "We spent time with all of these guys in Jamaica at Big Stan's mansion for the bachelor party weekend. They are the kindest, most normal, coolest guys you'll ever meet."

"We were at Big Stan's and saw how nice they were to you guys. How about those swag bags? $75,000 worth of goodies," Manish said.

"You were in Jamaica?" Desanctis asked, surprised.

"Yes, our job is to be everywhere and be invisible," Keyur answered. "Nobody knows we are around. If we can be discreet enough, you'll see one of us and wonder, where have I seen you before? You look familiar."

Manish continued, "And that's why you don't have to worry. We will keep you safe."

Everyone on the first helicopter remained oblivious to the events at the heliport. They happily enjoyed the flight to the Hamptons and chatted about the activities for the day.

Carrie talked about the vineyard on the Dryden Estate. "It had been dormant, and Donald has been getting it back up and operating over the last three years. His orchard has 50 acres of grapes. Maybe we can do a visit today and a tasting?"

"Yes, that's a great idea," Donald said. "I want you guys to check out what we are doing with a small vanity label called O&G. It's an homage to Oliver and Gill. Right now, I'm producing a chardonnay, merlot, cabernet sauvignon, and a red blend."

Carrie added, "I've been telling him to name the red blend Black Camelot."

Donald noted his agreement with Carrie, "My lady has the best ideas. We may release a limited edition for this summer."

He became energized as he talked about the vineyard. Marcia Cherry commented on it, "I see your enthusiasm for this. I know if you put your smarts and energy into this, it will be a success."

"Thank you, Marcia. I am quite excited about the wine. We are going to land at the vineyard, and you guys can see why. It is the only place large enough to land a helicopter. We have some guys coming in from the house to pick up the equipment for the shoot ."

"Guys? Whom do you mean?" Tom asked.

"Oh, just the landscapers. I told them about today, and they will bring some golf carts out to ferry what we need to the vineyard and the beach and back to the house."

Donald had a security team at the Hamptons house full-time since the attempt on his life at Harris Simmons. He thought the team was sent by Harris Simmons' security because Oliver Harris assigned them, but they were Society of Protectors members. As the choppers landed, Keyur received a text from the Voice that said four members were at Donald's Hamptons house. He breathed a sigh of relief and told Manish, "Four more of us are on the grounds. We've got the help we need."

Chapter Forty-Five

While they waited for Bronson Pagent to come downstairs, Yancey Stuart stared at his daughter-in-law. Her steely gaze concerned him. He said, "Dawn, be strong, but keep your cool. Remember, I've got three tickets for the Black Camelot weddings. I need my plus-one."

He then bit into another of the croissants Carmelita served while they waited. "I can't describe how tasty these are. You should have at least one."

Dawn muttered, "I'll pass. Croissants are fattening and terrible for your cholesterol. You've had enough for today."

Yancey shook his head. The soft, flaky, buttery crescents smelled like Heaven. They also reminded him of Dr. Ewell's warning, "Anything that tastes good, don't eat it."

This morning he wasn't going to heed his doctor's advice. Carmelita's croissants were too good.

They both heard footsteps descending the stairs. Dawn stiffened, and her glare grew steelier. Bronson appeared in the entryway, dressed in the same blue suit and power tie he'd worn days earlier when McClellan had visited. He had 15 identical blue suits. They made him feel strong. He hoped the image would work today as he walked into the room.

"Good morning. To what do I owe the honor of this morning's visit?"

Before Dawn could speak, Yancey stood and took charge.

His voice boomed. Dawn had never heard it so loud and strong. Yancey sounded like he was speaking into a microphone, "Dawn here is Robin Hood, and I am Little John. We are here to rob from the rich and give to the poor."

Bronson took a step back. He knew of Yancey Stuart, Sr. Everyone in New York real estate circles did. However, he had never met him nor experienced his commanding presence.

"Excuse me, Sir, what are you talking about? Robin Hood? What are you saying?"

"It means we are here to take all of your money. You had to know this day was coming. You were complicit in the death of my son and the ruination of our family dynasty. I should have had you killed."

"Wait! Uh, what? Uh, hold up. I'm sorry," Bronson stuttered. The old man's threat petrified him. He now understood what Phillips Warner had tried to explain.

As she watched her father-in-law change into the powerful and feared man he was in his heyday, Dawn slumped, and her eyes began to water.

When she began to whimper, Yancey snapped in his commanding voice.

"Nope. No crying. This is your meeting. Now sit up, Dawn, and take it from here."

The doorbell rang. Carmelita, who was eavesdropping from the kitchen doorway, ran into the living room and said, "You have another visitor, Mr. Bronson."

"It's Phillips Warner, Carmelita. Please answer the door and bring him in here." Bronson's calm voice concealed his panic.

Carmelita ran to the door and said in her thick Spanish accent, "Mr. Phillips. Hurry up. He needs you."

Warner rushed past her and into the living room. Bronson stepped back and Warner stood between him and the Stuarts. He said, "I'm Mr. Pagent's attorney."

"Today, you are on the wrong side," Yancey responded in a dark voice that intimidated his client moments earlier.

"Excuse me. What do you mean?"

"Tell him, Dawn. It's your moment. Come on, now."

"What is he talking about?" Warner asked as he turned to her.

She spoke up. Her voice was now clear and free of emotion, "We are here to collect from Bronson and end his reign as a corrupt real estate magnate. It's over. I want all of his papers, and I am here with my father-in-law to begin this process."

"What! Hell, no!" Bronson yelled.

"Shut up, Bronson," Warner snapped and turned to her. He looked at her with a glare. He was trying to eyeball her and find a weakness he could identify, but didn't see one. "Now, Dawn, what do you want?"

"All of it. Every damn red cent. I want everything liquidated. We are giving it all away," she said, and glared at Bronson.

She turned back to Warner and continued, "As Yancey said, I am Robin Hood. He's Little John. Your client is Prince John. You can play The Sheriff of Nottingham if you want and try to protect this fool. Remember who won."

"You'd better listen to this woman," Yancey said. He was satisfied that Dawn was in control and sat, crossed his legs, and said, "Get them, Robin, I mean Dawn."

Phillips knew who Dawn was and all about her storied past. "I liked you better as Madame Hot Temper."

"Madame Hot Temper's just warming up. Trust me," she said. "This is how it is going to go down. I have enough files to put your client in jail for bank fraud, wire fraud, tax fraud, bid-rigging, extortion, usury, and racketeering to start."

She then, with two quick side steps, slid ominously into the center of the room and stared down Bronson, who cowered behind his lawyer. Bronson hung his head as her stare intimidated him. Dawn wore a form-fitting green cotton mock turtleneck with tight green linen slacks and Louboutin loafers. Her red hair was bound in a long, thick plait that draped across her shoulder. Her arms dangled at her side as she stood with her legs spread shoulder-width apart. She clenched her hands into fists, gritted her teeth, and rolled her neck in a circle as if she was readying to attack. She glared at Pagent.

Yancey took notice and said, "Madame Hot Temper has warmed up, gentlemen."

Dawn glared at Yancey. He covered his mouth and apologized, "Sorry, Dawn. Go ahead and do your thing.

She turned back to Bronson and Warner and continued to lay out the consequences for not signing over the assets, "And that's just the start. He's potentially looking at white-collar prison for 30-40 years. If you pile on the racketeering and other mob-related activities, and oh yeah, countless sexual assault charges, your accommodations will change pretty quickly to Big Boy Jail. And judging by the *Revenge of the Nerds* bitch-boy look you are giving me right now, you don't want to end up there."

Yancey jumped in, "Bronson, you had to know this day was coming. That's how it works in this game. You reap what you sow. You didn't build this business with talent. My son bankrolled you with my money when you were struggling. You bit the hand that fed you and then stabbed him in the back and assaulted his wife, you piece of crap. You've profited as a lecherous predator and a disgrace, but you've made a lot of money. I suspect you have a fair amount stashed away in untraceable offshore accounts, right? I'm guessing $100 million, $150 million or more? And if you don't, that's dumb."

He got up from his chair and walked over to Dawn in the center of the room. She continued to eye Bronson like a lioness about to attack its prey. Yancey whispered into her ear.

She nodded in agreement. Yancey turned back to Phillips and Bronson, "This is what we are willing to do. You keep 25% of the liquidated value of all your assets."

He returned to his seat, crossed his legs, folded his hands in his lap, and waited for an answer.

Bronson finally spoke. He still stood behind his lawyer's physical buffer. "Hell, no. I won't do it. I'm not going down like this."

"Excuse me," Dawn barked. She walked over to her bag on the sofa and pulled out two folders. She held up one and said, "Club Fed here," then held up the other and said, "Big Boy Jail here."

She continued, "Oh, and think of this as a ticking auction. You lose 5% of your share every minute you delay. Given your initial rejection, I'm going to start the clock right now with 40 seconds left in the first minute."

Warner had heard enough and yelled, "We'll take the 25% deal. Stop the clock. We'll take it."

"No, Phillips, what did you do? I must fight!" Bronson screamed. "I won't do it."

Warner raised his hands in a T-sign to quiet Bronson and asked the Stuarts, "Excuse me for a second, please, while I confer with my client."

"Do what you need to do," Dawn said.

Phillips pulled Bronson into the spacious hallway and whispered, "I told you this was going to happen. Sometimes you have to pay the piper."

"I understand, but I can't, Phillips," Bronson protested.

"Hey man, do you know what's in those folders? And don't lie to me. Is it as bad as they say?"

"Uh, yes. I've done a lot of bad things."

Phillips looked at his client and gritted his teeth. "Don't be an ass. Can they implicate you in the conspiracy that led to the shooting at the strip club?"

"Probably," he said. "But…" he closed his eyes as he tried to find the words to protest.

Warner didn't let him. "I'm telling you, Bronson, you're lucky they are not leaving you penniless. You'd also be dead in Big Boy Prison in a week. They've got you. They win."

Bronson began chuffing, and his shoulders slumped.

"You okay, Bronson?" Warner asked.

"Hell no, I'm not okay," he rasped. "I'm in a pickle. I'd never survive prison, so you're right. I give up. They win."

Warner stood facing his client and braced both hands on Bronson's shoulders and said in a voice that he hoped consoled him, "I understand, it's not easy to give up your empire. But remember what I said. You will walk out of this with a lot of money. Let's go back in there and do what we need to do."

When they returned, Dawn walked back to the center of the room and resumed her glare. Yancey held up his phone. "I have my counsel, Hollis Tassie, on speaker. He's going to witness the terms of the agreement now. He will have an associate from his firm set up the paperwork and the liquidation terms."

Bronson and Phillips both sighed when they heard the name Hollis Tassie. "Don't say anything, Bronson," Warner said. "Let me handle it."

Phillips asked, "What happens if we have problems liquidating?"

"Then we'll assume 100%, and that means less money for you. We will only give you 25% of what you sell. So it makes sense to sell as much as you can."

"Can you give us 90 days?" Warner requested.

"That's reasonable," Yancey answered, and Dawn nodded her agreement. "We'll give you 90 days, after which stiff penalties will apply. You'll start to lose percentage points every day after that. You know how to sell a property, Bronson, so I suggest you start selling."

"Okay," Pagent said, pouting like a petulant child. "Do I have to sign anything?"

"We'll have documents there in an hour," Tassie said through the speakerphone.

"Jesus, this is not fair!" Bronson whined.

"Not fair? I'll tell you what is not fair!" Dawn yelled and crossed the room with cat-like quickness towards Bronson and Phillips. Bronson backed up to the wall with horror in his eyes. Phillips recoiled, too, startled. Dawn jumped in the air and threw a right cross punch that connected cleanly with Bronson's jaw. The blow knocked his head back into the living room wall. He squealed in pain from the crushing blow and crumbled to the floor. Two teeth fell onto his blue suit. Blood trickled from his mouth onto his white shirt as he slumped on the floor.

"Well damn, Madame Hot Temper. You didn't have to do that. Was that necessary?" Warner yelled.

"Yes, it was necessary. I went to jail because of this guy. I lost my marriage and my husband because of this guy. Hate, for me, has a first and last name: Bronson Pagent. He's lucky that's all I did."

"What is going on over there, Yancey? Is everything okay?" Hollis Tassie screamed.

"Everything is fine, Hollis. Just send over those papers and I'll see if I can wrangle you some of these homemade croissants. They are delicious."

. . .

On the ground at Donald Alexander's beach estate, Luke McFlemming and Mike Desanctis jumped off the helicopter and called Teddy Walker. He was expecting their call. The wheels of communication were at work. Keyur Patel texted The Voice, who called Walker and told him Luke and Mike had witnessed the heliport shooting.

"Teddy, I mean Chief Walker," Luke said excitedly.

Walker could tell the journalist was unnerved and frightened. He interrupted, "Luke, is Mike with you?"

"Yes, he's right here. We have the phone on speaker."

"Okay. Now listen to me carefully. The first thing I need you to do is relax."

"But, but," Luke stuttered. He was not ready to listen, and Walker was uninterested in Luke's grandstanding.

"Stop and listen, Luke," Walker barked as Luke continued to try and talk over him.

Walker then commanded, "Mike, take the phone and walk away. Let me speak to you alone for a second."

Luke was confused by this request. In keeping with his true nature to not share, he pulled the phone back and snapped, "No!"

Walker yelled, "Mike. Smack the hell out of him and take the phone. You can do it, Mike. Don't hesitate. Do it now."

Confused by the request to smack his colleague, Desanctis hesitated. The Chief of Detectives yelled again, "Dammit Mike! Do as I told you. Smack him across the face, and take the damn phone."

This time, Desanctis did not hesitate. He smacked Luke's face so hard that it dazed him and left a handprint.

Luke recoiled and grabbed his jaw but didn't give up the phone. "Dammit, Mike, was that necessary? You may have knocked a tooth loose. You're an ass for doing that."

"Just give me the phone, Luke," Desanctis said, reaching for it.

Smacking Luke felt better than he'd imagined. It even settled a few past scores.

"Hit him again. Harder this time," Walker said when he realized McFlemming had not given up the phone.

"Stop, Mike. Don't hit me. Teddy, I am handing over the phone now," Luke said. He glared and gave the phone to Desanctis.

Walker ordered Mike, "Turn off the speakerphone for a second, walk away, and talk to me."

As Desanctis walked away, Walker said calmly, "As you witnessed this morning, these guys are assassins. You are safe now. But I need you to hold Luke up. It's been a rough couple of months with his assault, and now this. He's fragile. Think of him as having post-traumatic stress disorder. He needs to understand that if he mentions today's shooting in his column, all of you will be in danger. Keeping silent is the best way for us to protect you all. Do you understand?"

"Yes, I understand," Desanctis said. It was all a shock for him too, but he trusted Walker, and if he said that an article would put their lives in danger, he was going to follow orders.

"Okay, Mike, now go back to Luke and turn the speakerphone back on."

Desanctis complied and told his colleague, "Sorry to hit you so hard. Are you okay, buddy?"

"Buddy, my ass. You could have broken my jaw or knocked some of my teeth out."

"I mean it, I'm sorry. Anyhow, please listen to Teddy. This is serious. All of our lives are in danger, and he wants to explain why. Just listen, okay?"

Walker interrupted them. "Luke, please stop worrying. There are forces at play, and they will be for a while. You are not a target and won't become one unless you run a story about what you observed this morning."

"But Teddy, four guys got shot in the head. We witnessed an assassination."

"Luke, there's a dark underworld of bad guys and evildoers that you'll never understand. There's also a world of people who protect you from them that you'll never see."

"You mean like the guys on the helicopter today?"

"Yes, Luke. They saved your life twice."

"What do you mean?"

"They are part of a larger team assigned to protect the Black Camelot crew. The protectors on the ground took out the gunmen before they could shoot down both helicopters."

"What was the second save?"

"The special protection group on the chopper used discretion by explaining to you what was going on. They didn't want you to panic and told you what to do. That's why you are talking to me now."

"What do you mean?"

"Before the helicopter landed, they instructed you to contact me. Let me be clear when I say this. You are the press. Had you attempted to report what happened at the heliport before speaking with me, you'd be dead. There is an order of magnitude to all of this, and I hate to say it this way, but your lives would be considered collateral damage."

Luke and Mike's faces turned pale. They were standing 20 yards from Jennifer, the Black Camelot crew, and the others. The Patel brothers walked around with their camera crew equipment and blended invisibly with the crowd.

"Four additional security team members are there today. They will protect all of you, but to guarantee that you stay safe, you must not report the shooting. It will put a target on your backs."

The two Celebrity Hacks looked at each other. They couldn't fully comprehend Walker's caution or why they might be in peril, but they trusted Walker.

Desanctis said, "Uh, wow, Teddy. It was a crazy morning, but I know you and trust that you wouldn't blow smoke at us." Luke nodded silently in agreement.

"Thanks, guys. I like you all, even when I am tough on you. It's my job to protect you, and I will use all of my resources to keep you safe. Just keep your head low as I ask, and let's get through this."

"Through what, Teddy?" Luke asked.

"As I said, there are dark forces at work that want to undermine everything. For now, let's get through these Black Camelot Weddings. If the attackers succeed, we will go from the Black Camelot Weddings to the Black Camelot War."

He continued, "Now, because I trust you, and I've told you what the consequences will be if you break your silence, I will share something with you."

"Tell us, Teddy," Desanctis asked. "What is it?"

"We've got 38 bodies to account for from the same white supremacist group over the last nine months."

"You mean dead bodies?" Luke asked.

"Yes, plus the four gunmen killed this morning."

"What?" Desanctis said.

"Yeah, and brace yourselves. Our records indicate that none of them are locals. They've come to New York for one reason: to kill those people you flew out to the Hamptons with this morning."

Luke uncharacteristically fell to his knees. Mike Desanctis did, too. "Chief Walker, we need to pray. We can't have this in our city. Mike and I are on our knees now."

"That is a great idea. Prayer always works," Walker said. "I am on this end praying with you."

"Lord Jesus," Luke began, "Please protect our city, our leaders, our friends against these enemies brought together by hate, envy, and misunderstanding. Render them powerless and put a shield of protection around our city and loved ones. Protect the city from this war. I ask that the war against Black Camelot end now. In your name, I pray, Amen."

"Amen," Walker and Desanctis echoed.

Walker then said, "We'll bring Jennifer in, too. We'll need everybody on the right side of the fight."

"You mean war, Chief Walker," Luke said.

"Luke. I'm afraid we're already in a war, but right now, the battle is to get through these weddings without any of our guys getting killed. And frankly, I don't want any more dead bodies in my city."

Walker knew the reporters were shell-shocked. He had considered telling them about the attacks in Jamaica and how close they had come to being massacred, but decided against it. The Voice had left it up to Walker whether he should tell the civilians or not, and the Chief of Detectives decided that was need to know information. The day's events had already given the reporters more than enough to keep secret.

Chapter Forty-Six

Teddy Walker arranged to meet with the Celebrity Hack Patrol and Charlie Humphrey at Café Cielo the day following the photoshoot.

They met in the private room in the basement where Walker solved the Harris Simmons murders. He said to Jennifer, "I wanted you here today to go over what I told your buddies yesterday. They saw something they wish they hadn't, and so the secret is out. I want to share with you, as I did with them, how important it is for the incident to remain our secret."

"They didn't tell me anything. What is going on, guys? Are you holding out on me again?"

Luke answered, "Jennifer, yesterday at the heliport, after we lifted off, four men with high-powered weapons took aim at your helicopter. Two other men took them down before the gunmen got off a shot. Remember the counter guys at the heliport?"

"Yeah, I do," she said and began to tremble nervously as she guessed the news was awful. "You mean the ticket guys."

"They ran out of the terminal and shot the assailants dead."

She gasped and grabbed her heart. "Get out of here, Luke. That did not happen. I would have seen it."

"No, it happened just like Luke said, TV," Desanctis chimed in, "and two security guys on our helicopter told us that if we reported the story, we'd put ourselves in the crosshairs of the team trying to kill the Black Camelot Crew."

"Jesus, Jesus, Jesus. Oh my God!" she said, covering her mouth with both hands in disbelief. "Don't play, guys. This has to be a joke, right Chief? Right, Charlie?"

"No, it's not Jennifer. You guys ventured onto something that was part of the dark side," Walker said. "Charlie, why don't you explain it to her."

"Jennifer and guys, we told you before about the white supremacist organization called BE. They want Black Camelot dead. There is another, even more sophisticated, hate group than BE called Pre-1860. We're pretty sure they want the Black Camelot crew dead, too. Teddy and I are retired from an organization named the Society of Protectors. They are the good guys, the people you never see, who snuff out crap all over the world. Bad guys, strong men, narco-terrorists, and now out-of-control white supremacist groups. Since you guys started this Black Camelot thing in New York, BE has been taking shots at them, and the Society has been taking them out."

"Jesus, what the..." and she stopped herself from cursing.

Humphrey continued, "Since the engagement concert nine months back at the Grand Ballroom, the Society has killed 38, including the four guys shot and killed yesterday. They badly want the Black Camelot crew, Jennifer. It could start a race war, and that's what they want."

Jennifer's shoulders slumped, and her eyes began to water. She shook her head, slammed her fist on the table, and yelled, "No. No. No," as tears streamed down her face.

"We agree," Walker said. "We can't let that happen, and so the attacks and our response, such as yesterday's deaths and the other bodies, must not be reported by you guys or anyone else. We have to keep this under wraps. And if you report on it, you will be in danger, too."

As tears rolled down her face, she said, "I can't believe this. I love those people. It was my idea to name them Black Camelot. I feel terrible that they are in danger."

Kung looked at Walker, Humphrey, and her colleagues, "Have you told Black Camelot about this?"

"No, we can't tell them," Walker said.

"But they have the right to know Chief. Don't they?"

"The damage is done, Jennifer. They are targets because the public sees them as royalty, and some Americans cannot accept the idea of black royalty. But, the Society of Protectors is committed to keeping Black Camelot safe."

He continued, "We have a major player under arrest. Your help on the Mac McClellan and Bill Trombetta rogue cops story was a big help. It took 15 years to get to this guy, but we now have him in custody. We have you guys to thank for that."

"So what's next? What will this lead to?" Jennifer asked.

"This is not going to go well for Before Emancipation. The Society of Protectors is super stealth. Eight protectors were with you yesterday. Two in the heliport that wiped out the kill squad. Two on the second helicopter, and four more on the ground in the Hamptons."

Jennifer grabbed her heart again, "Lordy, Lord, Jesus, I need a drink. I still think I should warn these guys. It was my fault. I came up with the Black Camelot idea to drive readers and fans to our celebrity web pages and columns. The Black Camelot crew got pulled into this because we branded them as New York City royalty. These are hardworking, self-made people dedicated to helping others and don't deserve this."

"That's why we have to go forward, Jennifer," Desanctis said.

Luke added, "I agree. We know who they are. Let these racists eat crap. Maybe if they pay attention to the coverage and realize that these guys earned everything and are just trying to live their best lives, they will stop hating and start loving."

Humphrey asked, "Where'd that come from?"

Before Walker could answer, Jennifer said, "He's had a split personality since he got knocked on the head a few months back. Today is a good day for him."

Luke smiled meekly. He was embarrassed by the teasing but managed a wise comment, "Everybody tries to knock old Luke, but y'all should think about how boring the city would be without Luke McFlemming, head of the Celebrity Press Patrol."

Chapter Forty-Seven

BE staggered into June demoralized. The arrest of the Confederate was the harshest blow. But the Society of Protectors didn't stop. They kept up the pressure to ensure the Black Camelot Weddings proceeded without incident.

Walker was able to secure files with information on numerous BE members, several of whom ranked right below the Confederate. He funneled this information to The Voice. There were hundreds of raids and attacks on BE members across the country. The raids led to 15 more deaths and scores of maimed members with broken trigger fingers and toes. Maiming became the Society's trademark and most effective deterrent as BE members would no longer be able to shoot a gun, handle a knife or run away from an attack. The Voice titled the offensive Project Maim because it forced a lot of racist terrorists into early retirement. He only told Walker about five of the deaths. Ten more were in New York and he decided to tell him after the weddings.

After Project Maim's early success, The Voice contacted Doug and Darryl Duncan, Keyur and Manish Patel, and Garry and Larry Miller to share the next attack plan.

"Okay, guys, I want to brief you on how we plan to move forward. Everything is still focused on keeping BE assassins out of New York and away from Black Camelot. We have the first wedding on the third Saturday of June, and here's the plan to make the city safe."

He continued, "With Project Maim, we've nabbed a lot of people in the top 100 of BE. Now we have a list of 1000 more who are mainly street toughs and goons. We are going to send them an electronic message to stay out of New York."

"Stand Down notices?" Keyur asked, surprised. "That's not going to work. Why don't we just go and kill them or continue with Project Maim?"

"I want to keep the violence down," The Voice said. "We have phone numbers, email addresses, home addresses, and photos of these guys. And sure, we could travel the country assassinating them, but that would attract law enforcement. And the risk is local law enforcement and politicians might be BE members or sympathizers."

"But they want a war, and they came into our town to try and start one. All is fair in love and war, right?" Darryl asked.

"True, Darryl. But that's not how we operate. I want them to live in fear and understand that we have targeted them and can reach them whenever we want. Remember, all these guys are aware of Project Maim. We want them looking over their shoulders, waiting for us to knock on their doors. Does that make sense to you?"

Darryl thought for a couple of seconds and realized it was a sound strategy. "That's why you are our leader," he said.

"Darryl and Keyur," The Voice continued, "This should make you happy. We have identified five people you guys must hit over the next week. Our records show they are the top lieutenants of the Confederate. We need them taken care of in five days."

"And the rush is why?" Doug asked.

"I want to send a second set of electronic messages to all of the members announcing that in addition to the 38 bodies, they include the 34 in New York and the Frat Boy team of four in Jamaica, that we killed the Confederates' top five lieutenants. And I will reiterate that we can get them whenever we want."

"Oh, goody, this will be fun," Darryl said.

The Voice continued, "You guys split the work on the top five as you see fit, but I need all this done this week. I need to report to my people that New York is open and Black Camelot is safe."

"Your people? Whom do you report to?" Manish asked.

"Suffice it to say, there are powerful people behind what you do. They support us because we are protectors, not random assaulters or killers."

. . .

A couple of days later, Bobby Joe Blain soiled his pants when he saw Darryl, Doug, Larry, and Garry walk into Jethro Bob's Lumberyard, the home repair company where he worked.

"Jesus Lord, what are they doing here in Nashville?" He said and ran to the bathroom to hide and clean himself up.

Six other BE members worked at Jethro Bob's. Bobby Joe knew they were all in trouble. He still walked with a limp and was on pain killers for the broken fingers and toes suffered during the Grand Ballroom fight nine months ago. He feared a repeat of that night for his five friends, plus Jethro Bob, Sr., the owner.

He tried to be quiet in the bathroom stall and hoped they wouldn't come in to look for him. He ran to lock the bathroom door when he realized he had forgotten to do so.

"Bobby Joe, we know you are in there," Darryl yelled from outside the locked bathroom. "We've made people shit on themselves enough to know why you are in there. We just wanted to say hello before the fun continues with your BE brothers out here in the lumber yard. You should clean yourself up and come out."

"Lord, help me, I am sorry, God," Bobby Joe prayed. He didn't want to say anything to Darryl. "Get me out of this fix, and I will go to register for classes at junior college tomorrow, I promise."

"I heard that," Darryl said. "We won't hurt you anymore, but you should come out for the fight. Garry Miller is stretching and getting ready for Jethro Bob, Jr., Ricky Boy, and Gator. Doug already took care of Dough Boy. He's pretty fat and didn't put up much of a fight, and Beanie Paul cried for his mama. We are making Jethro Bob, Sr. watch everything. We know he is a local BE leader and told him that after we get through all the young folks, we will put the hurt on him."

Outside in the lumber yard, Garry asked the three burly southern rednecks, "Okay, who is going to be first?"

"Da-da-damn, man, you are a wh-whi-white man. You are one of us. Wha-wha-what you fa-fat, fatten' with them for?" Jethro Bob, Jr. stuttered.

This response made Garry bristle, "Wha-wha-wha-what's your name, and did you say, fatten' when you meant fighting? I'm not a racist like you."

Garry's mocking Jethro Bob, Jr.'s stutter enraged him. He charged Garry angrily, and it was a mistake. Jethro Bob, Jr. misjudged Garry to be an easy foe because of his slight, five-foot-ten, 190-pound build. Jethro Bob, Jr. stood six-foot-three and weighed 280 pounds and thought he would demolish him. He charged Garry, planning to ram and tackle him. Garry didn't move or flinch until Jethro was an arm's length away, and then he unleashed a lethal blow to the larger man's nose. The punch stopped Jethro Bob, Jr. in his tracks. He staggered and fell to one knee and shook his head as he tried to regain his wits, but it was over once the full impact of the blow took effect. When Jethro Bob stood up, he dropped to both knees then fell backward in a spread-eagle.

"Timber!" Garry raised his hands over his head in a victory pose and yelled as Jethro Bob, Jr., fell backward. He looked at Darryl and winked. Darryl smiled appreciatively at his Society of Protectors brother's skill.

"Now that's a very impressive one and done," Darryl said.

"Hands of stone. I call it my granite blow. Now, who's next?" Garry asked. He stared at Ricky Boy and Gator and threw a couple of punches in the air as he danced in a circle like a prizefighter. "Let's go. I need a workout. I didn't come down here for nothing."

"Stop, stop," Jethro Bob, Sr. screamed in his thick southern accent. "I've seen enough. I don't want anyone else hurt here today."

Jethro Bob, Sr., opened his phone. Like his son, he stood six-foot-three and weighed about 280 pounds. He appeared to be in his early 50s and was wise enough to realize this was a fight he would not win today or in the future.

"Our safe house in the Bronx is at 2424 Van Cortland Boulevard. That's where all of our teams stay in New York City. I am supposed to send a group of ten people to raise hell this month. I'm not going to do that, but if you want to keep the weddings safe, you need to visit that place. I'll also put the word out to all my associates that they should stand down. But I have to tell you that there are some true believers out there. They may decide to come out anyhow. Until today, we here were true believers, too, but not anymore."

"Why are you giving up this information so easily?" Doug asked.

"We want to live. We saw what you did to my son. It's my fault that he is a member. Don't kill the rest of us. And like I said, we were true believers until what I just witnessed. Bobby Joe told us you guys were badasses. He still can't write his name and walks with a limp. I guess you had to see it to believe it. Just let us be, please."

The Van Cortland safe house turned out to be a critical tip to an incident-free summer of weddings. It was information the Society of Protectors kept from Teddy Walker. The Voice decided to keep the location of this safe house and the body count of ten true believers who chose to come to New York City from Walker until the Black Camelot weddings were complete.

Chapter Forty-Eight

The Society of Protectors' plan worked to perfection. The team took out the five top lieutenants of Before Emancipation. Afterward, Charlie Humphrey and Teddy Walker set up another meeting in Café Cielo's downstairs room with the Celebrity Hacks.

"Meeting here is becoming a routine. I hope the news is not as bad as it was last time," Luke said.

"The news is quite good," Walker said. "I am pleased to tell you that we've done a major cleanup at BE. These guys will not be coming to New York over the short term, if ever."

"That's fantastic news," Mike said. "It means we're safe, right? I've been trying not to worry but have to admit to sleeping with one eye open."

"Yes, it is excellent news, but you still can't report on what you saw or what you now know."

"But it does mean that the Black Camelot crew is safe, and no one has to worry. Right?" Mike asked.

"Yes, they are safe, and we will continue to protect them."

"Awesome," Jennifer said. "That is what matters most. If you need anything else from us, please let us know."

"I will, Jennifer. For now, we must ask you guys to maintain our secret pact to not discuss it with anyone else or report on BE attacks. We will always do our best to protect you."

"Thank you, Teddy," Jennifer said.

"I appreciate you saying that, Chief Walker," said Mike.

"I'm with the crew," McFlemming said. "We appreciate you protecting us."

"Great, now let's get some drinks. Luke, you are buying. I hear you have the biggest expense account," Walker said.

Chapter Forty-Nine

New York City police were ready for the first wedding on the third Saturday in June. Teddy Walker asked Police Commissioner Safity for permission to lead the security detail. Safity happily deferred the charge to Walker. His Chief of Detectives was the only other officer in his department who held enough clout to be held accountable to the Mayor.

Walker had 1000 uniformed officers on duty in the city plus 500 plainclothes officers. The processional of covered horse-drawn carriages ferrying the wedding party to Freewill Baptist Church, Central Park, and the Major Museum drew enormous crowds. The Commissioner and the Mayor had protested to Alexander and Mills about the huge police presence until an anonymous $50 million donation arrived at City Hall marked Black Camelot Weddings Police and Sanitation Overtime.

The NYPD was unaware there were 200 members of the Society of Protectors in the crowd. At Walker's request, the Voice had pulled together its top male and female members from across the world. They moved through the crowds anonymously and provided Chief Walker with a highly skilled defense team better suited to spot and neutralize terrorists than NYPD's rank-and-file officers.

He expected a crowd the size of the city's largest parades and anticipated that many would follow the horse-pulled coaches across the entire travel route. The crowd did not disappoint.

Carrie rode with her maid of honor, Debbie Techelle. They were in the last of the five carriages; Michelle and Danielle were in the fourth. Marcia Cherry and Sammy Rivers were third. Carrie's four other Harlowe friends and sorority sisters rode in the first two carriages. Adrienne Goolsby, a DC-based power lawyer, sat with Nikki Mussenden, the technology executive, in the second buggy; Susan Thomas, the Congresswoman from Maryland, and Margot Mosely, the renowned poet and current Diplomat to South Africa, were together in the first carriage.

Debbie asked Carrie as they looked out of the carriage windows at the thick crowds of sightseers, "Can you believe this? We are riding through the city's streets with a parade of people standing 10-15 deep for five miles just to catch a glimpse of you and your girls."

"This is unbelievable, Debbie. I'm overwhelmed. We have come a long way to this moment. I am wearing a $50,000 Patricia Norman dress. This necklace by Priscilla is worth millions. Remember when we were eating sardines and crackers in college?"

Techelle shook her head as she recalled their broke college days, "Do I? That was good eating, girl. Especially, the sardines in the hot mustard can."

"And how about when we would take a bottle of wine and stretch it with water?" Carrie said.

"Ooh child, we sure stretched it out, didn't we, Carrie?"

"Yes, we did. We had a lot of fun. Thank you for being with me through all of this, both good times and tough times."

"You are kidding, right? Thank you. I can't even begin to think about life without you in it. You are my best friend and my sister from another mother. You've always had my back, even when I was following stupid boys. You ever tell Donald or Kwame about the time you punched out that guy on the basketball team who was leading me on."

"Oh no," Carrie said. "He deserved it. That dude thought he was a player. He was a punk. You liked him because he was popular and had curly hair."

Debbie smiled and laughed at the memory. "I did. Oh, the stupid things we did when we were young. His hair wasn't even curly. It was a Jheri curl, and that Jheri curl juice was nasty. It messed up my good blouse."

"You can never tell Donald. I don't want him to know that I won't hesitate to smack a fool," Carrie said.

"Smack a fool! You kicked his butt in the cafeteria in front of everyone. I don't think that clown ate there for the rest of the semester. Susan and Margot started calling you, Mr. T."

"I pity the fool," Carrie said and made a fist and mean face, and they both busted up in laughter.

"Oh, what memories! Now, look at us. Look at that crowd," Debbie said. The best friends then leaned out the coach's window and squealed in excitement. When the other women heard them, they all leaned out of their coach windows and waved to each other and the crowd. The press caught a picture of all of them waiving with bright smiles. The photo became the most searched online photo of the year.

When they sat back, Carrie looked at Debbie and said, "I'm a princess. I'm on my way to marrying my Prince Charming. I just can't believe this. Can you pinch me?"

Donald and the groomsmen arrived at the church a full hour early. They spent 45 minutes making their way 100 feet from the church's entrance to the front row as they greeted many of the guests. They were overwhelmed by family, friends, business associates, politicians, and already seated celebrities. The guest list was a Who's Who of influential people. When they finally got to the front, Donald said to his brother Rick and Ron Cherry, "I'm glad we got here early.

Cathy Martin told me this was going to be intense, but my goodness. I am overwhelmed."

To make sure he was okay, and at Cathy's instructions, Ron and Rick tagged along with Donald until the ceremony started. Her orders were clear, "You don't leave him alone for a second. The magnitude of the moment will stress him out. Keep him calm."

The other groomsmen, Kwame, Tom, JoJo Littlejohn, Rote Tunz, TJ Melendez, and Greg Smith, were scattered across the sanctuary, busily conversing with friends, fans, and associates.

As Donald stood upfront, the invited members of The Guiding Force, Mauldin "Danny" Daniels IV, Wimer "Lax" Brockelman, Jack Zell Mulliken, John S.P. Curtin, Janet Bivens, and Jacci O'Connor, entered together. They were all accompanied by their spouses and sat together in the same row. They fit in with the distinguished collection of guests.

The room came to a hush as the last couple entered the church. All eyes were suddenly on the older man and the knockout redhead wearing dark sunglasses and a form-fitting light pink lace, off-the-shoulder mini-dress by Patricia Norman. The distinguished gentleman happily waved to friends as he and his guest made their way to their seats. He had the regal look of a politician. She, a movie star.

"Who's that?" Rick asked his brother and Ron.

"I have no idea," Donald said, "but she looks familiar."

"She, my friend, is Dawn Davis Stuart, and she is a killer," Ron answered.

"What? Be still my heart. I see why you'd call her that. She's a knockout," Rick responded.

"No, Rick. Ron meant that she is literally a killer. She shot her husband and, just a few weeks back, shot an intruder in her home," Donald said.

Rick quickly realized his error, "What? Do you mean Madame Hot Temper? Oh, man. I'm a big fan. I knew she looked familiar. I don't know if I should ask for her autograph or her phone number."

"An autograph might be safer," Ron whispered and smiled.

As she sat, every eye in the church was locked on her. Kwame and Donald wondered why she was in the row with the other Guiding Force members.

After the dramatic entrance, the loud chatter in the church lowered to whispers as many of the congregants engaged in hushed conversation. Everyone was talking about Dawn Davis Stuart's stunning entrance. It was a moment not lost on her father-in-law. He leaned over and whispered, "I think you made quite an entrance. I'm sure it's earned you some suitors."

Dawn's moment ended a few minutes later when the trumpeters blared to announce the bride's arrival. Inside, the crowd rose and craned their necks to see the bridesmaids and bride. Outside, the parade of onlookers gasped and cheered as the women departed the carriages.

"You ready for this, buddy?" Rick asked the groom.

"I am so ready, Rick. I can't wait."

"Good, my man. Mom and Dad just walked in. Let me escort them to their seats. Then I'm going to join the other groomsmen. I'll be behind you when this starts. Lean on me if you need to. I've always leaned on you. I got you today."

The bridesmaids made a dramatic entrance. They wore -lilac-colored, long mesh dresses with a V-neck and beaded waistbands designed by Sheila Diann. The designers were amongst the guests and smiled at the numerous nods of approval for their designs.

There was a collective gasp when the bride ascended the stairs and appeared at the sanctuary entrance. Guests were asked not to use cameras in the church but ignored the rules. They snapped pictures of the smiling Carrie, who wore a white, spaghetti strap, sleeveless chiffon gown custom-designed by Patricia Norman.

As she stood at the entrance next to her father, the noted heart surgeon Sebron Hubbard Sinclair, Donald leaned back on his brother and said, "Oh, my. Wow! My knees just went weak."

"I got you, Brother. I told you. I am here for you," Rick said as he stepped closer to his brother and held him up. "Catch your breath. You've been holding it down for all of us. I got you."

It took a couple of seconds, but Donald found his balance. "I'm better, Rick, thank you, little brother," he said and turned towards Carrie as she walked down the aisle.

Rick whispered, "Carrie is looking like she's right out of a fairytale. But this is not a fantasy. This whole Black Camelot thing is the truth."

"God smiled on all of us, Rick. I know it now. Look at her. Only God can make this happen. I'm marrying my Queen, and my friends get to marry theirs, too. After this, we do what Oliver Jr. told us to do."

"What is that, Donald?"

"He said, 'Do something good.' And that's what we'll do."

. . .

The wedding was a blur for Donald. His love for Carrie hypnotized him, and thanks to the majesty of the other Black Camelot weddings, he remained that way for the entire summer.

It was the same for Tom and Kwame. All three weddings went without a glitch as Teddy Walker, Charlie Humphrey, and the Society of Protectors kept BE and Pre-1860 out of New York. Cathy Martin's masterful series of weddings and the Celebrity Hack Patrol's coverage made the Black Camelot crew an even bigger sensation.

. . .

Jennifer, Luke, and Mike were exhausted but ecstatic. They grew their online audiences by 200%, and newsstand sales doubled. Readers had an insatiable appetite for wedding stories, pictures, and sidebar stories. The biggest sidebar story was about Dawn Davis Stuart. She was one of the most photographed subjects of the summer.

Paparazzi stationed themselves outside of the Stuarts' apartment building, hoping for a picture or an interview. Yancey Stuart held daily afternoon cocktail parties with them for a month until Dawn asked that he cease them. He agreed to scale them back to every other day.

"I have had ten guys call on me since the first wedding, but I now have a paparazzi trail whenever I leave. I'm not going to be able to go on a date with them trailing me and you having cocktails with them everyday."

"Ah, face it, honey, they love you. They want to know everything about Madame Hot Temper. Besides, I like having them around. It gives me some fun guys to talk to."

"Yancey, you've got me dressing in disguise and leaving out of the back entrance to avoid these guys," Dawn said. She pointed to a table near their free door that had an assortment of wigs, hats and sunglasses that she was using for disguises.

Dawn knew Yancey didn't care about her privacy and was enjoying his press friends. She feared he would sell out her secret exit and made a deal with him. "Don't tell about my exit, and I will come out every two or three days so they can get a picture. That way, you can still hold court with your new drinking buddies."

They agreed to continue that secret pact through Kwame Mills' wedding at the end of August. It also coincided with when they expected to get the money from the sale of all of Bronson Pagent's real estate holdings.

"There's a method to my madness Dawn. Yeah, I do like having these guys around, but I want to have a huge press event once we get Bronson's money. Getting these guys oiled up all summer will earn me at least one free press conference. I'm looking forward to announcing your Robin Hood moment."

"Dad, I wasn't born yesterday. You're still a big deal in this town. You can get the press out whenever you want. You just want new drinking buddies. That's okay. Enjoy yourself."

"Oops," Yancey, Sr., said and looked at his daughter-in-law with a sly, embarrassed grin and shrug of the shoulders, "you saw right through that one, didn't you?"

"Yeah, old man, that was weak," she said.

Chapter Fifty

The day following the last wedding, Teddy Walker and Walt Bigelow were exhausted. They looked forward to some long-needed time off. They sat in Teddy's office, happy about getting through the summer with all the Black Camelot members safe.

Kwame and Michelle were on their way to their honeymoon on a private island when Donald Alexander, his bride Carrie Sinclair, and Ron Cherry called Teddy.

Donald said nervously, "Teddy, something is going on here that is not good. I don't know if it is a prank or not. We just received a text from a guy who claims he is the Confederate's boss, and Chief Walker knows who the Confederate is. It said, 'Tell Walker. We have eyes on Kwame and Michelle. Revenge begins now.' Chief Walker, what does this mean?"

A jolt of stress ran through Walker's body. "Donald, when did you receive that text?" he asked.

"Ten minutes ago. Ron Cherry is here now for lunch. I shared it with him, and we called you. Oh, and the text also said, "We took care of Travis Pfaff. We ended him and his retirement early. We've got Trombetta, too, and are on our way to McClellan's. You wanted a war. Tell your people and the Society they have one now.'"

At that same moment, Walker's and Bigelow's phones beeped. Bigelow read the text aloud, "Chief Walker, you thought it was going to be that easy. The guy you have in custody is just a mid-level manager. The Confederate reports to me, the General. You guys and your Society of Protectors are good but tell them we have regrouped and are coming for them."

Another text followed, "Donald Alexander is a billionaire, and Kwame Mills is worth half a billion, but they're still black. In what world would there ever be black royalty? Coonville maybe, but not in America. We need them and all their fancy friends dead."

And then a third and final text came, "I decided that a bigger prize would be to kill them once they became kings and queens, so I let you have your weddings. We will destroy Black Camelot and the Society of Protectors. There are 53 dead bodies to account for, we are coming, and this is war."

Walker would have to tell Bigelow about the Society of Protectors, but first, he had to return to the phone call. "Donald, don't leave your penthouse. We will be sending a security detail right away. Everyone is in danger, Ron Cherry and all the Black Camelot members. Hang up the phone and stay away from the windows. We are at war. I will call you back in 10 minutes."

…………To Be Continued

Black Camelot's Days of War

Chapter One

"Captain Geoff, this is the Voice. We have a major problem and I need your help. How heavily armed are you guys?"

The level of urgency alarmed the pilot of the Fortress 5000. His boss's panic raised the hairs on the back of his neck.

The Voice didn't wait for a response from the pilot. "We need you to turn the plane around and head back to the island. There's a credible threat to Kwame Mills and Michelle Nubani. You need to head back right away and pick them up."

Yesterday, Kwame and Michelle were married in New York in the last of the Black Camelot weddings. Less than an hour earlier, the private plane piloted by Captain Geoff Stevens dropped them off for their honeymoon at Oliver's Oasis, a private Caribbean island 50 miles south of Puerto Rico.

"Roger that, Voice, we can turn this bird around and be back there in 30 minutes. And yes, we are armed and ready for just about any type of attack."

"Then tell your team to prepare for a fight. We've got notice from a Before Emancipation leader that they have eyes on Kwame and Michelle. I am not fully sure what this threat means, but I need you to get them off that island alive and without injury. Will there be any problems?"

"It's a private island, Voice. That means it has an open airfield without normal regulations. We will be at the airfield in 30 minutes. Do you want us to go to the compound to get Kwame and Michelle? Or will they meet us there?"

"Go get them," the Voice answered. Capt Stevens nodded and noted the stress from his leader as the Voice continued with the orders for the pickup.

"There is a panic room at the mansion on the grounds. I'm going to have them hunker down there. We've got a small team of Protectors on location. They arrived only a few hours before Kwame and Michelle. I'm concerned about the 10 miles of dense forest there. That means we could have an army of enemy BE fighters camped out in those woods. I need you to follow my S-three code, be smart, super-tactical and safe."

As he talked to Captain Geoff, The Voice thought about the team that took out four BE assassins during Kwame Mills', Donald Alexander's and Tom Wilson's bachelor party at Big Stan's compound.

"Geoff, a few months back we took out a kill squad of BE assassins in Jamaica. It was easy work for our guys. They waited in the woods until the bad guys walked almost right to them. The BE gang would love to pay us back with the same kind of response. Be careful, I don't want your team to walk into a hail of gunfire."

"We always are, Voice. You can count us being extra careful."

Stevens had now completed the plane turnaround and was headed back to the island. As he looked ahead the Voice said, "Captain Geoff, do you have any explosives or rocket launchers on the plane?"

"Sure. We've got a full artillery room in the lower deck. We can take down a skyscraper or two with the explosives we have on board."

"Great, that's exactly what we need. I'm going to need you to get some of that heavy artillery to our guys on the ground. Do a pass over the building and parachute some hardware to the backyard of the mansion. After that, circle back and land the plane on the airfield. The crew in the house can keep the bad guys at bay, especially if you can give them good ammunition."

"Okay, Voice. Is there anything else I should know?"

"Yes, we are sending a backup team of Protectors in from Puerto Rico. They will arrive in speedboats. It should take them an hour to get there. I would have sent them in by helicopter but we can't get one and a pilot on such short notice."

Twenty minutes later, Captain Stevens lowered the plane to 5,000 feet in preparation to land. He called his boss to report the sighting of three speedboats, with four guys on board each, hightailing it to the island. "Voice, I've spotted some speedboats that are suspicious looking. They are 10-15 minutes away from land and have machine gun turrets on each. Can you confirm whether or not they are our guys?"

"They are definitely not our guys. Our boats don't have turrets onboard. You need to handle this," the Voice answered.

"Not a problem," Captain Geoff said calmly. "I will launch an offensive from up here and take these guys out."

"Okay then. Do your thing; take care of these guys so we can get our people back here, safely."

The captain turned to his crew. They were crammed in the cockpit listening to his conversation. His co-pilot Adrina Crichlow knew what he wanted to do before the call ended.

Crichlow touched her shoulder-length, dark brown hair. "Bird Droppings, huh Captain? Ugh! That is so dangerous. And I just got my hair done."

He looked at her, flashed a tense smile and said, "Don't complain, my friend. You and Razor are the best at it. That's why you are on my team. I need you to do what you do best."

Edge Bottum was the third member of the crew and the most daring. Stevens and Crichlow nicknamed him Razor because of his fearlessness. He rubbed his bald head, smiled at Adrina and Captain Geoff, and said, "I'm ready for some action and I don't have any hair issues."

Stevens smiled back at Razor, as did the rest of the crew. "Okay, team I'm going to circle this baby. You guys go below deck and signal me when you are ready."

The co-pilot and Razor went below deck on the custom-built plane. The lower cargo was retrofitted as a weapons room that turned the private plane into a fighter jet. It included two rapid-fire machine guns, a cache of bombs that could be dropped on a location, M-16 rifles, grenades, gas masks, night vision goggles and other top-shelf military-grade equipment.

Bird Droppings was a special attack tactic perfected by Captain Stevens' team. Crichlow and Razor strapped themselves in the lower deck compartment, put on oxygen masks, and hit a button that opened hatches in the plane's floor. They would hang perilously by their straps and machine-gun their targets.

The attack team took care to fasten their straps and masks, as they would face wind thrusts of up to 150 miles an hour, and if the oxygen masks were not fitted properly they could suffocate.

Adrina and Razor had completed this attack dozens of times and in minutes strapped themselves into position. Crichlow, as the senior member, gave the instructions. "Okay Razor, you take the machine gun and pepper the boats. Make sure you get the engines, okay."

"Roger that, Crich," Razor said excitedly. He reached into his shirt, fished out his chain of a cross, kissed it, and screamed over the loud sound of the engine to his fighting partner, "I'm ready for some action and happy to lead the bird droppings with some cold iron steel. Good luck, Crich."

The co-pilot gave Razor a thumbs up and pressed a button on the wall for the plane's lower cabin intercom. She said through her oxygen mask, "Captain, we are ready for Operation Bird Drop."

"Good luck, you two," Stevens said. He lowered the plane's altitude, and Crichlow and Razor yelled in glee at the roller coaster-like plunge to 1,000 feet. "Hell yeah, Crich, whee, this is so much fun!" Bottum said.

Crichlow looked at her partner; they had been together as part of Captain Stevens' crew for five years. She knew how much he enjoyed these kinds of missions as she smiled and said, "You know you are crazy, Razor."

"That's why they call me Razor's Edge, Crich."

Within seconds, the plane closed in on the small fleet of speedboats. Captain Stevens confirmed them as the enemy and said, "I can see clearly that these are guys we need to take out. Show them our firepower before they turn around. Remember, these boats have heavy artillery turrets. We can't afford to miss. They can shoot us down at this low altitude."

"Roger that, Captain," Razor said as the bottom of the plane opened up. As 150 mile per hour winds gusted furiously on his face, he squeezed off a barrage of machine gun fire. The teams on the speedboats turned around terrified by the surprise attack from the sky as bullet fire pelted the water and their watercraft.

The speedboat attackers heard the private plane as it approached for a landing and turned to look at it, but had no reason to suspect the Fortress 5000 doubled as a fighter jet. The realization that they were under attack came too late.

Razor admired the carnage and explosions on the water, and yelled excitedly to Crichlow, "I've hit all three of the boat engines and at least six of the 12 targets."

"That's good shooting, Razor. I'll finish them off," Crichlow said and nodded as she looked at her partner's work. The co-pilot dropped six bombs as Captain Stevens circled the plane to make a pass over the now-stalled, bullet-riddled boats. The detonating bombs transformed the calm blue Caribbean waters into a massive ball of red fire and black smoke clouds.

Their mission accomplished, Crichlow hit the button that closed the plane's bottom hatches and removed her oxygen mask. The Canadian Special Operations Regiment Lieutenant and Society of Protectors member congratulated her partner. "Nice work, Razor. I'm sure we got all of them. Let's stay strapped in until the Captain confirms we are good to go."

She hit the intercom button on the wall and asked, "How did we do Captain Geoff? Did we get everyone?"

"Our visual scanners don't show any body movements. The boats are blown to bits, and I don't see any swimmers. You guys did great. If they survived they won't have any artillery, that's for sure. Nice job, team."

Razor smiled at Crichlow and gave her a thumbs up.

Captain Stevens continued, "Next, we have to drop the artillery in the backyard of the mansion before landing. You guys prepare the artillery to be parachuted."

From the island, a team of BE fighters had watched the plane attack. They stood shocked as the aircraft approached the island and roared over their heads. "Jesus," Team Leader Dixie Bill said. "That plane just wiped out all of our guys. My cousin Country Ticky was on one of those boats. Look at that ball of fire. It's impossible to survive that."

Dixie Bill fell to his knees and covered his mouth as his face turned pale. The dramatic explosion, machine gun attack and bombing a few miles off the coast of the private island that Kwame and Donald co-owned and had nicknamed Oliver's Oasis brought the rest of the BE members out from the woods. They had been helicoptered in two days earlier from Puerto Rico and had food, water, artillery and a mission: "Kill Kwame and Michelle Nubani."

The 12 men in the speedboats were only a backup crew. The 10 BE members on-site had been camping out in the woods since arriving. Up until now it had been fun for all of them.

After regaining his composure, Dixie Bill reminded them why they were there. "Gentleman, the General told us we are at war. You just saw what war looks like. The time for games is over. Get back in the woods and get ready. They attacked first, but we will attack last."

The team walked back to the camp set up in the dense forest a couple miles from the house. Dixie Bill was still stunned and said to himself, "It also is now personal; I've got to avenge my cousin."

As the plane whizzed by, Margaret Pasadena, the fourth person on the Fortress 5000 team, said to Captain Stevens, "I counted six, seven people standing on the beach. I'm assuming they were waiting to greet the guys we just wiped out."

Chapter Two

Bill Trombetta knew something was wrong. The two guys in the mega-home repair store were up to no good. His instincts were refined from all his years as a military police officer, New York City street cop and recently promoted detective. He knew bad guys when he saw them and his mind began to race as he wondered what they were up to.

Instinctively he patted his ribcage, felt for his gun and muttered, "Damn, I'm in trouble."

Trombetta was off-duty and had intentionally locked his gun in the glove compartment of his car. He'd run into the store to buy a few items for a small backyard project. Now, unarmed, he knew what he needed to do. "Let me go to the sheet metal department. I can get a couple of pieces of metal to make a shield for protection."

The seasoned cop walked quickly to aisle seven. He glanced back and saw the suspicious guys waiting at the cash register. "I don't know what's up with these guys, but I have to do something. What a bad time to be without my gun."

He pulled out his phone as he walked along aisle seven and texted his buddy Detective McClellan. "Mac, send some squad cars to Grills, Pools, Garden & Yard, the home repair store in the West Village. I don't have my weapon on me; it's in my car. There's a pair of bad guys here: white males, both in their mid-20's. I don't know what they are up to."

The veteran cop's suspicions were well-founded. What he didn't know was the guys were assassins, and he was their target. He just knew that his instincts were on fire. He texted his partner again. "Hurry up, Mac. Send help now."

In the sheet metal aisle Trombetta spotted what he needed, a row of iron slabs. He found a small one that he could use as a chest-plate, and eyed a larger piece.

"If I can get a couple of suction hand grips, this one will make a good armored shield and help me stop these guys," he whispered to himself.

Trombetta grabbed the two iron slabs and scooted his cart two aisles down where he found a package of hand grips and ripped it open. He stuck the small slab of metal in his shirt; covered his chest and heart. "It's uncomfortable but should do the trick," he said to himself.

His partner McClellan hung up and immediately called the West Village police precinct. "We've got a situation. Officer is in distress. Send a unit right away. Officer Bill Trombetta is at Grills, Pools, Garden & Yard in the West Village. Send patrol cars there now. He just texted me and reported that there are two bad guys in the store. We need to get there right away."

The dispatcher immediately put out a distress call, "All available units head to Grills, Pools, Garden & Yard in the West Village."

Two minutes later, a fleet of patrol cars with sirens blaring entered the parking lot just as Trombetta was affixing the hand grips to his shield. The bad guys heard the patrol cars, peeked outside, and the taller of the two said, "We can't wait for him to go outside. I saw him go down aisle five; let's get him now. Take two kill shots, and let's run out of the back entrance and get on the subway."

Trombetta kept a watch on the two men, and when they began walking towards him and flashed their guns, knew immediately why they were in the store.

The two gunmen opened fire. Trombetta didn't get his shield up in time and took a shot to the shoulder. Another, a head wound that creased his ear. The rest of the shots ricocheted off the shield.

"Why don't you put the guns down and fight like men?" Trombetta yelled. "I'll tear you apart. I'll even fight you both at the same time."

The tough street cop was hot. He'd never been shot and never used his gun on anyone. He believed that fists were how you settled scores.

"Keep shooting. Forget about two shots. We have to make sure we get him," the taller assailant yelled as the bullets continued to ricochet off Trombetta's shields. The hitmen continued to shoot until the police entered the front door, guns drawn.

"Stop shooting. Drop your guns!" the first officer yelled. He was joined by a cavalry of cops who ran in after they heard the gunshots. "Put your guns down, now!"

The assassins did drop their guns. But they were not going to wait for the uniformed cops to arrest them. They ran past the injured

Trombetta to the back entrance of the store and exited onto the crowded streets of the West Village.

The barrage of bullets had forced Trombetta to the ground. He lay there bloodied, just a few feet away from the two guns his assailants had dropped.

"They dropped their weapons and ran. Don't worry about me, get their asses!" Trombetta yelled.

"You're injured; we've got to get an ambulance here and will take you to safety. We'll find those guys. There's a gazillion video cameras in and around this store. Trust us, we'll find them," an officer said.

Author's Thank You & Review Request

Thank you so much for taking the time to read Black Camelot's Dawn & The Return Of Madame Hot Temper. This is the second book in the series. The third book is scheduled for July 2021 and the fourth in Fall 2022.

If you've read this far, I hope that means you've enjoyed Black Camelot's Dawn and will continue to follow the series.

Also please go to dariusmyers.com and join our mailing list to stay informed of future works.

Cheers,

Darius

Made in the USA
Middletown, DE
25 April 2023

29191785R00195